BUTTERFLY SKIN

SERGEY KUZNETSOV

BUTTERFLY SKIN

TRANSLATED FROM THE RUSSIAN
BY ANDREW BROMFIELD

TITAN BOOKS

Butterfly Skin

Print edition ISBN: 9781783290246
E-book edition ISBN: 9781783290253

Published by Titan Books
A division of Titan Publishing Group Ltd
144 Southwark Street, London SE1 0UP

First edition: September 2014

10 9 8 7 6 5 4 3 2 1

This is a work of fiction. Names, characters, places, and incidents either are the product of the author's imagination or are used fictitiously, and any resemblance to actual persons, living or dead, business establishments, events, or locales is entirely coincidental. The publisher does not have any control over and does not assume any responsibility for author or third-party websites or their content.

A CIP catalogue record for this title is available from the British Library.

Printed and bound in the United States.

I wanted to dedicate this book to two of my friends. They refused to read it and said they didn't want their names to be associated with it. So I dedicate the novel to my wife, Katya. She has absolutely nothing at all to do with this story, but her love helps me survive in this beautiful world.

As Joan was burning, she looked round and said:
"See, I have taken off my dress and shaved my head.
See, now I am not hiding anything,
The second dress I tear off is my skin.
Pluck at the veins and feel the flesh
There is only a single moment left."

Alexander Anashevich

1

YOU ARE TEN YEARS OLD, OR PERHAPS YOUNGER. YOU are riding in the subway with your mother, looking toward the front of the train through the transparent doors of the cars. Suddenly you notice that somewhere up ahead, something has happened: people jump to their feet in a strange state of alarm and run back against the movement of the train, as if they are fleeing from something, until they reach the locked doors between the cars – and they tug and tug at the handles... But then their faces contort as panic sweeps over their normal features like a wind driving ripples across the surface of a pond. Something invisible is approaching, something nameless and formless, more terrible than death, more horrible than a nightmare. Something they have known about and tried to forget all their lives.

And now the front cars slowly enter the transparent wall of condensed horror, but you can no longer bear to look at the faces flattened against the glass, the mouths opened in mute screams, the eyes bulging out of their sockets – you turn your gaze to the passengers still untouched by the horror, sitting in the nearest cars, and again you see that faint shadow of anxiety change to panic, you see them jump to their feet and run, run and pound on the locked glass doors... and the invisible wall gets closer and closer, advancing implacably, like in a dream. But you don't leave your seat, you don't feel for your mother's hand, you just think with relief that it will all soon be over.

These are only my fantasies. I was ten years old, or perhaps younger, and I often imagined this scene. As I got older, however, everything changed, it was no longer a wall, but more like a wave, a wave from a distant cold sea that froze the blood, a wave that swept along the train from the front to the final car. But now no one jumps up from his seat, everybody sits there until the shuddering contorts their faces like a hand crumpling a used tissue.

Yes, as a boy I certainly had a rich imagination. When I grew up a bit, I started telling other people what I used to believe when I was a child: that there was a place in the subway where hell seeped through into the tunnel in a thin layer of horror – and the trains passed through it so quickly that only really sensitive people noticed. I used to give the girls a suggestive look at the words "really sensitive." Sometimes it worked.

Now I know it has nothing to do with sensitivity. It is my own personal hell, my personal horror, my concentrated nightmare. The passengers will never have any idea about it, nothing will distort their faces, not a single hair will shift out of place. I am the only one who notices the signs, the only one who senses the approach, the only one who understands the language of the things and objects that warn me in vain of *the approach*.

The fine hairs on woolen scarves stand up on end, leather coats are covered with fine cracks, feathers creep out of down-filled jackets as if seeking escape, stockings grip legs even tighter, the colors drain out of the advertising posters, any moment now the glass in the windows of the car will rain down on to the seats, the handrails cringe under my fingers, the doors scream in horror. Everything stops, as if time has been switched off, the clatter of the wheels fades away, and suddenly you can hear what the two girls standing by the closed doors are talking about. One is small and skinny, with tousled black hair, the other is graceful, with long legs and light hair. Just a minute ago they were laughing and nudging each other as they discussed how they were going to spend their first pay cheque, but now their faces have aged ten years, and you hear the light-haired one say: "I can't believe she's gone," and see her wipe her eyes with a handkerchief as contorted as your own face, and the smaller one takes hold of her hand and replies: "And I still can't even cry."

And then the sounds get duller, space curls up round the edges of your vision like old wallpaper on a damp wall and everything goes dark before your eyes, as if the entire world is hiding behind those whirling black spirals: the sudden surge overtakes you, sweeps over you. You can't breathe, the outlines of your body blur within this black cocoon as despair and hopelessness congeal: reach out your hand and you can touch them.

The old horror of childhood? No, this is not horror, it is anguish, concentrated anguish, a stifling feeling, a constant ringing in the ears, the flow of your own blood, darkness, darkness – the dark cloud will hang on the folds of your clothes, cling to the contours of your face, to the hairs stuck to your forehead, to the gnawed ends of your fingers.

You carry this cocoon, this cloud, with you as you leave the subway. You will make conversation, discuss work, come to decisions, write business letters. You will flirt with girls, play with your children, smile at people you know, try to live the way you always do. But on days like this, if you reach out your hand, you can touch the boundary of hell: suffering oozes out of doors slightly ajar, flows across the walls of buildings, crunches under your feet like broken glass; every gesture causes pain, every touch makes you shudder convulsively; your skin dissolves, leaving only the naked bleeding flesh, just barely covered by the gray cloud of anguish.

Days like this are excruciating for me. In order to cope somehow, I start remembering the women I have killed.

2

AN ELECTRIC BEEPING. NOT A METALLIC CHIME, NOT the tinkling of a small bell, but the artificial trill of a microchip. The signal of an alarm clock bought in IKEA, a child's alarm clock covered in bright-colored soft plush, with a big dial and yellow hands. Out from under the blanket comes a hand, a thin hand, with a silver ring on the index finger, an arm with a faint scar just above the elbow. The little palm swats a blue velvet pimple, the ringing stops, the arm disappears.

You don't want to open your eyes, you don't want to wake up. As if through half-closed eyes we see the corner of a pillow, a braid of hair, the edge of a blanket. You want to sleep, with your head hidden under the blanket, swaddled up as tight as you can get, hidden away, as if you were nestling inside a cocoon, sleeping like that forever, ever since you were a child.

"Good morning!"

Who did you say "good morning" to in that muffled sleepy voice? There's no one else in the room. A patch of yellow sunlight – it matches the hands of the clock – on the bright-colored kilim by the bed, an open laptop with its matte screen reflecting nothing, a fluffy pink rabbit lurking between the wall and your body. Good morning, as if you were trying to wake yourself up. Yes indeed, good morning, Ksenia.

Yes, your name is Ksenia, you live in a rented flat, cheap, found through friends. That's about a third of your salary, everything's very Western, the way grown-ups live. You're completely grown up now, twenty-three years old, you work in the news department of the internet-newspaper *Evening.ru*. E-v-e-n-i-n-g dot ru, not a very well-known newspaper, second flight – maybe you've never heard of it, but our news section is good.

Outside the window there is rain, outside there is December, gray sky, not a single snowflake. You only imagined the patches of sunlight in your sleep. Slip your feet into the fluffy slippers, pick the white dressing gown up off the armchair, push the "Play" button and turn up the volume. The Gotan Project playing a remix of Gato Barbieri. That's how the morning starts.

On the way to the bathroom you can't resist looking at your email. Five messages, including four pieces of spam, two of them offering to increase the size of your penis and your breasts. You don't need either – you don't have a penis and your breasts are just fine.

What do you look like? Thin, short, with tousled black hair, lips puffy from sleep, big eyes that simply refuse to open in the morning. You look at the fifth message. Aha, from your friend Olya, good that it's not about work. But then, how could it be about work? You went to bed at three and got up at eight – at that time everyone's asleep, no one's writing work emails.

You walk through into the bathroom, turn on the shower and freeze in front of the mirror, trying to put the day together in your mind. What's in store for us today? The usual stuff first thing in the morning, then a talk with Pasha about money, lunch at the coffee house, Mom's birthday, she asked you to be there at seven and not be late. You take off the dressing gown with a sigh and look in the mirror, already dewy with condensation: it's damp, steamy and warm in here, the way you like it.

The bruises on your breasts and shoulders are barely visible, but your thighs – oh, that's quite a different matter. And the welts on your buttocks sting in the scalding water. Yes, you like your body to retain its memories of your assignations for a long time. You like to be hurt. You have a small collection of various amusing gadgets at home, black leather toys, whips, gags, nipple clamps. On good days you don't see anything unusual about your preferences. The way you think about it is more or less like this: sometimes I want to dance the boogie-woogie in a club in the Kropotkinskaya district, sometimes I ask someone to beat me and hurt me. Sex is like dancing; the important thing is to have a good partner. That's the way you think on the good days, but on the bad days you remember that sex is not dancing, and it's not easy for someone with your tastes to find a worthy partner. It's not easy, but you cope one way or another. More or less.

But you're not coping too well, to be honest. You parted company with your last lover a week ago, it's over between you now – that's why, instead of the sweet pain of gratification, your skin is smarting with the nagging pain of separation.

You turn off the shower, rub yourself down with a towel and your raw spots ache. Smiling, you walk through into the kitchen and put the kettle on. The music from the other room is almost inaudible. You look at the clock: you still have enough time for a cup of coffee.

This is how the day begins. Outside the window, a colorless sun in a gap between December clouds. Good morning to you, darling Ksenia. Don't forget to dress warmly, there's a strong wind today. Don't forget to take the present for Mom, your cell phone, money, ID, travel pass. Don't forget – you have a lot to do today, darling Ksenia, take good care of yourself. Ah yes, and the keys too. Don't forget them, please.

3

AND SO... ONCE UPON A TIME A LITTLE GIRL LIVED with her mommy and daddy, went to the kindergarten, then to school, danced and laughed and never cried. Mommy and Daddy got divorced, school came to an end, the little girl went to work and now, six years later, here she is sitting in a tiny office cubicle with her strong fingers pounding away at a keyboard, her tousled hair more or less held in place by a hair slide, her painted lips pursed in concentration and not a trace of the morning's relaxed mood left in her voice.

"Ksenia, are we putting the news about Berezovsky at the top or is everybody already pissed off with him?"

"He's the one who's pissed off. What else have we got, apart from Berezovsky?"

"I'll just take a look."

This is an ordinary day. The Little Lady of the Big House. It's just a title – Senior Editor of the News Department – a pitiful staff of three, plus the freelancers. True, they're all a few years older than you, and some even have formal qualifications in journalism. Think of themselves as professionals, shit! Sharks of the pen, jackals of the keyboard, freebooters of the computer mouse. There was a time when you had to have sharp words with them, it's true, but now you have them all in line, working at full stretch.

Alexei from the next desk asks on ICQ Internet Messenger:

"how are you doing?"

She answers: "ok" and then asks: "when will I have the interview?"

"I'm just typing it up." Yes, he's sitting there in his earphones, deciphering it.

Daily work inevitably becomes routine: making sure they choose the right news, correcting mistakes, telling off the young girl translators, deciding who to take commentaries from today. A couple of times a week you end up with good material, something you can really take pride in, not feel ashamed of. But then, you don't feel ashamed of what you put out every day either, although there's really not that much to feel proud of, except maybe the successful start to your career: after all, at twenty-three you're already the department's senior editor. The boss. It's funny.

Ksenia likes her job. She enjoys rummaging through the news and she enjoys coordinating, managing and controlling even more. In a few years' time she'll be a good manager, although it's not yet clear where. Maybe she'll become a genuine senior editor, get into paper journalism, if Putin doesn't grab all the newspapers the way he's already grabbed the TV channels. Or perhaps she'll go into pure IT business. "IT" stands for information technology, and it's part of everything to do with the internet. In America they like to add the letter "e," from the word "electronic," but in Russian it's not always convenient to add that letter. You definitely can't add it to the word "business," for instance. "You know," Ksenia explained to one of her foreign friends, "the combination 'eb' in Russian is the same as 'fuck' in English. So you get 'fuck-business.' I can't even say that to one of my friends, let alone my mom."

Ksenia likes her job. She enjoys feeling confident, successful and prosperous. She likes being able to do everything at once: edit an interview, instant message, look through the news. By twelve they'll put the first section of material out on the web, and then she can go to the cafeteria with Alexei, read the latest jokes at Anecdote.ru, call in to see Pasha and have a word about money.

Pasha Silverman, Ksenia's immediate boss, the editor-in-chief and founder of the newspaper Evening.ru, had no interest at all in journalism until the age of thirty-seven.

He moved from the Chechen capital, Grozny, to Moscow in the late eighties – just in time: first there were no more Russians left in the city, then there were no Chechens, and then the city itself disappeared. By the mid-nineties Pasha was heavily involved in advertising, but during one of the repeated market carve-ups, he got squeezed out of TV and billboards, and by the beginning of the next decade all that remained of his former glory was an internet agency, which was lifted up on the rising wave of the investment boom of 2000.

When Pasha first came to the internet, the major form of advertising was banners – little rectangular pictures at the top, bottom or side of the internet page. If the picture caught someone's attention, he clicked on the banner with the mouse and found himself on the advertised site. Basically, that was all there was to it. You could take money for the number of people who would see the banner (that was called "pay-for-views") and for the number of people who clicked on the banner ("pay-for-clicks"). Since then variations had appeared – square banners, pop-up window banners, flash banners and lots of other wonderful technical innovations – but the general principle hadn't changed. The technology made it possible to show the advert to the right audience on the right site – that was called "targeting" – but basically Pasha made money out of people looking at little pictures on their computer screens and occasionally clicking on them for some reason or other.

Pasha had always believed that dealing in advertising was dealing in something unreal. That didn't frighten him: it had been explained to him many years before that in mathematics imaginary numbers like the square root of –1 were just as important as ordinary numbers. Trading in advertising in virtual space was a double unreality – and just as the number *i*, which didn't exist in the normal scale of numbers, made it possible to solve equations and create graphs, the ephemeral banner advertisement allowed Pasha to consolidate his own business and help others to build theirs. Pasha liked the idea of working with things that weren't real – perhaps because there wasn't a single stone left standing in the city where he had spent his childhood.

A couple of years earlier the logic of business development had led Pasha to the idea that it would be good not just to trade in views on other people's sites, but to have a platform of his own where he could show his own banners. He decided to set up a newspaper, intending at the same time occasionally to publish *advertorial*, or paid articles, especially since the time for elections was approaching and the political parties and independent candidates were still prepared to pay well for such material – although, of course, not as well as in the nineties, when the elections were really fascinating.

As an advertising man, Pasha was convinced that to get *high traffic* all you needed was the right kind of promotional campaign. After six months he realized that an online newspaper was not the same as washing powder or a new model of cell phone. The competition in internet media was pretty stiff, and Pasha sacked almost all his editorial staff and took on new people to replace them. One of these was Ksenia, and today Pasha knew it was her energy and talent he had to thank for the large numbers of people who read the news on his site, even if Tickertape.ru did provide much broader coverage.

Ksenia has a sense of style: she can make any banal news story entertaining – news about the economy comes out as a story about urgent daily realities and the experts' comments sound like providential revelations. Pasha has raised her salary twice during the last year, but now, seeing her sit down in a chair and cross her legs, he regrets that he allowed himself to be sold on the idea. I won't give her another kopeck, he tells himself, and smiles amiably.

"How're things, Ksenichka?"

"Fine, thanks," she replies.

Tousled hair, stubborn lips, strong thin arms wrapped round her knees. She doesn't like Pasha's familiar use of a diminutive "Ksenichka" – to everyone else she is just Ksenia, even to her lovers. And she doesn't allow anyone except Olya to call her by her childhood name "Ksyusha." Only Olya can pronounce "Ksyusha" in a way that doesn't remind her of the fifth class at school and mocking children's rhymes.

But Pasha calls everyone by familiar pet names and he has

persuaded her to accept Ksenichka – persuaded, sold, soft-soaped – he told her that he was prepared to address her formally as Ksenia Rudolfovna if she wanted, but he asked her please, please to let him say "Ksenichka" sometimes, because otherwise he wouldn't be able to do his job properly: *I'm not young any more, it's too late for me to learn new ways*. Ksenia agreed and, of course, now he called her nothing but Ksenichka. Since then she had seen over and over again in business negotiations how Pasha extorted advantageous conditions while emphasizing that he had absolutely no right to them and was only asking as a personal favor. Maybe, if Pasha was not coping well with his business, it wouldn't work – but when it came to PR support and advertising promotion, he was the best there was, and the clients let him have his way.

"How're things, Ksenichka?"

"Fine, thanks."

"Fine?" Pasha repeats, turning his monitor toward Ksenia. "Let's just take a look at our rating. Look, this is Rambler – and what spot are we on?"

A screen with light-blue strips running across it. The Rambler Top 100 Ratings – the most important rating on the Russian internet, the unofficial table of ranks, a kind of independent audit. With meters set up on almost every site in the Russian internet, measuring the *traffic*. Ever half hour Rambler generates new ratings of sites according to about fifty subject categories. Whoever gets the most hits has the highest rating. Of course, everyone knows that this rating can be hyped up but even so, the advertisers take their bearings from it, and the small investors use it to decide if their money's working hard enough.

The liquid crystal display of Pasha's monitor shows the "Media and Periodicals" section. As usual, Tickertape and News.ru are fighting for first place, while Evening.ru is in the doldrums somewhere between ten and twenty.

"What do you expect, Pasha?" says Ksenia. "That's what comes of being tight-fisted. You know yourself that within the limits of the present budget I do the impossible."

Her face turns even more stubborn, her lips squeeze together angrily.

"Ksenichka, darling," Pasha replies, sitting on the edge of the desk, "how can you call it being tight-fisted? Look, in the last year I've raised your salary twice. Sure, the first time was when I put you in charge instead of Lena, but the second time was simply because you deserved it, and that's all. But you tell me, have you started working any better since then? Or, rather, will you start working any better if I give you another two hundred dollars?"

"If I say yes," says Ksenia, "you'll say I'm not putting in enough effort, so I don't deserve a pay rise, if I say no–"

"Then I won't give you a raise anyway," Pasha says with a nod. "You understand the whole thing. Every employee has a natural limit: after that, no matter how much you raise their pay, you won't get anything more out of them. Now, if you came up with some special kind of project – one that generated lots of advertising and lots of traffic! – then I'd give you a separate budget. And, of course, part of that budget would go toward a raise for you. But sorry, I won't give you any money just like that."

"What kind of project would you like to have?" Ksenia asks with a smile.

"I don't know," Pasha answers with a shrug. "Something that would fit into the concept of our publication and also attract readers. And wouldn't be like what our friends in the other internet media have."

I get it, Ksenia thinks with a nod. Magical fairytale stuff – I don't know what it is, but bring me it.

"I'll think about it," she says, getting up.

"You have to understand my position," Pasha says apologetically. "I haven't got a lot of money, the election advertising didn't come up to expectations... well, not entirely up to expectations."

"I sympathize," Ksenia says morosely, and for a moment Pasha remembers that he is lying shamelessly: business is going well and there's plenty of money, but that's no reason to start giving it away to the staff. Because if someone works for seven hundred and fifty dollars, there's no point in giving them a thousand. At least, not until someone else starts trying to poach them. And so before every conversation about a raise, Pasha tells himself "there's no money, there's no money, there's no money" until he starts to believe it – and then he can repeat these words with a clear conscience. In the unreal world that he inhabits, it's the only way.

Ksenia has only a vague idea about all this. But even so, she goes back to her desk feeling quite satisfied: now at least she knows what to do. She just has to come up with some project, then go back to Pasha and start the conversation by saying: "Remember, you promised me..."

She doesn't take offence at his obvious lies about the election campaign money: deep in her heart Ksenia suspects that if she were in Pasha's place, she would act the same way. She enjoys observing her boss: he is far from stupid and there are things she can learn from him. Her colleagues sometimes complain that they're pissed off with Pasha, that he's so mean. They might be pissed off with him, and he might be pissed off with them, but who else do we have apart from Pasha? she asks herself. A good boss who's sociable without fraternizing too much and is friendly without any harassment.

Before joining Pasha's Evening.ru Ksenia used to work as a journalist in the internet section of the Moscow branch of a Western publishing house. Almost all the employees were local, but the office was still dominated by an extreme spirit of American political correctness: a strict dress code, no jokes about sex, no flirting. Her friend Marina, who dropped in occasionally, used to joke that the tea in the plastic cups was about to freeze solid in the positively benevolent atmosphere of the place, but at the beginning Ksenia had actually liked the atmosphere there. Coming to work with her nipples still itching after the clamps and fresh bruises on her thighs, she used to smile to herself and think complacently that her colleagues would recoil in horror if they only knew how she spent the nights. Ksenia had good career prospects, with a chance of moving from the internet department to the advertising department, and she was already mulling over this option. From the age of nineteen, when almost by accident she had found herself as an assistant in one of the laboratories of the Central Institute of Economics and Mathematics, she had always been involved in the web, and sometimes it seemed to her that real life and real business were not here, but out in the *real world*. But all that came to an end rather sooner than expected, at the out-of-house pre-Christmas party.

They rented a guesthouse outside Moscow. Some people were thinking of going back to the city, but most were intending to stay overnight. The table was laid in the banqueting hall, the Big Boss proposed a toast in fairly decent Russian, the local DJ turned on the strobe lights, the Euro-pop started playing – and an hour later, as she watched her colleagues hopping about friskily, Ksenia was reminded of the old school dances. She liked to dance and she was good at it, but this mawkish oompah-oompah didn't inspire her. When she was a bit younger, she used to bring her favourite CDs with her – but this wasn't the right occasion for that. She shrank back against the wall and exchanged a couple of words with Liza from the marketing department, who was wearing an unusually short skirt and was already slightly drunk, and then she went to the table to pour herself a punch. When she leaned over, someone's hand gave her buttock a gentle squeeze. Two fingers landed precisely on a fresh mark, a long diagonal bluish-black stripe, but that wasn't important – before Ksenia even realized what she was doing, she swung round and struck out.

Fifteen years earlier, when karate emerged from the underground, her parents had immediately sent her brother Lyova to a club. Lyova had practiced his blows on his little sister and tried to teach her a couple of *katas* and *mawashis*. Ksenia was a bad student and she thought she'd forgotten everything in the years since then, but her body's memory proved very retentive: her blow landed with perfect precision.

Something squelched under Ksenia's fingers and she was amazed to see blood spreading across the white shirt of the deputy director, ruddy-faced thirty-five-year-old Dima. He had started off as a Komsomol businessman, but come off the road on the steep curve of the 1990s and ended up as a common-or-garden executive, or, to use the modern term, a manager. Now he was on his way up: if you didn't count the Big Boss, Dima was the third most important person in the whole office. Fortune seemed to be smiling on him again, and perhaps that was why he didn't move aside and pretend nothing had happened, but tried to hit Ksenia back, and she saw her own right hand move in a slow-motion movie sequence to deflect the blow, and her left hand swing and jab once again into that astonished pink-and-red face.

Afterward, as she tried to thumb a lift on the snow-covered highway and rubbed the stinging knuckles of her fingers with the bitten nails, Ksenia blamed herself and wondered: *Did I break his nose or just split it?* Yes, Lyova would have been delighted with her, but Ksenia felt ashamed anyway. Good girls didn't behave like that, and neither did bad ones. Maybe he had touched her by accident, and she had just struck out without bothering to check? Ksenia felt so upset she could have cried – but she never cried. When she got home, she rang her lover at the time and asked him to come over and be rougher than usual: maybe so that the drops of blood would take the place of her uncried tears.

After the holidays she gave in her notice: not even because of that guilty feeling she'd had, and certainly not because she was afraid of revenge. In a single instant Dima had suddenly ceased to be a boss for her. It wasn't the harassment, it was just that Ksenia couldn't respect a man who had let through two of her amateurish blows in a row.

But she's sure of Pasha. He doesn't confuse the office with the bedroom, and if anything did happen, he'd catch her hand. Or hit her himself.

And anyway, Pasha avoids direct conflicts. He knows nothing about Ksenia's sexual preferences, but he understands her very well – far better than many of her lovers.

It was like this: the two of you were in a large group of people you didn't know very well, some friends of Sasha's, at the birthday party of one of the girls from his class at school, someone he used to be in love with. Sasha called to collect you, and before you went to the party you made love, never suspecting that it was the last time. At the party people started talking about sex, and you couldn't resist saying that you liked rough sex, BDSM, to be exact, also known as "playing": what do you mean, you don't know what that is? Well, it has a triple meaning: BD is bondage/discipline; DS is domination/submission; and, well, SM is sadomasochism, that's obvious. In principle, these are all different things: some people who play like bondage, others like submission, and some just like pain for its own sake, but sometimes someone likes all of them together, although I'm pretty much indifferent to bondage. Everybody stopped talking, as if they were embarrassed, and Sasha said something like "That's too much for vanilla people like us to understand. I never thought you were such a pervert." You immediately tensed up. Although, of course, that was his right, if he wanted, he could stay in the closet, as the fraternal fags put it, let him pretend to be a decent, *vanilla* individual, if he felt so ashamed in front of his friends. You got up and walked into the kitchen. Sasha followed you. "Get on your knees and take me in your mouth," he said, and you flew into a rage. You never promised to submit to him anywhere except in the bedroom, no 24/7, and you had no intention of sucking him off in the kitchen at a birthday party for an old classmate he used to be in love with when he was a delicate little boy and no doubt incapable of beating a girl so hard with a riding crop that the marks on her buttocks took a week to heal. "I don't want to," you said and then, remembering your games, he tried to grab you by the hair and force your head down, and then you said it again, feeling yourself getting angrier and angrier: "Don't," and he said: "If you don't do it right now, it's over." And then you pushed him away and said: "Then it's over."

"If you don't do it right now, it's over." That was the last straw. Not the vanilla public image, not the demand to suck him off. No, it was those nine pitiful words that decided everything. Sasha could have tried to break your will and force you down on your knees (oh, how glad you would have been to suck him off then!) or retreated smoothly, pretending it was all just a joke. You would both have forgotten about it, and the next time at your place you would have been his submissive slave again, but those words – *if you don't do it right now* – those words meant he lacked the strength of will to be a genuine master, and he lacked the wisdom to realize it. A pitiful attempt at blackmail, a little boy moaning and telling his mother: “If you don’t buy me that railway engine, it means you don’t love me anymore.” So it means I don’t love him, you thought, and that was the most terrible thing, because the words – the ones he said and your reply – couldn’t be taken back now. You couldn’t pretend they were never spoken. That evening you deleted him from your ICQ and put his telephone number on your Motorola’s blacklist.

Moscow is a small town, you’re bound to meet again – but never again will you lie on the floor in front of him, with your hands tied above your head and your eyes closed so that you can’t see which breast will take the next blow from the double length of telephone wire.

4

AFTERNOON, AND THE CARS ARE ALREADY BUMPER to bumper. The creeping afternoon traffic jam. Bolshaya Nikitskaya Street looks like a river covered with drift-ice in spring. Olya, that is, formally, Olga Krushevnitskaya, a successful businesswoman of thirty-five, an IT manager and co-owner of a small online shop, maneuvers in her Toyota, cursing through her teeth. On her way to have coffee with her friend, she repeats to herself: "So, what was it he said? *I wouldn't even shit in the same field.* Just slammed the door and walked out. And what am I supposed to do now? No point in complaining – they warned me: Olya, you'll come unstuck with these two, there'll be hell to pay."

Three years earlier Olya herself invited Grisha and Kostya (that is, Grigorii and Konstantin) to join her business. Or rather, the business wasn't hers then: Olya was a hired manager on a salary, and she only managed to grab herself a quarter of the business when the shop was bought from the first owners – who, by the way, got three dollars for every one they had put in. That was the way they set up the shares: money from Grisha and Kostya, and from her – knowledge of the market and experience, three years of hard graft. But at the very beginning of the whole thing, someone at the Internet Business Club told her: those two bears will never get along together in your little den.

They won't get along together in my den. Won't shit in the same field. They'll take their money – then it's goodbye and farewell to Olya's business. Wolves. Bears. She'd served them faithfully for three years, fed them with her own flesh and blood, interest on profit, flattery and lies. You know how much I like working with you, Grisha. Believe me Kostya, in our business everything depends on you.

Our business? But that wasn't right. Olya had always thought of the business as hers alone. She had started it and kept it going for all these years, she was the only one who had the vision and understood the development plans, who could anticipate the future. But she had honestly torn chunks off to feed the wolves, trying to forget that wolves were always looking back to the forest. She had held out for three whole years, and now Grisha and Kostya were both bolting from the common field, back into their homeland in the depths of the forest to look for Little Red Riding Hoods – or anyone else they could find to gobble up.

Olya stops at a traffic light, pulls down the mirror and looks at herself. A well-groomed thirty-five-year-old woman. An elegant arm lying on the steering wheel with a bracelet of dark stones round the wrist. A prosperous businesswoman, the co-owner and general director of a small internet shop. No, she didn't look a bit like Little Red Riding Hood, it wasn't so easy to gobble her up. She knew every bush in this forest too – and she wouldn't go to her granny's little house, she'd go into the dragon's cave, then we'd see which of the wolves would risk following her in.

And there's the first miracle of this lousy day: a silver BMW pulls away from the curb at just the right moment – and Olya parks her Toyota. She jumps out on to the pavement, trying not to step in the dirty puddle of melt water, slams the black, mud-splattered door shut, presses the button on her remote and, just as she's walking into the Coffee House, she hears the quiet beep of the security system. That means everything's all right. Now she'll try to choose a table by the window and on the way take a moment to check that everything really is all right. When you live on your own for a long time, you get used to things: to the laptop that should have been changed ages ago, to the bracelet that you were given, hanging round your wrist, to the car that you ought to sell, but can't bring yourself to. You don't admit it to anyone except yourself, but you feel a kind of inner kinship with it. Six years for a car is like thirty-five for a woman: still running, but with the price tag falling faster every year. And so you look after it as if it were your own body – regular services, fresh oil, BP gasoline, comprehensive insurance. And there's the result: great condition, not a single scratch, as good as new.

Her friend Ksenia, who she calls Ksyusha, is already sitting at a table, toying with a cell phone in a kitschy bright-pink fluffy case.

"Look what I've bought," she says. "Isn't it just delightful?"

Olya politely takes the mobile in her manicured hands and buries her fingers in the pink fur.

"It reminds me of something," she says.

"Aha," Ksyusha agrees, "my rabbit, remember, I showed it to you?"

Yes, the pink rabbit. Every over-aged Little Red Hiding Hood should have her own pink rabbit: that way there's something to give the Big Bad Wolf when he comes knocking at the door of the hut. But Olya doesn't have any fluffy toys, and you can't put a case on a Sony-Ericsson P800. All she has is an aging Toyota, well-preserved, but already doomed.

"I was thinking," says Ksyusha, "if you crossed a cell phone and a rabbit, what would their children be like?"

"Well, fluffy little mechanical devices," Olya replies. "Like the rabbits in the Energizer advert."

Little rabbit girls hop around in the dark forests of Russian business and shudder at the roaring of the big bad wolves who can't share the same field, only the same forest. Because in the field there's no one to eat, but in the forest there are fluffy pink animals and aging Little Red Riding Hoods who aren't mobile enough to avoid the wolves' teeth.

"You've got everything mixed up." says Ksyusha. "A cell phone isn't a mechanical device, it's a communications device. They'd probably be telepathic rabbits."

"There was some story about telepathic rabbits," says Olya, "remember?"

"Na-ah," says Ksyusha, "I haven't read very much. I mean, not as much as you."

That's probably a good thing, not to read so much, Olya thinks. She spent almost thirty years stuck in the gingerbread house of their library at home and Petersburg University's castle in the air. Probably it really is a good thing not to fritter away your time on books, not to know every word of Brodsky's *To Urania* and *A Part of Speech*, smuggled into the country by other lovers of poetry like yourself, but to find yourself out in the dark forest right away, before you got midway through life. To find yourself there without even being able to recognize the hidden quotation (at least one) in that last phrase, but not to feel daunted when you met the wolves, panthers and lions – or whoever it is that Dante and successful IT managers ran into along their way.

"So what happened to the telepathic rabbits in the story?" Ksyusha asks.

"I don't remember," Olya replies. "I think they've all been eaten before the story even starts. Before anyone has even realized that they are telepaths."

"Bang-bang, aye-aye-aye, see my little rabbit die," says Ksyusha, citing the old children's song. And she knocks her cell phone over as if it has been hit by a hunter's bullet.

Olya smiles, and her lips cramp at the memory of two wolves glaring at each other from behind the trees in the dense forest of their joint business.

"Listen, Ksyusha," she says, "I need your help. Will you help me?"

Ksyusha suddenly turns serious – a businesswoman, IT manager, senior editor in the news department of a popular online newspaper – she sets her thin elbows on the table and leans her head to one side, as if to say: I'm listening, come on Olya, tell me what's bothering you.

And Olya tells her.

Three years ago, at the height of the investment boom, two major internet companies decided to invest in the shop that Olya managed. They bought it from the first owners, gave Olya her twenty-five percent, and divided up the rest between them. Two major companies? Actually just two investors, two men who had known each other since before the internet. Kostya and Grisha, Konstantin and Grigorii. Friends and competitors, rivals and comrades. For three years their furious skirmishes didn't interfere with the business; it remained a joint interest, until this December when they quarreled big-time over dividing up the funds from the election campaign. And this morning Grigorii slammed the door of Olya's office and shouted "I wouldn't even shit in the same field." The little online shop – a rather trivial business by Kostya's and Grisha's standards – turned out to be the little goat from that other children's song that took it into its head to go wandering into Dante's dark forest at just the wrong time. The situation was tragic in an entirely literal sense – Olya's business was about to sing its farewell *goat song* and become a ritual sacrifice in a squabble between two former friends.

She can repeat the old familiar move and bring in a big new investor to buy the business from Grisha and Kostya. There isn't anyone like that in the Russian internet – but Olya knows who she could go to. If, that is, she can really take the risk of going to him – because Olya doesn't like this man. He's an outsider, someone from a different and dangerous world, from offline, ordinary business, business that makes Kostya's and Grisha's wild, remote forest look like a tidy English park.

Olya explains all of this to Ksyusha now, explains it carefully, trying to avoid any allusions to Dante, jokes about the little gray goat and goat song – because she's not sure that Ksyusha knows about scapegoats, Dionysian sacrifices and the birth of tragedy out of the spirit of music. After all, Ksyusha didn't graduate from the history faculty in Petersburg; immediately after school she set out like an emancipated Little Red Riding Hood along the winding path to a place where there had never been any granny, but there was at least some faint hope of earning your own piece of bread and butter.

As Olya tells her story, Ksyusha watches the way she waves her hand, and the way the bracelet on her wrist shimmers. Large dark stones, as dark as Olya's eyes. Olya waves her hand beautifully, she draws beautifully on her long cigarette holder, she talks beautifully and even sighs beautifully. If Ksyusha could fall in love with a woman, she would definitely fall in love with Olya. You might say she has already fallen in love: at the negotiations three years earlier she said "Wow!" to herself the moment she saw this tall woman with the well-groomed hands, short light-tinted hair and deep, dark eyes. They discussed the terms for yet another advertising campaign, and Ksenia thought she wanted to be like Olya someday. Perhaps she simply liked Olya's way of inclining her head during a conversation, smiling with just the corners of her mouth and waving her hand fluently when she rejected an unacceptable proposal. Ksenia even liked the not exactly old-fashioned, not exactly provincial Petersburg way she smoked a cigarette, drawing in the smoke through a long cigarette holder. On that first occasion they got through the business quickly and spent another forty minutes talking about all sorts of nonsense, she can't remember exactly what now. They immediately started calling each other "Olya" and "Ksyusha," and now they meet a couple of times a week, and Ksyusha is glad her premonition didn't deceive her: it was friendship at first sight.

"And so," says Olya, stubbing her cigarette out in the ashtray, "I want to ask you to make some inquiries about him, about this man. I don't really know anything about him, but you're a journalist, so you can manage it, right?"

5

KSENIA WALKS THROUGH THE PASSAGE FROM ONE subway line to the other in a dense crowd of people, in a vortex of deep human waters, a subterranean reflection of the traffic jams on the Moscow streets. Instead of frosty Tverskaya Street with its smell of petrol, there is the stale air of Pushkinskaya Station; instead of the stench of tobacco in the front seat of a private car acting as a taxi, there is the smell of sweat in the stuffy carriage. Save fifteen, no, twenty minutes and two hundred, no, one hundred and fifty rubles, get there for seven as she promised, not be late at least this once.

She was never late for business meetings or assignations, but somehow she had never managed to get to her mother's place on time, ever since she was a child, when it used to take her an hour to get home from school, stopping for a chat with Vika, and then with Marina, who she called Marinka, saying goodbye ten times on every corner, and then deciding to make a detour anyway, walking to the garages first, and then to the bus stop. It took her fifteen minutes to walk to school and an hour to walk back. She had to be at the dance studio by three. Ksenia didn't really have to hurry, but her mom was nervous anyway, she said she would go crazy, times weren't what they used to be, now they didn't even let little children go to school on their own, let alone Ksenia, a beautiful ten-year-old girl, the delight of any pedophile, a future Lolita, the light of her parents' lives, the fire of God only knew whose appalling loins. Ksenia was stubborn, she forbade her mother to meet her, swore she would come home on time, but she still came late. Her mom made a show of drinking her decoction of one-hundred-percent natural valerian from virgin forests somewhere in Siberia or the Urals, her mom clutched at her heart, her mom said her daughter didn't love her at all. Ksenia persuaded herself that these reproaches were a proof of love. Not of her love for her mom, of course, but of her mom's love for her. Because if her mom didn't love her, why would her mom get so anxious?

Lyova was already in eleventh grade at school and he was regarded as quite grown up already, he had even applied for a place in college amid a general atmosphere of approving indifference: who could ever doubt it, of course he would get in. Ksenia heard Lyova telling a friend or a girlfriend on the phone that if not for the army he would never have applied for college; who needed an education now? And he probably wouldn't be a physicist, there was no money in it, unless you went away to America. Afterward, many years later, Ksenia was surprised at how much he knew about everything in advance: he had been right twice over – he didn't become a physicist and he went away to America.

She was always home late from school; only once, when half the class, including Vika and Marinka, was off sick with flu, she came on time and ran into Slava in the entrance of the building (he was the one, by the way, who never wanted to be called "uncle" – just Slava, that was all) and he hesitated, as if he was embarrassed about something, mumbled "Hi" and hurried off to the bus stop. She walked in, shouted "Mom, I'm home!" and through the half-open door of her parents' bedroom she saw the crumpled sheets and didn't understand at first, then her mom came out of the bathroom wearing a robe over her naked body, with her hair all clumped together. "What are you doing here so early? You could at least have rung the doorbell." She'd never asked Ksenia to ring the bell before, Ksenia had had her own keys since third grade, and now as she stood there in the corridor Ksenia started blushing uncontrollably, as if she'd done something unforgivable, almost criminal. She whispered, "Sorry, Mom, I didn't think," and went to her room, trying not to look round at the grinning door of the bedroom and burning with shame, feeling like a criminal for having found out something she wasn't supposed to know. The latest number of Mom's *AIDS-Info*, the sex education tabloid, was lying on the floor beside her bed, she'd been reading it yesterday before she went to sleep, she was proud that her mom and dad weren't like other girls' parents, they didn't hide anything, on the contrary, to her grannies' horror, they had explained everything to her at the age of six with a little book translated from French, so that now, at the age of ten, Ksenia knew absolutely *everything about that*. But today this pride and this joy had disappeared somewhere. Ksenia felt ashamed. She would rather not have known what had been going on only half an hour earlier in her mom's bedroom. It would have been better if she didn't read *AIDS-Info*, but read what all the girls did, something like Alexandra Ripley's continuation of *Gone With the Wind*. She wanted to cry, but she'd forbidden herself to do that, big girls didn't cry. Ksenia never cried, and anyway, what point was there in crying, tears wouldn't help her grief, her mom was right, it was Ksenia's own fault, she shouldn't have come back at the wrong time, if she was so grown-up already and understood everything so well. And so Ksenia sits there in her room, takes the textbooks out of her briefcase and starts doing her homework. Mom always said: if you feel like crying, go and do your lessons. Especially since she has a test tomorrow, and she has to get an A.

Ksenia walks through the passage under the stone vaulting of the Stalinist subway system. There are little wind-up khaki-colored soldiers crawling along the wall, with their machine guns chattering, but the toy guns can barely even be heard above the noise of the crowd. The soldiers crawl along as if they are delirious, with their entire bodies squirming, squirming as if they are dodging blows, as if in erotic ecstasy, crawling as if their legs refuse to carry them, crawling to some unknown destination, invalids continuing a futile war, a war that was over long ago. They will survive and ride through the carriages in the underground in metal wheelchairs, collecting money in paratroopers' berets, crippled, with no legs, either drunk or stoned. Ksenia will lower her eyes into her book, trying not to look at them, trying not to remember how every time she encounters pain, suffering and physical deformity, people who have lost arms or legs, it is like some kind of prediction that could affect her personally. The same way she used to feel frightened by articles about psychotic killers, sadists and perverts who tortured their partners by hanging them from a hook in the ceiling by their outstretched arms, covering their bodies with the parallel stripes of scars, welts and bruises. It's still there, that aching pain of separation, now what have you done, where are you going to find another lover like that? But it's over – don't you understand that? It's over.

Ksenia walks through the passage. Clattering heels, dark business suit, short winter coat. One thin hand lightly holding the purse in place on her shoulder. Walking through the passage. Twenty-three years old, a good job, excellent prospects. Walking through the passage.

6

THE ROOM THAT USED TO BE KSENIA'S IS HER MOTHER'S study now. There's a computer on the desk where she used to do her lessons all those years ago. There are dictionaries on the shelf where the pink rabbit used to sit. Every time she comes here, Ksenia gets a bitter feeling. It's not that she would really like to keep everything just the way it was. But perhaps she would like the flat where her childhood was spent to have remembered her for a little bit longer. It seems to Ksenia that her things have disappeared so easily because she herself was only an accident in her mother's life, an accident who was easy to forget. Forgotten. She never admits these suspicions even to herself: of course not, after all, she knows how much her mother loves her, didn't her mother talk about love all the way through her childhood, and specifically about her love for Ksenia? There was never a word spoken about her love for Lyova, that was somehow taken for granted, not a subject for discussion. Almost everything to do with Lyova was taken for granted – but from early in her childhood Ksenia can remember her mom's voice saying how much she did for her, for Ksenia: she gave up a trip to London when Ksenia was six months old, she didn't sleep at night when Ksenia was ill, she didn't divorce Dad for all those years, she put up with his drunken friends and weeks-long work assignments, with his coming home after midnight whenever there was a deadline for delivering another *computer program*, and all so that her daughter would have a father, at least some kind of father, although it was hard to call him that. "How many times a week do you see your daughter?" She used to hear that from the next room. "You don't care about anything at all apart from your job, but it's not as if you even earn decent money. If not for Ksenia, I'd have divorced you ages ago." She covered her head, trying not to hear, but a pillow was poor protection against her mom's loud, harsh, piercing voice, that voice she loved so much. Ksenia lay there with her eyes closed and her hands over her ears, she swaddled herself in the blanket, trying not to hear those words – and she lay there in the same way on those other nights, when Dad went away on his assignments and Mom had visitors and they drank wine in the kitchen and laughed in the corridor. Mom would come in to kiss her goodnight, looking beautiful in high-heeled shoes, smelling of perfume and wine, and Ksenia went to sleep surrounded by those smells and the quiet laughter coming through the half-open door. Then she would wake up in the night and cover her head with the pillow, trying not to hear her mom's heavy sighs suddenly breaking through the silence, sighs that changed into a deep, frightening scream. Once she asked Lyova why their mom screamed in the night and he said she was "too little to be asking questions like that" and Ksenia blushed, because there was nothing in the little French book about sighing and screaming, and Lyova gave her a gentle slap on her bottom and led her off to play at Sarah Connor and the Terminator.

That was their favourite game. First Ksenia had to do a chin-up on the children's sports frame, and then Lyova appeared from the hallway, holding a toy pump-action shotgun and shouting "I'll be back!" and Ksenia screamed "It's him, it's him, I knew he would come!" and made a dash for it, and Lyova pursued her all round the flat. The skirt covering her childish knees trembled in terror, Ksenia ran and ran until Lyova squeezed her into a corner, grabbed both her wrists in his fist and said: "Calm down, Sarah, I've come to save you." Their parents didn't like this game – perhaps because one day, during a gallop along the corridors of the imaginary insane asylum Ksenia (Linda Hamilton) and Lyova (Arnold Schwarzenegger) caught the cable of the VCR standing on the old Soviet "Ruby" TV and the video went crashing to the floor. Fortunately, it wasn't damaged, apart from a crack in the silvery plastic. It was symbolic, said Dad, that when they played Terminator, they knocked the video recorder over. After that their favourite game was banned, which only made them like it all the more. When their parents were out, Ksenia ran round the flat time and time again, choking on her fear and fatigue as she anticipated the feeling of Lyova's strong hands, the crunching of her wrists and the calm voice that spoke at the peak of her terror: "Calm down, I've come to save you."

Standing in the corridor where Lyova once used to pursue Ksenia is aunty Mila, a small brunette the same height as Ksenia, or perhaps even shorter. She's standing on her toes, kissing Valera (or Vadim? – Ksenia can't remember) who is married either to aunty Sveta or aunty Lera – or was married first to one and then the other. They take no notice of Ksenia, perhaps they're too absorbed in what they're doing, or perhaps they're too used to the idea that Ksenia is only Masha's daughter, still just a little girl – funny, she looks so much like Masha, but she isn't beautiful at all.

Today Mom is wearing a green dress that she brought from America when Ksenia was fifteen. She kisses her daughter on the cheek and for a second the half-forgotten smell of perfume and wine is back again.

"See, I'm not late," Ksenia says.

"You could at least have gone home to change," her mom replies. "This is my birthday party and you've come dressed for work."

"I'm sorry," says Ksenia, lowering her head. "I just didn't think."

"Never mind, it's too late now," says her mom, giving her a gentle nudge in the side. "Go in the kitchen and help Sveta with the salads."

They've already drunk to their hostess, the birthday girl, our beautiful Masha, to this house and to love, yes, of course, to love. Mom never laid tables crowded with food, like the parties at Granny's house. She preferred the *à la fourchette* approach, even though she still cooked a whole series of different dishes:

hors d'oeuvres, salads, entrees and then tea with cake. Mom was an excellent cook, so good that Ksenia couldn't even hope to achieve such perfection. That was probably why now, when Ksenia celebrated her own birthday, she simply bought ready-made food or invited everyone to a café or a club: it didn't cost much more, and you didn't have to clear up in the morning. But Mom! Mom was a born cook. Dad always said that if no one needed translators any longer, Masha could always get a job in a restaurant. He used to say it every time they had guests and one day aunty Lelya, Slava's wife, couldn't stand it anymore, and at the end of Dad's tirade she added "as a waitress." Mom ran out of the room and slammed the door, Dad went running after her to apologize, and he never mentioned the restaurant again, while aunty Lelya, a beautiful plump blonde, carried on turning up at the important events with Slava, twisting the corners of her mouth without saying anything as she waited for the chance to put in her drop of poison. This annoyed Ksenia and one day, when she was already fifteen, she actually said to aunt Lelya – it was while the two of them were cutting the vegetables for the salads in the kitchen – "You don't like my mom, do you?" Lelya shrugged her white shoulders under her loose-fitting semi-transparent blouse and answered: "I don't really have any reason to like her much. Your mom's never done anything good for me" – and at that moment the knife in Ksenia's hand slipped, she shrieked, the blood spurted into the plate and the salad was ruined. The scream brought her mom running in, she grabbed Ksenia's hand and lifted the cut finger to lips painted the same color as Ksenia's blood, kissed it several times and shouted into the flat: "Lera, bring the first-aid kit!" Then she sat Ksenia on her knees, stroked her hair and kept stroking it until aunty Lera and aunty Sveta stuck a plaster over the cut with a glance of reproach at Lelya, who briskly threw the salad into the rubbish bucket and started slicing everything all over again. Ksenia didn't cry, but she felt resentful and ashamed, not because of her finger, but because a few minutes earlier, for just a second, she had thought there really wasn't any reason to love her mom – as if she loved her for some reason or other, and not just because she was her mom, the best mom in the world, the only person who loved Ksenia, the most beautiful, the sexiest, the kindest.

Lelya had got divorced ages ago and married some German from the Siemens office; she didn't come to the parties anymore. Slava still attended all the birthday gatherings but, looking at him today, Ksenia thought for the first time that he was five years older than Mom, really old, his beard was almost gray, he was almost completely bald and his face was covered with wrinkles. He'd got drunk very quickly and now he was passionately trying to persuade the other guests in the kitchen about something or other. Ksenia didn't remember all of their names any longer. They were talking about the explosions in Moscow, about Berezovsky, the FSB and Zakaev, and if they weren't her mom's friends, Ksenia would have put in her own two cents' worth and explained how it was all done, how the media created events and put out exaggerated conspiracy theories that were designed to lay the truth bare and obscure it in equal measure. Whatever you might say, she was the only person there who had any direct connection with the mass media, although the guests probably didn't know that, because her mom usually just said simply, "My daughter does something on the internet." Ksenia's achievements paled in the light of the brilliant career ahead of Lyova: after the third year at college he had gone away to America and suddenly been transformed from a physicist into a businessman with an MBA and an unbelievable annual salary.

And there they are talking about Berezovsky, Zakaev and the FSB: Slava, who never wanted to be called "uncle Slava," Vadim (or Valera), who had been kissing aunty Mila, uncle Kolya, who never objected to the word "uncle" and liked to tickle Ksenia when she was little, and after she turned fifteen took a liking to kissing her when they met, pressing her against himself so tightly that one day she had to say "don't" in that voice that already worked on men even then, regardless of their age or how intimate she was with them. When Ksenia grew up, that "don't" served her as an effective replacement for the stop-word that they wrote so much about on the BDSM sites, because that "don't" worked even on the most arrant of dominants, who liked a girl to come crawling to them on her knees, hanging her head and exposing her breasts, submissively handing them a riding crop or a paddle; that "don't" stopped even them without any advance agreement about a stop-word. So it's not surprising that uncle Kolya recoiled at Ksenia's response as if she had struck him, struck him with one of those *katas* that Lyova had once tried in vain to teach her. After that uncle Kolya was always emphatically polite, but his eyes still followed Ksenia as she walked round the room.

And there they are talking about Zakaev, Berezovsky and the FSB, and her mom comes into the kitchen in her green dress and high heels, with her lips the same color as Ksenia's blood, enveloped in a cloud of perfume and wine, she comes into the kitchen and looks at them, all steamed up already and shouting at each other as if their words can change something in this world, as if they can stop the suburban trains and apartment blocks being blown up, stop the soldiers raping and killing, make the bullets pass through the flesh without damaging it, like a ray of light passing through a cloud of dust, make the federal forces and the Chechens suddenly stop making money out of this war and turn the pain into pure joy, happiness and love. Her mom looks at them, smiles sweetly and says: "What excitable boys you are... and you know... you all have something in common, and I know what it is..." and then she gives them the look that Ksenia remembers so well from her childhood, the look that heralds sighs in the night, she looks at them, smiles sweetly and pronounces these words so loudly that they can probably be heard by her girlfriends in the next room, the former or present wives of these gray-haired boys, and they understand perfectly well what the men who have gathered here today all have in common, what unites them above and beyond their excitability, the smell of alcohol, the mid-life crisis, imminent old age and inevitable death.

Ksenia walks out of the kitchen and opens the door of her room – the room that was hers. The light is off, but as always the street lamp is shining in through the window, and by its ghostly light she sees aunty Mila standing on tiptoe and kissing someone enthusiastically... but who is it? What difference does it make, these people have known each other for so many years, they've probably all slept together as couples, perhaps even as threesomes and foursomes. Ksenia closes the door, there are loud voices in the large room, Zakaev, Berezovsky and the FSB are in the kitchen, and she decides not to go into the bedroom, not because the childish prohibition is still in effect, but it would simply be awkward to see two fifty-year-old people making love in the bed that to Ksenia is forever her parents' bed, although her father hasn't spent the night here for many years now. But whoever might be in there, it would certainly be a primal scene, Ksenia thinks. Just the month before, Olya had finished explaining to her about psychoanalysis, childhood traumas and the Oedipus complex – all the things she hadn't remembered from *AIDS-Info* when she used to read it, in those days when her parents' bedroom really belonged to her parents.

Ksenia walks along the corridor: the sound of voices, Leonard Cohen singing in the room, uncle Kolya walking toward her, opening his arms wide, and for a moment Ksenia cringes in fright, because she suddenly has a very clear vision of her right hand sinking into his solar plexus. This vision is so real that Ksenia takes a step back, and just in time, because Sveta comes out of the room carrying a pile of plates and falls straight into uncle Kolya's embrace. The top plate falls and breaks, Ksenia ducks into the bathroom and locks the door behind her.

She is shuddering in revulsion, despair and arousal. There are clothes pegs hanging on a line, she chooses a green one and a red one, then sits down on the edge of the bath and pulls down her skirt and panties. There is a tight ball of warmth rolling about somewhere below her belly, she pulls up her shirt, unfastens her bra, bites on her lip to stop herself crying out, clamps the clothes pegs on her nipples – first the red one, then the green one – closes her eyes that are filled with tears of pain, puts her right hand on her clitoris and the fingers of her left hand into her vagina and starts to masturbate.

At moments like this she doesn't have to think about anything. She forgets about her mother and her father, she forgets about the Evening.ru office, she forgets about Sasha, she forgets about her own loneliness – until eventually the pain and the pleasure climax and intersect, merging into one.

Still in the darkness of her closed eyelids, Ksenia unclamps the clothes pegs, freeing her nipples, and they flare up, sending a final tremor through her entire body; there's a salty taste in her mouth, she must have bitten her lip after all. Then Ksenia opens her eyes and looks at the pattern traced out by the small tiles on the bathroom floor that she has known since her childhood. A dark skirt, black panties, two clothes pegs – red and green – today's *MK* tabloid newspaper, open at the "events" page, a blurred photograph and a large headline: "Moscow psycho kills again."

7

I REMEMBER VERY CLEARLY THE FIRST TIME IT happened. When I realized that I would kill soon.

It was evening, I was masturbating in the shower. The jets of water were streaming over my skin, my prick seemed huge. It was swollen up as if all the blood in the world had flowed into it, that evening when I realized for the first time.

I always found it hard to come quickly. Except perhaps when I used to toss off as a kid, after waiting for my little brother to go to sleep. I used to imagine Roman patricians raping female slaves by the hundred, or barbarians on prancing horses bursting into Rome to dishonor and kill. I don't think I was the only one who imagined such things: naked flesh was only accessible in the form of classical statues, sex was taboo and it seemed quite impossible that women could do it of their own free will. So I used to imagine Red Indians in the deserts of the Wild West, standing beside a wagon and tearing the clothes off the juvenile granddaughters of a gray-haired patriarch with a biblical name. A chief with the noble profile of Gojko Miti , the star of the East German Westerns, would tell his deputy – or whoever it is that Red Indians have: "I'll rape the youngest one, you rape their mother. Then we'll swap."

I didn't know any other verbs. In my fantasies they never said "fuck" – I thought that word sounded vulgar, and I never heard the word "screw" until I was nineteen, in a dubbed version of Russ Meyer's film *Faster, Pussycat! Kill! Kill!* The characters in my fantasies didn't fuck or screw. They preferred to rape or even dishonor. "I'll dishonor the youngest one, you dishonor their mother. Then we'll swap." I was a bookish boy and it couldn't be helped – I could never find the right words. Although, as you recall, I certainly had a rich imagination.

Sex was taboo, and even the word seemed almost obscene. In my adolescent years they used to write it on walls in English, beside the word "prick." It was hard to believe that the word "sex" even existed in the Russian language.

Then I grew up and learned about the right words and the warmth of women's bodies. I was considered a good lover, they used to think I was taking care to please the girl and that was why I took so long to come. In my young years this was highly valued. But in fact, the reason I didn't come for a long time was not at all that I was concerned to satisfy the girl moaning like a wild animal with her eyes closed somewhere underneath me. It's just that in order to come, I had to imagine a knife slicing through skin, blood streaming from the wound and a severed nipple falling to the bloody floor. Imagine flayed scalps, a stake transfixing someone from anus to throat, little girls, with breasts that are still tiny, weeping, down on their knees with their hands cut off.

All the blood in the world, yes all the blood in the world.

Imagining such things is not really very pleasant – especially when a woman you love is lying beside you. And so I used to take a long time making love, holding back right to the end, only letting my imagination off the leash when I was really tired. When I was tired or when it got too boring. Then I came quickly, in the same one or two minutes as my peers who were regarded as quick finishers.

That evening I was home alone. I stood there masturbating in the shower, the jets of water were streaming over my skin, but not the jet of cum, no, the jet of cum was still biding its time. All in all, it was a comic scene. A grown man who has been tossing off for so long he's starting to get tired. You know, like in the joke: "change hands" said the doctor. I did change hands, and more than once. The jets of water were streaming over my skin, my prick seemed huge, the fantasies that used to bring me to orgasm flashed past one after another in front of my closed eyes. But nothing happened.

All in all, it was a comic scene. But I didn't find it funny at all. When I was tired I sat on the edge of the bath, looking at my prick, which was still aroused, its head as huge and red as if all the blood in the world had flowed into it. As a young child I had already guessed what the world around me was like. I didn't even have to watch TV, I already knew anyway. Although I do remember the anchorman on the Sunday politics program explaining that in America a rape took place every fifteen minutes. The Sunday politics program, a fatted hog, a privileged swine. Every fifteen minutes. Only in America.

My parents sat beside me, watched the same screen, listened to the same words. Not a single muscle twitched in their faces, as if this had nothing to do with them – incredible, every fifteen minutes a woman weeps and struggles with tears of despair in her eyes, her scream smothered by a sweaty palm. I didn't know then how much time one rape takes, but I did understand that just as one rapist started cooling off, the next was setting to work – on the other side of the country, with a different woman. Believe it or not, I felt that this concerned all of us, not just the ideological struggle, the conflict between two systems and TV propaganda.

I was fourteen years old, I already masturbated, imagining youthful plantation owners flogging black female slaves with canes – but at that moment I wasn't thinking about my fantasies, I wasn't aroused – after all, I didn't feel aroused when the TV news told us about the labor camps in Cambodia, and Soviet war films showed Nazi German newsreels with dump trucks piling up skeletons covered with skin from the concentration camps. I wasn't aroused – I just felt I'd heard something that was directly connected with my life.

I was fourteen years old, it was my life then, and it was still mine now. I sat on the edge of the bath and my prick seemed huge, and I realized that somehow I had to tell people about the world I had lived in for as long as I could remember. I was a bookish boy, but I could never find the right words. Perhaps because I had seen them too often on paper.

This is a comfortless world, a world that has no place for hope, where death is inevitable and suffering is routine and unendurable. This is a world in which children's heads are piled up into pyramids in Rwanda, to make it easier to count them, a world in which a thirty-year-old man sits on the edge of his bath in Moscow and cries because he can't come, he can't come even when he imagines how, strip by strip, he tears the skin off a fifteen-year-old girl who is begging for mercy, a girl who has no more tears, because her eyes have been gouged out.

He cries precisely because this picture is the only thing that arouses him.

8

IF ALEXEI ROKOTOV HAD NOT BEEN BORN IN 1975, HE would never have become a journalist. If he had appeared in the world a couple of years earlier, he would have been a computer programmer, and five years later he would have become a financial manager or a lawyer. But at the time when Lyosha was fifteen, there was no better profession in the country than that of journalist: *Sixty Seconds* on the Petersburg TV channel every Friday, *Outlook* on Channel One every Saturday, the magazine *Spark* in the mailbox. Every week the journalists made a small revolution by opening the eyes of the populace to the atrocities of the communists and the wretchedness of Soviet life in general. The indestructible colossus was reeling to cries of "but the king is naked!" and the bold cartoons in the newspapers seemed like a premonition of imminent victory.

Lyosha remembered one of the cartoons very well. Two ants were standing beside the flattened body of their friend, a huge foot was disappearing up into the sky, and one of the ants was saying: "You know, they'll come up with some way of getting rid of them soon." It seemed to Lyosha that the sole hovering above the ants' heads was the clay foot of a colossus, and the fear of it was only a game fostered by the state's lies. And there was no profession better than the one that could crush those lies – that was why Lyosha Rokotov began studying to enter the faculty of journalism, hoping that five years of hard toil would raise him up to the heavenly heights inhabited by the bright but distant stars of Liubimov, Nevzorov and Korotich. This was the dream he used to spur himself on for the first two years of study, but then he noticed that somehow his dream had grown tarnished. Either his former idols had changed, or Lyosha himself had begun to suspect that the way the world changed didn't really have anything to do with what they wrote in the newspapers. During the communist putsch of 1991 he stood in the cordon to protect the rebellious White House and even photocopied several flyers in the office of a friend who had gone into business. Lyosha and his friend must have printed the wrong number of copies or got their timing wrong – by the time they overcame their fear and started handing out the proclamations, the flyers were already out of date and it was time to print new ones. Hundreds of the flyers remained lying in Lyosha's room for ages, like a prophecy of the times when the main question concerning the press would not be "how can we print?" but "how can we distribute?"

When Lyosha was in his second year of study, a small civil war took place in Moscow. This time he was among the crowd of idle onlookers who watched as tanks bombarded the building he had defended two years earlier, and he wandered round the streets of Moscow alone, trying to understand what was happening. But when a man only a yard away from him fell to the ground, killed either by a stray bullet or a shot from a sniper, Lyosha realized that the antithesis of the lies was not the words that they wrote in the newspapers, but the fresh frosty smell in the air and the nausea that rose up in his throat at the sight of brains oozing out onto the asphalt.

He realized that never again could he talk about the danger of communist revanchism or the right policy for economic reforms – just as he had known earlier that he could never write for the newspaper *Pravda*: in short, by the end of October, Lyosha Rokotov had difficulty even understanding what he *could* do.

The only thing he liked out of everything he read was the "Art" column in the newspaper *Today* – and he decided he ought to start writing about books, films and exhibitions. As a trial run, he volunteered to report on the conference "Postmodernism and National Cultures" taking place at the Tretyakov Gallery. The editor of the student newspaper to which Lyosha promised the article said he should try to get an interview with Charles Jencks, the famous architect. Lyova only found out that he existed two hours before the conference started, there was no time to go to the library but, despite his apprehensions, the interview went really well. Jencks put forward his project for the reconstruction of the burnt White House: a blue facade, streaks of red where the burn marks were and a white top as a symbol of reconciliation. Amazed by the visiting star's cynicism, Lyosha didn't even bother to ask if he knew that those were the colors of the Russian tricolor. Jencks said: "If the White House is going to be white again, that means a decision has been taken to pretend that nothing happened." Lyosha remembered those words many times – especially in the company of his colleagues who repeatedly mouthed magic formulas about the market and free competition. Once, in the late eighties, he used to believe in this abracadabra himself, but now it sounded strange, to say the least: it was becoming clearer and clearer that the system emerging in Russia had only the remotest of connections with the theories of Adam Smith and John M. Keynes. For some reason Lyosha recalled the old cartoon with the two ants, and it didn't seem funny anymore. The White House was painted white again, and the huge foot remained poised in the air, blanking out half the sky. Jencks was right: nothing had happened.

Lyosha thought more and more often about the fact that most people didn't want to have their eyes opened. They were prepared to forget about the terrible past for the sake of a quiet life. There was a certain mature wisdom in this, but it was beyond the comprehension of Lyosha's youth. Now perestroika seemed to him like a brief moment of truth in which the population of one sixth of the world's land surface suddenly found itself face to face with the wretchedness and horror of human existence. But the moment had been too short: people were only too glad to put the wretchedness and horror down to the bloody Soviet regime and pretend that it was all nothing to do with them. They were too busy: they were learning how to lick the asses of the new authorities – just as their parents had licked the communists' asses twenty and thirty years earlier.

Lyosha never did write any more about culture, but at the

Tretyakov Gallery conference he met redheaded Oxana, a final-year student at the Russian State University for the Humanities, who was happy to explain everything he didn't understand in the presentations. A day later she continued his education in the Academy of Sciences apartment on Vavilov Street that had been left at her disposal for two weeks while her parents were lecturing somewhere on the east coast of the US. Of course, Oxana wasn't his first woman, but it was the first time Lyosha had found himself in bed with a girl who could not only abandon herself to pleasure, but also sweep him away with her to places where what happened to the power of the people and free speech seemed entirely trivial and inconsequential – if only because in those places freedom had no need of speech and all the power belonged to Oxana, since she was the only one who knew how to get there.

They were married six months later, and Lyosha quickly grew used to thinking of himself as part of "we." By the time he graduated from university, this "we" already consisted of three parts, like the trinity of colors in the Russian flag. Little Dasha forced him to a fresh look at the question of which publications the young journalist Rokotov would like to see his work in. The 1996 elections were coming up, the Russian oligarchs were spending freely to support Yeltsin, and Alexei realized there wouldn't be another opportunity as good as this for earning money for a long time. And in addition, no matter what, he still preferred President Yeltsin to the communist leader Zyuganov, and in agreeing to take part in a regional offshoot of the youth program "Vote, or You Lose!" Alexei wasn't even really sinning against his conscience all that much – and that feeling was so intoxicating that just for a moment Alexei believed he really did have a brilliant future ahead of him.

Now, almost eight years later, he realized he had been mistaken. All the major events that convulsed the mass-media market had passed him by: during the battles over "Svyazinvest," the conflict between Primakov and Yeltsin, the election won by Putin and the closure of the opposition TV channels belonging to the same oligarchs who had once supported Yeltsin, he had remained equally distant from big politics and big money. Now he had a modest job as a reporter in an insignificant online newspaper that wasn't even in the top ten on Rambler. His female boss was five years younger than him – precisely the amount of time that he had wasted on studying at university.

Six months earlier, when Ksenia Ionova became senior editor of the news department, she had informed Alexei and his colleagues that their terms of employment had changed. Now they had to arrive at ten o'clock, submit a strictly specified amount of copy every week and also maintain contact with their readers in online forums. Evgenii had tried to object: "Ksyusha, no one's IT editorial staff comes to work before twelve, not at Tickertape, or Gazette, so why should we?" Ksenia told him in an icy tone of voice that when they overtook Tickertape and Gazette, they could come to work at twelve too. If Evgenii Andreevich liked sleeping in in the mornings, then he could work for Evening.ru as a freelancer. "I'll decide for myself," Evgenii muttered, but he was wrong, because now Ksenia decided everything: a week later he was fired when he arrived in the office at midday yet again.

"I value what you write," Ksenia said, "and I'm sorry we weren't able to work together in the same office. But I'll be glad to publish your material. We can discuss the matter of fees if you like."

Evgenii's articles really did appear from time to time on the Evening.ru site, and perhaps he hadn't really lost too much money. Apart from that, history does not judge the victors: three months later the popularity of the news section had doubled, and although Evening.ru was still a second-flight publication, Alexei and his colleagues soon began to respect this skinny young woman with eyes as big as a manga heroine and a voice as icy as the Snow Queen.

But now as she sits opposite him in the local cafeteria, the ice in her voice has almost melted. She stirs the sugar in her cup and smiles. She reminds him of an ordinary final-year student, almost the same as Oxana ten years earlier.

"It's a good interview," Ksenia says, "it's just a pity he doesn't want to be named."

"He's afraid," Alexei replies, "but if necessary, I have his signature."

"It's not that, it's just that the readers don't trust an anonymous source as much." She drinks a mouthful of coffee from an old cup that goes back to the days of Soviet public catering. "He definitely doesn't want to be named?"

"No way," says Alexei. "It's a matter of professional etiquette as well. Supposedly he has no right to discuss his colleagues' actions."

"The anonymous investigator from the Moscow Public Prosecutor's Office speculates to the dictaphone about whether the murders attributed to the Moscow Psycho really all have been committed by the same person." Ksenia lowers her tousled head to the printout.

"*These murders, which have created such a sensation recently, don't in fact have all that much in common. The victims are females between the ages of fifteen and forty, who have first been raped, although in a number of cases it's hard to tell, because their sexual organs have been cut out, burned away, or scalded with boiling water. In almost every case there is evidence of torture lasting several hours – cuts, burns and wounds – but there are virtually no bruises. The common factor in all these cases is that the bodies have deliberately been left in places where they will easily be found. It's possible the killer wants to be caught, which is often the case. The famous Chicago serial killer William Hance even wrote above the bodies of his victims: 'For God's sake, catch me before I kill again!' However, we can't be entirely certain of the motivation in each particular case: perhaps the killer is taunting the police or enjoying the sensational reporting in the newspapers. But to get back to...*"

"I wonder why everyone likes to say that when the press writes about these things, it provokes the serial killers?" Ksenia asks testily. "Anyone would think Chikatilo was a media star. And anyway, if I remember rightly, there were plenty of psychotic killers in the Soviet Union, and everyone knew about them, even though there was never anything in the papers."

"Aha," Alexei says with a nod, "my parents told me about Mosgas."

"Who?" Ksenia asks, and Alexei is surprised: five years is a big difference. An entirely different generation, they never knew the Soviet regime, they learned about psychotic killers from *The Silence of the Lambs*. He explains:

"Well, he pretended to work for the Moscow gas supply, checking for leaks. He used to ring the doorbell and say 'Mosgas,' and when people opened the door, he hacked them to death with an axe. There was even a joke about it. The husband comes to the door: 'Who's there?' – 'Mosgas.' – 'Come in, come in. The axe is in the bathroom, my mother-in-law's in the kitchen.'"

Ksenia smiles and says:

"But they caught him when he went to a building where they already had electric cookers."

A strange kind of joke, Alexei thinks and then, seeing his baffled expression, Ksenia explains.

"I've never had a gas cooker. Why would I open the door if I heard the word 'Mosgas'? For me that would be as strange as opening the door to the words 'Mosmunicanal' or "Transsib.'"

She puts down her empty cup and reaches for the dessert. Thin, strong hands with the nails bitten down, not so nice, but if she took care of herself, she'd be way sexy. A ring at the door. Mosmunicanal. Ksenia in the doorway, the psycho just outside. Alexei thinks her icy tone and steely composure would probably be of help.

"*...But to get back to the question of whether the same murderer is responsible for all these crimes*," she reads aloud, "*then the killer's ostentatious behavior could be misleading: once the press has written about this, any murderer could fake the psychotic's signature. I think our press was rather hasty in spreading panic about this.*"

"Interesting logic," says Ksenia. "We shouldn't spread panic because there might be several psychos in Moscow and not just one. We certainly have some remarkable people living in this city."

"Well, a killer doesn't have to be a psycho," says Alexei, taking his interviewee's side, "it could be a domestic killing that the murderer disguises as one of a series."

"A domestic killing with the sexual organs cut out and signs of torture," says Ksenia, wiping her fingers with a napkin. "Like I said, we certainly have some remarkable people living in this city."

Alexei nods, then can't resist asking:

"But it's a good interview, isn't it?"

Just look, he thinks, six months ago I'd never have believed anyone who told me this girl's opinion would matter to me. Maybe it doesn't even matter now: all I'm doing is asking the boss's opinion about new material. That's perfectly normal.

"Yes, it's good," Ksenia replies with a nod, "but this is already the tenth interview on this story. It's all done right, it's all good, but what's going to make the reader, well, I don't know, remember it, I suppose? Make it different from the other dozen?"

"Of course," Alexei says, "it would be better if we caught the murderer. But that only happens in Hollywood movies."

"No," replies Ksenia, getting up. "It's not our job to catch the murderer. But the thought nagging away at me is how we can come up with something else, make this a serious subject of discussion."

Five years' difference, oh yeah. Make this a serious subject. As if it was still the late eighties and Perestroika, when people really were interested in serious subjects.

"And another thing," Ksenia says, "There's something I wanted to ask you, not to do with work. What do you know about this man?" And she mentions the name.

"Why do you want to know?" Alexei asks.

"It's not for me," says Ksenia. "It's for a girlfriend of mine. She's wondering whether she should go to work for him."

Ksenia repeats the man's name again, and Alexei shakes his head and says:

"No, I've never heard of him before. But I can take a look on Google."

"I've already looked on Google," Ksenia replies and hands him the printout of his interview. "You think about how much more you can squeeze out of this psycho."

Alexei thinks that there was a time when he would have grabbed at this opportunity. A great beginning for a Hollywood movie. An independent journalistic investigation. But it is some years now since he stopped expecting his work to bring him fame or even satisfaction. Maybe he should never have joined the journalism faculty. He ought to have been a computer programmer, or even a lawyer, if it came to the pinch. Normal human professions.

9

THE DARKNESS OF THE MOSCOW WINTER EVENINGS. A bright-colored kilim on the floor. A one-room flat for two hundred and fifty dollars a month. A matte laptop screen. A black TV screen. Ksenia, sitting in the only armchair with her legs pulled up, chewing on her nails. Stay home alone, don't think about Sasha, watch TV, read books, surf the web. Nothing feels right, she's all fingers and thumbs, everything's wrong: the cheap pirate DVDs she bought at the underground station get stuck, the movies are boring and affected, like some kind of *Ripley's Game*, tell me, who on Earth watches this stuff, the latest Murakami that came out last week has already been read and brings no more pleasure. Stay home alone, remember Sasha, stand pensively gazing into an open drawer, masturbate, stretching your breasts so far by hanging weights on the nipples that they leave bruises. Come quickly, but still feel the same emptiness inside. Stay home alone, don't think about Sasha, remember Sasha, stand there holding a long sewing needle, figuring out the best place to jab it in. It's a bad sign, you know it is, bad: in a little while now you'll start cutting yourself.

Put the needle away: remember instead how it all started. You had just finished tenth grade, and Mom was just about to go on vacation to Greece, supposedly with aunty Mila, but actually with aunty Mila's current husband. She'd been complaining for a long time that they didn't have any money, Ksenia's father didn't really pay the alimony properly, she'd have to borrow, and then work for six months without any weekends off – stupid contracts, legal documents, forced labor for a translator.

"Then stay at home," Ksenia said in a fit of teenage fury and in reply was accused of being heartless, egotistic and callous.

"I've no place to lay my head in my own house!" Mom shouted. "When I'm dying, no one will give me a glass of water. I do everything for you, and you don't want to let me go away for two weeks' holiday! Lena's daughter's already earning money, you're the only millstone, still left hanging round my neck."

Lena's daughter was three years older than Ksenia, but that wasn't important. Ksenia bit her lip and said she would get a summer job, and Mom wouldn't have to work all fall without any weekends off. When Ksenia told her father, he tried to protest, and even phoned her mother, but she snapped back: "This is a very good thing, let the girl get used to financial independence. Or she'll grow up a loser like you."

That was the final argument in every row, and it successfully blocked all her dad's attempts to interfere in his daughter's upbringing. Ksenia remembered that when she was in fifth grade, just after they got divorced, her mom said she had to work harder at her studies so there was no point in her going to the dance studio three times a week. Ksenia liked dancing; when she danced she felt like she grew up and became as beautiful as her mom – in high-heeled shoes, enveloped in a cloud of perfume and wine – and her dad always came to the performances and admired her and told her "you're my little beauty," but in fifth grade it all came to an end. Ksenia sat in her room and did her lessons in order not to cry and in the kitchen Dad, who had come for the weekend to see his daughter, tried to explain something to Mom, but she just kept repeating: "If the girl wastes her time on nonsense like that, she'll end up a loser, like you."

And this time too, her mother said to her father: "It's a good thing, let her get used to being independent," but she told Ksenia that she was a fine girl, of course, but really there wasn't any need, the family had money anyway, "if you're doing it for me, there's no need."

"Oh no, Mom," said Ksenia, "it's just that I think it's time I started earning some money."

During the holidays Ksenia and Marinka found jobs as couriers from an advertisement. There wasn't a lot to the job: collect correspondence from several firms and deliver it to the addresses shown. True, it took almost all day, but they promised to pay them a hundred dollars a month. Over the summer that would mount up to three hundred, not really a lot, but a decent sum, enough to stop her feeling like a sponger.

Mom left on June 25, and the next day Marinka phoned and said she wasn't going to work because she was ill. Ksenia asked what was wrong with her, she said she'd caught a cold and Ksenia started getting ready, although she hadn't liked the sound of Marinka's voice. She was already half way out the door when the phone rang again: through her tears Marinka confessed that the evening before the man she handed in her list of jobs to had raped her.

"I got back in the evening," Marinka sobbed, "and there was no one in the place apart from him. I followed him into the office, as usual, and he asked if I'd like some tea. And I said yes, because I'd got caught in the rain and I was frozen. He put in a little splash of cognac, and then started making passes at me and, well..."

"So did you let him, or did he rape you?" Ksenia asked.

"I don't know," Marinka answered, "I kept saying 'I don't want to.' In America it would be rape."

"And what are you going to do?" Ksenia asked. "Will you go to the police?"

"No, of course not! I just won't go back there anymore, that's all."

"But what about the money? They still haven't paid you anything. Don't be stupid, Marinka!"

"Well, that means there won't be any money," Marinka sobbed, "I won't go back there again. Why don't you just stop hassling me?" she said and added after a pause: "He said I could call him Dimochka."

And for some reason, that was the moment when Ksenia's fury turned everything black in front of her eyes. That "Dimochka" stung her far more than the rape, more than the fact that Marinka was willing to forego the money as long as she never had to go there again. Ksenia knew these fits of fury – because of them the kids in her class thought she was crazy and were afraid to tease her even in elementary school. But just then Ksenia recalled what Lyova's *sensei* used to say: you mustn't allow your negative emotions to take complete control of you, you must direct them, put all their energy into the blow. And so she carried her fury with her all the way, like a glass of water, trying not to spill a drop. She had a picture in front of her eyes all the time: the villainous Dimochka tearing Marinka's clothes off, her matte skin gleaming dully in the semi-darkness of the office with its cheap "European-style" refurbishment, her light hair billowing out in a halo round her head. The picture was blurred, not because Ksenia couldn't remember Dimochka's face properly, but because the mist of her fury prevented her from seeing any details.

In the office Ksenia took the list of jobs and the correspondence as usual, and only then asked in an icy voice if the managing director was in. Dimochka, a tall, balding middle-aged man, gave her a surprised look through his spectacles and asked why she needed to see the manager. I just do, Ksenia said in a voice that immediately made him take her right across the office to reception.

"Galochka," he said to the secretary, "this courier girl here wants to have a word with Arkadii Pavlovich, I don't know what about."

"Arkadii Pavlovich is busy," said Galochka, without looking up from her computer monitor.

"I'll only be a moment," said Ksenia, opening the door of the manager's office.

Five minutes later Dimochka, blushing bright red, was standing in front of the manager. His lips were trembling and the eyes behind his spectacles were swollen with tears.

"She wanted to..." he babbled.

"You stupid prick," Arkadii Pavlovich hissed, "she's under age! It's a criminal offence! Even if she did want to!"

Ksenia had calculated correctly: people of the older generation didn't know what the age of consent was.

"We're prepared to pay compensation," said Arkadii Pavlovich, "I'll deduct whatever you think appropriate from his salary."

"I'm not sure I want to talk about compensation," said Ksenia. "When a girl takes money for a man having sex with her, it looks more like prostitution than compensation. I'd just like my colleague to be given what she's already earned. If possible without coming into the office."

Ten minutes later Ksenia left the office with Marinka's hundred dollars.

"There, you see," she told her friend, "you even earned it for three days less than me."

But the following day turned out to be Ksenia's last day at work too. The first client she came to noticed that the package had been opened. There was nothing in it but a letter, and he was supposed to have received a small sum of money as well. Three hundred and fifty dollars, nothing to worry about, we'll sort it out in a moment, he told the hysterical Ksenia, and dialed the number of the office. Of course, Dimochka swore that when he gave Ksenia the envelope it was sealed and the money was inside. He took his revenge on Ksenia in the manager's office.

"They start with blackmail and move on to theft," he said.

Even if Arkadii Pavlovich understood what was going on, he didn't see fit to do anything. They agreed on a compromise: they considered that Ksenia had lost the money, and so they wouldn't go to the police either (Dimochka couldn't hold back his smile at that word "either"), and they wouldn't ask Ksenia to make good the loss, because they realized she was just a girl and she didn't have any real money – we're not some kind of vicious brutes, are we, Ksyusha? But, naturally, it was out of the question for her to carry on working or to be paid for June.

Ksenia realized she had been set up. The rich grown-ups had put the little girl in her place! Of course they had! They couldn't have some pint-sized chick throwing her weight around, demanding her rights! There, take your rights, three hundred and fifty conventional units of currency, there's our divine kindness for you, we won't go to the police *either*! Ksenia remembered that lesson for the rest of her life: you must never relax even in the very simplest job. You couldn't trust anyone but your very closest friends.

She spent the whole evening watching TV dry-eyed, repeating

to herself *big girls don't cry.* Her mom said crying meant admitting you were helpless, admitting you'd been defeated, but what you had to do was fight. No, big girls don't cry, I have to think of something, Ksenia kept repeating to herself, but even so she didn't tell Marinka she had been sacked without being paid. Not because she was afraid of Marinka's sympathy, it was just that Marinka would have suggested splitting her money, and Ksenia didn't want to take anything from her. It was enough that Marinka had been raped. Ksenia didn't say anything, even when Marinka phoned and admitted that she'd decided to go back to work from July 1, because Dimochka had phoned and apologized, and promised that nothing of the sort would ever happen again. But then, Marinka's voice had a familiar vibe of excitement to it, and it occurred to Ksenia that something of the sort could very well happen again.

"Actually," said Marinka, "it was quite interesting really, I've never had any men so much older than me."

All right then, Ksenia told herself. So I was a fool. So I should have kept well out of the whole business. They would have sorted it out for themselves. She felt a bit annoyed with Marinka, but her resentment was weak, as if she was feeling it through a thick layer of felt, or rather, through the cocoon that was wrapping itself round her tighter and tighter.

Stay home alone, don't think about Marinka, watch TV, read books. Nothing feels right, you're all fingers and thumbs, everything's wrong: it's your own fault, you're to blame for everything. You wasted an entire month. You didn't earn any money, and it doesn't look as if you're going to earn any. You waded in to save Marinka, who coped perfectly well on her own. You forgot that first of all you have to think about *Mom.* What are you going to say when Mom comes back from Greece? Leave the curtains closed for days on end, never change your clothes, never go outside, slouch around the apartment in nothing but a T-shirt, smoke the grass you found in Mom's desk, float in a scalding-hot bath, drink black coffee and feel as if the apartment is full of gray threads of cobweb… they mesh together round your body, weaving into a cocoon, drag across the parquet in pellets, like a convict's ball. You'll never achieve anything. You can't work, not even as a courier. You're no good for anything.

You tried masturbating, but that didn't help for long. At that time you still managed without any additional equipment, your fantasies were enough. Ever since you were little you liked to imagine yourself as a princess abducted by fierce bandits, or a young lady sold into the sultan's harem. When you got a bit older, the pretentiousness of these scenes began to irritate you slightly, so gradually the settings lost their splendor and everything was reduced to the interaction of two or three bodies, ropes, a gag and a whip. The imaginary torment is better than thinking about what *Mom* will say when she finally gets back: the pain and the shame were the same as in reality, but your dark subterranean fantasies worked like an alchemical retort, smelting them into pleasure. It swept over you in a warm wave and retreated, leaving behind on the seashore snatches of thoughts, fragments of images, a despair so solid, it felt as if you could touch it with your damp fingers.

Despair? No, this is not despair, it is anguish, concentrated anguish, a stifling feeling, a constant ringing in the ears, the flow of your own blood, darkness, darkness – the dark cloud will hang on the folds of your clothes, cling to the bulges of your face and the hairs stuck to your forehead, the gnawed ends of your fingers.

One morning you woke up in a puddle of blood. At first you just thought your period had started, but then you realized that when you went to bed, you took a knife with you and covered the insides of your thighs with cuts as you were going to sleep. You couldn't remember anything, not this time or the others. Fortunately the cuts weren't deep and the knife hadn't caught any veins, but you were frightened.

You had to do something – and you forced yourself to go outside. You bought *Megalopolis-Express* from a newspaper kiosk and an article found by chance gave you the answer to the question "What should I do?" You phoned Marinka, and a week later you met your first dominant lover. He was called Nikita, and your body still responds to that name, even though eight years have gone by now. Nikita is far away, and none of your other playmates can console you either. You put your toys away in the cupboard and tell yourself that tomorrow after work you'll definitely go visit someone, just in order not to stay home alone. Go visit someone, get drunk, come back home and fall asleep straight away.

It would be good to visit Olya, you think, it would be good to sit in front of the TV with your arms round each other and watch *Love Actually* or some other romantic movie. Olya likes romantic movies the same way you like Italian horror movies. A good idea, but it won't work – tomorrow's Vlad's birthday. Olya promised to help, cook, clean up, wash the dishes. A grown woman, and she still can't say no to her brother, But then, you wouldn't have said no to Lyova, if he asked you to do something for him. A pity, it's hard to ask from America. Hey, Lyova. Would you like me to come over to New Jersey and wash the dishes?

Yes, Lyova went away, Nikita went away, Vika went away, so many others disappeared off to God knows where, but Marinka's still here. Ksenia's on the point of recalling that old incident, the false rape, the childish sense of grievance. But you can't stay annoyed with Marinka for long. When you get right down to it, some girls can't say no to sex, others like to be beaten until they bleed – we all have our own strange tastes, it's no big deal. So no more sitting here with your arms wrapped round your knees: pick up the phone and dial Marinka's number. What are old friends for if you can't go to see them when you feel totally wiped out?

Hello, hello, says Ksenia, just you try telling me you're busy tomorrow evening.

10

"LOOK, IT'S REALLY LOVELY, ISN'T IT?" – AND MARINA slips the T-shirt off one shoulder.

Marina has a beautiful T-shirt: her lover brought it from California. It's handmade, he says, the old ex-hippies make them, that is, simply hippies, because the ex-hippies all became yuppies, they all became VIPs, and CEOs. The T-shirt is covered in bright swirls of color, acid style it's called. As it happens, Ksenia has never tried acid, she doesn't use drugs at all, if you don't count coffee, grass and tea. She hasn't tried acid, but she knows what the word "acid" means as an adjective, and she knows Marina is very fond of this word, although she thinks Marina hasn't tried acid either, but then, you can never quite be sure of anything with Marina. There are acid drawings hanging on the wall, the computer monitor on the bar stool is displaying acid patterns that are almost the same as the hand-made T-shirt given to Marina by her Californian lover. "With patterns like that, who needs acid," says Marina, breathing out the sweet smoke.

The T-shirt really is beautiful. With a T-shirt like that getting high is easy, with a joint or without one. Only you couldn't go to the office in a T-shirt like that, that's for sure. But Marina doesn't have to go to the office, she doesn't have any subordinates or any bosses, but she does have a handmade T-shirt that her lover brought from California.

And now she slips that T-shirt off one shoulder. "Look," she says, "it's really lovely, isn't it, look, I can't see for myself, tell me, how do you like my little darling?" It's not really all that beautiful, to be honest: there's a large blurred pink patch on her skin, like a cloud, overlying the tattooed outlines of a dragon.

"Wow!" says Ksenia, "that's really super. But you used to have a butterfly there, what did you do with it?"

Marina hides her shoulder back under the beautiful T-shirt, shakes her straw-yellow hair and knocks off her ash – *oh, I haven't smoked for so long* thinks Ksenia – and smiles:

"I used to have a butterfly, but I covered it over with the dragon. He emerged from the butterfly, like a butterfly emerging from a chrysalis, get it?"

Of course, what's not to get? Dragon emerges from butterfly, butterfly emerges from chrysalis, from the large blurred patch as pink as a Barbie doll box.

"Remember the pink box Vika's Barbie doll came in? She had the first one in the class, it cost crazy money, from abroad?"

"Of course I remember," says Marina. "You don't forget your first Barbie, it's like your first man."

Ksenia laughs. "You've definitely had more men than dolls."

"Go figure, I used to be so stupid," says Marina, "such a fool, I wanted a girl so much, so that she could have my dolls, but now I understand that a boy's much better. Just look at him, just look, only nine months old, and you can already see he's a real man, my little Chinese mandarin, my little orange, my precious little sweetie pie."

She picks Gleb up in her arms, kisses his little nose, his narrow eyes, his floppy my-little-elephant ears.

"Ma-ma," says Gleb and crawls away again.

Marina hasn't got any furniture, apart from a large mattress at the far end of the room and the bar stool with the monitor glowing on it. Marina used to call it her cybernetic altar, and Ksenia prefers not to think about the kind of rites that were celebrated in front of it during the night. And now here they are sitting on the floor, on a rug as shaggy and huge as a polar bear pelt, the one on which our world stands – according to the legends of northern peoples unknown to the ethnographers. Or perhaps, according to these legends, the whole world is the back of an immense polar bear, and we creep about in its fur, like little Gleb on this huge rug in his mother's one-room apartment, while she sits there with her oldest and dearest friend. Marina's wearing a beautiful T-shirt, handmade, brought from California by her lover, but Ksenia, as usual, is wearing a business suit, all dressed up, in full regalia and war paint, strong lips, big eyes, half an hour in front of the mirror in the morning. Even when Marina used to go to the office, she still didn't wear business suits, she was a designer, a creative girl, almost bohemian, she preferred the ethnic style, men liked that, it suited her – but then, what had style got to do with it? Men had always liked her, with her long legs and that halo of bright hair round her head, with that constant smile that some called whorish and others called innocent.

"You're really going overboard," says Ksenia. "Remember what you used to say when you were pregnant? A boy is an enemy inside, like Intel Inside, you could even hang the logo on your belly. Because men and women are two different species, not simply the male and female of *Homo sapiens*."

"Go figure, I used to be so stupid," says Marina, "such a fool, I wanted a girl so much, and I was so furious about this pregnancy, such a dimwit, remember?"

How could she ever forget it? Japanese cinema week in Moscow, free entry, a hall full of people fighting for seats, illegible subtitles, someone's head blocking out half the screen. Marina politely asks him to get down a bit and then summarily presses the head down with her hand, *why's he acting so stupid, doesn't he understand plain Russian?* But when the lights come up she sees that he doesn't – slanting eyes, yellowish skin, oh, how embarrassing. Marina says "Arigato," hoping that in Japanese one polite word can take the place of another, the man laughs and tells her in English that he's not Japanese, although he does have some Japanese friends he was supposed to meet here, but they don't seem to have come, and he didn't understand very much, to be honest, Japanese with Russian subtitles – he had almost no chance. Perhaps a girl who speaks English so well could tell him what actually happened?

Marina told him, and they drank to friendship between peoples in the nearest restaurant, and then caught a taxi and kissed in the back seat, and Marina, who was already a little bit drunk, felt terribly curious, because she'd never had any Asian men. And is it true that Asians can, well, you know, I mean, well, in bed? The Asians do it much better on a mat than on a bed. What do you mean, a mat? He points down past his feet, at the rubber mat, ah shit, yes, on rice-straw mats, right?

They couldn't find a straw mat in Moscow, though, so they tried it on the bed, and on the rug, and then Marina looked at the clock and suddenly remembered that in the morning her lover from California was supposed to call her, the one who would later give her the beautiful T-shirt, handmade, with the acid design, that she was wearing right now. And right now was when eighteen months had passed since that night, which wasn't hard to figure, if you knew the age of the child and the average duration of pregnancy in females of the species *Homo sapiens* – that is, of course, if you still believed they were members of the same species.

But a year earlier, on a depressing winter evening just like this one, Marina had sat on the floor in just the same way, with her legs crossed, with a T-shirt pulled over her large belly, and said the boy was an enemy inside, and some kind of Chinese into the bargain, like his freaking dad.

"Why didn't you call him?" Ksenia asked then.

"I don't have his number," Marina answered. "I gave him mine, but I didn't take his. That is, he wrote it down for me, but I left it on the table in the kitchen, because I was so dimwitted in the morning, which isn't surprising, we worked so hard, made an entire child together, slaving away for four hours, we were absolutely soaking."

"Why didn't you take any precautions?"

"Go figure, I was so stupid," said Marina, "such a fool, I took precautions the first two times, and then I ran out of condoms and he wasn't so hard any longer, and I said, *ah go for it,* because I really wanted to, and anyway, I'd heard there was much less chance of getting pregnant from the third ejaculation in a row. And in general I was planning to take the morning-after pill, but I was so stupid I fell asleep at home, and then I forgot everything. I forgot absolutely everything, I even left his phone number on the kitchen table, but I wouldn't have called him anyway, since he didn't call, so what if I did get pregnant, I should have been more careful, right?"

"It's a good thing he was disease-free, or you wouldn't just have been pregnant, you'd have been HIV-positive."

"Don't say that, don't hassle me, I don't tell you that someday one of your sadist lovers will simply cut your throat."

"You don't? I hear that from you all the time."

"And now you can frighten me by saying I'll die in childbirth."

"Whatever next! I wouldn't dream of it. You'll have a beautiful baby, strong and healthy."

That was what they'd said a year earlier, and that was the way things had turned out, there's the baby, strong and healthy, crawling around on the white rug as if it were the back of a female polar bear, not a male bear, because it's his mom's rug, his mom's room, his mom's apartment, his mom's little Chinese boy, her little mandarin, her little orange, who's my tasty little boy? "That was why I got the dragon tattoo," says Marina, "to have a bit of the East, because if I have a Chinese son, then I'm a little bit Chinese myself, aren't I? And don't worry about the pink patch, that'll be gone by summer, and right now I've got nobody to show it to, apart from you."

"Wow," says Ksenia, "what does that mean, nobody? What have you done with all your men, your lovers from the four corners of the earth, every age and color, the ones you find it so interesting to be with, because you've never tried that kind before? Have you really exhausted all the combinations, have you really had everyone you could ever imagine, even a hundred-year-old Afro-American with a touch of Inuit blood, the result of a short visit to Alaska before the First World War by a battalion of marines, what is it they call them in America – Seals? Polar bears?"

"You laugh as much as you like," Marina replies, "I've found the most important man in my life, just look at him, just feast your eyes on him, he's the best, the most beautiful man in the world, look at his face, look at his balls, look at his prick – I've never seen such beautiful balls and such a beautiful prick on any man. And, you know, I've seen plenty in my time."

Yes, you really have seen plenty of men, I know. And has

your eye really wearied of looking, has its lens grown dull, has the keenness of your gaze dimmed? Where's the Marina I could never take to anyone's place, because she immediately started looking around to see who she could drag off to screw in the bathroom? Where's the Marina who, if she couldn't get to sleep, used to count her lovers the same way other people count sheep or elephants, and always fell asleep before she'd counted them all? Where's the Marina who used to know everything about the sexual preferences of every man in Moscow and the countries served by Sheremetyevo International Airport? Where's the Marina who introduced me to Nikita at the age of fifteen when she found out that I was into playing? Where's the Marina I used to love so much that for her sake I would have become a man for just one night?

She's sitting on the floor with her legs folded underneath her, wearing a handmade T-shirt from her lover in California, and the acid pattern on the fabric is like a radiance shining from her belly, and the acid pattern on the computer monitor is like a blessing from the cybernetic gods, and little Gleb is crawling around near her, like a celestial Inuit child on the back of the Great Polar Bear Mother.

11

LOOK HOW THE TIME OF MY LIFE IS PASSING, THINKS Olya. Look how the time is passing, I'm already thirty-five years old. Eight years ago I came to Moscow from Peter. A year ago I bought myself an apartment. Eight minus one is seven, seven years in other people's places, two of them in the same apartment as Vlad and his constantly changing mob of friends. So seven minus two leaves five. Five years on my own, five years as my own woman. Five plus one makes six. It's six years, because when I'm in my own apartment I'm alone too – there's nothing to be done about it, that's the number.

Numbers are my specialty, thinks Olya, drawing in the smoke through the long cigarette holder. How did a humanities girl from a cultured Petersburg family develop such a fondness for numbers? Maybe it's all because of the chess. I used to have a grade two ranking, after all. I used to be able to figure out the alternatives pretty well. Black and white squares, letters on the horizontal rows, numbers on the vertical ones.

Numbers are my specialty. I started off as an accountant, I was an IT manager, and for three years now I've been an executive director, the co-owner of a small company. Cashflows aren't much different from computer networks, the figures add up to numbers, the numbers line up in columns, the columns gather together into tables, the ones and zeroes march through the wires and when they come out they turn into a picture, a word or another number. All this is called financial accounting;

all this is called the internet. The place where finance meets the internet is the precise spot where I'm located.

The spot where I'm located physically just at the moment is called "The Hollows" after the holes under the low tables to accommodate the customers' legs. It has the cheapest Japanese lunch in Moscow, one hundred and forty-nine rubles. Numbers are my specialty, they're always with me, even at lunch. Ksyusha's twenty-three, I'm thirty-five, so she's twelve years younger than me. If I'd got pregnant straight after my first period, my daughter would be exactly the same age. I'd like her to be like Ksyusha now. That's if it was a daughter, of course, and not a son. She'd call me "Mom," and I'd stroke her hair and say "don't worry, Ksyushenka, everything will be all right, you know I love you." I'd stroke her tousled black hair, because it's very important to have someone who loves you.

When I was twenty-three, I didn't understand that. I thought there were lots of other things in the world far more important than the love of one woman for another. For instance, the love of a man for a woman, or a woman for a man. In fact, it was Vlad who taught me that lesson by explaining that the love of a man for a man means a lot too. Vlad is five years older than me. Twenty-three plus five is twenty-eight. He came out of the closet at twenty-five, so I'd known for three years that my brother was a homosexual. That means since I was twenty.

I'd like to have a daughter like Ksyusha. But it's not possible. I slept with a man for the first time at the age of twenty-two. I was so confused and in love that I didn't take any precautions, so if I'd got pregnant then, my daughter would be twelve years old already. Exactly the same age that I was when Ksyusha was born.

Look how the time of my life is passing, thinks Olya, the time is passing. Grisha and Kostya aren't talking anymore, and today I got the bill for an ad that was shown on the sites of Grisha's holding company, and I didn't like it. Numbers are my specialty, and I don't have to go digging last month's out of the files to notice that something's wrong with them. After lunch I'll go back to the office, call Grisha and ask him what happened, where have all the internal discounts disappeared to, isn't my shop part of his holding company anymore – and I'll be prepared to be told no, that thirty-seven point five percent of the shares still belong to Kostya, my company isn't part of the holding company, so it will have to pay the same as everyone else. We will pay the same as everyone else. That is, I'll pay the same as everyone else. I know in advance that's what I'm going to hear. Numbers are my specialty, so I know what the people who write these numbers are going to tell me. I know the numbers, I know the people. But not all of them.

Last week I asked Ksyusha to find out about That Man, the Big Investor, but Ksyusha's not saying anything, as if she's forgotten, or she couldn't find out, and I suddenly realize that it's hard for me to raise the subject again. I look at her, dark circles under her eyes, nails bitten down almost to the quick. Poor Ksyusha, what's happening to you? How can I bother you with my own business? I'll cope on my own somehow. Somehow or other.

Because we all have moments when we realize there's something wrong with the world around us. And it takes all our strength not to cry in front of other people. And then everyone hangs on the best way they know how.

Numbers are my specialty, numbers reassure me. My daughter would be the same age as I was when Ksyusha was born – and that means that in some cunning way Ksyusha is my daughter, if only for a moment.

Look how the time of my life is passing, thinks Olya, the time is passing. Yesterday Vlad was forty, there was a big birthday party...

I went to the Auchan hypermarket with him, she thinks, he asked me to go and I went, we bought so much stuff that the receipt they printed out for us was a yard and a half long, we loaded the car right up to the gills and took it all to his place. I'm a really good sister, Ksyusha, you know that. I cooked everything, laid the table, and then the guests started arriving, his guests, you understand, bohemian types, the regulars from the Mix Club, theater stars, DJs, VJs, I don't even know who else, thirty-eight people, even more than Vlad was expecting. Thirty-eight plus two makes forty, exactly his age, strange, isn't it? And all those thirty-eight people looked right through me, no, thirty-nine, because Vlad didn't notice me either. Even though there was a time when I lived in the same apartment as some of them. And don't think there were just gays there, there were straight men too, some with girlfriends, but they just looked right through me, as if I was a waitress in an expensive restaurant. As if there were thirty-nine of me too, and I was standing there beside every place setting as still as a statue. Can you understand how hurt I felt?

Yesterday evening I went out onto the closed balcony with the cold December wind blowing in through a little gap, I pretended I wanted to smoke, I took out my cell and dialed Ksyusha's number. Of course, I know it off by heart, numbers are my specialty, but it's entered in my phone as number 2, because number 1 is Oleg's number, and Vlad's is number 3, even though I remember all these numbers anyway, I have a good memory for numbers, which is hardly surprising, with my specialty. You were temporarily unavailable, Ksyusha, so I won't tell you now about the way I stood on that cold glazed balcony, pressing my forehead against the window frame and sobbing because I felt so hurt. I would have liked someone to put their hand on my shoulder, pat me on the head and say *don't worry, everything will be all right, you know*, but we were separated by a distance of twelve years and miles of frosty air, frozen concrete and Moscow ground crammed as full as a birthday cake with water mains, underground utilities, telephone cables and fiber optic internet lines, with all those ones and zeroes running through them and turning into pictures, letters and other numbers when they come out.

It takes all our strength not to cry in front of other people. I wiped away the tears and went back into the kitchen to wash the dishes. Vlad asked me to do it, he's always hated it, ever since he was a child, there are gays who like housework, but I'm unlucky. I went back into the kitchen to wash the dishes, and now, sitting here at a low table in The Hollows, I don't tell Ksyusha how I dialed her number on that balcony filled with the chill of December, I just ask *why does Vlad treat me like that? Maybe it's because he's gay?*

Ksyusha laughs, pushes away her miso soup and reaches for the sushi with her chopsticks. "Listen, Olya," she tells me.

"Don't you of all people turn homophobic. We all know plenty of fags who get on perfectly well with women, quite splendidly in fact. But your brother, your brother is just a straightforward heel, I'm sorry. A talented stage director, a society celebrity, whatever – but still just a straightforward dominant-type heel, so stop beating up on fags, they're fine guys. And it's not true that they're afraid of women, it's you who's afraid of men, otherwise you wouldn't let them treat you like a doormat."

I wonder, if I had a son, would he be gay? I know it isn't inherited, especially not from an uncle on the mother's side, but maybe a bad example is infectious. Oh, what am I thinking, why bad? Ksyusha's right, I feel so ashamed. Just different. A different example is infectious. That's more politically correct, definitely.

As if she can read my mind, Ksyusha laughs and says it's not a matter of political correctness at all – she learned about the existence of homosexuals at about the same age she learned how men and women screw, and from pretty much the same source.

If she were my daughter, she wouldn't have spent her childhood reading *AIDS-Info*: even after I lost my virginity, I still thought that newspaper was incredibly vulgar and horrid and, to be quite honest, I still think so. If Ksyusha were my daughter, I wouldn't have let her read all sorts of filth, I would have taught her to love poetry instead.

My mom always loved poetry, and she still loves it. A cultured Petersburg family, Dad a retired army officer, Mom a teacher of German. Dad always used to laugh at her and say she'd have been better off if she'd learned to cook instead of how to conjugate German verbs. Dad died three years ago and Mom... Mom's in Peter, and she still loves poetry, but somehow I don't like it as much as I used to. I don't call her very often. It's a good thing Vlad doesn't forget to call. He's probably a better son than I am a daughter – even though his life is such a mess and he's always changing partners.

"You know," says Olya, "he's the only family I have. My dad died, my mom's in Peter, and to be quite honest, I don't know what to talk to her about. She keeps sounding me out to see if I'm thinking about having a baby, especially now that I have an apartment in Moscow. As if the apartment could give me a child.

With the electric cable, say, or the telephone wire."

Olya sees Ksyusha smile at those words, sees her dark eyes turn even darker, as if a tunnel opens up inside her, and all of Olya's words fall into it, to be transformed into images or memories, the same way ones and zeroes are transformed into pictures or letters. She prefers not to know what lies at the bottom of wells like this, what other uses her friend knows for telephone wire or electric cable, so she repeats what she already said: "You know, he's the only family I have."

Ksyusha pours herself some green tea with a trembling hand and takes a hasty sip, as if her throat has gone dry, then says in a hollow voice, as if she's shouting into the well:

"You just shouldn't let him treat you that way."

"He's my brother," Olya says, "he's always treated me that way, you know that, since we were kids."

"That's because you're not a masochist," Ksyusha says. "If you allowed yourself to be tied up once a week and whipped with that telephone wire, you wouldn't let anyone treat you like a doormat for the other six days."

I wonder, thinks Olya, when she says "treat you like a doormat," does she mean that literally? For a second she imagines Ksyusha naked, lying on her back, and someone wiping the sole of his shoe on her taut nipples. It's so hideous, God almighty, she thinks with a shudder and she too takes a sip of green tea, as if her throat has gone dry. She's afraid of pain, she loves Ksyusha, and she doesn't like the thought of anyone hurting her.

"Six days," Ksyusha says, but Olya immediately converts that into hours, because even the longest and most varied kind of beating is only a few hours, three, or five at the most. So we have to subtract those five hours from twenty-four times seven.

Ksyusha explained to me once that 24/7 is a kind of contract. When the submissive partner, typically known as the "sub" or "slave," places herself at the disposal of the dominant partner (typically known as the "master" or "lord") for twenty-four hours a day, seven days a week. I've never drawn up any contracts like that because, even though my specialty is to do with numbers, it lies at the point where finances meet the internet, not the point where pain meets pleasure. And from the point at which I'm located, I simply can't see that other point where Ksyusha is located from time to time and, to be quite honest, I'm afraid to look in that direction, it frightens me and gives me a bad feeling.

I wonder, thinks Olya, drawing in the smoke through the long cigarette holder, if Ksyusha were my daughter, would she be able to teach me about life the way she's doing now? Would she try to persuade me to go with her to dance the boogie-woogie at a club in Kropotkinskaya district? Would she be able to explain some of the things about sex that I still don't understand even now, although I'm twelve years older than she is? But if we convert years of life into men, I'm afraid my number will be smaller. So it turns out that I'm more like Ksyusha's daughter, if we count our ages as the number of men we've had in our lives, although we've never performed any calculations of that kind. Olya is an innocent little lamb, who barely managed to lose her virginity, and Ksyusha is an experienced woman, a treasure house of wisdom, a well of vice.

Well then, it's a good thing Ksyusha isn't her daughter, although it's not clear where she could get any other daughter from, after all, your apartment can't give you a child, even if that apartment is in the "University" subway district and you'll be paying off the loan for it for another eight years. Eight years, look how the time of my life is passing, the time is passing.

In eight years Ksyusha will have her own apartment too, she'll have her own business, or simply a good job. A little tousle-headed black pawn who will become a queen on the eighth horizontal row.

They bring the check, and Olya automatically verifies it, although she knows they don't make mistakes here. And then Ksyusha says:

"You know, I wanted to ask you to check the numbers in something." She takes a transparent folder out of her purse and holds it out to Olya.

"Check it? I'll be glad to," says Olya. "Numbers are my specialty, you know that. But what is it, Ksyusha? An information site?"

"A special project," says Ksyusha, "a supplement for our Evening."

That's good, Olya tells herself, now I can remind her. But not straight away. First take the folder and take a look at what's inside it.

"Politics?" she asks. "The election?"

We make an unreal world, Olya tells herself, an unreal world of numbers, wires and luminescent monitors. Politics, elections, the Russian internet, banner shows, hits and traffic. An unreal world, an unreal life.

"No," says Ksyusha, shaking her head and setting the locks of hair swaying at her temples. "Not politics, more like crime. I want to do a special project on the Moscow Psycho – I think it's far more important than any election."

Far more important than any election, yes, that's what Ksyusha really does think. Olya knows that. Don't complain about the unreality of your world, Ksyusha once told her, are you sure you want to see the real one? I know how, I've told you many times. Pain doesn't lie.

The transparent folder lies on the table between them.

"I'll do it tomorrow, okay?" Olya says, but she doesn't reach out her hand.

Ksyusha nods, and then Olya says:

"Listen, do you remember I asked you to find out about someone..."

"Of course," Olya answers, "I looked on the web and Googled his name – there's nothing about him."

Googled his name, thinks Olya, I did that myself. Numbers are my specialty, and Google's the best search engine on the web, but even so, it can only find what's in the internet. And That Man keeps everything secret, he doesn't give his name to the newspapers, and he's not mentioned on Dirt.ru.

"I Googled him," Olya replies, "I thought you would enquire through your own channels..."

"Of course," Ksyusha answers, "I'm sorry, I'm going through a bad patch right now, and I got kind of tied up. I asked around, but no one knows anything. But I'll ask Pasha too, the next time I talk to him."

"Thanks," Olya replies, "thanks and sorry for pestering you. It's just that I need it very badly – and as soon as possible."

If she were my daughter, thinks Olya, I'd still be reluctant to put pressure on her. I'd still say *thanks and sorry for pestering you*, but even so I wouldn't let her do a project on a murderer who cuts girls' breasts off and gouges their eyes out. But she's not my daughter, so all I can do is take the folder and put it in my purse.

"No, thank *you*," Ksenia answers, getting up.

It's snowing outside, like in a Japanese movie.

12

IT IS GOOD TO KILL IN WINTER. ESPECIALLY IF IT HAS snowed overnight, and the ground is covered with a delicate blanket of white. You put the bound naked body on it. The blood from the wounds flows more freely in the cold frosty air, and the warmth of life departs with it. If you are lucky and she does not die too quickly, she will see the solid film of ice cover what was flowing through her veins so recently. Red on white, there is no more beautiful combination than that.

They say freezing to death is like going to sleep. Put her head on your knees, watch as the pupils glaze over, as the eyes close, gently stroke the cooling skin, rouse her occasionally with searing blows of the knife, so that she shudders in pain and returns to life for a moment, catch the final glimmers of consciousness in her eyes, sing a quiet lullaby, touch her forehead like Mom did when you were ill as a child and she checked to see if you were feverish. Repeat that gesture all these years later, check, feel the skin getting colder and colder every time, as if the Snow Queen is wafting her breath over her, notice that the blows no longer make her shudder. Then you can cut the ropes, take the gag out of her mouth, sit down beside her and cry, watching as your tears mingle with the blood that is already starting to congeal.

It is good to kill in spring. Especially when the first leaves are opening and the forest you look out at through the window is covered with the delicate green mildew of new life. On days like this it is good to gather fresh branches of pussy willow, full of spring sap, and go down into the deep basement where she is already waiting for you, crucified on ropes between the floor and the ceiling. Take out the gag, let her scream, walk round her a few times, and then strike the first blow. Gradually, shriek after shriek, her thighs, back, stomach and breasts will be covered with a network of weals and a reddish mildew of blood. Then loosen the ropes, put her on her knees, lean down and ask what her name is. It's very important to know the girl's name in order to call to her when she's leaving, to keep her here as long as possible.

They say in China bamboo grows so fast that if you tie a man to the ground, the young shoots pierce right through his body overnight. I wish the spring grass had the same strength, so that the new life and the new death would fuse into one, and the red drops would freeze like flowers on the broad leaves of the snowdrops blossoming in her crotch, on the yellow inflorescences of the dandelions growing up between her breasts that have already been torn open by the thrust of the bitter wormwood. So that she would be lying there, still alive, among all the flowers that have grown through her body, and her final breath would mingle with their spring scent.

It is good to kill in summer. The naked body is at its most natural in summer – most natural and most defenseless. Hammer a dozen pegs into the ground of the yard, bring the weakened girl up out of the basement, tie her down quickly, without giving her a chance to gather her wits, spreading her arms and legs as wide as possible and not forgetting to check the gag properly, because in summer there are people everywhere and there will always be some do-gooder who will hear the screams and knock on the gate in the tall fence and ask what is going on here.

I would like to take him by the hand and lead him over to where the girl is lying naked, like someone on a nudist beach. She knows she is going to die soon. I would like to tell him to squat down and look into her eyes. That is what terror looks like, I would tell him, that is what despair looks like when it condenses so much that you can touch it. Do not be afraid, touch her hand, touch the slippery watering spheres of her eyes. I will give you one of them as a souvenir, if you like.

But if the gag is inserted properly, there will not be any scream, and you will have to look into her eyes alone and listen closely to the shuddering of the body that responds so subtly to each new stroke, each new flourish of the design that you burn into her skin with a magnifying glass. The heat of the sun, so highly concentrated that it can't help but move her. The flesh chars, the small pink mounds of the nipples darken in front of your eyes, the clitoris can no longer hide in the undergrowth of the hairs that have been shaven off, or in the hood of skin that has been cut away in advance.

Do not forget to wipe the sweat off her forehead, do not let it flood her eyes, let her see the sky, the sun and the green leaves. Have a damp towel ready, remember what Mommy used to do for you when you were sick, wipe the sweat off her forehead, look into her eyes, try to find the glimmer of your childhood anguish in them.

It is good to kill in autumn. The blood cannot be seen on the red leaves and the yellow leaves float in the crimson puddles like little toy boats. Tie her to a tree, arm yourself with a set of darts and play at St. Sebastian with her. Remember, a dart lodges best of all in the breasts, and there is no chance at all that it will stick in the forehead.

Leave her tied there overnight, if you like. In the morning you will find her freezing cold, but still alive. Untie her from the tree, take her into the warm basement, take the gag out of the mouth torn by its own silent screams, let her cry a little, feed her the breakfast you have cooked yourself, and then take her tenderly, as if this is your wedding night, and you have been waiting for it for two years. Lick the drops of blood off the marks from your darts—in a certain sense they are Cupid's arrows too. When you come, tie her up again, take her out into the yard and start all over again from the beginning.

Autumn is a time of slow dying. There is no need to hurry.

The leaves will have time to shrivel, the branches of the trees will be denuded, the leaden clouds will drift across the sky. On one chilly rainy night go out into the yard and approach the unconscious body slumped helplessly in the ropes and look to see what is left of the woman you brought here a month ago. If you are lucky, she will survive the daily crucifixion between the branches of the old apple tree, the blows of the darts, the tender, stifling lovemaking in the cellar, your rough tongue licking her fresh wounds. Pick up a lump of soil swollen with rain and rub this mud over her tortured body. We shall all lie in earth like that sooner or later. Look at her one last time, take the gag out of her mouth and hope that the sound of the pouring rain will drown out her final screams. Take a knife and kill her with a few blows, before winter begins.

That's what my calendar is like. My four seasons. Pictures from an exhibition.

I'd like to write a book like that. A beautiful and bitter book, in which the beauty of nature and the beauty of death would merge into one. But unfortunately I cannot do it, for everything I have said is a lie.

When you kill, you do not think about the seasons of the year. When you kill, you just kill. And there is nothing inside you but horror.

Horror and arousal.

13

"MAKING A SITE LIKE THAT IS CHILD'S PLAY," OLYA writes on ICQ Messenger. "If you have a blog engine, then it's three days' work, including the design."

"I have a blog engine," Ksyusha replies, "it's at Evening.ru, and we can put it in here too."

"I don't understand where you're going to get content from. You export what Tickertape has written about this monster, and then you run all the interviews you can dig up in the press. Then what?"

"We have to make this site the place all the information flows to," Ksyusha hammers out briskly on the keyboard, "a place where people who think of themselves as specialists on this sort of thing can publish their articles."

"An expert site?"

"Well, yes. An expert site with a strong community-oriented component. A system of forums, a chat room, blogs."

"You think people will go for it?"

"Of course they will."

"Okay, they'll show up once from the banners or the links, but what's going to make them come back? What are they going to discuss in the forums?"

"Suggestions about the psychological profile of the killer, previous similar cases in history, possible motives... there's plenty of stuff!"

"You idealize our subscribers. Everything you just mentioned is material for expert articles. The simple reader will only visit a forum for one reason: to say what should be done with this man when they catch him."

"All right. If that's so, we'll drop the forums. But I think the site could become a gateway for the public to talk with the authorities. The police could use the site to warn the people of Moscow, people could report their suspicions, demand that measures be taken, etc."

"You're an idealist ☺. What makes you think the authorities are prepared to talk to the public?"

"☺ The authorities need to exploit every possible channel for getting information across. They won't close the site down, and they won't take it away from us either. That's too much hassle – they'll have to give us interviews and write press releases for us. Apart from that, we'll get the charities and non-profit organizations involved: psychological help for parents of the victims, fundraising for those who can still be helped by money, announcements of people who have gone missing. My experience as a journalist tells me there'll be more than enough content ☺."

"OK. If that's right, your site will get into the news programs. And you get five or seven thousand unique visitors a day."

"Wow! We're in the Rambler top ten! ☺ ☺"

"☺ And then we'll start selling advertising and make it into a commercial project."

"Will we sell a lot?"

"You won't make much on banners. But the targeted ads – that's a real wow!"

"And where will we get them from?"

"All the fitness clubs that have anything remotely like courses of self-defense for women; online bookshops who sell books like the hundred most famous killers of our time; CDs and DVDs like *Murder Ballads* or *The Silence of the Lambs*. The promotion company for any new film about a psycho – and they come out every month. Shops that sell weapons for self-defense. And there must be something else I've forgotten."

"Is this all realistic?"

"IMHO yes. You collect the material, and I'll find the clients."

"Wow, at last we'll be working together!"

"Like in the good old days ☺."

"Okay, all I have to do now is talk to Pasha."

The medium, as Marshall McLuhan once said, is the message. That is, the means for the mass distribution of information is more important than the information itself. Or to put it slightly differently, the messenger is the message. Marshall McLuhan was a Canadian academic who studied means of communication. He died a long time ago, and his most famous phrase was spoken about television. It would be amusing to hear what he would have said if he'd seen the internet. But Marshall McLuhan isn't saying anything and there's no way he can know if his prophecies came true. Anyway, almost fifty years ago, he forecast that with the appearance of national TV, local dialects would die out. Well, now half a century has passed and what's happened? Local dialects are still the same as they were – and not just in Russia, but in America, where there's far more TV around. This alone would be enough for the Canadian academic McLuhan to be forgotten forever. But in our business, as I know only too well, what's valued is not how accurate a prediction is, but how neatly it's formulated, how catchy the idea is. The form is the content, the messenger is the message, a rose is a rose is a rose.

I've been working as a journalist for ten years now, and I have a pretty good nose for ideas. Not that I've come up with anything absolutely brilliant all that often, but when it comes to grasping other people's ideas, I'm as good as it gets. And now this evening, as I'm sitting in the Rake Restaurant (fabulous design and equally fabulous low prices), having dinner with my boss Ksenia, I understand immediately what she has in mind. This special project is going to be a real bombshell. Because we can take the subject away from the gutter press and do it so people won't be ashamed to visit the site. We'll create an environment where they can express their secret fears and secret desires. And the environment is the intermediary, as Marshall McLuhan didn't say. Ksenia says it's an intermediary between the authorities and the public, but I think it's between every one of us and our most secret dream.

I've been working as a journalist for ten years now, and most of my bosses were firmly convinced that journalism is a form of PR. Commercial PR, political PR, election PR. Our big boss Pasha Silverman once read somewhere that the ideal photo model should have a completely blank face, so that you can draw anything you like on it. And he's very fond of saying that a journalist should have a completely blank brain, so that you can draw any idea on it. I feel rather offended when I hear that, and not just because I have a very high opinion of my own brain. Deep in my heart, I still believe that a journalist is an intermediary. If not between the public and the authorities, then at least between people. Someone who can tell some people about others.

I regret that I didn't go to Chechnya four years ago. Oxana lay down across the threshold, with her red hair that hadn't started turning gray yet flowing free, like Andromache.

"You're not going to make our children orphans," she said, "you're not going anywhere."

"It's pretty safe there," I lied.

"It can't be safe there," said Oxana, "remember Moscow in '93, isn't that enough for you? And anyway, you'll come back from there a sick man. Normal people don't go to war voluntarily, especially to a war like that."

I tried to protest, but I already knew I wasn't going anywhere, because a profession is all well and good, but I had a family, Oxana and two children. And so the Second Chechen War happened without me, if, of course, you can say that, bearing in mind that I put information about explosions and casualties on the news every day. But I still regret that I didn't go. I thought being there was a debt I owed to the boy who went to the faculty of journalism in order to conquer the lies of the state, a debt I ought to repay.

That evening when I decided to stay in Moscow, Oxana and I made love again. We don't make love very often, especially since our second child was born. Six years of marriage will cool any ardent passion, but that evening I threw her down on her back and forced myself into her body desperately, as if I was knocking at a locked door. I came quickly and suddenly burst into tears.

During the years we've been together, I've made love to many women, but I've never wanted to cry with my arms still round them, or as I unclasped my embrace immediately after the final eruption. But that evening I lay with my face pressed into her red hair and sobbed, without even knowing why, and Oxana stroked my hair and looked up at the ceiling and kept repeating *Lyoshenka, Lyoshenka*, perhaps thinking some thoughts of her own. The speaker is more important than what is spoken – and I pressed my entire body against her and felt like Hector, who never did see his Troy.

My big boss Pasha Silverman likes to say journalism is part of PR. I feel rather offended when I hear that, but the senior editor in my department, the young girl Ksenia, just shrugs her pointy shoulders. She's five years younger than me, and she has five years' fewer illusions. All second-flight publications live on advertorial, she says – maybe that's why they're second flight. Ksenia herself never writes articles to order, because the message is the messenger, the text is the author, and advertorial kills you as a professional. Take that road, she says, and you can earn fifteen hundred a month quite easily – but you'll never earn more.

Ksenia wants more. She's twenty-three years old, and she's my boss. You can't write anything on her face, except what she herself wants. Big eyes, harshly made-up lips, tousled hair. A girl who grew up early. In two years' time she'll have her own car and in four she'll have her own apartment.

I think that's why she thought up this special project, because even if you wanted to, there's no way you could put any written-to-order material into it. What good is the Moscow Psycho to anyone? Before the election, the subject could have been used to attack the Moscow authorities, but now nobody needs this story. So this will be genuine journalism, completely unadulterated by PR. Almost an independent investigation, in an area a million miles away from politics – if such a thing is possible in Putin's Russia.

Ksenia says this project is an intermediary between the authorities and the public, but I think it's an intermediary between every one of us and our most secret dream. If it all works out the way she's planned it, then in a month's time the newspapers will be standing in line for an interview with her. I know the way the media market works too well to be wrong about that: in a month from now the skinny young girl from a second-flight online newspaper will be a star. Tousled black hair, big eyes, hard mouth, emphasized even more by lipstick. She's beautiful, I think, she'll look good on the TV screen. In the nineties she would definitely have made a brilliant career. It's not certain that they'll want to see her on air now, but she's destined for more than the fifteen minutes of fame promised by Andy Warhol, whose own fame lasted all the way from the fifties to the car he was supposed to have painted for the TV Series *Brigade* in the late eighties.

I wonder if Ksenia realizes what we're starting here? What a scandal this whole story will be – not the site itself, but the story of a twenty-something girl devoting a site to a psychotic killer? How many people will say, without even visiting the site, that she's making propaganda for violence and provoking new crimes?

"Maybe we should drink a toast to success, what do you think? I think what you've come up with is great. To be quite honest, it's really got me going, I haven't felt anything like it for ages. Why don't we have a shot of vodka apiece, and then go home?"

14

KSENIA TELLS ALEXEI ABOUT THE SITE, LAYING OUT the printouts of the interviews and news in front of him: there are occasional black and white photos, indistinct, almost completely obliterated by the poor-quality printing. Alexei listens, nods and sometimes chuckles approvingly. A thirty-year-old man, the father of two children, a boy and a girl, isn't it? – I ought to make sure of that somehow, so as not to get it wrong. He probably feels bad because I'm younger than him and already the boss. He doesn't show it, though.

Black and white sheets of paper on the table, try not to look, try not to read a single word by accident. What must be going on inside the head of a man who cuts off women's nipples, burns patterns into their bodies, puts the eyes squeezed out of their sockets into their anus and vagina? Better not ask yourself that question because then you'll have to ask yourself what's going on inside your own head when you haven't known what to do with yourself for a week and every evening as you go to sleep you masturbate, imagining these very details, no, don't look down at the print-outs, because if you do, that dark wave will sweep over you again, and the space around you glowing in anticipation of a celebration will start eddying and curling up behind your back until there's nothing left apart from the heat that fills your whole body, the tight ball rolling around below your belly, the itching, the pain, the anticipation of pleasure.

What's going on inside your head, I ask you, what's going on?

"You and I are sick people," your lost lover Sasha used to say while you washed his cum off your hair in the shower. And you, wincing at the touch of the water on your lacerated skin, used to answer him: "No, darling, you and I are normal healthy people. Do you know how the really sick people behave? You ought to be screaming at me now: *You bitch, look how low you've brought me, I'm not like this!* And he used to come up to you, stroke your fresh weals tenderly and say, "Yes, I am like this," and smile his most touching and open-hearted smile. And then, you used to say, "we could behave like some psychotic killer in a bad movie and swear to each other that we won't do it again."

"We will," he promised, "we definitely will." But now you know we won't do it again, it's over.

Alexei has brought your shot of vodka, shit, this is just the wrong time, I wonder if it's the same for ordinary vanilla people, the arousal sweeping over you just at the most unsuitable moment? If you told this nice thirty-year-old boy, *I'd like you to take me to the restroom put me down on my knees and fuck me in the mouth*, he'd probably choke on his vodka. But he has lovely hands, a bit like Lyova's hands, strong, with long fingers. I wonder how it would feel if he caressed you with them from the inside, if he squeezed your nipples? Better not think about that, though, just drink up quickly, yes, here's to success, to the success of our project, look at your watch, say I guess it's time to go home. Collect your coat from the cloakroom, yes, thanks, that's very kind of you. I wonder if it's true what they say, American women won't let men hand them their coats, or is it just a lie? It's probably a lie. But then, who cares. Say goodnight, take a taxi, go home.

The two of you walk outside, Alexei's mobile rings and he answers quite loudly, so you can't help hearing: "No, Oxana, I'll be delayed a bit longer. Pasha's asked me to discuss a special project with him." So Pasha asked him! His Oxana must be the jealous type, then. A boy and a girl or two girls. Now's the moment you ought to ask. You ask: "How are the children?" He answers: "Fine, thanks, but they've been sick this last month. Some kind of really terrible flu." So it's still not clear *who* he's got.

A taxi stops, he asks: "Where are you going?" He says: "I'll take you." You pile into the back seat, and on a corner he presses himself against your thigh, as if by accident, and he stays there like that and says that for every item in the real world there ought to be a corresponding item in the virtual world, so that ideally every event should be honored with a special project, it's a pity no one has the resources or the money to do it, and you try to think what kind of special project could be made out of the story of your split with Sasha. Photos of the participants, a description of the tortures that he invented and the ones you invented, with separate sections for the ones you had time to try, and the ones that remained dreams: a few texts of cultural analysis, a link to the resources of the Russian BDSM community – SMLife, bdsm.org.ru and Bondage.ru, plus a few blogs. A link to your other web projects. Sasha's CV. An mp3 file with a reconstruction of your final conversation. The hostess's reminiscences about how Sasha used to be in love with her at school. A photo gallery: your buttocks before and after an assignation. Alexei really does have strong hands, so really, perhaps you could – close your eyes and reach out your lips for a kiss. Of course, he's your subordinate, you mustn't offer him the full program, you can limit it to vanilla sex, the standard, simple nookie.

After all, a man's prick is better than a dildo. At least there's some variety.

15

HE'S NOT A STUPID MAN, THINKS KSENIA, BUT THE most important thing is that he has flair. He'll agree because he realizes it's a dead cert.

The three of them are sitting in Pasha's office. Silverman behind his desk, half hidden behind the PC monitor, Ksenia and Alexei on chairs, shoulder to shoulder. More like companions-in-arms than lovers, thinks Ksenia.

She's a beautiful girl, thinks Pasha, but the most important thing is that you can feel the drive she has. You don't often find that kind of drive in Moscow girls, I would have taken her for a provincial, from somewhere in Ukraine or the south of Russia, or Peter at the very least. I can tell that sooner or later she'll squeeze that hundred-dollar raise out of me, especially since the project she's suggesting is a dead cert, an excellent idea, it's a pity I've got to say no.

And he does say no, and Ksenia's not even surprised, because she's already read this "no" in his face, but Alexei, restraining his indignation asks: "Why not?" A good partner, Ksenia thinks about him, good, but too impatient. It would be interesting to see how he dances. Although I'd probably have to spend six months teaching him first. Just look how complicated everything is for me: whether it's for dancing or for bed, I need highly qualified specialists. And what's more, the qualifications are different: so all my dominant lovers turn out to be lousy dancers. Maybe I really ought to teach him to dance the boogie-woogie, I'm still going out dancing alone, like some girl looking to get picked up.

She's not saying anything yet, pausing for effect, thinks Pasha, clever girl. I remember when I put her in charge of these idlers six months ago, I was sure they'd gobble her up, but just look – everything turned out fine.

"Because the times aren't right," says Pasha and thinks to himself that he can't remember when the times ever were right. During his childhood, during the period of Brezhnev's lies? Or later, when all the Russians were forced out of Grozny by the Chechens, and then some other Russians razed Grozny to the ground? When those two apartment blocks were blown up on the edge of Moscow? When those hostages were taken in the theater near the Dubrovka subway station? Yes, he asks himself, when were the times ever right? He doesn't know the answer, but he does know for certain that they aren't right now.

"But it's not even politics," says Alexei, and Ksenia remembers him explaining that this site could become the intermediary between people and their most secret dreams. She thinks: what kind of dreams did he have in mind?

"In this country everything's politics," says Pasha. "It's a brutal, bloody, shocking project. And right now everything has to be nice and peaceful. Try watching the TV in the evening sometime."

"As long as you keep on thinking like that," Alexei suddenly shouts, "we'll never get out of the second ten on Rambler. Look at Gazette, read their columns! They write about whatever they want. And look at where they are on the ratings and where we are."

He's getting too worked up, thinks Ksenia, as if he didn't know it's pointless to shout at Pasha. You have to take what you can get and wind up the conversation. She's starting to feel sad: they haven't got anywhere with Pasha, she should finish up quickly, maybe she'll be in time to go dancing this evening.

"Gazette.ru is financed by YuKOS," replies Pasha. "So maybe you'd better look at where Khodorkovsky is and where we are."

"But listen..." Alexei says, and Pasha explains he doesn't mean we'd all be put in jail, he's only talking about... err... their degree of financial independence. "So I won't give you any money for this, he says. "But I will support the advertising."

He's not a stupid man, thinks Ksenia, but the most important thing is that he has flair. Maybe our project really is no good? And I only like it because I… well, because it interests me. Maybe, I should drop it? thinks Ksenia, and out loud she says:

"Thank you, and I wanted to ask you to let us have us the blog engine you have on Evening."

She's a beautiful girl, thinks Pasha, but the most important thing is that you can feel the drive she has. She has strange interests: two days ago she asked me if I could make enquiries about a certain man. And she added pointedly: through my own connections. I don't like jerking my own connections about, and I almost always refuse, but this time I agreed. "Is it to do with work?" I asked. "No," she answered, "no, of course not, it's personal business." Personal business, thinks Pasha. What kind of personal business could she have with this forty-year-old businessman with a criminal past who has survived two attempts to kill him and has three criminal prosecutions pending? A man whose business partners go missing in broad daylight. Of course, personal business is personal business, but it's not nice to think about it. When we finish this conversation, I'll ask her to stay behind and show her the note they drew up for me.

"Give us the blog engine you've got on Evening," says Ksenia, and Pasha shrugs.

"Take it, and take my programmer too, he's on a fixed rate anyway. Do you want me to find a good designer?"

"I have a designer," Ksenia replies, "an old school friend of mine. We'll agree terms."

I'm going to do this after all, thinks Ksenia, if something can be done, you should do it. If only to find out whether it works or not.

"All right then, that's settled," says Pasha, smiling, and asks Ksenia to stay, and he thinks to himself: how can I tell her I'd like to support their project? It's an excellent idea and a commercial dead cert – but something inside tells me I'd better steer clear of it, or else sooner or later I'll start thinking about the fact that there's a man walking round this city who amuses himself by cutting out women's intestines and hanging them round their necks like garlands of flowers. I don't want to think about that, there are already too many things I'm trying not to think about too much. About having to say "no" when you want to say "yes." About businessmen whose partners disappear without trace. About piles of rubble that appear where buildings used to be. Sometimes it feels like I waste most of my energy on trying not to think about such things. I waste so much energy on it and every day as I walk through the city, I shudder when I see a heap of debris where only recently there was a restaurant. It feels like my nightmares are becoming reality, but it's not that, it's just Mayor Luzhkov clearing space for new skyscrapers, clearing it with a gusto that sometimes makes it seem like the terrorists have learned to use a new kind of explosive – so silent that it doesn't produce any echo in the newspapers or the conversations of the citizens.

I'm not going to get any boogie-woogie today, thinks Ksenia, no dancing to Indigo Swing and Jump4Joy, no chance to invite Alexei to join me. What is it Pasha wants to say to me, he's not a stupid man, and the most important thing is that he has flair.

Pasha puts a folder of printouts on the desk.

"You asked me to check this man out through my contacts," he says. "Read it here, I won't let you take it out."

Ksenia reads, and Pasha carries on thinking about the serial killer, about Putin's politics, about piles of rubble on the streets of cities. Even so, he thinks, the ruins are produced by inanimate machines. A detonator, hexogen, a trigger mechanism, a bomb hatch. The person who presses the button doesn't see the bloody scraps of bodies go flying through the air. The dust from the ruins doesn't settle on his clothes. The person who takes the decisions doesn't see their consequences. He lives in the same unreal world as all of us.

"Impressive," says Ksenia, closing the folder, "and a girlfriend of mine was thinking of setting up a business with him."

"I wouldn't advise it, Ksenichka," replies Pasha.

"A horrible man." She carefully lays the folder in the middle of the desk.

No, thinks Pasha, he's not horrible, he's an ordinary man. The one who presses the button, the one who sets the machine working.

"Not so very horrible," he says, "it's just that in his business the rules were different from the very beginning."

"Haven't you ever wanted to change the rules?" asks Ksenia. "For instance, we could behave as if there was no Putin TV and Khodorkovsky wasn't in jail."

Pasha laughs and thinks: she has drive, she's a beautiful girl. I wonder if she has a boyfriend – or whatever it is they're called nowadays?

"You could have said yes to us today," says Ksenia, "after all, everything you said was just excuses. Explain to me what the problem is. Don't you believe in this project?"

"Listen, Ksenia," he says, "we both know this is an excellent idea. It's a commercial dead cert. But you know, you said *he*..." – Pasha nods toward the folder – "...is a horrible man. But then, all he's done is pay the money, give the orders and, and fly off to Spain or Greece to give himself an alibi. We can understand him. For him the murders – if there really have been any murders – are just a way to redistribute property. Redirect the cash flows. When you get right down to it, he's been living in a world of abstractions for a long time already. But this man you want to set up the site about – he lives in the same city as we do. Goes to the same shops. Probably eats in the same restaurants. And what he does, he does himself. With his own hands."

16

You got away, the only one, you got away.

You had little feet and hands
And shoulder-length brown hair
A pubis shaved with just a thin line of hair untouched
by the razor
And I thought a cutthroat had never touched your
body before
There are so many things you don't know in this life
But we have time

I undressed you, unconscious, on the table in the
concrete basement
And stood there for a moment, listening
As a string started quivering somewhere inside me
Like a tuning fork responding to an old familiar melody
Like a faded leaf clinging desperately to the branch
In the gusts of autumn wind

You had a Walkman, I crushed it under my heel
You won't need it now, I'll teach you a different music
The faded leaves out on my lot
Could not cling to the branches
They lie on the cold ground and wait for you

I ran my hand over your stomach
Gently rounded, like a little hill
Perhaps you thought "I've got fat this summer, now I
must lose weight"
Believe me, I have known many women
Closer than anybody else
I tell you, as sincerely as the razor
Slicing through the skin:
You have a lovely body

Your body is lovely from its outer coverings
To its inner depths, to the moist pink depths
of the mouth
The red muscles, the yellow fat, the blue veins
Visible even now beneath your summer suntan skin
Two white triangles, front and back,
Where the swimsuit was

Now you have nothing to hide

Something quivers inside me, like music playing in a
crushed Walkman
Wait, and you will hear it too, you will respond

You said "I must lose weight, slim down"
Let me tell you that losing weight is very simple
Like a tree dropping its leaves in autumn
I'll teach you how when you wake up

Her eyes were closed, but I remembered their color
They were brown with amber-yellow veins
When I first saw them, I could feel
The world grow still around me, curling up like a scroll

Brown eyes with amber-yellow veins
The plump lips of a teenage girl
Who kissed all evening in the empty corridors at school
While dance music thundered downstairs in the hall

Oh, what a shame to stretch that mouth with a rag or
 a gag
But I wanted so much to go outside with you
Where the faded leaves were lying on the cold ground
Waiting for you

I gave you an injection to make you sleep soundly
And then I took a needle and thread
My granny taught me to darn things
She said "No need to throw away what can be darned"
Yes, the war generation, poverty and hunger
They weren't bothered about being overweight at your age
They were hungry all the time anyway

I finished and then wiped away the blood
Licked it off with my tongue but it still wouldn't stop
It was like a kiss
My eyelashes trembled on your cheek

I tied your hands together
Little hands like a child's
They could easily slip out of the ropes
I tied them tighter

I put shackles on your legs so you could walk, but not
 too fast
I knew straight off you weren't one of those girls
Who give themselves with tears and make no effort
To get their own way

We will have plenty of time, I said to you
We'll get to know each other better
I'll show you things you never thought you'd see
Your body will reveal its mysteries
And you will know there was no need to worry
About how much you weigh

You're not really heavy, I can easily carry you in my arms

I'll tell you how I've lived for all these years
Without you here beside me
Tell you about the world where I was born and I grew up
I'll lead you into its forbidden groves
Where flayed skin hangs on branches
Like faded leaves
Where a little boy can't sleep
Listening to the trembling growing louder
As if someone is choosing music
To make the tuning fork respond

You sat there on the porch
Faded leaves lying at your feet
Your lips pressed tightly closed
The white triangle below your stomach
Bisected by the thin line of hair
Glowed in the evening twilight

It was a peaceful autumn evening
In the cool air
Sounds carried well
Somewhere in the distance a dog barked
And a train hooted

You opened your eyes

You had brown eyes with amber veins
When I first saw them, I could feel
The world grow still around me, curling up like a scroll
Like a fallen leaf on the ground

You didn't try to stand, you simply tensed your arms
As though testing the strength of the ropes
Red muscles, interwoven tissues
Little mounds on your forearms
Under the skin that was still tanned
And then you suddenly did something with your face
I didn't understand what happened

A fountain of blood spurted out
Your mouth opened
And you screamed

It was a peaceful autumn evening
In the cool air
Sounds carried well

Before I realized what was happening
I darted to your side but you kept on screaming
A single note, like some broken mechanical toy
AAAAAAAAAAAAAAAAAAAAAAA
I darted to you, and in one swift stroke
I slit your throat

Forgive me.

It was autumn, people closing up their dachas for the
winter
The whole village full of visitors
Sounds carried well in the cool air

Now there will be nothing more
No music and no trembling

I'll never know how your skin comes away
Or peel your breasts, like two halves
Of a single orange

The sound broke off as if someone stamped on a
Walkman
You clung to life for one more second
Like an autumn leaf in a cold wind
Clinging to the branch

You lay there in my arms
Your lips, the plump lips of a teenage girl
Were torn to shreds

I didn't think you had such strength in you
Maybe my granny taught me darning badly
Or I was a careless pupil

While the dance music thundered downstairs in the
school hall
I wanted to kiss you in the empty corridors
I wanted to walk with you up the dark stairs of a
school
Where every classroom holds new pain and new
humiliation
And the graduation diploma is a gob of spittle in the face
And a shout of "get lost"

I was the only pupil in that school
I'm still amazed that they made such a big building for me
My dad, mom, granddad and two grannies who
survived the war
But failed to teach me to darn properly

I took you in my arms and carried you to the
basement
You were really light, believe me
You didn't need to worry about your weight
I put you on the table where a few hours earlier
I undressed you, and then turned out the light

Standing on the steps, I turned to look:
The white triangle below your stomach
Glowed in the darkness of the cellar
Bisected by the thin line of hair
Like a razor

17

IT'S EASY TO BE UNFAITHFUL TO YOUR WIFE. ESPECIALLY if you happen to work in one of the liberal professions. You can be delayed at work, you don't have to sit in the office all day long and, when all's said and done, you can even work at weekends: the latest issue has to be put to bed, or you need to do an exclusive interview. The important thing is to find a place, because finding a woman is no problem. Women in the liberal professions are liberal-minded when it comes to friendly sex. But it's better not to sleep with your colleagues – apart from the female journalists there are always the female designers, page makers and photographers.

Three years ago I even met a girl courier, only sixteen years old. She was as curious as a little squirrel and every time I came up with a new place and new position for her to give herself to me in, teaching her the psychogeography of the city and sexual acrobatics at the same time. We opened the season in a cubicle of the editorial office restroom, where I dragged her after the bottle of wine with which we had celebrated her first pay packet. Then came an attic, the stairway of a Stalinist skyscraper, a basement, where my courier suddenly started feeling dizzy and I had to drag her back out into the fresh air, stumbling over the pipes and tearing my jacket. Then the driver's cab of a dump truck that had been left unlocked overnight, a building still under construction and – the brilliant crowning moment of our affair – a room in the Rossiya Hotel, where I saw her completely naked for the first time: her navel was pierced and she had a little rose tattooed on her left buttock. The girl used to wear boots with thick soles and she only put on a skirt for her assignations with me – because it was too awkward taking off the trousers with numerous pockets that were her uniform on every other day. That evening in the hotel we completely satisfied our mutual curiosity and when we parted, I think we took away only the very best of memories.

I knew all the places where I passed the time with my little courier very well. With my practiced eye I could tell immediately which entrance would be best for our next brief encounter. I prefer the ones where the elevator and the stairs are separate and you can feel safe on the landing of the top floor. As I grew older, however, I started preferring girls who had their own apartments. Fortunately, there were more and more of those, nowadays even students try to rent a place to avoid being crammed in with the old folks, never mind Ksenia, who's my boss, after all, and not even the memory of her lips clasped round my prick can change that fact. But even if we forget about that, it really would be embarrassing for a respectable grown-up man to carry his young companion off to a basement, like some spotty teenager. There were still hotels, but they have been getting more expensive with every year that passes, and I can't bring myself to pay a fifth of my monthly salary for two hours in my lover's arms. I'm a family man after all, the father of two children, the husband of my wife.

It's easy to be unfaithful to your wife. Especially if your wife also happens to work in the liberal professions and has a liberal outlook on life, if you have an open marriage and she is willing to close her eyes to your infidelities. She sits on top of you, closes her eyes and starts swaying smoothly to and fro until she suddenly explodes into a long, drawn-out sigh and collapses, pressing down on you with her heavy breasts and scattering her red hair that is starting to turn gray. Holding her carefully by the buttocks, you make two or three thrusts into her and shoot your load too. And that's it, *finito*, you can open your eyes. In our sexual duet Oxana assigns the passive role to me, and even that doesn't happen very often. It's a long time since I last managed to persuade her to vary our games – the times when the young student of the Russian University for the Humanities demonstrated the fundamentals of sexual acrobatics to me on the carpet in her parents' parlor were consigned to oblivion long ago. She likes to be on top, and I don't know what's more important here – subtle points of physiology or the desire to dominate. In our family life the missionary position has been an exotic exception. The last time we tried it was probably on the day when Oxana refused to let me go to Chechnya.

It's easy to be unfaithful to your wife. Especially if you know why you do it. If you wake up one morning with the feeling that your life is passing by pointlessly, squeezed between the routine of work and the routine of family. I love my job and I love my family, but I resent being an ordinary correspondent who does an occasional interview for a second-flight online newspaper. In professional terms, I'm a successful failure. Successful – because I do actually earn the kind of money I can bring home without feeling ashamed. A failure – because after a year even I can't recognize my own articles. Everything would have been different if I'd had the talent to become a columnist like the ones who write for *Gazette* – then my friends would quote my columns to each other when they met. Or if I could have gone to Chechnya.

I don't regret the choice I made. I chose my family, but even in my family I still feel like a successful failure. My children love me, my wife supports me at difficult moments. In the final analysis, we drag this cart along together – my interviews in Evening.ru and Oxana's articles in *Harper's Bazaar* or *Elle*, added together, provide our breakfast, lunch and dinner, which is what five billion of the six billion inhabitants of the Earth toil for. I'm a very successful failure, I love my wife and my children. But I feel cramped in our life, just as the four of us are cramped in the two-room flat left to us by Oxana's parents.

Sexual acrobatics with women I hardly even know – that was the only war I could set out for. Basements where water slops under your feet, stairways where the glass from broken bottles crunches under the soles of your shoes, abandoned buildings scheduled for demolition, a hoarse cry, a palm covering a mouth – for me these are Gudermes, Mozdok and Grozny, which I never visited. I never made it as a journalist, but at least as a man

I don't feel like a loser. I remember all of them, from the young girl courier with the pierced navel to the forty-year-old American journalist with whom I celebrated Yeltsin's victory with oral sex in the sumptuous luxury of the Radisson-Slavyanskaya Hotel. All of them from the first-year student Natasha, who seduced me six months after my wedding, to Ksenia, whose ear-splitting shriek I only heard for the first time last week. These memories are my invisible trophies, photographs brought back from places where I didn't have to feel like a failure.

It's easy to be unfaithful to your wife. You just have to know the boundary that you must not cross. You just have to remember all the time that these women are doomed to become memories, invisible trophies, and your wife will be with you unto death. It's very easy to respect your wife, especially if you've lived with her for ten years and you have two children. Sexual acrobatics is impossible with a body you know as well as you do your own; it's like trying to kiss yourself on the heel. Your bodies have been ground to fit each other, they have no need of superfluous movements as they sway in synchronized motion on the waters of Oblivion in the most erotic rhythm a man and a woman can know. This rhythm is called "we shall grow old together," and it is measured out by the water boiling in the kettle in the morning, the New Year chimes on TV and the rare long, drawn-out sighs in the air of the bedroom at night. Every morning you wake up together and every night you go to sleep together, every day you watch the gray hairs growing through the red tresses, every month you breathe in the smell of unborn children leaving her womb when their time comes. And when Oxana is sleeping beside you, you put your arms round her and as you fall asleep you wonder what invisible trophies her memory holds. Sexual acrobatics is impossible with a body you know as well as you do your own; and so is infidelity.

18

I LIKE WEEKENDS. I DON'T HAVE TO GET UP AT NINE o'clock in order to be at work for eleven, I can lie in bed, then take a shower, stand in front of the mirror and watch the drops of water slithering down, the same way my body sags more with every year. I once promised myself that the bathroom in my own apartment would have a mirror right across the wall – I must have seen that in a video, in some dubious erotic tape that was a fifth-level derivative of *Emmanuelle*, some German soft porn or Scandinavian movie about the interminable adventures of five, six or seven buxom Swedish girls in every country in the world. My female friends and I, all decent, high-minded girls from the history faculty of what was then Leningrad University, sometimes used to get together in Katya's apartment to discuss Nabokov and Brodsky, and then watch porn. Liza once brought genuine hard porn with pricks, full erections and all the works, but I found it distasteful and went hurrying off home, citing an exam that was still two weeks away. Well then, it was on one of those relatively innocent tapes that I saw a bathroom covered in mirrors, I don't remember what was going on in there, but the idea of it stuck in my head and now here am I, Olga Krushevnitskaya, a thirty-five-year-old woman, IT manager, successful professional, standing naked in front of the mirror, all on my lonesome.

Of course, Oleg and I did once try to screw looking in the mirror. I don't remember what they showed us when we were young, but in the movie everything must have looked far more sensuous. In reality your feet slip on the bottom of the bath, screwing and looking in the mirror at the same time is very uncomfortable, and in the end the curtain collapsed on our heads, like in another movie so terrifying that I switched the TV off at that point and felt glad that I was all on my lonesome in the apartment, so I didn't have to feel ashamed in front of anyone or lie about having to study for an exam.

Ksyusha probably likes watching movies about psychos, maybe she even gets aroused by stories of men in masks wielding massive choppers and pursuing squealing girls. The girls in those movies always have huge breasts, like those numerous Swedish girls on Ibiza and the Mediterranean islands. So I don't have to worry, I'm safe, my breasts are quite ordinary, size B at best, and they've started to sag in the last few years.

It would be good if I already had a child: then, when I looked in the mirror in the mornings, I'd understand that my breasts have sagged because a little boy or girl drank milk out of them and pounded me with his or her little fists. Looking at my sagging breasts, I'd think about my child, but as things are I only think about how time is passing and the way my body is drooping like a candle left out in the hot sun. Drooping further every moment even now, as I stand in front of the mirror in the bathroom, all on my lonesome.

Oleg says he likes my body, that it's a mature woman's body, a really experienced body. I don't want to disappoint him, but my body isn't all that experienced, except in waking up alone in its own bed. My sexual experience has been limited to the men that I have loved. There have been very few of them – probably because I've always remained a girl from a cultured Petersburg family, where Mom explained that the most important thing in life is love, and so the word "sex" was never even spoken in our home. It's an effort for me to fall in love, I fall out of love slowly, and I was always envious of my girlfriends who had holiday affairs, as if they weren't Petersburg girls from cultured families, but five, six or seven Swedish girls who had moved from Ibiza to Koktebel, Repino or Sestroretsk near Petersburg.

To be quite honest, the ability to make hard work of falling in love is all that remains in me of the girl from the cultured Petersburg family. Girls like that shouldn't live in their own apartment in Moscow, they shouldn't drive a Toyota, not even one that's six years old, and they certainly shouldn't weave intrigues against their own shareholders. Delicate Petersburg girls from the humanities faculty don't ask their friends to use their journalistic contacts to check out potential investors with a distinctly criminal past, two partners who have disappeared and three criminal cases pending. Decent girls prefer to read about men like that in books or, at a pinch, watch them in the movies. To be quite honest, even Grisha and Kostya, my present shareholders, are not the most appropriate company for a cultured Petersburg lady, even if both of them do have a college education.

I feel a bit sorry to hand Grisha and Kostya over for this man to gobble up – and not even because he'll find some way to pay them far less than the business they want to destroy is worth, but simply because I like them. We understand each other, because we're very much alike. We're all traitors.

I was supposed to study the nineteenth century, and Grisha and Kostya were supposed to study theoretical physics. We were supposed to live poor but honest lives. I was supposed to deal with words and dates, not numbers, and Grisha and Kostya were supposed to search for black holes or something of the kind, not the loopholes in the law that allowed them to make their first money. We've never spoken about this, but I know that we understand each other.

We are traitors, and betrayal is only hard the first time round. It's hard to quit your job and go away to Moscow. It's hard to tell yourself: "I can grow this business." It's hard to say for the first time: "Mom, I can't talk now, I've got a meeting" – and hang up. After that everything just happens. You buy an apartment in Moscow, you grow this business, you get used to paying your parents' bills. You have no difficulty in delivering up Grisha and Kostya to a man who will shaft them – and perhaps shaft you too.

It's only hard the first time round – in business and in love. Hard to take your clothes off in front of a stranger, hard to respond to a kiss for the first time, hard to accept the attentions of men you don't love at all. It was like that with Oleg. He wooed me for six months, sent me flowers, invited me to restaurants. He was a head of department in a major bank for which the firm I worked in was putting together a website. At first I thought Oleg was too pompous, then I thought he was too pushy, then I told myself he wasn't from my social circle. Once when we were dining together, I was feeling unwell, I had a sore throat, so I hardly said a word. When they served the dessert, Oleg took a little box out of his pocket. Inside it was a bracelet of dark red stones. He put it on my wrist and kissed my fingers, one by one. At that moment I realized I couldn't postpone the inevitable any longer. You're a big girl now, I told myself, how much longer are you going to string the poor man along? Let him have it this evening, he'll never show up again, and you'll be quits.

Oleg always took me home, but this time I let him come up to the apartment. At that time I rented a one-room apartment near the Dynamo subway station, and he carried me straight from the hallway to the bed. We started making love and I suddenly felt what was happening wasn't right. I could hardly breathe, my throat was smarting as if it had been scraped with sandpaper, I was helpless and passive, so Oleg spun me about like a lifeless doll. When he came, I just carried on lying where he'd put me five minutes earlier. He got up, leaned over me and asked: "Is there something wrong?" But I just waved my hand toward the door as if to say – go! He got dressed, walked into the kitchen, drank some water and came back into the room. "Are you sure there's nothing you need?" he asked, and I shook my head again and waved my hand toward the door. He shrugged, kissed my unresponsive chapped lips and said: "Forgive me, apparently I..." and left without finishing what he was saying. It was only hard the first time round – so hard that in the morning I had a temperature of almost a hundred, and I stayed in bed for an entire week. Oleg came to see me every day, he brought me food, medicine and flowers. There was something old-fashioned about it – and that was how we became lovers.

I moved from near the Dynamo station to the Sokolniki district and then bought an apartment near the University subway, and during those years Oleg and I met once a week, sometimes less often, sometimes more, and had dinner at a restaurant. He told me about his work and sometimes mentioned his wife and children – simply in passing, as something that was taken for granted. It was from him that I first heard about the man I want to hand Kostya and Grisha over to. Oleg said that if I wanted to see this man, he could arrange a meeting.

Yes, we used to meet, dine at a restaurant and then make love. Oleg kissed me goodbye when he left, and I was left all on my lonesome, a girl from a good Petersburg family where they used to say that the most important thing in life is love.

Standing in front of the mirror all on my lonesome, I thought that maybe they didn't simply say that, maybe they really believed it. I still believe it even now, but I wouldn't admit that to anyone but Ksyusha.

Ksyusha often laughs at me. She says: you ought to screw more often, then you wouldn't confuse sex with love. She says that if I'd had five or six men instead of one during this period of more than three years, I could say which one of them I love, but the way things are I just love the one who happens to be at hand, as they say, or rather, the one who has been between my legs. Ksyusha, by the way, doesn't say "between your legs," she avoids euphemisms in general, and so, by the way, do many Petersburg girls from good families. I never used to say things like that, and I never say them now, not because I'm embarrassed, but because a long time ago they became simply a work tool for me, a jargon that my business partners use, especially the suppliers. It would be strange to use words like that in ordinary everyday speech – for me it's as strange as calling the check from the Auchan hypermarket a *payment document*.

But whatever Ksyusha might say, I think that if instead of one man I had five, six or seven – numbered like those lascivious buxom Swedes – I wouldn't be able to love any of them. I would have several times more sex, but there would be no love left at all. My kind of girl can't do it like that.

"Ksyusha," I asked her one day, "have you ever been in love? Genuine girly love, like in the movies?"

"Probably, in fifth grade," Ksyusha answered, "and perhaps with Nikita, my first BDSM lover. Apart from that, no, never. I told you, you need to screw more."

It sometimes seems to me that Ksyusha and I are very much alike. I've never seen her Lyova, but I imagine him as being like my Vlad; if he was in Moscow, he'd make her wash the dishes after he had visitors. I'm sure that by my age Ksyusha will have her own apartment too, and a good car, perhaps even better than mine. I imagine that this morning she's standing in front of the mirror in her bathroom too, a bit of a journalist, a bit of an editor, just a little bit of an IT manager, but in any case a successful professional, and thinking about me. Every one of us has a little secret: I have my Oleg, Ksyusha has her strange predilections. But then, what kind of secret is that, she doesn't try to hide it, although, to be quite honest, I still feel embarrassed. The other day we were sitting at the chessboard tables in the Atrium mall, and I remembered how I used to play chess at school and reached the second grade, and Ksyusha told me she used to go to the dance studio and how glad she was six months earlier when she found a club where she could dance the boogie-woogie. The bar is shaped like a carved wooden arbor and the winter sun shone with unusual brightness through the glass walls. I thought that in ten years' time Luzhkovian architecture would meld into the urban environment of Moscow, and people a bit younger than Ksyusha wouldn't be any more annoyed by it than I am by touristy Arbat Street. So we were having a nice chat, and I was telling her about the shoes I'd bought the week before, and suddenly Ksyusha said in a perfectly genteel tone of voice: "And yesterday I bought myself a lovely scourge with lead tips on it. An absolutely classic cat-o'-nine-tails. It was damned expensive too, but you can't expect the men to get anything, I have to get everything myself." She said it so loudly that the people at the next table heard and probably realized quite clearly she wasn't saying she'd bought a wonderful little kitten with nine tails. I immediately felt embarrassed and wanted to leave.

I'm afraid of pain and I don't understand Ksyusha. Oleg once bit the lobe of my ear too hard and the arousal instantly disappeared. There was a time when I used to watch videos that were fifth-level derivatives of *Emmanuelle*, German soft porn, the interminable adventures of Swedish girls in every corner of the world: what happens on the screen can't really be true – at least, not in the world I live in. But now I stand in front of the mirror in my own bathroom – a thirty-five-year-old woman, IT manager and successful professional, and I think: my friend likes to be tied up, beaten and humiliated, and I realize that if they knew about Ksyusha, even the five, six or seven Swedish girls from the island of Patmos would be embarrassed.

19

THE FOUR OF YOU ARE SITTING IN THE COFFEE INN – your lover Ksenia, Ksenia's friend Olga and Ksenia's school friend Marina. You got together today to celebrate the opening of your new site. You managed to get it done in time for the New Year after all; now you can relax over the holidays. You'll come back after the Russian Christmas and finish the job properly, meanwhile the site can hang there in test mode, there are only half as many people on the web during this period anyway.

You've been writing and talking to each other on ICQ for two weeks, but this is the first time you've seen Ksenia's two friends. Olga looks as if she's over thirty, but you've never been able to tell women's ages very accurately. She lights up a cigarette in a long holder, and you notice a bracelet of dark stones on her wrist. Marina looks younger than Ksenia, maybe that's because she's not wearing any makeup at all, there are no clasps in her light-colored hair and it swirls round her head every time she moves. Marina is wearing jeans and a sweater, she smiles at you amiably, but then seems to forget that you're there. She doesn't work anywhere, but she can always be reached on ICQ; she has her office at home, and the computer stands on a bar stool in the middle of the room, like a cybernetic altar. You don't know that yet, and you probably never will, unless Marina invites you to visit her, or Ksenia tells you about it. Marina calls her friend "Ksenia," but Olga calls her "Ksyusha." You don't think your intimacy as lovers will ever get that far.

You yourself didn't expect the site to be so good. Detailed accounts of all eleven known murders, commentaries by criminal investigators on all of them. The cases grouped according to various factors (several different classifications to choose from). A map of Moscow showing where the bodies were found. The precise date and time when each body was found. The approximate time of each murder and when each girl went missing. One long interview with the deputy head of the Moscow General Prosecutor's Office and two in even greater detail – with employees of the procurator's office and the criminal investigation office, who both declined to give their names. A section titled "A Brief History of Murder in Moscow" with detailed analysis of the cases of Ionosian-Mosgas, Vedekhin the Satyr, Golovkin the Boa, Oleg Kuznetsov and Sergei Ryakhovsky from Balashikha. And also including excerpts from Nikolai Modestov's book *Psychotic Killers: Blind Death*, a detailed account of the biggest serial killer cases in Russia.

Alexei is especially proud of the "Theory" section, which was suggested to him quite unexpectedly by Oxana, who dug up several articles of sociological analysis in her archives from the old college days. There was a long analysis of the case of Gilles de Rais, the famous child killer, Marshal of France and companion-in-arms of Joan of Arc, who was burned in 1440, and also an article by Pierre Klossowski about the Marquis de Sade, which, to be quite honest, you haven't actually read yet.

Olga, who has some experience in putting together community-oriented sites, suggested that instead of just one forum they should make several: "Discussing the cases," "Theory and History," "Why does it happen" and "Evidence." The last forum was intended for those who suspected that they might have seen or met the killer. "Most likely it will be nothing but rubbish," Olga sighed, "but if there is even the slightest chance, we have to take it. And anyone who was afraid to state his suspicions publicly could write in using a special form."

You look at Olga and think: aha, so she's the one Ksenia uses as her model for a businesswoman. If things go on like this, in ten years' time Ksenia will have a car parked at the curb too, and she'll have that strange glint in her eyes that you've seen so many times in the eyes of successful single women over the age of thirty. Many people take it for frigidity, but you know it's the congealed salt of tears that were never cried, buried deep behind the pupil, from where they can't be lured out by the paroxysms of love or the warmth of a man's embrace. Except maybe if he went up to her, stroked her unnaturally light hair and said: "Don't worry, everything will be all right, you know it will" – but it would be really strange to act that way with a woman he hardly even knew.

They discuss banners and argue over whether they can use photographs of the victims.

"I think they'll be clickable," says Ksenia, "so what's the problem?"

"The other sites might refuse to put them up," Olga objects, "something like that happened a year ago, during the theater siege. But maybe I'm confusing things."

"What have the other sites got to do with it," you unexpectedly find yourself saying, "they have families. Have a heart, girls."

Everybody falls silent for a minute, and then Ksenia says:

"All right, then we'll use banners with parts of the map of Moscow: say, the name of a subway station and an arrow with the words 'Psycho kills here.'"

"I'll have that done for the morning," says Marina, smiling and shaking her light hair.

You always used to think it was best not to sleep with your colleagues – after all, apart from the female journalists there are the female designers, page makers and photographers. Probably you were wrong, it's actually really nice to know, as you part this evening in the hallway, that you'll see each other again in the office, where once again Ksenia will be clad in the benevolent armor of a businesswoman, the armor that slowly peels away under your kisses and embraces and shatters completely with that ear-splitting final shriek. Perhaps for the first time in your life you're content with yourself both as a man and a professional and Ksenia is the witness to both your triumphs.

It seems that this evening, as you raise a glass to the start of your project, you don't feel like a successful failure any longer.

20

THEY PLAYED SNOWBALLS, LIKE LITTLE CHILDREN, slid down icy slides, first on their feet, and then on their backsides, on a piece of cardboard: so much for Ksyusha's sheepskin coat, so much for Olya's fur. In a cheap eatery they drank vodka out of little plastic glasses and gave the brush off to two teenagers who took them for two girls their own age at first, and then for mother and daughter. They showed their Moscow residency registrations to a flaxen-haired police lieutenant, and he handed back their passports with the words, "Carry on enjoying yourselves, girls."

They still had three days left to relax and enjoy themselves. The two grown-up girls, one, let us say, a journalist and the other an IT manager, but both successful professionals, only five minutes away from stardom, the creators of the most popular site of the year just beginning, have made themselves hoarse singing karaoke in the Yakitoria and now they are soothing their throats with hot saké.

"I think this is the best New Year holiday of my entire life," says Olya, who has almost managed to forget that Oleg wasn't able to get to her place either on December 31 or on January 1, and she wasn't even expecting him after that, because on the morning of the 2nd he and his family had jetted off to Thailand, and so this was the third day Olya and Ksyusha had been doing the rounds of Moscow's clubs, restaurants and snack bars, chasing after each other and falling backward into the rare snowdrifts with their arms and legs held out, leaving an imprint like a five-pointed star or a snowflake.

"It definitely is for me," answers Ksyusha, who has either really got drunk for the third day running, or is simply so happy that the mere memory of this happiness should be enough to last her for the rest of her life. The year ended splendidly, they launched the site, she consigned Sasha to oblivion, released her erotic stress, and now she was moving into the New Year young and free, a girl ready for any changes up ahead.

On December 31 Alexei had phoned to wish her a happy New Year; she was a bit surprised, she didn't know whether to put this down to zeal from a subordinate, a confirmation of friendship or an attempt to suggest to her that good things come in threes and their two evenings together should be continued in the New Year. We can sort that out in the New Year, thought Ksyusha and simply put Alexei out of her mind. It was good with him, but he wasn't her type. He ought to be better at the boogie-woogie than at sex, but she'd get round to that later.

"I've remembered a great joke," says Olya, pouring out the remains of the saké, "about a teacher in an elementary school. After the holidays she walks into the classroom and starts dictating a math problem: two young, interesting, cultured girls bought six bottles of beer in a shop for thirty kopecks (*I don't actually remember for how much, it's an old joke, but that's not important*), a bottle of vodka for four rubles twelve kopecks, 'Seawave' processed cheese for, let's say, fourteen kopecks and a bottle of cheap sweet 'Crimea' wine… oh my God, why did we drink that wine!?"

Ksyusha laughs, finishes her saké and walks toward the door.

"Your place or mine?" asks Ksyusha.

"Mine," Olya declares. "It's closer."

"But I've got a New Year tree," Ksyusha parries.

Two young interesting girls, successful professionals only five minutes away from stardom, stop a car in holiday-time Moscow. They pile into the back seat and both try to explain the way, interrupting each other. The driver, with bristly gray hair and blue eyes that have faded to white, turns down the old Soviet songs on the radio and says:

"Don't worry, girls, I've been behind the wheel for thirty years. Just tell me the address and I'll get there."

They drive through the Moscow streets, there are festive lights strung across facades without any walls behind them, and the gaping windows of the gutted buildings are full of the black night air.

"Just look at what Luzhkov's doing, will you?" says the driver. "Have you heard, there's a plan to knock down all of Tverskaya Street? Can you imagine it, girls? Thirty years I've been in Moscow, and I don't recognize the city. It's like after the war, honest it is."

"Never mind," says drunken Olya, "they'll put up new buildings, better than the old ones. Moscow's like that... it can take anything."

Olya's from Peter, she has a special attitude to the capital city, but the driver doesn't know that, he turns the radio down again and carries on abusing Luzhkov. He smells of sweat, but there's not a whiff of stale alcohol and that surprises Ksyusha, who is still regretting that they don't sell saké to take out at the Yakitoria. Absorbed in these important thoughts, she misses the moment when the driver moves on to discussing the war in Chechnya.

"My father and his friends came back from the Second World War, so I knew them, they were good-hearted people. But they come back from Chechnya mean."

"The men are like the war they fight," Ksyusha snarls, already wondering how she can ask the garrulous driver to shut up. Really, why do conversations about politics have to come as a free supplement with every journey across Moscow?

"And they say there's a psycho on the loose in the city," the driver continues, "so you take care now, girls. Of course, he won't bother two of you, but just as a matter of principle."

"I know," replies Ksyusha, immediately interested, "but where did you hear about it?"

"They were just talking about it on the radio, I picked up Moscow Echo by mistake, they said there was everything about him in the computer, like, on the web: who he kills, how, when he kills again."

The two young interesting girls, successful professionals,

only five minutes away from stardom, start hugging each other and laughing loudly on the back seat, and the blue-eyed driver scratches his stubbly gray hair, mutters something to himself and turns the radio back up.

"It's a success, Olya, it's a success!" Ksyusha shouts, skipping up and down in front of the computer. She hasn't taken off her sheepskin coat yet, the snowflakes are turning into little puddles on the parquet floor, and the corner of the kilim by the bed is already getting wet. Olya comes back out of the kitchen, where she was putting the kettle on, her short light-tinted hair stuck to her forehead, a fluffy sweater with a high neck, flared jeans with a flowery pattern stretched tight round her thighs. Yes, you couldn't turn up for negotiations in the bank dressed like that. My God, how good it feels to forget about the dress code for a week! She glances over Ksyusha's shoulder and says in a satisfied voice:

"Fifth place, congratulations!"

In her time she has worked on projects that climbed into the top ten on Rambler, and not in the subject listings either. She's thirty-five years old, and for five of those years she has worked in the Russian internet, she's not easily surprised. It's much more fun to slither down icy slides and play snowballs like little children, drink vodka from little plastic glasses and saké from little ceramic jiggers.

"Attagirls, good for us," says Ksyusha, skipping up and down and shrugging her sheepskin coat off straight onto the floor. "We did it! Yes!"

She slaps her little hand with the bitten fingernails against Olya's well-groomed hand and the phone immediately rings, as if the clap has woken it up.

"Oh, shit," says Ksyusha, reaching for the phone. "Hello, it's me, Happy New Year, who's there?"

She hears her mother's voice and a wave of fright sweeps over her – what's happened? Mom never phones for no reason. Is everybody all right? What's wrong? What a hoot, they actually mentioned my name? This is a big deal, Mom, supermegabig.

What do you mean, why? Because it's my job. Because I'm the editor of the online newspaper Evening.ru, a journalist, even a bit of an IT manager, Mom, but in any case, a successful professional, and this is my new project. What do you mean, you took a look at it, and it's nothing but filth? What do you expect to find on a web page about a psycho who's killed eleven girls between the ages of fifteen and thirty-eight in just the last eight months? No, Mom, I can't close down the project, no, I won't withdraw my name from it.

Ksyusha never cries. But now she stands there with her face buried in Olya's fluffy sweater, right between the two breasts that are size B at best, and Olya strokes her hair and says: "Don't worry, Ksyushenka, everything will be all right, you know I love you" – and feels that for a brief moment her strange fantasy has become reality and she has acquired a daughter she can be proud of, the daughter she has loved and waited for all her life. Everything will be all right, Ksyushenka, she says, let's go and have some tea, let's go and have a wash, and I'll wipe away your tears and kiss you on the forehead, and put you to bed, just don't cry.

"I'm not crying," says Ksyusha, the good editor, the successful professional only five minutes away from stardom – and she lifts up her face with streaks of mascara on her cheeks, and Olya laughs and says: "oh sure, your face is all wet and your mascara's run."

"That's the snow, Olya, the snow," Ksyusha replies, "you know I never cry, it's just the weather, it fell off my hair, look how hard it's snowing outside."

And now here they are sitting in the kitchen, two young interesting girls who are suddenly sober, as if there never was any vodka in little plastic cups or saké in ceramic jiggers, drinking tea from mugs with the word "Rambler" on one and "Evening.ru" on the other. Without any makeup Ksyusha's face looks completely defenseless. Yes, thinks Olya, like that I'd say she looks eighteen, certainly not twenty-three. Twenty-three minus eighteen would be five, twelve plus five, yes at seventeen I could easily have had a child, that is, of course, if I hadn't waited until twenty-two to lose my virginity, and then only because I was madly in love.

"She's right, of course, she's right," says Ksyusha, "now her friends will think I work in some online tabloid like the *MK* newspaper, they won't even go and look at what we've done. Probably they're right, it is propaganda for violence, maybe we really are provoking the psycho into committing more murders?"

Olya leans down to her and takes her hand. Covers the little palm with her large, well-groomed fingers that manicurist Liza works on twice a week, soaking them, cutting away the cuticles round the half-moons, polishing and varnishing. She takes the hand between her palms, looks into Ksyusha's deep black eyes and says:

"My little girl, no one provoked Chikatilo, that was in Soviet times, everything was kept quiet, and what happened? Fifty-something dead bodies. We both read it. Nobody provoked Ottis E. Toole and Henry Lucas, and they boasted that they'd killed more than five hundred people. In Gilles de Rais's time the internet didn't exist, I don't think there were even any newspapers – and did that help the poor little children? Don't upset yourself, Ksyusha, we're doing everything right. It's your job, you're the editor of an online newspaper, you make the news. Remember, every time terrorists take hostages, they blame the press and say that if the journalists didn't make such a fuss, it wouldn't happen."

"Maybe that's right?" says Ksyusha.

"No," replies Olya, "I think it's completely the other way round: if someone wants to be famous, wants to produce a dramatic effect, nothing will stop him. If you don't write about terrorists, they'll poison the water supply and explode nuclear bombs. If this psycho really wanted people to know about him, he'd start killing twice as often, three or four times as often, even more brutally. So that the rumors would circulate without any help from the newspapers. So what we're doing is good, it's necessary. Don't upset yourself – a person's worst enemies are his closest neighbors. My Vlad's no bundle of joy, you know that. The important thing you must remember is: your parents should be proud of you. They have to be."

Of course, I could say that I'm proud of you, thinks Olya, but that probably wouldn't be any help to you. You know very well that I love you and I'm proud of you and happy to be your friend – but, unfortunately I am only your friend, and not your mother, and you're not my daughter, because how could I possibly have such a grown-up daughter?

The phone rings again, "I'll say you're not here," says Olya.

"No, no, I'll answer it," and she runs into the room and comes back, shrugging her pointy little shoulders.

"It was Dad. He said he'd heard about me on the radio and called to say well done."

"There, you see," says Olya, and Ksyusha thinks that her dad's praise doesn't mean much, he never achieved anything in his life, so he can't really judge how successful his daughter is. "There, you see," Olya repeats, and she looks in Ksyusha's cupboard and finds the bottle of Baileys that she brought the last time and, and there are just two glasses left, "So let's drink to the New Year, to our success, to all our wishes coming true in the New Year."

They open out the bed, Olya comes out of the shower, wrapped in the spare sheet instead of a towel, switches on Ksyusha's hairdryer and her light-tinted hair starts dancing around her head. If you don't go to work for four days, the wrinkles on your forehead dissolve, the features of your face soften, and even if you look in the big mirror in the bathroom at the other side of Moscow, you'll see that time has stepped back from you just a tiny little bit, Olga Krushevnitskaya, a thirty-five-year-old woman who should forget at least once a year that she's a successful IT manager, a genuine professional and a specialist in numbers.

While Olya dries her hair, Ksyusha stands in the bathroom with the door closed, biting her lip. Olya said it was late and she didn't want to go home, and Ksyusha said "of course," and now she's angry with herself, because it's awkward to turn on the vibrator with Olya there and it's altogether too awkward to take the nipple clamps out of the box. She goes to the small shelf, picks up her vanity case, unzips it, takes out a little mirror, wraps it in a towel and breaks it against the edge of the bath.

Then, sitting on the floor, she selects the very sharpest splinter and jabs it with all her might into the inside of her thigh.

Olya has already dried her hair. She looks at her sweater hanging on a chair and sees a black spot where Ksyusha's mascara has smudged across it. That's a strange picture, thinks Olya, like the Turin Shroud or maybe a Rorschach test.

21

IN A CONCRETE BASEMENT, ON THE SMALL PLOT OF land round my house, in the forest near Moscow or in an elevator, I try to tell people about myself. If I were a writer, words would be my helpers. But the way things are, my helpers are a knife, a scalpel and a blowtorch.

But these girls, so beautiful, so touching in their defenseless nakedness, still innocent, even though they start having sex at fourteen nowadays – they don't understand a thing. They ask "why me?" they think at that moment about themselves, about their own inevitable death, they can't understand that perhaps what is happening to them is more to do with the whole world than it is with them.

Since they were children they have been raised to believe that the world is beautiful and wise. The glossy paper of the magazines, the glitter of the TV screen, the daily lies of the newspapers – all these conceal the truth, but not the truth about terrorism, corruption or theft, no, they conceal the truth that the world is as full of suffering as a freshly carved hole is full of blood.

It's not true that when you kill you forget everything. At every moment of my existence I am aware that what I do is absolutely monstrous. But that does not stop me – and so my very existence proves that there is something wrong with the world. I think it would be easier for me to accept this world if I did not exist.

And so all I want to do is destroy the lies, to speak out so that people can no longer pretend they don't hear me. So they can't carry on living as if they don't know. I cut off the nipples, rip open the abdomens, melt the fat of bodies that are still alive with a blowtorch – and that is my way of speaking.

I scream with their voice, I send them to bear witness to my pain and torment, to the world in which I live. I slice through skin as if I am ripping apart the curtain of falsehood and lies. I take out the hot kidneys, the liver, the heart as if I am touching the raw bloody centre of being with my bare hands, the place where there are no lies, where suffering and despair are no longer cloaked by anything. The scream becomes a howl, then a groan. These are the sincerest sounds. Pain knows no falsehood.

But they still don't understand anything, and then everything ends, the thread snaps, and someone else's life shrivels away under your hands like a butterfly skin, and even if they have understood something, the understanding dies with them. Perhaps it is what kills them. Sometimes I think that no one is strong enough to endure such pain. Sometimes I am astonished that I am still alive.

These girls, so beautiful, so touching in their defenseless nakedness, don't understand a thing. And I live in the hope that perhaps one of the readers of the Moscow morning tabloids with *the soul-chilling details of the latest victim of the Moscow Psycho*, yes, that one of them will understand me. Because, when you read in the newspaper on your way to work that the body of an eighteen-year-old girl has been found with her own intestines wound round her neck and her severed hand stuck in her tattered vagina – when you read that, something has to change in the world around you, surely? You can't just close the newspaper as if you've been reading an article about one more football match, a Duma election, or the details of the local pop-star's new affair.

That is precisely why I take what is left of them – so beautiful, so touching in their defenseless nakedness – to places where they can be found by people – mushroom pickers, young mothers with baby buggies, couples seeking solitude.

I often think about suicidal killers who have selected a good vantage-point and fired off several clips from their automatic weapons before the police shot them dead. I think about the

Chechens and the Arabs who have blown themselves up in the middle of festive crowds in Russia or Israel. The Washington sniper, or the two fans of Marilyn Manson who shot half a school before killing themselves in Littleton, Colorado. Whatever it was you wanted to say, your cry went unheard. You were written off to politics, insanity and the influence of pop-culture. We need to resolve the conflict in the Middle East, stop the war in Chechnya, introduce measures to prevent mental illness and ban rock concerts. Then the world will probably be a better place, won't it?

And even though the idea of dying at the dense heart of an explosion or being transformed into the happy rapid-fire chatter of a warm gun sometimes seems unbearably tempting to me, I still despise it a little. That is working with the masses. However much I might rely on the newspapers and TV, in the first instance I always address an individual – like the poet who shows his poems to his beloved before printing them in an edition of a thousand.

When you address an individual, you speak far more sincerely than when you are trying to get through to all the people. I would like to believe that those who will read about me in the newspapers will appreciate my sincerity and perhaps, in the end, understand me.

Sometimes I am frightened by the thought that everybody already knows all about what I am trying to say. That the people I meet in the street know as well as I do that they live in hell, but they have accustomed themselves to this idea, learned to live with it. That every one of them is surrounded by the same cocoon of despair and anguish. That I am a failure, the one lousy sheep in the flock, an idiot who has brought a revelation from the day before yesterday, the bearer of Bad News that nobody wants to hear, because they all know it already.

Sometimes I think that everybody lives in hell, but they have accustomed themselves to this idea. But only for a moment, and then I calm down. No, that really can't be true. It's not possible to accustom yourself to hell, that's what makes it hell.

22

THEY SAY THE MOSCOW SUBWAY ONCE USED TO BE bright and clean. It probably was too, at some time. But Ksenia never saw those days. Either they were over before she was born, or she doesn't remember very well what the subway looked like when she traveled in it with her parents, not on her own. Olya now, she can't stand going down under the ground, but Ksenia likes it.

Olya says that a while ago she started smelling urine in the underground. That the smell wasn't there seven years ago, when she'd just arrived in Moscow, but that it's appeared now. Ksenia tries to remember more clearly – and it seems to her that it has always smelled like that. The smell has always been around – you just had to forget about it. But I try not to forget about it, thinks Ksenia, I don't know why.

She sits in a half-empty car, looking at the sticker with a picture of a baby chopped to pieces on the window opposite her. Ksenia knows that below it there is the laconic slogan "Thou shalt not kill," or a little poem about the evil of abortion: *murderers of those unborn/when your fiendish work is done/may your nails be bloody and torn*. This child that has fallen to pieces makes Ksenia insanely angry, she thinks how she herself would gladly rearrange the faces of people who paste up things like that. With a razor, in roughly the same way as shown in the picture. But then, nobody else is taking any notice of the sticker; those four passengers facing Ksenia can't see it, it's up above their heads.

Strange people ride the Moscow subway at half past midnight, thinks Ksenia. One man is tall, with hair that is unshorn and uncombed, wearing a long coat and jeans that are wet up to his knees. A bottle of beer is standing between his feet and his face can't be seen, because he has lowered his head and his shaggy locks hide it. He's probably sleeping, thinks Ksenia, but it would be really interesting to know, for instance, what color his eyes are, if his nose is long or short, if his expression is fierce or, on the contrary, good-natured. Maybe he looks like the charming fascist in the film *Brother 2*, or maybe he's like uncle Yura, Mom's friend, who disappeared from the scene a long time ago. Sitting beside him is a couple: a peroxide blonde, white jacket and a skirt that barely covers her podgy knees in black tights. She looks about thirty-five or forty, but the way blondes of that kind spend their lives, she could be twenty-five or even twenty-three, the same age as Ksenia. Her companion is an elderly man in a black Chinese down jacket, with the flaps of a gray suit jacket protruding from under it and trousers to match. A briefcase is standing on the floor between his feet. He has one arm round the blonde's shoulders and is clutching her paw in his other hand. He has a dull wedding ring on his ring finger, but the blonde doesn't have anything on her hand apart from a little cheap silver snake. A strange couple, who are they? Two people in Moscow on business? Lovers? A cheap whore and her client?

Ksenia looks at the last passenger, a fat man who reminds her of one of the two hogs that little Chihiro's parents turn into in the Japanese cartoon film, *Spirited Away*. He's wearing a short sheepskin coat, unbuttoned, his shirt is stretched tight across the stomach that sags down over his trouser belt, one button has come off and through the gap she can see a black vest, or maybe hair. He has a dirty crimson scarf draped round his neck, all three of his chins are lying on his chest, his gray eyes are open and their gaze is surprisingly intelligent. Poor man, it's probably some hormonal thing. God preserve us from such afflictions.

Ksenia sits opposite them, all alone, a small, slightly built girl, Greek sheepskin coat, high boots, leather purse on her knees. She's going home after visiting Vlad Krushevnitsky, the well known theater director (she hasn't seen even one of his shows) and a regular at the Mix Club (she's never been there even once), Olya's brother – oh yes, that reason's quite good enough.

Despite what Olya had said, Vlad's place was clean, well, just like any solitary male's. Maybe even cleaner than solitary straights' places. Naturally, Vlad didn't look anything like the stereotype homosexual: he didn't have bulging muscles, he didn't wear leather trousers or a feather boa – at least not at home when he was expecting his young sister and her friend. Neither did he dye his hair or wear eyeliner, although in the bathroom Ksenia saw a collection of creams that any girl would have envied, except perhaps Olya, whose collection was even bigger. Vlad really did resemble Olya, with a certain distinctive expression, a strange combination of soft features and a fierce, intent gaze. Although, at those moments when Olya's face softened, there was nothing left in her eyes but merriment – play snowballs, like little children, down the icy slide on her backside! – so Vlad's face was made up of Olya's two halves: the Sunday Olya and the workday Olya.

"Olya, bring us something from the kitchen to nibble with the drinks," he said, and went into the sitting room, gallantly allowing Ksenia through first.

"Something to drink, Ksenia? Don't mind if I call you by your first name, do you?"

So, he's gallant, gentle, charming. He poured Jack Daniel's and shouted: "Olya, bring some ice!" As if he was calling to a servant, really, just as if she was his housekeeper. Amazing that she allows herself to be treated that way. But why am I getting so uptight about it, after all – it's their business, I shouldn't interfere, I'm just a guest.

Strange people live in Moscow apartments, thought Ksenia, examining the room. One wall was completely taken up by bookshelves, there were a couple of pictures hanging on another. Ksenia thought she recognized one of them: a Dutch artist, wasn't it, who drew endless biomechanoid creatures? On another wall there was a man hanging upside down with one leg drawn up and his stomach slashed open so that his entrails tumbled out, straight onto his face.

"A friend of mine painted that," said Vlad, "he's not in

Moscow now, he's traveling in South-East Asia. He sent me a letter from Cambodia recently, he says there's a place where the skulls of all the people killed during all that mess are piled up. A huge mountain, and they had to put it behind glass because the tourists were pilfering them. A pity. Andrei would have brought me one. I'd have had a genuine Cambodian skull in the house."

What a nice man, thought Ksenia, God preserve us from brothers like that. A Cambodian skull, for fuck's sake.

Olya came back from the kitchen, ice in a big mortar, sliced French cheese, carbonade of beef, sliced tomatoes. Strange, at home Olya never served food like this, she just cut bits off things or broke them with her hands. Ksenia looked at Vlad's well-groomed hands and thought: I wonder if he goes to the manicurist Liza twice a week too, so she can soak his fingers, trim the cuticles round the half-moons, polish the nails and gradually turn them into little works of art, exactly like his sister's nails? Listening with half an ear, Ksenia heard that Vlad has been offered the chance to direct a play in a certain very fashionable theater, but there are absolutely no good plays, absolutely none. So he will clearly have to write it himself, and that's why he invited Ksenia round – Ksenia, shit, not Ksenia and Olya, what a creep – to talk to her about her work. That, is, not actually about her work, but about the special project she's doing.

"Yes," says Ksenia, "I know, Olya told me, of course. What is it that interests you?

Her voice is gradually assuming an icy tone, a portent of anger. The special project that she is doing. That *they* are doing! She looks round at Olya – she's sitting motionless in her chair, the bracelet on her wrist glitters slightly, her black eyes are deeper than usual.

"I'm sure," Vlad explains in the meantime, "that this killer is one of us, that he's gay. Very many serial killers are homosexuals – you must know that, as a specialist. John Wayne Gacy Jr. killed more than thirty teenagers. Jeffrey Dahmer drilled holes in his lovers' heads and poured acid into them, Joseph Kallinger even killed his own son, and the Fisher from the Moscow region admitted he didn't have a family because he was afraid that if he had a son, he would kill him too. But he still killed eleven boys in his concrete basement, and he even killed some of them in front of others. And what about one of the first Russian serials, Anatolii Slivko? The legendary young pioneer leader, who tortured more than thirty boys and killed eight – supposedly all as part of an 'experiment in survival.' He was one of us too, you know! And just recently in Peter, Igor Irtyshov killed eight boys after raping them first. He ripped his last victim's anus open with his bare hands and tore his guts out."

She looks at Vlad's well-groomed hands, so much like his sister's hands: the fingers are trembling slightly. Ksenia has never seen Olya's fingers tremble, but she knows that trembling very well, the trembling of arousal. She lowers her eyes to look at her own hands: the fingers with the bitten nails are lying motionless on the arm of the chair.

"But not just the ones who killed boys," Vlad continues. "The mothers of Charlie Manson, Ottis E. Toole and Henry Lee Lucas sent them to the first year of school dressed as little girls. Robert Joseph Long, who killed nine women in the early eighties, was born with large female breasts, the famous William Hance, one of the first American serial killers, liked to dress up in women's underclothes. And remember the killers who liked to work in pairs, the famous Roy Norris and Lawrence Bittaker, who adopted the nickname 'Pliers' because that was his favourite instrument. They picked up Californian girls on beaches and drove them off to secluded spots, where they tortured and raped them. They were caught when they started acting like this Moscow killer of yours: they dumped the dismembered bodies on the lawns of a suburb of LA. They liked imagining the respectable fathers of families finding that carrion under their windows early in the morning."

Look, Ksenia, look, she tells herself, this is what a man who is aroused by thoughts of violence and death looks like. Don't turn your eyes away, how are you any better than him? What right do you have to condemn him? Maybe you should put your glass down on the table, get up out of your armchair and hug him, the way you hug Olya? Maybe this is your real family, your adopted mother and father? – and incidentally, they live separately too.

"I want to do a play about this. About the fact that all

those people were killed by the hypocrisy of society, killed by homophobia, by the closet that generations of homosexuals were locked into. I imagine the Moscow murderer as a titan, an evil genius, a spirit of the air imprisoned in a human shell. I want to do a play about the power that acts through him, about the power that oppresses all of us. About the power that is called 'be like everyone else.' Do you understand me, Ksenia? I'd like to make it a one-person show, just him sitting there on a chair and telling everyone about how he tried to become a real man, how he wanted to treat women the way his father treated his mother, how he was afraid of being a wimp, a weakling, a fag, a pansy, a queer. That's what I'll call the show: *Fag*. No, not because of Burroughs' book, *Queer*, but in honor of that old TV program back during perestroika – you probably don't remember it, Ksenia, you were too young. That's what it was called, *Fag*, and it told the story of some poor young guy from Peter, I don't remember what he did, Article 121 of the Soviet Criminal Code was still in effect, but I hadn't been hiding who I was for a couple of years already. And I remember when I saw that program what I felt wasn't fear, although of course there was fear too, but fury. And just at that moment I wanted to kill somebody – so, in memory of that moment I'll call the play *Fag*. A play about the fact that anybody could be a serial killer."

Ksenia looks at the passengers. Strange people ride the Moscow subway at half past midnight. Any of them could be a serial killer. Now Lanky will throw his greasy hair back off his forehead, and he'll have colorless eyes, thin bloodless lips, a mouth with no teeth in it. Lying in the pockets of his coat are a scalpel, a knife and surgical forceps. Hanging round his neck, under his T-shirt, a necklace of women's nipples. Hanging from his ear lobe on hairs pulled out by the roots is a little bag of skin torn off the breast of the eighteen-year-old student Masha F. (the body was found three months ago in Bitsevo Park). Lying in the little bag are eyes gouged out of the faces of twenty-year-old Kristina P., a salesgirl in an all-night kiosk, and twenty-year-old Darya K., a resident of Rostov-on-Don. Analysis will discover his skin tissues under the nails of eight of the eleven victims – if the analysis is ever carried out, because now Lanky gets up, knocks over the bottle, hunches over and goes tumbling out of the open door. Ksenia never does get to see his face. Strange people ride the Moscow subway at half past midnight.

"And all the time," Vlad continues, "photos of the victims will be shown on the backdrop. Not photos of them mutilated and chopped to pieces, but ones where they're young and happy, alive and in one piece. We have to make the straights in the audience want these girls, feel lust, get them aroused and make them feel their hard-ons as they listen to the story of how the girls were killed!"

Vlad slapped his own crotch, slapped it with a well-groomed hand so much like Olya's hand. Yes, Ksenia noticed, he really does have a hard-on. Not for me, I hope.

"And then," says Vlad, "those men in the audience must feel guilty. *What's this,* they have to ask themselves, *I hear about someone being skinned alive and I feel aroused? What a monster I am really!* And if I can manage to convey that mixture of horror, arousal and guilt, if I can infect the audience with it, then I'll be able to explain what makes a homosexual into a fag. Because this whole story is not about love for men or boys, it's a story about horror, arousal and guilt. It's a story about my parents, who spoke aloud about love, but behind closed doors they told me that if I ever laid a hand on a penis, I'd go blind. Later, when I was grown up, I learned that they often frighten boys like that, to stop them masturbating. They mean the boy's own penis, you know, but for some reason I imagined my father's huge one, the large penis of a grown man, which I had seen once when we went to the bathhouse. And I imagined myself touching this penis – and my eyes immediately melting out of their sockets. It was only here, in Moscow, that I realized I had relived the myth of Oedipus, who blinded himself after he killed his father. I'd like to kill mine, but I can't, he died of cancer three years ago. When I was a kid I used to think: I want to kill him because he's always shouting at Mom, especially in front of guests, but now I know I want to kill him because he couldn't even tell the simplest of stories for frightening children properly. But he's already dead, so that's it." Vlad takes a sip of whisky and looks at Ksenia with his well-groomed fingers clutching the glass tightly. "So I guess that's why I want to do this play. To say that where horror, arousal and guilt meet, there's always a corpse – real or imaginary."

Strange people ride the Moscow subway at half past midnight. In his briefcase the Business Trip Man has a gag, chloroform and a rope. As they walk through a dark alley, he will furtively take out the bottle, moisten a piece of cloth and cover the blonde's mouth with it, just as they are passing a car parked in the shadow. He will tie her up, stick the gag in her mouth and hide her in the trunk. Then he'll start the car, check by the light of the headlamps that he hasn't left any clues and drive to the place where he has set up his torture chamber. On the way he will stop at McDonald's and take his time drinking a strawberry milkshake, picturing the hell the tightly bound girl is going through every minute he spends savoring the pink frothy liquid.

Ksenia sees this as clearly as in a movie – and at that moment the couple get up and walk to the door, the blonde laughs and hangs her cheap purse over her shoulder, the Business Trip Man grabs his briefcase and in the doorway he looks back at Ksenia with bleary, unseeing eyes. Ksenia watches through the window as they walk along the platform, still arm-in-arm.

Dear girl, Ksenia wants to cry out, *take your little hand out of his arm. Wherever you might have met this man, no matter how long you might have known him, whatever bonds there might be between you – run, run and don't stop. Set the heels of your cheap boots clattering along the frozen Moscow streets and your short skirt flapping above your podgy knees. Take off that white jacket, it's too conspicuous in the darkness, run, run quickly. Try to hide as well as you can, and may the silver snake on your finger protect you.*

But the train is already leaving the station, and Ksenia is left alone in the car with the final passenger. Yes, strange people ride the Moscow subway at half past midnight, thinks Ksenia, and at that moment the hog raises his eyes and looks at her intently, keenly, straight in the face.

"Why are you telling me all this?" she asked Vlad. "It's not very likely I can help you write this play. Everything I know is on the site, so..."

Vlad put his glass down on the coffee table.

"I don't know why," he said, "I guess I want to ask if it's possible. What do you think of the idea? Are these murders like what I'm talking about?"

"I don't know," Ksenia replied, "but what does it matter? In any case, you're telling your story. About horror, arousal and shame. It doesn't matter how things really were for this psycho."

"Yes, yes, it doesn't matter," Vlad repeated after a pause, "thanks, it doesn't matter. What I really wanted to say was something else, I thought it would be such a stylish, dynamic show, nonconformist, in the style of Gregg Araki and *Fight Club*, but now I don't even know if I'm going to stage it. It's not just that it's a very personal story, well, about my mother and father, what I told you just now. It's our job to tell personal stories, I know that. I'm not ashamed of it, not even slightly ashamed. A grown man shouldn't feel ashamed of his feelings. Ultimately it's nobody's business but mine and my parents'. I feel I can't go on living if I don't talk about it, if I just say nothing. My silence will turn everything I do – as a director, as a man, as a lover – into a lie."

"Yes, you're right," said Ksenia, "of course you must stage this play. It's a powerful story."

She felt awkward: she never went to the theater, she avoided theater-lovers and people who worked in the arts. Marina was her model of a creative person – and now this man, who was old enough to be her father, had confessed his intimate vision to her.

"You know, Ksenia," Vlad continued, "there's only one person whose opinion is important to me. And if not for you, Ksenia, I would never have been able to tell Olya about this. Because they're her parents too, after all. They're her mom and dad, our mom and dad."

Ksenia looked across at Olya, sitting in an armchair with her hands over her face, in a pose of still mourning. All the way through their conversation neither Vlad nor Ksenia had looked in her direction even once.

"I'm afraid that now she'll never want to speak to me again," says Vlad, still not looking at Olga. "In reality, I haven't had a father or a mother for a long time, and I know I'll never have children. She's the only family I have."

His voice breaks off. He seems about to burst into tears. The ice has melted in the mortar; the empty glasses are standing on the table. Olya takes her hands away from her face, those well-groomed hands so much like her brother's hands. She goes over to Vlad and says:

"Stop it. You're the eldest. Don't you dare cry. You're my brother and I love you. You're the only family I have too" – and she put her arms round him.

Ksenia notices that even at this moment they don't look at each other, but look at her, as if she attract their eyes, or maybe she becomes a living camera who has to preserve this picture forever on her retina: brother and sister embracing in the middle of the room and gazing straight into the lens like in a traditional family photograph.

Then they sat there for a long time, talking about cinema, which, after all, Ksenia knew more about than the theater, looked at the first Russian gay magazine with the strange title *Queer* (a new word that had only appeared in Russian recently) and discussed Vlad's plans for going to Thailand or India. They drank almost half a bottle of Jack Daniel's, and when Ksenia started getting ready to leave, Vlad said:

"Olya, clear the table please and wash the dishes" – and then Ksenia left without waiting for her friend, and now here she was in the subway car, face to face with the final passenger. Yes, strange people ride the Moscow subway, she thinks, and at that moment the Hog raises his eyes and looks at her at her intently, keenly, straight in the face, and in that look she reads a story of repeated humiliation, school nicknames, interminable ordeals in diet clinics and the gastroenterological departments of hospitals, she sees the anger and frustration of an intelligent, strong man who has been obliged all his life to feel ashamed of his body. He looks at her without lowering his eyes, but she lowers hers and looks away.

Strange people ride the Moscow subway at half past midnight. And not one of them arouses desire, only pity or fear.

23

THIS TIME SHE DIDN'T GET TO MARINA'S PLACE UNTIL the evening, when Gleb was already sleeping on the huge mattress in the room with his legs tucked up under him as if he was still crawling in his sleep. Marina puts the kettle on, she's wearing a Chinese robe embroidered with dragons, her straw-colored hair is twisted into a complicated knot with a chopstick from Yakitoria sticking out of it.

"Go figure," she says, "I'm not really sure at all that he's Chinese. Maybe he's a Korean or even a Kazakh. A sure-fire move: make out you're a foreigner, speak English, all Asians look the same to Russian girls, and nobody knows Chinese anyway. And you can ramble on as much as you like about Hong Kong and the reunification of China and then take someone home and screw them on the bed or the floor, because you won't find any straw mats in Moscow in the middle of the night in any case."

Ksenia laughs:

"Come off it," she says, "I've seen plenty of Kazakhs! Your Gleb's a typical Chinese, a perfect little baby Mao."

"I don't care if he's Korean," says Marina, "he's still the most beautiful child in the world."

She pours the tea – green, of course, what else, if she's wearing a Chinese robe, with a chopstick in her knot of straw-colored hair? I wonder when Marina will decide to dye her hair black, because there aren't any light-haired Chinese girls? And then, I wonder, will that be followed by plastic surgery to alter the shape of her eyes, nose and mouth? Maybe I'd better take a good look at this Marina, in five years' time there might be no more left of her than there is now of the Marina she used to be only nineteen months ago.

Ksenia takes out an envelope and puts it on the table.

"What's that?" asks Marina.

"Your money," says Ksenia, "call it your pay or your share of the profits, whichever you like. Olya sold the title sponsorship to the film company 'West,' they're releasing the movie *Monster*, so now Charlize Theron and Christina Ricci are plastered all over our site."

"Ooh, look at all that," says Marina, glancing into the envelope. "I wasn't really expecting anything, I thought it was kind of a favor for a friend." She puts the money in her pocket and a dragon seems to gulp it down. "Will there be more work, or have we already finished?"

"There'll be more," Ksenia replies. "We have to do a section called 'Conversations with the Psychologist,' and readers have sent us new material about serial killers. I had no idea so many people were fascinated with this stuff. In the West they even have the concept of 'serial killer groupies,' you know, like rock musicians have. There was an appalling case in the eighties when a journalist who was writing a book about a serial killer fell in love with her subject."

"And what did he do?"

"He used to dress up as a policeman, stop women driving in their cars alone, then torture and kill them, the usual thing. Anyway, when they caught him, they proved seven or nine murders, but they suspected there were far more. And when he was already in jail, this writer deliberately killed a woman and left his semen at the scene to confuse the police. But she slipped up somewhere and they put her away too, although afterward she escaped, and I think she's still on the run."

"Just like in the movies," Marina laughs, "so was he good-looking, this psycho?"

"Judging from the photos, not very," says Ksenia, "but how can you tell? We wouldn't look too lovely in police photos either."

"Oh, come on now," says Marina with a proud jerk of her

head, which finally shakes the chopstick out of her hair and the straw-colored splendor across her shoulders again – oops – and she laughs.

The steam above the kettle is like a Chinese dragon in profile. Ksenia goes over to the window, the white flakes flutter against the glass and Marina hugs her round the shoulders.

"Tell me, do you get off on this stuff?"

"Me?"

"Yes, you, you. Don't act so dimwitted. Which of us is the submissive masochist with a partiality for torture and self-mutilation?"

Ksenia sits down on a chair.

"Well, in any event I wouldn't try to rescue someone from jail," she says, "but it's not the same every time I read about it. Sometimes I get aroused, but more often it's just loathsome. To be quite honest, it makes me afraid to think how many perverts will flock to our site. And they're not just sadomasochists who get together quietly on the SMLife web site or other places for people who play, but genuine creeps who like to discuss torture and murder."

"So we're doing a good site," says Marina, pouring cooled water into the baby's bottle, "because people need to read about all this."

"What for?" asks Ksenia. "I understand why I need to. At least I get aroused sometimes. But what would you read it for?"

"Maybe I don't have any need to," Marina replies, measuring out infant formula from a can with a spoon. "But one of my lovers told me about this theory. Go figure, all our deepest problems come from the way we were born. There's, like, four stages: while he's lying inside and hasn't got a care; when it gets cramped and he starts getting uptight; when he slips down and he gets really uptight and, finally, when he's born. So if he starts slowing down at any stage – say, he took too long getting through the birth canal, or else he got stuck in the womb for a while – then that's the stage they have to go through at the symbolic level, so to speak. And supposedly it turns out that all the sadists or SS types in the concentration camps – they got stuck at the third stage. Go figure, blood and shit all around you, you're twitching away like grim death, crawling toward that pure, clean light. So, to make everything hunky-dory you have to get it together and work right through this stage to the end."

"Meaning – kill someone?"

"No, killing doesn't help at all. Because you have to solve the problem at the symbolic level. Go figure – read a book, look at photographs, go to the movies – or to our site. So you could say we're helping these people."

"What about masochists?" Ksenia asks.

"I don't remember," replies Marina, "either the second or the third stage. Don't get in a sweat over it. The main thing is to know that you're okay."

"I know that," says Ksenia, "I'm okay, sure. But it's a pity I don't know how I was born, and it's too embarrassing to ask Mom."

"I'd ask mine," says Marina, "if I wanted to know."

"I guess that's because you have a child," Ksenia replies and Marina laughs in a way that makes Ksenia ask: "Admit it, you just made all that up, didn't you?"

"Oh no," replies Marina, screwing the teat onto the bottle, "I started thinking about it straight away. You don't think I'd help you with a site I thought was harmful, do you?"

"I don't know," Ksenia laughs, "maybe out of friendship?"

"Not even out of friendship. I've got a growing child, I have to understand what's good and what's bad."

24

It's hard to explain how it happens
Simply at some moment I realize
There she is, a girl I can tell the story of my life to

Richard Trenton Chase, Vampire of Sacramento
Explained to Robert Ressler, agent of the FBI:
"I never chose anyone
I walked along the street and tried the doors
If a door is locked
It means you're not welcome."

That's what I do too
Sometimes the door is open, sometimes not
You have to go up and touch her hand

She was sitting opposite me in the subway
She was wearing a simple dress,
Straps on her shoulders and beside them
More straps from her bra
Everyone wears them that way in Moscow now
It's rather vulgar
And it doesn't arouse me at all

But she had very beautiful arms,
The shoulders, the forearms, and especially the hands

With long, agile fingers
And well-groomed nails
I guess a couple of times a week
The manicurist Liza, Galya or Masha
Soaks her fingers, trims the cuticle round the half-moons
Polishes and varnishes
Gradually transforming the nails
Into small gleaming pearly shells

When I looked at those hands
The train seemed to stop
I got up and approached her
Although my body was still
Sitting there without moving
I approached her and looked into her eyes

The eyes are the most important part of any woman
Even lying on my open hand
They still retain a particle of her soul
Rolling between the hills of her breasts
Tumbling into the deep hollows
As if they are saying farewell
As if the soul before it departs
Is making its final inspection
Of the body already abandoned

She had wonderful eyes
Dark eyes, as dark as the darkness of a basement
Where the light has been turned off
And the door has been locked

As a child I was afraid of the dark
My parents used to laugh at me
And ask what I could see there
I couldn't answer them then
But now I know the answer:
What I saw there was this darkness
The darkness that suddenly condenses out of the brightest day

Enveloping me in a cocoon
As if a huge pencil
Is obliterating the whole world
With its sweeping black spirals

Those were the kind of eyes she had
And I knew straight away
That I could talk to her
And she could answer me.

For all I want to do is talk
When I read in the newspapers
That I hate women
And I hate people, I know it isn't true
I love people
I wish I could make love to the whole world
But I don't belong to the Earth
The deep darkness speaks through me
And I must be heard

And when they scream – it is me calling for help
Alone in the wilderness of the big city
Oh Lord, I call out to Thee,
Hear me

But the scream breaks off, there is no answer

I sat back down and the train moved off
No one noticed anything
No one notices when for a few moments
They fall out of time and belong to eternity

The girl in the summer dress
With two pairs of straps on her shoulders
Turned to her friend and raised
A beautiful hand with long, well-groomed fingers,
She started making gestures
And her friend answered in the same way

They were deaf and dumb

I got out at the next station and walked home alone
I couldn't talk to that girl, not to her
Even if she could read my lips
She would have shut her eyes tight
Even if I cut off her eyelids
She could still not look at me

She can't talk to me
Nobody can
Nobody will hear

Sometimes I remember her
I think we understand each other anyway
I talk with my hands too
With my arms soaked to the elbows with blood
And the darkness condenses in our pupils

They say love is when you understand each other
without words
But in reality
Explaining yourself without words is very easy
A scalpel, a cigarette lighter, fishhooks and boiling oil
Are more eloquent than all the poetry in the world
When the subject at hand is pain
And at bottom I have nothing else to talk about

I'd like to find a person
I could talk to in words
I dream of a girl who would listen to me
Nod and weep and repeat
Yes, yes, I know, that's how it is
A cocoon of darkness, black spirals
A huge pencil obliterating the world

She would say: yes I know
Then take a razor and slice her own skin

To let out our pain
So that somewhere else, outside the cocoon
We could meet again
Like brother and sister

I think, if I met a woman like that
I could die happy

25

TWO DAYS. OR RATHER, FIFTY-TWO HOURS. USUALLY her body works like an ideal chronometer. Twenty-eight days. Nine o'clock in the morning – and you could put the flags out, or whatever it was they used to say. Their gym teacher liked to check in his diary that the senior girls weren't getting off too often: "I know you," he growled, "give you half a chance and you'll be exc. full point every week." "Exc. full point," that is, "excused with a full point" was what the girls were supposed to say if gym class coincided with *those days* – so that it wouldn't be confused with "simply excused," when the doctor allowed you not to go to gym for two weeks after the flu or a serious throat infection.

Olya's period started late, in ninth grade, but then almost immediately it was twenty-eight days, six hundred and seventy-two hours, nine o'clock in the morning, spot on every time. Not a single miss. She used to sympathize when every month at least one of her college friends feverishly counted the days and then went running off for the "mouse test." They said that if the girl was knocked up, the mouse died – and Olya used to imagine that up in heaven where the souls of people and animals meet, a little mouse with wings was already waiting for the soul of the unborn child doomed to be aborted.

She had never had to worry about the mice, or the present-day quick and humane pregnancy test. All her life it had been twenty-eight days, six hundred and seventy-two hours, nine o'clock in the morning: the first day was Tuesday and it was over by the weekend. Only now it is already Thursday, one o'clock in the afternoon. She is fifty-two hours late.

And still nothing.

They are having lunch in the Clone, which is door-by-door with the Coffee Inn on Bolshaya Dmitrovka Street. The waitress brings the menu. Vlad gestures round the room:

"When I get back," he says, "this will all be gone. This is the end of days. Luzhkov will tear it all down – the Clone and the café next door."

"Oh come on!" Olya says incredulously.

"Yes, redevelopment. They've already said so, definitely. So, if you haven't been here before, take a look: a historic place. You've no idea how much time I've spent here."

Outside the windows snow is falling, and Vlad tips some newly printed photographs out onto the transparent tabletop.

"Look," he says, "Andrei sent them from Goa. This is the house he's rented. And that's our beach, this is the sunset over the ocean, and this is Andrei himself."

Andrei is standing in tight swimming trunks, tanned and smiling. Olya thinks she vaguely remembers him. Tall, thin, awkward, she thinks he's a DJ, or a VJ, Olya's not too sure about the difference, and Vlad never introduced them properly.

"He had a small beard at your birthday party," she says.

"Yes, he did," Vlad says with a nod, "he shaved it off in Thailand."

Every Muscovite wants to go to Thailand in winter. It's warm and sunny there, the level of comfort is almost European and the prices are almost Asian. True, they say there's AIDS there too – but you can take precautions.

All her life Olya has hated taking precautions. She has always reassured herself with the thought that effectively she has a steady partner, he wouldn't give her any infections, there's no need to be afraid of pregnancy, her body works like a clock, all she needs to do is count the days. And she certainly knows how to count, that's for sure.

She glances at the face of the clock to the right of the bar: fifty-two hours fifteen minutes.

"Just imagine," says Vlad, "for us this will be, well, like a honeymoon. Because that's what he wrote to me from there, that he can't live without me. That I'm the love of his life."

Apparently congratulations are in order, thinks Olya, but she doesn't know how to do it: after eight years of small talk and orders to do housework – *Olya, bring some ice!* – suddenly to hear Vlad talk about his life! So he's in love. So he's having a romance. Of course, how could it be any other way? After all, he's a boy from a cultured Petersburg family too, a family where they used to say that love is the most important thing. What difference does it make whether it's for a girl or a boy?

"He says there's no homophobia in Thailand. According to the local Buddhism, there are three sexes: male, female and all the rest. All the rest – that's us. And most importantly, all the sexes can attain liberation."

And no need for any excuses, Olya thinks automatically. Three sexes, well, well. For her gays are still men, it's stupid to separate them off into a separate sex, although politically correct Ksyusha would support the idea. But a third sex is like a third color in chess: as if red or green pieces have suddenly appeared between the white and the black.

She wonders if schools in Thailand have three changing rooms. With "M," "F" and, probably, "N" written on the doors? Neuter gender, as in grammar. If they have one in Thai, that is. In their school there were only two changing rooms: for those who knew what "exc. full point" was and those who had no idea it even existed. It was a great girls' secret, they all knew you mustn't tell the boys about it on any account. She wondered how the boys did find out about it. Were their fathers supposed to tell them, or did they cover it in some anatomy lessons that she'd forgotten? Or perhaps the secret of female menstruation was part of a man's initiation, and his first woman was supposed to tell him about it? If that was right, then Vlad still didn't know what "exc. full point" was.

"If I was a musician," he continues, "I'd move there to stay. But as it is, I need the language. I'm a theater director, after all."

He pronounces the word "director" with pride. She has seen two shows and understood almost nothing, maybe she just doesn't like the theater, maybe the gay aesthetic fails to move her. But how strange this is – at the age of thirty-five suddenly to acquire a brother. To learn that as well as going shopping at Auchan with her and sending her to get ice from the kitchen, he loves some Andrei or other and is proud of his profession. I guess Vlad doesn't know anything about me either, thinks Olya. Should I tell him something about me now? Or is their new relationship still one-way traffic – brother talks, sister listens?

"Maybe you could come and visit us?" says Vlad. "We could fit you in easily enough, we've lived together before." He laughs. "Remember how we lived in the Preobrazhenka district for two years?" Olya remembers. The jolly times of the mid-decade: either there was no money at all, or suddenly there were incredible amounts of it. The music in the apartment never stopped – acid house and Goa trance – there were pills scattered across the dining table, there was always someone high and someone coming down from a bad trip. They were jolly times. But not for Olya. Every time she came home she was afraid she'd find three or four strange men in her bed with pupils dilated halfway across their faces, enthusiastically making love. True, it never happened – all the inhabitants of the flat fastidiously respected the privacy of the only woman.

If we'd lived in Thailand then, thinks Olya, I would have had "F" on my door and all the others would have had "N." That is, if they know how to write Russian in Thailand. Vlad could stay there if they do.

"I don't think I could stand that again," says Olya. "I kept expecting you all to start explaining to me in chorus how to give good head."

"Well only for the sake of good relations between the sexes," Vlad replies. "Thank God, we were all decent guys. Nobody laid a finger on you."

"That would have been all I needed!" Olya laughs.

Those were jolly times – but not for her. Olya ran off to Moscow after her second man, a forty-year-old professor of Slavonic studies, who first taught a one-semester course at St Petersburg University, and then carried out some research or other, funded by some foundation or other, in the State Archives in Moscow. Naturally, he had brought his wife and daughter with him from America. They even had lunch all together a few times. Olya was supposedly some kind of assistant and she actually received one hundred and twenty dollars a month. But when Olya's mother discovered – while Olya was still in Peter – that her daughter was having an affair with a married man, she made a terrible scene: "It's not enough that my son's a fag, my daughter's a slut too." Olya was surprised to find that she felt more stung by the politically incorrect term "fag" than the predictable "slut," and when she went to Moscow, she didn't call home once in two months, thank God, Vlad regularly reported that she was all right. For the first time in her life Olya felt free of her parents' power – excused without any points.

"Well, there wouldn't be that kind of mess in Goa," Vlad reassures her, "we've all grown up and settled down. Andrei never touches any hard stuff. Nothing but hash now. No speed, no ecstasy, no coke – complete and total chillout."

"Did Andrei live with us too?" asks Olya.

"What do you mean? Of course!" says Vlad, surprised. "We've been together ten years, near enough. We can hold the anniversary party soon. For the last year we've been quarreling pretty much all the time, but really – he's my greatest love. It's for life, together forever, surely you must have noticed?"

"Well, we don't really know much about each other at all," says Olya, glancing at the clock: fifty-two hours, thirty-five minutes. But the minutes aren't important. Simply fifty-two and a half hours.

"That's true," says Vlad, sticking his nose in his plate, "that's true. But come and visit us anyway, you'll like Andrei for sure, he's wonderful."

"No," says Olya, "first, no money. Second – problems at work."

"What do you mean, no money?" Vlad asks in surprise. "Borrow it from somebody, you can pay it back later. And what kind of problems?"

Olya sighs. There are actually two problems. One is called "Grisha and Kostya" and the other is a delay of fifty-two hours and forty minutes. And where, by the way did, she get the idea that boys have no way to find out about menstruation? They advertise panty-liners everywhere nowadays, everyone's been in the know for ages. Blue liquid. Just at that moment she would have preferred red liquid, red like the revolutionary banners. She wonders if in Cambodia under the communists the flags were red, or some other color? In Cambodia, where according to Andrei, the skulls were kept behind glass so they wouldn't be pilfered for souvenirs.

"There's actually only one problem," says Olya, "the two investors are fighting and destroying the business. I was thinking of bringing in a third investor to buy them out, but Ksyusha made enquiries about him for me and, to be quite frank, I'm afraid."

"Why so?"

"Well, you see," Olya explains, "in our industry so far no one's been killed. But this man, the external investor, well, it seems that's the way he's used to solving his problems."

"You're having me on," says Vlad, delighted, and calls over the waiter to order coffee, "this isn't the nineties, they don't kill people anymore."

"I wouldn't like to try testing that out," Olya replies.

"But why are those two fighting?" Vlad pushes his plate away and looks at Olya as if he really does intend to listen carefully and give her some sensible advice.

"They fell out over the election money," Olya says with a shrug. "They're old rivals anyway."

"Wow," says Vlad, "what a great subject. I wanted to write a play about that: two businessmen, they've been together since school, friends and rivals, powerfully attracted to each other – which they're afraid to admit... I just didn't know what ending I ought to come up with. For Moscow, I guess they ought to fall in love with each other and go away, say, to Thailand, but if I take them to the West, they can kill each other. Which version do you like best?"

"The Moscow one," Olya replies.

"Well then, arrange it," laughs Vlad, "let them give free rein to their feelings!"

And what do I know about their feelings? thinks Olya. Nothing. No more than about the feelings of my own brother. No more than about the feelings of Oleg and the other men

I've loved. What about Ksyusha? she thinks. Yes, Ksyusha's a different matter. But all the same, why does she have to have the bruises and the blood?

And, by the way, about blood. Fifty-two hours and fifty-two minutes.

"Anyway, sort things out with these two fags of yours and come," says Vlad. "Maybe we'll all stay there, damn the theater. I'll take up mime, say, or ballet – you don't need language for that. Maybe Andrei and I will adopt a boy – they say that's no problem in Asia. We'll live with you – you'll be the mom and we'll be the dads. In the mornings we'll go swimming, and then we'll sunbathe. Andrei will teach him music, you'll teach him to read books and I – I'll teach him to act." Vlad looks pensively at the smoke from Olya's cigarette dissolving into the air. "You know, sometimes I think I would have made a good father. I think I understand what children need."

"And what's that?" asks Olya.

"Just to be loved. For what they are."

Vlad stops, musing wistfully, and Olya realizes he has already set out the stage: Andrei sitting with a tin-whistle in his hand and one foot resting on a big drum, a dark-skinned little boy playing in the sand with Vlad, and Olya, the communal mother, standing there holding a book – from the distance you can't make out what it is. The boy raises his head and speaks in international language – "mama." And this scene is so impossible, so unreal, that Olya stops counting the hours and minutes and realizes it's time to accept the facts, go to the pharmacy, buy a pregnancy test and get the answer that she already knows.

The mouse would never have survived the news.

26

EIGHT DIFFERENT FOLDERS OF DOCUMENTS, TWO with newspaper clippings. A metal mesh tube with two pens and three pencils sticking out of it like aerials, the sharply pointed leads make her heart skip a beat. Keeping pencils like that on your desk is like carrying a razor around in your vanity case, but you can't explain that to Taniusha, who is responsible for Pasha's office housekeeping. An ergonomic keyboard that supposedly doesn't make Ksenia's exhausted, bitten-down fingers so tired. An optical mouse with a red laser eye on its flat sole. A Samsung liquid crystal display monitor. This is what the desk of a young professional, a journalist and IT manager, looks like, the desk of the rising star of the Russian internet, Ksenia Ionova. "We met the blogger and the producer of the Moscow Psycho project in her office to ask..." Oh, shit, I have to make it a rule to insist that they show me the text before they publish, I'll just phone Pasha, to apologize. "In her office!"

Ksenia knows now what fame looks like. Modest fame, low-key, but even so, fame. Thankfully people don't recognize her in the street yet, but when she was at her dancing class one girl came up to her and said she'd heard her on the radio, she realized straight away the voice was familiar. Yes, three recordings for radio, ten interviews for the online press, a few articles in the major newspapers – that's fame, isn't it? It's a different matter that so far fame is no reason for giving up work. So it turns out that very little has changed in Ksenia's life. Every morning she looks through the breaking news, gives the girl translators a roasting, sends Alexei to report on something and tries to get commentaries from Moscow newsmakers on the latest event of the day. For other people she may be a newsmaker herself, but in her own editorial office she's a journalist, the senior editor of the news section. Her personal project – all right, hers, Olya and Alexei's – is their own personal business, it has nothing to with her job, Ksenia doesn't even need to be reminded of that.

It's time to sort out those papers. It's funny to recall that her elementary school teacher once told them computers would save the forests from being cut down: paper wouldn't be needed anymore. She should see the offices of internet companies. But then, Ksenia doesn't have a very clear idea of what offices looked like before the appearance of computers. She wonders if they had typewriters on every desk. Or did people write the draft versions of contracts by hand?

Last year's report from the Public Opinion Foundation is dispatched into the waste paper basket as outdated. A print-out of the movie theater programs for December 15 – an attempt to catch the film *Underworld* on the big screen, she missed it last time – goes into the basket too, all twelve pages of it. The rough draft of the business plan with Olya's remarks – into the basket. A list of people for Alexei to interview, printed out before the meeting in the café and left on her desk two weeks ago, goes the same way. A print-out of the news on Evening.ru for January 8, with glaring errors, corrected on the web, but preserved as a caution to the guilty parties – into the basket. What's a folder of contracts doing on my desk? Into the accounts department! An envelope with photographs of New Year celebrations – into my purse. A folder of newspaper cuttings about my beloved self – into my purse too.

Ksenia has a special album and a large cardboard box from IKEA at home for photographs. The newspaper clippings will be confined to the bottom drawer of the desk, which contains her entire personal archive: a few letters, the check for her last dinner with Nikita, for a satanic six hundred and sixty-six rubles, a sentimental dried rose (Ksenia remembers who it was from), the cover of a Dario Argento video cassette with his autograph,

Vika's hairclip, which was forgotten at Ksenia's place and not returned before Vika left for Germany, an incomplete list of Marina's men covering three pages, drawn up three years ago when Marina stayed the night at Ksenia's place, a clipping from the *Megalopolis-Express* newspaper from 1995.

The article caught Ksenia's eyes that morning when, after washing the blood off her slashed thighs – not for the last time, alas – she decided to go out into the city, walk as far as the nearest street stall and buy something to eat. Too bad, she hardly had any money left at all – she hadn't wanted to take any from Mom, she'd been sure she was going to get her pay, but now it was screw you, Ksenichka, no pay for you. It turned out that during the week when she hadn't left the building, a kiosk selling books and tabloid newspapers had appeared where the vegetable stall used to be. Ksenia bought *Megalopolis-Express* because one of her mother's guests had said it was the only newspaper that was possible to read. And anyway, the titles of the others didn't mean anything to her. When she reached a shop, Ksenia bought a bagful of food, went back home and sat down to read, dropping sour cream on the newspaper from her tomato salad. The photos of semi-naked girls were definitely only improved by these white and pink blotches.

The article was included in the "Confessions" section, right smack between the replies to readers' questions ("Dear editor, please tell me if it is possible to get pregnant from oral sex...") and stories about a sect of Satanists who were despoiling graves outside Peter. Ksenia's attention was caught by the sentence in a frame at the centre of the page: "I cut myself with a knife, confesses *M-E* correspondent Maya Lvova." Ksenia vaguely remembered that Maya Lvova specialized in intimate stores about her sex life – two years earlier Ksenia and Vika and Marina had had lively discussions about Maya's reminiscences of how she was deflowered – obviously in anticipation of their own defloration. This time Maya Lvova wrote in her typical ornately explicit style about how a year earlier she had suffered severe depression as a result of the death of her mother and other events of a personal nature. "I hadn't gone out for a month," wrote the correspondent, "I blamed myself for everything that had happened. So great was my despair that I attempted to end my life, inflicting clumsy cuts on myself with a kitchen knife." However, a faithful friend was on hand to take the failed suicide off to her dacha, where Maya made the acquaintance of a handsome and masterful man not much older than herself. The entire tone of Maya's article made it clear that this man was a rather well-known individual and so she could not give his name, preferring – entirely in keeping with the style of the newspaper – the euphemism "my demon." "On our first night," she continued, "I simply could not become aroused. Yes, I desired him insanely, but it was as if my body had died! And then my demon turned me over onto my stomach and slapped me several times on my buttocks, which were quivering in anticipation." Later, when she re-read this article. Ksenia always giggled at this point, imagining Maya Lvova's fat thighs quaking like jellied meat on a wobbly table. However, in the summer of 1995 Ksenia was in no mood for merriment, and she read all the way through to the happy end in a single breath ("...can be bought in certain sex shops in Moscow, but my demon prefers to import them from abroad.") Carefully lowering an unfinished tomato onto her plate. Ksenia dialed Marina's number, trying to contain the thrill of arousal or, as Maya Lvova would have said – *the quiver of anticipation.*

That was how Ksenia met Nikita, her first dominant lover – and he taught Ksenia most of what she still likes in bed now. Despite all the men Ksenia has had since then, Nikita is still her first, in a class of his own. Their affair only lasted six months: then Nikita went away to America, where he is now quite well known in the BDSM community of San Francisco. Ksenia had to find others who were capable of satisfying the appetite for submission and physical pain that had suddenly awoken within her. It wasn't easy, but it was worth the effort.

"For me, ordinary sex is like beer for someone who likes vodka," she explained to Marina. "It relaxes you, it's a pleasant drink at negotiations or with lunch. It's convenient, as a matter of fact. And it's the same with sex: after a good vanilla lover I feel really relaxed. If I like the man, I enjoy having him near me – you know, I like the male body in general – but all that's not what I'm talking about at all. When they beat me, put me on my knees, hurt me or humiliate me, the world goes away. The space around me seems to curl up, even before I come – and in cases like that I can come for a very long time – well anyway, almost immediately I'm in a different place. Maybe I'm liberated from my body, I don't know. In the specialist literature it's called subspace, meaning 'submission space' as far as can tell from the descriptions. I guess for me the difference between vanilla sex and play sex is the same as it is for you between kissing and the normal sexual act. You like to kiss, but you're hardly willing to give up the pleasure you get from screwing."

"I read somewhere," replied Marina, "that highly successful businesswomen have leanings like that. They have to keep everything under control at work, but they let themselves go in bed."

"Probably," said Ksenia, who still wasn't a successful businesswoman then, and shrugged her skinny shoulders. "Maybe. But I think there's more to it than that."

She made no secret of her own leanings, but several sad experiences had taught her that men get frightened when they find themselves in bed with a girl for the first time and, in addition to a condom, they are offered a selection of two whips, handcuffs, lashes, a leather paddle, a riding crop and nipple clamps linked together by a frivolous little silver chain. Some instances were positively tragi-comic. Once at a party at a club Ksenia met a superbly built young guy with blond hair, a genuine blue-eyed Slavic folk-epic hero. And his name was something ending in "slav," just as it ought to be, maybe Svyatoslav or Miroslav. He was a friend of a distant acquaintances of Ksenia, and after countless tequilas with lime and salt, they caught a taxi and went tearing off to Ksenia's place, because it turned out that Stanislav, aka Rostislav, lived with his mom and dad. Everything would have been fine, but along the way the youthful hero bit Ksenia on the neck, hugged her so hard that her bones cracked and, in addition, jabbed his cigarette into her knee, as if by chance. If not for the tequila, she might have realized that Vyacheslav, aka Mstislav, simply didn't have very good control of his arms and legs, but Ksenia, who hadn't had a BDSM lover for two months, became so aroused that they were barely even inside the apartment before she started eagerly demonstrating her new acquisitions.

"What's that?" asked Slava, gaping at Ksenia with his astonished blue eyes.

"This is a riding crop," said Ksenia, "and this is a lash. They're used for beating women, as you know."

The folk-hero lover reacted unexpectedly: his eyes glazed over and he slumped to his knees from his full heroic height, disgorging onto the linoleum three limes and one squid salad – that is, all his solid refreshments for the evening. Ksenia spent the rest of the night feeding the epic hero tea and listening to confused apologies. When it was nearly morning her maternal instincts got the better of her, she stroked Slava's hair, led him into the bedroom, undressed him and five minutes later, trying hard not to hit a false note, she moaned that he was a wonderful lover. Since neither of them had slept all night and Ksenia didn't even have the strength to moan properly, she wasn't really hoping to deceive him, but even so, she felt she had done enough to heal the wound inflicted on his sensitive male soul. Then she said it was time for her to go to work, and led her failed lover to the subway by the most tangled route possible so that when he finally sobered up, he would never be able to find the way back to her apartment. Naturally, she gave him a false phone number, with one digit changed, as she always did in such cases. When she phoned Marina that evening, she summed up: "Maybe it was the worst sex in my life, but it's one of the funniest stories."

So now, bearing in mind her bitter experience, Ksenia is in no hurry to involve Alexei in her semi-taboo games. Certainly, she does leave a leather paddle or a cat-o'-nine-tails lying around in conspicuous places, but Alexei's indifferent glance skims over them and he probably takes them for part of the interior design. They get together every two weeks, Alexei apologizes to Ksenia because he can't manage it more often, but she doesn't tell him she wouldn't agree to more often anyway. Combining a light affair like this with work has proved to be rather convenient: as a manager she would actually say that Alexei has started working better. Though maybe the reason for that is the success of their project: the man is thirty years old, after all, and so far he has nothing much to be proud of.

After throwing the papers in the basket and rearranging the

folders, Ksenia sits down on her chair again. In the bottom corner of the monitor the ICQ icon is blinking – someone once wittily dubbed it "a flower on the grave of the working day." Ksenia clicks on the yellow rectangle and a message appears: "Hi!"

"Hi," Ksenia answers and dives into the user's details.

No first name or surname, just the nick "alien," written in English – highly original – and the only information given is the sex – male. In the "About" section there's a flashy text in English that looks like the introduction for some character in a computer game: "I'm a monster in your chest. I'm a really nasty one. And in a few hours, I'm gonna burst my way through your ribcage and you're gonna die. Any questions?"

"Do we know each other?" asks Ksenia.

"No," the other person replies, "but that can be fixed, can't it?"

Ksenia sighs. From time to time bored men come knocking at her ICQ door, wanting either to flirt or just chat. As a rule it only takes a few lines of conversation before she consigns them to the eternal oblivion of "ignore."

"I'm not sure I want to fix it," she replies hostilely.

Ksenia wonders if this one will start writing flirtatious nonsense like: "Ah, why are you so grumpy, darling?"

"All right," says the man, "let's not introduce ourselves. Let's just talk."

"What about?"

"What should people who don't know each other and are never going to see each other talk about? Their most intimate secrets, of course. So tell me, Ksenia, what is your most cherished secret desire?"

Ksenia looks at the Samsung liquid crystal display monitor, at the tube of metal mesh with two pens and three pencils standing in it, at the neat piles of folders and papers. Career, money, success? You could hardly call those desires secret, and in any case, they're not even desires – they're the inevitable future or, rather, a premonition of the future. For a second Ksenia's thin hands hover motionless above the ergonomic keyboard.

"I'm an ordinary girl," she types. "I want to find a man who will understand me and make me happy."

27

I OFTEN THINK ABOUT WHY THIS HAPPENED TO ME. There are many theories explaining why people lure solitary girls into their basements, torture them for days and then kill them.

Of course, there are simply the creeps who the girls won't put out for, or who are afraid they won't put out, vicious little boys ready to break a beautiful toy just because it doesn't belong to them. I don't think that's really my case.

And they like to talk about homosexuals, victims of repressed sexuality who hate women or are afraid of them. These men obviously had problems with their mother and father, as well as with society in general, Article 121 of the Soviet Criminal Code, jokes about fags, a spacious closet with a tenth of the male population inside it. I don't think that's me either.

I would actually like to be gay, for some reason they find it easier to talk about pain and love in the same sentence. I once read a story in which two boys in love are standing with their eyes closed on the shore of the ocean and they suddenly hear the screams of a dolphin that has been cast up on the shore, and the local lads are amusing themselves by jabbing it with pitchforks. And it is clear to the reader that those screams have an absolutely direct connection to their love. If I could write a story like that, I wouldn't need to kill.

And then there are the schizophrenics, God's own fools, to whom He speaks, or the Devil does – some Sam, Beelzebub or Belial. In Russia I guess they could hear the voices of Stalin or Hitler. After all, even Chikatilo wrote that he felt he was a partisan. Anyway, they hear voices that order them to kill – and that's definitely not about me.

I haven't heard any voice, neither God nor the Devil have spoken to me, nobody has given me any messages. I am here completely alone. I think that if someone did speak, God or the Devil, no matter who, I wouldn't feel so lonely and I wouldn't need to kill.

I've read Stanislav Grof, the Czech psychologist, who cleared off to California at the right time and experimented with LSD and special breathing techniques. He believes there are four perinatal matrices that determine a person's life via the process of birth. And the third matrix, the journey through the birth canal, is what engenders serial killers and sadists. I was so intrigued that I even asked my mother how it all happened, and whether that stage was the most difficult for me. I can't be sure that she really does remember but, as far as she can recall, it was just an ordinary birth, nothing that surprised the doctors. So this isn't my story either.

I have conscientiously read the American books, taking great care to buy them abroad and not attract the attention of the postal service or some department at Amazon.com that analyzes orders. They all say the same thing: repressed sexuality, child abuse, parental cruelty. To be quite honest, I'd only be happy if I knew my father raped me at the age of five in a drunken fit or my mother used to make me watch as she was screwed by the clients from whom she earned the money for a bottle of vodka or a shot of heroin. It would be a real stroke of luck if my brother had been eaten during the famine years, as Chikatilo's brother was.

I even invented a past like this for myself, false memories masking goodness only knows what. Yes, as a boy I certainly had a rich imagination. I had many fantasies – but in reality I had a happy childhood. I would prefer it to be the other way round – that would mean I've simply been unlucky. Shit happens, as the Americans say. I've been unlucky, but the world's just fine, I can leave the damned newspapers and their readers in peace, let them live as they like.

If I knew this was just my problem, I'd go to an analyst and I wouldn't need to kill.

If I went to an analyst, I would ask him just one question: why do I always kill girls? Why no men or boys? If I killed boys I could say, like John Wayne Gacy, that they are all me. I would quote Denis Nilsen, who said: "I always killed myself, but it was always someone else that died."

But I don't kill men, I don't touch people who are like me. I kill women and girls who are still very young. Why them? Yes, of course, I sleep with them, they arouse me. But what I want to receive – understanding, sympathy and forgiveness – I would receive from men too.

I don't think my sexuality is all that seriously repressed. And in general, it seemed to me that sex really had nothing to do with the whole business. So one day I decided to hold an experiment.

I thought: I wonder, can I kill a woman
But feel no arousal as I do it
Not masturbate beside her body
Not make her take me in her mouth
Or give herself to me in various positions
Mostly uncomfortable and humiliating?

I thought I would choose a woman at random
One for whom I feel nothing
Kill her quickly and walk away from the scene
Of course then, when they find the body
It will not be as impressive as the installations
That I set up in the forests outside Moscow
To please the mushroom pickers and young mothers
with their buggies
And couples seeking solitude
This killing won't make people think about the cruelty
of life
But maybe they will understand something about the
suddenness of death
And that's a pretty good result as well

I chose the office building where I used to work
I knew the side entrance, no ID needed there
And no security cameras inside, that was important
I walked up to the third floor, called the elevator
Not sure what I was counting on, but I was lucky
I've read that serial killers often are
Even Chikatilo was arrested twice and then released
But right now that is not the point.
The doors opened. There was a woman in the elevator
Aged about forty-five, not very beautiful
And wearing a cheap trouser suit
I guess she thought was business style
A bookkeeper or something of the kind
Her hair cut in a fussy style
And light in color, almost red.
Obviously dyed, with natural red hair the skin
Is never like her skin
Believe me. I should know

She aroused no feelings in me
Believe me, there were no vibrations
My penis lay curled up and sleeping soundly
The doors closed and I stepped behind her
And put one hand in my pocket,
To take the knife and cut her throat
It would only take two seconds
And I would get out on the next floor
Send the elevator with the body on up to the top
And then walk down the stairs to the side door
But as I took a tight grip on the handle
My penis suddenly turned hard inside my jeans
Hard as the Vendôme column or the Alexandria pillar
As if all the blood in the world had flowed into it at
that moment
I let go of the knife. The experiment was over

And as she stepped out of the elevator
I saw a gray strand running through her hair

I guess they missed it at the hair salon
Or left it gray on purpose, I don't know
But when I saw that scattering of ash
In that fussy light-red hairstyle
Suddenly I felt a great tenderness
And I thought that this woman
Had lived more than forty years, loved and been loved
Buried her loved ones and perhaps had children
Had wept and laughed – and now the ash was settling on her head
And in forty more years would overwhelm it
Like Pompeii or Herculaneum

When I thought about that I wanted to run after her
Beg her forgiveness for my worthless life
Hug her and press my lips against that strand of ash.

My penis was still standing hard
In my tight jeans, causing me pain
Distracting me from the tears pouring down my cheeks

For the first time my arousal had saved someone's life

28

ON THE WAY FROM THE CLEAR PONDS SUBWAY TO THE Discreet Charm of the Bourgeoisie restaurant Ksenia notices a gap between the buildings, as if a tooth has been pulled out. There had been a restaurant in the basement there, she came here with her parents to celebrate Lyova's wedding. Ksenia was fifteen and Lyova, correspondingly, twenty-one. Ksenia already knew the bride well by then: a tall girl with brown hair and a tendency to put on weight, and a large nose that stood out on her face like a foreign growth. She smoked Marlboro cigarettes, and wore baggy sweaters and tight jeans that looked absurd on her already voluminous backside. It was a mystery what Lyova saw in her, but one Sunday morning as she came into the kitchen, Ksenia saw Mom standing there stroking Lyova's hair and repeating: "What else can you do?" Ksenia only got her hair stroked when something happened: when she cut her hand, sprained something or simply fell ill. In fact, when she fell ill, her forehead was touched rather than stroked – to see if she had a temperature. So Ksenia thought that Lyova had been expelled from college and she asked spitefully: "Thrown you out, have they?" She was fifteen, and the times when Lyova used to chase her all round the apartment, making her pretend she was Sarah Connor, were long past. "I'm getting married," Lyova replied. "To Lyusya." "Well, congratulations," said Ksenia and turned round and ran to her room. For some reason she wanted to cry, but Ksenia never cried.

Later, when Lyova went to propose formally, Ksenia asked Mom: "Is she knocked up, then?" Mom nodded and Ksenia said "I see," and went to phone Marina. She herself was so afraid of getting pregnant that she carried condoms around with her even then. You could never tell, maybe some rapist would suddenly attack her on the way home – she imagined herself running away from him across a dark courtyard, down some steps with used syringes crunching under her feet, through basements full of slapping water, gasping for breath like Sarah Connor and then, when there's nowhere left to run, she stops, trying to calm her pounding heart, and says calmly: "Put this on." Of course, Lyusya had got pregnant on purpose, Ksenia didn't doubt that for a moment, but even so, as she lay there at night in the room that was empty without Lyova, she imagined the cells dividing inside Lyusya's ungainly body, swelling up in the impenetrable darkness and turning into a baby. As Ksenia fell asleep, she felt as if the blanket pulled right up over her head was that womb, the womb in which there was a basement restaurant where they had celebrated Lyova's wedding in a modest gathering of fifteen people.

That summer, while Ksenia was defending Marina's honor and meeting Nikita, the newlyweds dragged out their honeymoon in the Crimea to a full three months, and when they came back the child that Lyusya was supposedly expecting had disappeared without trace. Ksenia never did ask Lyova straight out what had happened: was it a miscarriage, an abortion, or had there never been any child at all and Lyusya had simply lied? The child disappeared, then Lyusya disappeared, moving out of the apartment that the young couple rented without any great fuss and going back to her mother. Lyova said he would stay in the apartment for the two months that had already been paid for, but four months went by and Ksenia realized he was never going to come back home. A year later he went away to the States and when they parted he said "I'll be back," and winked at Ksenia as if to say: don't be sad. But she had already worked through all her sadness two years earlier, when Lyova got married and Lyusya was pregnant with a child that later disappeared without trace, as if it had never existed – the same way the restaurant where they celebrated the wedding had disappeared now.

Olya loved The Discreet Charm... maybe because it was close to the salon where her hair was styled and she had her hands manicured twice a week. Two pairs of hands on one table: Olya's soft, well-groomed hands, freshly anointed with creams and fragrant oils, and Ksenia's little hands with bitten nails and one little silver ring. A small figurine stands between them, a ceramic or stone idol with square eyes and teeth that take up half its face.

"Vlad asked me to give you this," says Olya.

"How sweet of him," says Ksenia, although, of course "sweet" is a rather strange word, this is a figure out of a nightmare. "Who is it?"

"Some Mexican god," says Olya, drawing on her cigarette through the long holder. "Vlad went there last year and brought back a whole heap of all sorts of junk. But he says this is the real thing, not a fake."

Ksenia strokes the fine honeycomb surface of the stone. She wonders if it's Mayan or Aztec. At school she read that the Aztecs' prisoners fought with wooden swords against fully armed Aztec warriors and the Maya believed that for the world to continue to exist they had to make liberal gifts of blood to the gods several times a year. During the ritual sacrifices, the blood flowed in streams down the steps of the pyramids. If this really was a Mexican idol, everything he saw in Ksenia's bedroom would seem like children's games to him.

"I got a funny business proposal," says Olya. "A company that wants to advertise with us. They run historical tours to Tula."

"And they think our site is the right targeting?" Ksenia chuckles. "Maybe they're a bit confused."

"Don't laugh," says Olya. "You know what kind of tours they run? Torture in the time of Ivan the Terrible! The clients are sort of doing the tour of the local kremlin, and suddenly the *streltsy* spot a sneak thief trying to pick one of the tourist's pockets. They take him down into the vaults and..."

"Oh, come on!" says Ksenia. "You're putting me on."

"Listen, they've flooded the Russian internet with their spam, everybody already knows this wonderful story. They promise to show the genuine old Russian tortures – lash, pincers, fire, boiling oil and melted wax on naked flesh…"

"…and quartering," Ksenia adds. Olya laughs.

When the Spanish conquered Mexico, they quartered all the high priests. There's no way of telling now whether they tortured them in search of gold or they simply went berserk in the wake of the slaughter that was taking place in the streets of the city. But maybe, thinks Ksenia, that was the outcome the priests wanted, because they knew that this last blood spilt on the steps of the sacred pyramid was their final chance to postpone the end of the world.

Somehow Ksenia had missed out on the standard old Soviet stories about Young Pioneer heroes being tortured to death, and she had never found the image of young Komsomol girls facing the porous chalices of their breasts filled with their own blood very exciting. One of her short-lived dominant lovers had been a fan of the National Bolshevik Party, Nazi memorabilia and the film *The Night Porter*. Maybe he was good in bed, but the black leather, death's head and peaked cap with the high crown always gave Ksenia a fit of the giggles and put a rapid end to any erotic arousal.

Instead of Zoya Kosmodemyanskaya lying naked on the bloody snow, ever since she was little Ksenia had always imagined a South American Indian priest with his arms and legs cut off, lying on the stone platform of the sacred pyramid. In his dying ecstasy he forgets the pain and in his final moment he resurrects in his mind the heyday of his people and its culture, which has now disappeared without trace, in the way that unborn babies disappear when they are spat out of the impenetrable darkness of their mothers' wombs, in the way Lyova's wife disappeared, in the way that even the restaurant where they celebrated his wedding had disappeared today.

"And another thing," Olya continues, "I've been approached by an association for the support of women who are victims of domestic violence. They want us to make a free page on the site for them."

"But what have they got to do with us?" asks Ksenia.

"They say that domestic violence and psychotic killers are two faces of the same male sadism. The humiliation of a woman in the family and a murder somewhere in the forest are links in a single chain. And so on and so forth."

Ksenia recalls Vlad shouting: "Olya, bring some ice!" and the Mexican figurine suddenly grows heavy in her hand.

"We'll make them a page," she says, "no problem. We should help our sisters. But I'd advise them to learn karate and wu-shu."

"I'd advise them to get a good business education," Olya laughs, "and go to work for a year. That's an experience more frightening than karate or wu-shu."

"What about that man," asks Ksenia, suddenly remembering, "the one you asked me about, remember? Are you going to work with him?"

Olya shakes her head.

"I haven't decided yet," she says. "My partners don't leave me much choice. If things go on as they are, they'll destroy the business before spring."

"I understand," says Ksenia, but in actual fact, she doesn't understand, because no matter how much she would like to know her way around in business, she is merely a successful journalist, maybe a decent IT manager and a successful professional in areas where, thank God, you don't need to know about business.

They are already choosing their dessert and waiting for the coffee to arrive when Olya finally makes up her mind and says:

"You know, I think I'm pregnant."

Well there's a surprise, thinks Ksenia, and asks how late Olya is, and then asks the question to which she already knows the answer: *Yes, of course it's Oleg's, you know it is*, and then asks if he knows, and Olya says: *Of course not, I haven't decided what to do yet* – because she's a good girl from a cultured Petersburg family, not some kind of Lyusya in baggy sweaters and tight jeans who'll drag a man off to the registry office at the slightest excuse, and then to the uterine restaurant, where the new family unit swells up like an embryo in the womb, only for everything to disappear without trace afterward. No, Olya hasn't decided what to do yet, because she doesn't want to break up a family, and Ksenia suspects she couldn't break it up anyway: men don't leave their wives for mistresses they've been seeing for four years, instead of that they take new mistresses and start seeing different girls who manage their contraception better and don't allow the sperm cells to fuse with the egg cells in the inner darkness, so that they can swell up into the embryo of a new life.

"No," says Olya, "I haven't made my mind up about anything yet, I'm afraid to raise a child alone, I couldn't handle it, but maybe I'll keep it, because I'm already thirty-five years old, and I can't be sure there'll be another chance, and I love Oleg, and if it's a boy it will be like him." And as she talks about it, Ksenia places her hand that has never been manicured on Olya's fragrant well-groomed hand and strokes it gently, saying: "Whatever you decide, I'll be with you," and then she realizes that in her other hand she's clutching the Mexican figurine with square eyes and a toothy smile that takes up half its face.

29

KSENIA, KSENIA, KSENIA, ALEXEI REPEATS TO HIMSELF as he walks up the step of the pedestrian underpass. I love you, I love you, I love you. How strange it is to say that. How many times he has heard it on double beds in hotel rooms, in hallways where the doors slam with a dull thud, in unlocked attics where the cold autumn wind blows, how many times he has looked into eyes that were waiting for that answer, and he has never said it once. But now he repeats it to himself, like a mantra: kseniakseniakseniaIloveyouIloveyouIloveyou. Now he knows you can never tell in advance how love will come, a skinny little girl with her hair always tousled, with the nails bitten down on her frail hands, with a crystalline icy note of authority in her voice. You can see her every day, and your inner voice won't say to you: "Look, this is your love, your destiny, the blood in your veins, all your *yeses* and all your *nos*, it is the most important thing that has happened to you in the last ten years," and if it does say it, you won't believe it, and as you switch on the computer, you'll say what you've always said – "hi" – and as you switch off the computer, you'll say "see you," and you'll spend six months sitting in the same room as her like that, still not knowing what this is going to mean to you. And then you'll seduce her easily and several weeks later you'll pay the price for that ease when you finally understand. Be honest with yourself, you've been a good lover to many women, but you've never loved them. You're probably a good man but a little cool-blooded, no point in trying to deny it, it's God-given, there's nothing to be done about it. A body, in order to grow old together, children, in order to raise them together, your gold shimmering hair, with silver graying threads, ten years together, eternity together, dearest Oxana, forgive me, forgive me for what has happened to me. I didn't want this, if I'd known I wouldn't have lied to you that evening: *No, Oxanochka, I'll be delayed a bit longer, Pasha wanted to discuss a special project with me. I'll tell you all about it when I get home.* What will I tell you, Oxana, what will I tell you, if even these words that you will never hear are a lie? because even if I had known, I would still have put my arms round her in the taxi, kissed the lips that were offered, taken the elevator up to the apartment and made love there, still thinking that I was having sex. And two weeks later, when we launched the project, I would have looked at her again and again and just like the time before, I would have seen her tousled hair, her skinny shoulders, her strong lips outlined with lipstick, her frail hands with the bitten-down nails – and once again that tender feeling would have smothered me. Dearest Oxana, forgive me for what has happened to me, I hope you will never find out about it.

We make love very rarely and, God knows, I try very hard to keep it that way. Because if I could get to her apartment block every evening or at least a few times a week, the day would come when I couldn't control myself any longer. I would go down on my knees in front of her and say Ksenia Ksenia Ksenia here I am, your awkward colleague and infrequent lover, this is me, just as I am, the father of two children, the husband of my wife, look at me, take me for your own, make me small, put me in your pocket, write me to the hard disk of your laptop, keep me here. I want to kneel in front of you and kiss your frail hands and caress your thighs where I can see the blood pulsing in your veins through the thin skin, watch your lips part and open like flowers of flesh – kiss, caress and watch and repeat, repeat like a mantra kseniakseniakseniaIloveyouIloveyouIloveyou, like a monk who has lost his faith and no longer expects these words to bring salvation. I realize all this means nothing to you, dearest Ksenia, forgive me for what has happened to me. I hope you will never find out about it.

Alexei walks into the entrance, calls the elevator and tells himself for the hundredth time: you can analyze it and try to explain it – analysis isn't important and explanations aren't important. Yes, I've never slept with anyone I work with before, yes, we've created the finest journalistic project of my life, yes I've always liked girls who are just twenty-something years old. But all these "yeses" and all the unspoken "nos" don't change a thing, because what comes out in the end is still kseniakseniakseniaIloveyouIloveyouIloveyou.

Roman Ivanovich opens the door. Roman Ivanovich is wearing a wool tracksuit and the beads of sweat on his bald patch are visible even by the light of the dusty ceiling lamp in the hallway. Roman Ivanovich has spectacles with thin frames on his nose, and his big nose is like a foreign growth on his face.

"I'm sorry," he says, "I've forgotten your name."

Alexei introduces himself and Roman Ivanovich nods, asks him to repeat his patronymic and pushes a pair of tattered house slippers over to him with his foot.

"Put them on, put them on, Alexei Mikhailovich, let's go into the study, I'll show you the materials there and answer your questions."

Roman Ivanovich lives alone, his study is in the large room, and all three walls are covered with shelves full of files. There is a computer covered with a towel standing on a desk in the corner.

"Shall I tell you how I became involved in all of this?" he asks, and Alexei nods.

Roman Ivanovich goes across to a shelf, takes a file, puts it down in front of him and begins.

"The point is that I come from Rostov-on-Don. And the Don happens to produce a large crop of serials. The famous Chikatilo and Mukhankin, as well as Tsurman and Burstev, and many others as well. They say the environmental conditions are bad, but then, where are they good nowadays, in all honesty? Well, I became interested in the reasons for all of this. I started studying, analyzing, comparing. They say it's their childhood traumas. Chikatilo's younger brother was eaten during the famine, and when Mukhankin was born, his mother tossed him out on to the doorstep to his father and shouted: 'Take him, I don't want him!' The Americans also confirm that most serials were humiliated and raped as children. Henry Lee Lucas's mother made her son watch as she, begging your pardon, copulated with her lovers – and so he killed her when he was seventeen! Joseph Kallinger's adopted parents flogged him and threatened to castrate him, and when he was eight they simply raped him. They say you can find some terrible childhood memory in every serial killer's life, but believe me, Alexei Mikhailovich, that is by no means true. I have read a lot, and analyzed a lot. Anatolii Slivko, the famous psychotic killer who was a Young Pioneer leader, for instance, had a perfectly happy childhood.

"And then there is the very popular theory that these are men with sexual problems of some kind. They say Chikatilo was unable to perform the sexual act normally and even after he killed his victim, he would push his sperm into her with his finger. And as for the cannibal Spesivtsev from Novokuznetsk, his penis, begging your pardon, had rotted away from syphilis. And then there are the sodomites, also known as homosexuals or, as they say nowadays, gays. There are quite a number of them among the serial killers. Supposedly they take revenge on women because they're afraid of them. I will not deny it, no, I will not, that does happen – but that is only one class, so to speak. However to all appearances, this Moscow psycho of yours is not one of them. All the women have been raped while alive, many of them repeatedly.

"But why are we just sitting here talking like this? I'll go and make some tea, and in the meantime, you take a glance at the file, I've collected some interesting material for you here, perhaps you might publish some of it. There are no atrocities here, don't you worry about that, these are the serial killers' letters. This is from David Berkowitz, New York's famous Son of Sam, look what a touching letter it is: 'I want to make love to the world. I love people. I don't belong on Earth.' He wrote that a long time before he was caught, you mustn't go thinking that he's trying to justify himself to the court. 'To the people of Queens, I love you. And I want to wish all of you a happy Easter.' Look, there is even a photocopy of the last page, there. You can read English, Alexei Mikhailovich: 'Police, let me haunt you with these words: I'll be back! I'll be back!' Familiar words, those, are they not?

You must have seen *Terminator*, I'm sure. I'll be back, this is who he's quoting, now do you understand?

"And this is the last will and testament of Andrei Romanovich Chikatilo, from my own home parts. 'I ask you to exile me, like Napoleon, who destroyed millions of lives, to an island – an uninhabited volcanic rock in the North Kuril Crest or to the tigers of the Ussurian taiga. On the wild island I shall feed on moss and God's dew, as in my childhood I fed on nettles and other wild grasses.' Now there's real loneliness for you, Alexei Mikhailovich, that's what it's like. But do drink your tea, Alexei Mikhailovich, drink, and let me tell you this: you can analyze as much as you like, you can try to explain – analysis is not important and explanations are not important, that is not the point.

"I have read the specialist literature and the most various explanations. Take the famous Roy Hazelwood, from the behavioral science unit at the FBI – you've seen *The Silence of the Lambs*, haven't you? They show him in that, and that is the way things really are. Well then, from what I've read, Hazelwood absolutely refuses to talk about these matters. He says: "My job is to catch them, but when it comes to why – other people can try to understand that." Do you know why he says that? Because he knows a great many facts, almost like I do. And in this matter, Alexei Mikhailovich, the more you learn, the less chance you have of actually understanding anything. Let us be quite honest: we do not know where serials come from. They exist, that's all.

"Some say that sexual prohibitions are to blame for everything. The Americans like to tell us that three quarters of serial killers come from their country. And that that is because there is so much violence on television and sex in advertising. This is all nonsense, Alexei Mikhailovich, non-sense. Take Chikatilo, Mukhankin, Dzhumagaliev, Alexander Chaika, Gennadii Mikhasevich – were they in America then? No. And Pedro Alonso Lopez, who killed more than three hundred girls, was he from America? No. Did he kill them in the States? No, he killed them in Peru and Ecuador.

"Yes, in America they are better at catching them, that is true. But even so, Ottis and Lucas rode around the country and killed people. Do you know how they did it? They drove along a road until they saw a broken-down car or, say, a car with a courting couple in it. Then they stopped and killed the man quickly, but they took the girl with them and raped her by turns, then shot her too. Ottis used to call this a 'free breakfast.' Well, nobody even connected these killings together! They were caught because of an unlicensed gun that Lucas had – and he only confessed everything after that! And then there is Mike DeBardeleben, who was arrested for passing counterfeit bills, and they found a whole house full of video recordings and photographs of his torture sessions. The famous Ed Gein was arrested on a charge of stealing a cash register. And he was the psycho to end all psychos! Hitchcock based Norman Bates on him, and he was the model for Harris's Buffalo Bill in *Silence of the Lambs*. But both of them – Buffalo Bill and Norman Bates – are mere snot-nosed punks compared to him. Ed Gein made necklaces out of women's nipples, goblets out of skulls, wastepaper baskets out of skin, sculptures out of noses, tongues and vulvar lips. He was a genuine virtuoso.

"And on this point, Alexei Mikhailovich, I have a theory of my own. Does this not remind you of something? Necklaces, goblets, corpses? No? Ah, how ignorant you are. And yet, all the books have been published in Russian for a long time now, you know. These, Alexei Mikhailovich, are the traditional attributes of wrathful Hindu deities. And not only Hindu deities, of course.

"Let me tell you – this is all a matter of ritual. It is not necessary, by the way, for the serial killers themselves to understand this. Well yes, they do say that Ottis's grandmother was a Satanist and many others also practiced, so to speak. But in point of fact you and I are educated people, we understand that Satanism is just a word. There are, so to speak, certain forces. Why, for instance, are there, in point of fact, so many serial killers in America? Why, because until relatively recently human sacrifice was practiced there. Did you know that they call southern California 'Psycho Valley'? Well you should, having taken an interest in this subject. There have been very many serial killers there. The Hillside Stranglers, Angelo Buono and Kenneth Bianchi, or Bittaker and Norris, I could tell you about them for a long time. And it's not all because the area round Hollywood is thick with starlets and other easy meat. Look: this is the place closest of all to Mexico, where five hundred years ago the Maya and the Aztecs offered up human sacrifices.

"You ask, why then are there no serial killers in Mexico? But you don't know that. I don't suppose you have heard about Ciudad Juarez? More than three hundred and seventy women were killed there in ten years. One woman every ten days. The self-same thing: nipples cut off, indications of torture, bodies in the desert. They still can't find the killers even now, I've counted five, no, six conspiracy theories, I won't detain you by reciting them to you.

"What I want to say is this: in ancient times people were in contact with their own death. All the religions, not excluding Christianity, tell us about human sacrifices. God sacrifices His own Son and they crucify Him. And do you know why this is so important? Because men are not animals, that's why! A wolf will never kill a wolf, but one man finds it easy to kill another. Do you know why? Because man is the only animal who knows about his own death. And human sacrifice is one of the ways of understanding your future death. A way of thinking the unthinkable, so to speak. You have to try to look into the eyes of someone who is dying and read in them what will later be reflected in your own eyes, do you understand? That is why the sight of someone else's death is so attractive. Take *Highway Patrol* on the television, with all the dead bodies they show. And then there is your site. Public executions continued until the invention of television. The path mankind has chosen is to adopt surrogates: the place of sacrifices is taken by Hollywood movies and news programs. And that, of course, is a very shameful thing.

"Yes indeed, the fact of the matter is that people have banished the ancient rituals from their lives, do you understand? Just think, if Christ appeared on Earth today, where would he find Caiaphas and Pontius Pilate, in order to redeem our sins on the cross? Why, Jesus would have to look for a new John Wayne Gacy, a new Chikatilo, a new Ted Bundy, a new Ottis and Lucas… Two thousand years ago Jesus hung on the cross for six hours and that was enough to redeem the sins of men. But in two thousand years too many sins have accumulated and six hours isn't enough now. The Canadian serial killers Karla Homolka and Paul Bernardo, nicknamed Barbie and Ken, tortured fifteen-year-old Kristen for several days. And Hazelwood tells us about a man who didn't kill his victims until the forty-eighth day. But, of course, you are right, time is not the most important thing, what is important is the degree of suffering. Do you know that in Golovkin's burial ground they found ten-year-old boys who were entirely gray? Have you ever seen an image of a gray-haired Christ? And after that, will you tell me that he suffered greatly?

"And do you know what else I will tell you, Alexei Mikhailovich? The new Jesus will be a woman. A new Joan of Arc. Because almost all of them, almost all, kill women. That is why people visit your site, that is why I have many, many friends with whom I correspond all around the world – because people sense that perhaps any one of these so-called psychos could become the source of a new redemption. But of course, we won't write about that in the interview. The ignorant masses have no need to know that, do they now, Alexei Mikhailovich? We shall wait for our Christ, our Joan."

He shows Alexei out into the hallway and Alexei looks at the beads of sweat glinting in the light of the dull lamp and thinks: *Where does he get these affected manners, how can he still be like this? Wool tracksuit, slippers, this way of talking straight out of the nineteenth century?* – and in the doorway he asks:

"Are you retired now?"

"Why would I be retired?" Roman Ivanovich asks in surprise. "I'm only forty, how could I retire? I'm a school teacher, a teacher of Russian literature. And a good teacher too, I think. You know, sometimes it is a pleasure to listen to what really young people have to say. Only recently we were looking at Mayakovsky, following an expanded program, so to speak – I included a couple of rather interesting poems. There I am in the classroom, you know, and one of the A-students, a girl, is up at the blackboard running through the lesson. She says Mayakovsky was trying to shock the bourgeoisie with his line 'I like to watch children die.' Of course, that is the right answer, that is what it says in all the books. Shock the bourgeoisie. So I listen and look at her. Sixteen years old, her figure is all in place, you know what I mean, but she is still an absolute child. And I was filled with such joy, I simply do not have the words to express it. You know, the little fool doesn't understand that it's all much simpler than that; that if someone says 'I like to watch children die,' all it means is that he enjoys watching children die. And nothing else. And the bourgeoisie has nothing to do with it. And he is not interested in shocking anyone. It's hard to understand that at sixteen, of course. Unless, that is, you happen to attend Columbine High School in Littleton, Colorado. But here in Russia, thank God, we have all that still to come, do we not, Alexei Mikhailovich?"

"Yes indeed, Roman Ivanovich," Alexei replies hastily, and as he rides down in the elevator, he thinks how lucky he is to live in a world of normal people and to have a wife, two children and a woman he loves.

30

EVEN SO, IT FEELS GOOD TO BE A STAR, THINKS KSENIA, after all, I always knew that journalism was my true calling. That I could put together a good project, and people would be interested in it. Sometimes it surprises even me the way I know what interests other people. After all, it's hard to believe I can find people who will share my own preferences. It is hard to believe and, in fact, I'm not having any luck finding them. I wonder when was the last time I had proper sex? Not vanilla sex with my colleague Alexei, who is actually my subordinate, but real sex, the kind of play that leaves you bloody and bruised, with that sweet trembling in every part of your body? Six weeks ago, that's when it was.

I don't get it, thinks Ksenia, how can a girl like me create something that normal people find interesting? Although, after all, I am curious about all sorts of different things. I'm curious about the way they roll up rice, seaweed and raw fish to make sushi, although I've seen it done several times, and Olya even promised to come to my place some day and teach me how to make them, but I still don't understand how it works. I'm curious about the way a body starts moving to the music of its own accord after six months' training, I'm curious about the way people dance and the things they talk about. About the way with some people you can tell at first sight you'll be friends for the rest of your life and with others it takes years and years before you figure it out. I'm curious about why people change when they have children, and about why they have children too. I wonder about whether the people I remember, remember me; I even wonder about whether the ones I forgot a long time ago still remember me. I wonder who I have forgotten and whether I'll ever remember them again.

I'm curious about lots of things, thinks Ksenia, but I happen to have made a site about a psychotic killer, and people find it interesting. What do people feel when they see our banners? A map of the subway with one station circled and the words "psycho kills here." Shock? Curiosity? Horror?

I realized it a couple of weeks ago: I was sitting in the Atrium with Olya, in the café with the chessboard tables. Olya was telling me something about the chess tournaments she played in as a child, when suddenly I saw the huge sign behind her, on a concrete building from the old Soviet days. Through the bluish glass of the mall windows the letters looked like the broken shards of an amphora lying under water. The sign said MOSGAS.

Mosgas was the most famous Russian serial killer before Chikatilo. If it had been a banner, I'd have clicked on it. But at the time I didn't say anything to Olya, I don't know why, I just carried on drinking coffee and listening to that string jangling inside me in a joyful, liberating premonition of horror.

If it had been a banner, I'd have clicked on it – and people do click on the banners that all of us invent and Marina draws. Every day I get letters thanking me, but more often they advise me to see a psychiatrist, because I'm a sick bitch who gloats over other people's suffering and takes pleasure in cruelty. These people wonder what my sex life is like and if I often get fucked, as they call it. They wonder if I'm frigid or, on the contrary, if I'm a nymphomaniac. I wonder, by the way, is it possible to be both at once? But I'm not really interested in the answer to that question – especially since I'm not frigid and I'm not a nympho.

People are curious about my life, thinks Ksenia, and that means I've made an interesting site, because they like to wonder about the people who made the site. People like to wonder about other people, it's true. But I try not to wonder about the man who is the subject of this site – although it's hard not to wonder about him. Who is he, and what goes on inside his head? What is he like in everyday life? Was he abused and raped as a child? Does he have an incurable illness? Does he hate the world? Or does he only hate women? I wonder about this – but I try not to, because it's impossible to think about him without hating him. And what right do I have to hate him, if I get aroused myself when I read about nipples that have been bitten off and lips that have been cut out?

I think someone with my tastes has no right to judge others.

People wonder what's inside my head, thinks Ksenia, but no one's asked me about that in an interview yet. I guess all that's still ahead of me. Look, today I got a letter from Maya Lvova, the woman to whom I owe so much, asking for an interview. She says she's interested in talking to me. It would be interesting for me to meet her, I think, and I answer yes, by all means, let's have a talk, it could be tomorrow, or Friday, whatever suits you best. She used to like doing sensational interviews, she might ask what's inside my head. I wonder what I'll tell her?

I wonder what's inside the head of the man I chat with every day on ICQ. I should ask why he called himself "alien," what he meant by that. I wonder if he really doesn't know who I am – although, to be quite honest, I shouldn't exaggerate my own fame, he might not listen to the radio or read the internet newspapers, and even if he does read them, I can't be the only girl in the world called Ksenia Ionova, why should he remember that name in particular?

Every day Ksenia reads the forums on her site. She's curious about what people talk about after they visit the site to find out about the Moscow Psycho. When she invented the site, she thought all she would do was give people information, put them on their guard, and counter the spread of rumors. But now she's not sure anymore that people visit the site for information – they come for something else.

We really admire you, Ksenia reads. You're a cool dude. I think these babes deserve to be carved up, because they don't put out for us, heh-heh, it's signed Beavis and Butthead. Heh-heh, that really is interesting, thinks Ksenia, and reads the next thread. We'd like to meet you, because WE HATE this world too. WE'RE SATANISTS! Just recently we went to a graveyard, turned the crosses upside down and hanged a black cat. We were going to burn it, but max wouldn't let us, because he's a wimp and a tosser. It's signed "666" and there's an answer under it: why don't you lads go and have a drink instead of bothering with this sick f***ing rubbish? It's signed "777" and the asterisks are there because Ksenia installed an obscenity filter on her computer and it replaces all obscene words with asterisks.

I wonder, thinks Ksenia, what these people have inside their heads? Why do clueless teenagers, smart-ass jokers and pimply-faced wankers all come flocking to the smell of blood? She remembers that after one of the murders committed by Chikatilo, the mother of the victim received a note: "To the parents of the missing girl. Hello, parents. Do not grieve. Yours isn't the first and she's not the last. We need ten of them by the New Year. If you want to bury her – look in the leaves of the Darovsky Plantation. Black Cat the Sadist." They didn't find anything in the leaves of the Darovsky Plantation, the body was hidden somewhere completely different, when Chikatilo was caught he said he never wrote this note, but he really did kill another ten people before the New Year. Who was this joker, this black cat the sadist, this distant relative of the black cat that was hanged, but not burned and – she would like to hope – never even existed.

I was on my way home yesterday, Ksenia reads in the "Suspicions" forum, and this young guy tagged along behind me! I spotted him in the subway, on the escalator. He was giving me this strange kind of stare (OMG), but then I forgot about him, only later, in the passage on the way to my line, I saw him again, it was like he'd tracked me down! He was walking in front of me and then he turned straight onto my platform without even hesitating! I was shit scared, so I let the train go and pretended I was waiting for someone, and I stood there in the middle of the station for a while and then got into a different car from my usual one. There was no one there, so I stopped worrying, but when I got out at my stop (I don't want to say where I live, in case this psycho reads your stupid forum), he was standing there (OMG!) like he was waiting for me (OMG!) I took out my cell phone and called my boyfriend and said real loud someone was following me and I wanted him to meet me. Then my boyfriend came and this psycho must have got scared and he disappeared. So it was all right in the end. But tell me, everyone, what should I do, because I'm afraid he might be stalking me? And it's signed "Fluffy."

I wonder, thinks Ksenia, why she didn't approach a cop? Even if she was afraid, I wonder why she didn't go to a cop afterward? Why didn't she give him a description? Why doesn't she even give one here? What if this man really was the serial killer they've been trying to catch for the last six months? I wonder what she has inside her head? How old is she? What does her boyfriend look like? Is all this true, or did she make up the entire story so she could get her boyfriend to come to the subway station, and then wrote it down, because she started believing it herself? I wonder how this psycho could tell which station she was going to? Ksenia knows that killers often stalk their victims for months, she knows that many of them can get inside their quarry's head and guess in advance where she will go, what she will do and what words she'll respond to. Ksenia knows about this, but she's still curious.

I wonder, thinks Ksenia, why she wrote in? Maybe the answer she wanted to read is: *Dear Fluffy, I felt so frightened for you when I read your story. I can imagine how frightened you were!* But what she feels like writing is something quite different. *Why, oh why, Dear Fluffy, didn't you give us his description? Why, oh why, you hysterical idiot, don't you go to the police? Don't you care?* is what Ksenia wants to write, *or are you just stringing us along, you infantile little fool?* But she doesn't write anything and moves on to the next forum.

You girls who like to hang out on this site, Ksenia reads, how would you like to be given a real slamming? How would you like to be had by a real man? Write to me at *sadist_cruel_master@yandex.ru*, and we'll get together in my cozy little basement. First I'll give you a good flogging on your bouncy little backsides, then I'll make you lick my huge great dong, while my dog stretches your tight wet little holes for you. You'll be begging me to give you a good screwing but first I'll hang weights on your tits that'll stretch your nipples down to the floor, or tear them right off, ha-ha, and then the lads and I will shaft you so hard that when you leave in the morning you'll be crawling on all fours, and even the celebrated Moscow psycho would be disgusted by your huge tattered holes!

You are a sick creep, Ksenia reads, children visit this site, clear out. What's the moderator up to, Ksenia reads, get this filth out of the forum! People, come to your senses, think what you're writing, Ksenia reads, the dead girls' families could see this. What abominable filth, Ksenia reads, what kind of scum writes in to this forum? Yes, Ksenia reads, we're scum, we're here for a laugh.

All this, Ksenia reads, is because people have forgotten Christ and sunk into depravity. All this, Ksenia reads, is because the most important things in Russia now are money and financial gain. All this, Ksenia reads, is because the Russian people have forgotten their pride.

All this is becos its those little Russian bitches own folt. No one will raip a desent girl, she WON'T GO with a man she doesn't know. My sister always dresses desent, she doesn't go rownd with her bra showing like all these sluts.

Do the victims' families read this, Ksenia wonders, do they visit the site? Do the people who write in remember about them? I always used to think it was immoral to pester someone in mourning with questions, but now I think maybe I was wrong. Maybe people need to read about what kind of girls they were – Maria Z., age twenty-three, Dasha A., age sixteen, Julia B, age twenty-fIve? So they'll stop being dismembered bodies and just for a moment at least become girls who loved and wanted to be loved, who dreamed of having children and meeting *their* man, who hoped for happiness, looked out the window in the evening and thought about what they were going to do tomorrow, laughed at jokes, sobbed at funerals and expected to die when they were old, surrounded by loving grandchildren. When I look at their photographs, Ksenia thinks, I want to cry, but deep in my heart I know there's a strange truth in everything that has happened. That our future is made of dreams and daydreams, that it bursts like a shimmering rainbow soap-bubble, like a toy balloon pricked with a knife, a scalpel or a piece of a mirror broken in the bathroom. That I, a young interesting girl, a successful professional, the senior editor of a news department, only five minutes away from stardom, can feel a deadly horror pulsating beneath the thin soap-bubble membrane of my rainbow-bright future, like a heart beneath skin that has been slit open. Maybe, thinks Ksenia, that is why I made a site like this, because I'm curious about this horror.

But I really must write something to this Fluffy, Ksenia thinks, or she'll never wise up. Only I wonder just why she annoys me so much? I guess it's because I would have acted differently in her place.

I think, Ksenia reads, that sooner or later they'll catch you. And now let me tell you what they do with your kind on the inside. Everyone'll have your ass, you'll be licking the ***t out of the slop buckets, and when you get out, we'll find you anyway and kill you, but not straight away.

I think, Ksenia reads, that when they catch him, he should be interrogated properly. They should bring our special agents who interrogate the Chechen killers back from Chechnya and let them interrogate this psycho, and then he'll tell them everything.

I think, Ksenia reads, that capital punishment is too good for subhuman monsters like this. They should be tortured, to make them realize what they've done. I think, Ksenia reads, that first they ought to strip his skin off, but not all of it, or he'll die too soon. And then stick a pointed stake up his anus and attach electrodes to his nipples so that he twitches like a frog. And they ought to hang him upside down, because I've been told they stay conscious longer like that.

I wonder, thinks Ksenia, what's inside these people's heads? *I've been told they stay conscious longer like that.* Who told him that? How did they test it? Sometimes I don't believe they hate this psycho. Sometimes it seems to me they can feel the killer inside themselves. Sometimes it seems to me that he's been living inside me for a long time, swelling up like an embryo in the darkness of the womb and one day he'll come bursting out, break his way through my ribcage, burst out and say: *Hi.*

"Hi," Ksenia says into the phone, "how are you getting on? I'm fine too. I visited a forum and what's going on in there made my hair stand on end! Maybe we should get a moderator? Figure out how much it will cost, this is really getting embarrassing, take a look and read it for yourself. Or maybe we could have coffee together at lunch time," says Ksenia, "we haven't seen each other since last week and I miss you."

"No," says Olya, "I'm sorry, I can't today, I have to see the doctor."

"Is something wrong?" asks Ksenia.

"No," Olya replies, "everything's fine, I've just decided not to keep the baby."

"Do you want me to go with you?" asks Ksenia.

"No, there's no need," Olya replies, "I'll call you if I need anything."

Dear Lyusya, Ksenia reads mechanically, *I know you still visit this forum. So I'm telling you, for what you did last Friday I'm going to catch you and cut your womb out, and all your guts with it.*

Dear Fluffy, Ksenia writes, *I was so frightened for you when I read your story. I can imagine how frightened you were! I hope the psycho won't follow you anymore. Hang in there, and if anything happens, write in again, all of us here are very concerned about you.*

31

IN MOSCOW IN SUMMER YOU LEARN TO MOVE IN SHORT bursts, as if the street is a sea in which you have to swim from one island to another. Air conditioning in the bedroom at home, air conditioning in the car, at work, at the club. In the gaps between, your shirt instantly becomes soaked under the armpits, you're the first to find the smell of your own sweat disgusting – and no deodorant will save you. Islands in the sea, yes, I'd prefer the Cote d'Azur or at least Greece, or even, if it comes to that, Turkey, where my friend Mike's wife is on vacation right now with their seven-year-old son. Mike tells me Lyuba calls him and complains, says it's tough for her on her own, and threatens that next year she won't go anywhere without him.

Mike would be glad to go, the beach is better every way than a stuffy night club, where the air conditioning can't handle the vapors exuded by hundreds of bodies, most of them appealingly young. If you think of this club as an island and the heat as water, then the place is about to suffer the same fate as Atlantis. Not much of an island, in other words.

I used to differentiate between the Moscow clubs, I used to think that was important. I used to think one was fashionable and another was outmoded. Now they've all fused into a single dance floor ablaze with lights where the young things dance – the new clubbing generation that has come on the scene. They skip around to music that I have no more clue about nowadays than I do about the clubs; they skip about like puppies having fun in a dog park.

Mike wipes the sweat off his face. Good old Mike, endowed with a figure that allowed him to impersonate his own "protection" during the post-Soviet capitalist frenzy of the early nineties: he put on a fierce expression, crossed his arms on his chest and sat there at negotiations without saying a word. "I don't really look like a gangster, do I?" He used to say to me. "I'm just a regular Moscow boy." Ever since those days he still has the habit of wearing a gold bracelet and signet ring.

We're sitting right beside the dance floor, and I spot you straight away: skin-tight pants down to just below your knees, glittering shoes with high heels, a short top, already wet with sweat. Hair dyed in streaks, ginger on light yellow – straw color, almost white. So far I can't see your face, but the hemispheres of your buttocks are twitching rhythmically, sending me greetings. I pretend I haven't noticed you, we order two beers and I sit there half-turned away, still following you out of the corner of my eye.

Mike would be glad to go, the beach is better every way than the swelter of the city, but in the construction business summer is the hot season in every sense of the word. So Lyubka and Sevka are down there in Turkey, and Mike's here with me in a club with a name that's not really important. He hangs his jacket on the back of his chair and straight away I can see the spots under the arms of his light-colored shirt. No deodorant can save you. "No," he says, "you should never stay in this city in summer."

I look at you, you've turned in three-quarter profile and in the beams of light wandering around the dance floor I can make out a snub nose, rather sweet, and a two-tone bang that falls over your eyes every now and then. Before Igor went away to America to get his MBA, he had a little dog like that, one day he had it clipped, and the poor thing spent two weeks behind the curtain, with the fringe falling over its eyes instead of the hair that had been cut off. What kind was it now? A fox terrier, was it?

Mike is complaining about builders who don't want to work and clients who set impossible deadlines. He can understand the builders – you can't put air conditioning into an unfinished building. In that respect my office is far more pleasant. The waves of heat beat against the glass like the waves of the Mediterranean on the cost of Turkey where Lyubka and Sevka are suffering so terribly – if, that is, you can believe what she says on the phone.

Right then, Mike works in the construction business, but I wonder where you work? I used to differentiate between girls, I preferred educated professionals, I used to think that was important. Now that I know a lot more about women than I ever did before, I realize there's no great difference between a homeless tramp (provided you give her a wash, of course), a secretary and a successful businesswoman with an MBA of her own. Women are differentiated by the texture of her skin, the shape of their nipples and their lips, the density and size of their breasts and how easily the skin comes away from their muscles. Stop, I tell myself, stop.

Lyubka and Sevka are suffering by the sea down in Turkey and on this sweltering Friday evening Mike is sitting on the edge of a dog park and eyeing some girl, like a regular Moscow boy. In hot summer Moscow it's not that difficult to find yourself some girl, especially on Friday evening, especially if you know how to look. So far he hasn't noticed you, the fox-terrier girl with the twin-tone bang, red and straw-colored, red and white. Now you've turned to face me, little mouth, big eyes, snub nose, top tight across your breasts. Size C, probably. A pity I can't see the color of your eyes.

The music falls silent for a second and I can hear the noise of the air conditioner vainly struggling to transform the sweltering Moscow air into a pitiful simulacrum of a sea breeze. The sea is too far away, the wind can't reach this far, maybe that's for the best, it means it can't carry the news to Lyubka on her Turkish beach about the way her husband is eyeing the twenty-year-old girls skipping about in a dark night club where the air conditioning can't handle the sweltering Moscow air.

"I'll go have a dance," says Mike, and I nod to him as if to say go on, maybe you'll pick someone up.

It would be good if you had a girlfriend. Mike likes tall thin blondes, Lyubka used to be one once, but after Sevka was born, first she plumped out, and then she stopped dyeing her hair, saying everyone thought blondes were fools and that interfered with her work. Bearing in mind that she's a lecturer in some college of the humanities it's hard to understand what it could interfere with. As if anyone could make a brilliant career there.

It's not easy for Mike to find a tall thin blonde, even in hot summer Moscow. Even on Friday evening. Tall thin blondes aren't very fond of men who are over thirty and weigh more than 220 pounds. On the dog park of the dance floor Mike looks like a bewildered bear. He suddenly turns out to be almost a head taller than everyone else, or maybe he's just bigger. He dances the way they once used to dance at college discos: waving his arms around, stamping up and down on the spot, jerking his head, which many years ago used to be surrounded by long, flailing hippie hair, but now it looks as if a bear has just climbed out of the water and is trying to shake itself dry. Drops of sweat go flying in all directions – I guess that's not very sexy either. The little hares, doggies and pussycats cringe out of the way, watching Bruin with a mixture of fear and mockery. The way the guy gets it on is a gas, but who the hell is he: what if he turns out to be a gangster and starts a shootout? I used to differentiate between gangsters and regular Moscow boys too. I used to think it was important.

The fox-terrier girl squeezes her way through toward the bar, but she can't get to it. She looks round, trying to find someone, I wave to her and point to an empty chair. Naturally, she comes over. "You're a great dancer," I say. The fox-terrier girl smiles with her little mouth and says "thank you." She has a high voice with just a bit of a whine to it, exactly the kind a little puppy ought to have. "What can I get you?" I ask.

You look at the menu, adjusting your two-tone bang. Your skin's just a little bit dusky, or maybe that's the lighting, but two glittering silver rings stand out on your ring finger and index finger. You choose a martini with juice. Now that you're really close I can take a good look at you: a yellow top soaked in sweat, big gray eyes, snub nose. I wonder what kind of noses fox terriers have and, by the way, what your name is. You say "Alice" and I smile in reply as if to say that's a beautiful, wonderful name. Without waiting to be asked, you start telling me about yourself.

When you speak, it's not important what it's about. What's important is your intonation, which words you put in what order, the way you wrinkle up your little nose, the way you pick up your glass of martini with your dusky fingers. I can see straight away that you're a good little girl, not some kind of little scrubber, just a good little girl who's used to obeying her elders. You're used to obeying, so when I say, an hour and a half and four martinis later, *Let's go to my place*, you won't object, you might just ask for my cell phone to call your mom, if you live with your mom. I can spot obedient girls anywhere in any crowd. Stop.

Mike comes back – alone, just as I thought he would. "Listen, you don't happen to have a blonde friend, the peroxide giraffe type? My friend's bored and he'd like to have a dance or even just have a drink with someone. Take no notice that he's such a big brute, in actual fact he's a regular Moscow boy." You half get up and start looking round the room for someone. Your dusky stomach shows under your short top, gathered in below the navel by the elastic of your red panties, which creep out half an inch above your tight pants, in the style of this summer.

Mike sits down on a chair, you introduce yourselves. Your hands lie beside each other: Mike's big hand with the signet ring and massive wedding ring, and your little hand with the cheap silver rings on the dusky fingers. So you work as a secretary and you call yourself a "receptionist," which sounds a lot better, of course, because you know what everybody thinks about secretaries. They're wrong to think that, by the way. I would guard a good secretary like the apple of my eye and protect her – not only from my colleagues and partners, but from myself. It's very hard to find a good secretary. In hot summer Moscow it's much easier to find a girl who's prepared to sit at your table and drink a martini – the third glass, by the way – and tell you all about her life.

Outside the heat has probably eased off, but in here the waves of swelter are still slopping about. When I was twenty and a bit it didn't bother me either although, to be quite honest, there weren't any clubs like this then. But you like it here, it would be unfair to drag you away so soon.

"Shall we have a dance?" I say.

"Okay."

Right then, silver shoes, yellow top, already dried out a bit, dusky stomach between the yellow top and red panty elastic, two-tone bang. Right then, a secretary. Immediately after school you tried to get into college, the economics department, and failed both times. But you're going to keep trying anyway. It's hard to find a secretary in Moscow who isn't going to try to get into college to study economics or law, well, good luck anyway. I used to think a good education was important too.

You live with your parents and your elder sister, who happened to get into the law department at college, at the third attempt, in fact, but she graduates next year. At your sister's age girls in my generation were already getting married and having children, but the new clubbing generation obviously isn't in such a hurry.

Stop.

It's as if someone is waking up inside, starting to toss and turn inside my chest; as if he's getting ready to break through my ribs and come shooting out. But I only came to the club to relax. Like any regular Moscow boy. But all evening a phrase, a glance, some minor detail has kept throwing me back into the danger zone, where there's nothing but stop, stop, stop. As if you're walking along an endless corridor, opening new doors all the time – and suddenly you fall through one of the doorways into hell. And until you open it, you don't know what's behind it, but when you do open it, it's too late and you can't even understand straight away what happened, what it was that Alice said.

Ah yes, she studied in the department of law at Moscow University. Like Alice's sister. I took the student ID out of her purse, big, short-sighted eyes, she couldn't see a thing without her glasses, I had to try to find her new ones, take the risk, for that week when... Stop, I tell you, stop.

But I can see you're a considerate girl, you ask: "Are you feeling okay?" No, little Alice, I'm feeling monstrously not okay, but in your place I wouldn't try to find out anymore about it.

"It's stuffy in this club of yours," I say, which happens to be true, by the way, and we go back to the table.

Right then, she's a little puppy dog. She'll be a puppy even in the old age that she still has to live to see. Her bang will be gray, her skin will dry out, but maybe she'll keep the way she walks and the way she laughs. How much more does anyone need, really?

An hour and three martinis later I make eyes at Mike to let him know it's time for us to move out, and Mike also gets up, with a sigh, and says he'll go and dance for a while, although it looks like it's obviously not his evening in this club tonight. Alice says in her shrill voice that she was glad to meet him and Mike gives a confidential nod in my direction and says: "You watch yourself with him, he's a real psycho."

Stop, fuck it, stop! I can feel myself starting to turn red. You could blow your cover like that, stop, tell yourself to stop, and smile like this, the way people smile at a tired old joke that has nothing to do with reality.

An air-conditioned island. Genuine coolness. Silk sheets, a bottle of champagne beside the bed. Little post-pubescent fox terriers are into stuff like that.

Modern female fashion keeps no secrets. You even know the color of the panties in advance, the only surprise in store for you is the angel tattooed on her left shoulder. "That's my guardian angel," Alice says, and starts kissing me, sucking my tongue into her little mouth. Pausing to catch her breath, she explains that she doesn't like fingers *down there*, she likes it with the tongue, her breasts shouldn't be squeezed too hard, but her nipples are a genuine erotic zone, and she can hardly ever come without having her clitoris fondled, so I shouldn't be offended if she helps herself out at some point.

The new clubbing generation. Girls who know their own bodies the way the girls of my generation knew the discography of Pink Floyd. Life is too short, why waste half the night on exploration? Better tell him up front, so he knows exactly what to do, because in hot summer Moscow it's so hard to find a man who understands you without words.

Night, but the heat's as bad as ever. You find the smell of your own sweat disgusting. The waves of sweltering heat pound against the window panes, maybe you should take a trip to the sea? Take the fox-terrier girl Alice with you, stay in some small hotel, screw in the evenings and in the afternoons lie on the beach, dripping with sweat, just like you are now, as if you hadn't taken a shower. Alice the fox-terrier girl obviously sweats a lot in general, that must be the way the way the glands are arranged under her dusky skin (stop), or maybe she always gives it everything she's got, no matter what she's doing.

There was a time when I really liked all these sexual acrobatics and I differentiated between my partners according to their flexibility and inventiveness. I used to think that was important. But just recently I find I prefer the banal missionary position. If all we're doing is having sex then, at the end of the day, that's pretty boring. Stop. Stop.

Right then, we've already been moving in perfect synchronization for a long time already, Alice's red and light-yellow braids of hair have become completely tangled together on the pillow. As always, I don't come for a long time, lots of women actually like that. Then Alice starts howling like a dog, and in response I start feeling cold. I ought to get up and turn the air conditioning down, but Alice clings on tight with all four paws, lying on her back with her big eyes closed and her little snub nose wrinkled up. Suddenly her entire body shudders, look at that, we managed it without stimulating the clitoris, we carry on.

I used to think it was very important for the girl to come at the same time as me. Then it was explained to me that a skillful partner could simulate orgasm so well that even she couldn't tell the difference. Yes, sex is an artificial thing, too, like the coolness in this bedroom. There's too much falsehood in it. Stop.

The obedient little girl Alice, the fox-terrier girl, a puppy to old age. She keeps going, she can't stop, although she's gasping for breath and she's soaking wet, so that any moment now she'll slip across the silk sheets straight onto the floor, onto the shaggy carpet, there now, I knew it. She doesn't even open her eyes, trembling all over.

The little girl Alice whimpers as she lies on the floor, a dusky little body on the light-colored carpet. She twitches spasmodically, especially if I wave my hand through the air. Like an electric shock. Stop. Like the shock of a sudden blow. Stop.

Where is she now? Because she's not in this body. Where has she gone? Stop. Stop.

This has happened to me a few times before. If the girl is

easily aroused, I can't come for a long time, and she remains in that state of arousal... well, in short, this is pretty much what it looks like. Quite an impressive sight, but today for some reason, I feel sad.

Alone in my own bedroom with a dusky body on a light background lying at my feet, trembling and whimpering. A little fox terrier on a rug.

Alone.

There are tears in my eyes.

I walk to the remote that I left by the door, push the buttons, walk into the kitchen, pull open the drawer of the kitchen table (stop), pour a glass of water and ponder for a moment, then down it in one and walk back into the room with a second glass. I pick Alice up in my arms, sit her on the bed and give her a sip. Again, again, that's a clever girl, well done, good girl.

I put my hand on her forehead. When I was little, my parents only ever touched my forehead to find out if I had a temperature. But I like simply to stroke. Stop. Simply to stroke.

"Shee-it," Alice says in a hoarse voice. "What was that?"

I shrug.

"It happens," I say, "you kept coming too long."

"Shit almighty," she says, "at one point I was looking down from the ceiling. How do you do stuff like that?"

"Well," I say, "Mike told you I was a psycho. I guess that's what he meant."

She's trembling all over, and I wrap her in a blanket, swaddle her up tight and sit her on my knee. Two-tone bang stuck to her forehead, snub nose. How I love her like this, tired, drained, exhausted. Little Alice puts her head on my shoulder and I feel that now she is like the daughter I don't have.

I don't have a daughter and I haven't seen my son for eight years.

I run my hand over the damp two-tone hair and there are tears in my eyes. I press myself tightly against Alice, and at that moment she sees the condom dangling limply off the end of my prick.

"What d'you mean, you *still* didn't *come*?"

I hastily roll the rubber off and reply guiltily:

"Oriental techniques, you know."

I told you: women think I'm a good lover because I can manage not to come for a long time. Stop. Stop. Stop.

Leaving in the morning, she left behind
Her little silver ring. On purpose probably
She left her number on the back of her company card
Red and light-yellow hair,
Dusky skin, big gray eyes
Feeble yelping in a cool bedroom
In the middle of hot summer Moscow

Three days later it hit me
Remembering her, suddenly I saw
All the things I could have done with her
She had elastic skin
I told myself I mustn't think about it
Nipples with large areolas
A little mouth the gag would have ripped and bloodied

I don't know myself why it hit me so hard
It doesn't often happen retrospectively
I guess it was the way she came that did it
An orgasm is called a little death
There were so many, I wanted to see the big one

I thought it would only be fair
She came so many times and all the evening
I just kept repeating "stop, stop, stop"
Now we could balance our accounts
I would ejaculate time after time
And she would tell me "stop!
Please stop and let me go!"
She probably couldn't come like that
Not even if I touched her clitoris.
(I like touching girls' clitorises too
Cigarette lighter, pliers, scalpel
And other quite surprising instruments)

I pictured how her face would look
When she realized what was happening
I would bring her to my dacha
Without any drugs or ropes,
She would walk downstairs of her own accord
And only in the basement would she realize

The little mouth would form a perfect circle
Opened in a helpless scream
The red and yellow hair
Would instantly be soaked in sweat, but cold this time.
Horror would make the big gray eyes grow even bigger
Then she would squeeze them shut and maybe cry

Although in general it was against my rules
When I picked Moscow girls up in the clubs
I never took them to the dacha
Like any regular Moscow boy
First of all, it was quite dangerous
In general I tried to separate the two halves of my life
Many serial killers do the same
William Heirens thought up a doppelganger for himself
His name was Mr. Murman, that is, Murder Man
I also have an alias for my second self
Or, perhaps, my first

When I picked Moscow girls up in the clubs
I never took them to the dacha
Like any regular Moscow boy
But dusky little Alice, the fox-terrier girl
Haunted my mind, and the little ring
In the bathroom kept catching my eye
I really ought to give it back – and I started wondering
Where I could have put the card with the cell number
And the name of the firm
Maybe my cleaning lady threw it out
An old, but energetic woman
Who comes to me on Wednesdays

Perhaps the air-conditioned breeze
Carried it off to the Mediterranean Sea
Where Lyubka and Sevka are on vacation

Or maybe the tattooed angel
Really can save
The secretary girl who calls herself
A receptionist

You were lucky, sweet Alice
Fox-terrier girl
And now, after all this time
I'm truly glad. A little death
Is quite enough for a little girl
Live to be old, eternal puppy,
Gray bang, dry skin, children, grandchildren. And
education
Since you think it's so important

Some day on vacation by the sea
A grown woman, running through your one-night
stands
The same way other people count sheep or elephants
Remember me, the sugar daddy from the club
The silk sheets and the cool conditioned air
The heat outside, the way suddenly you saw the room
From a bird's eye view

It's called out-of-body experience, dear Alice
There are other ways of inducing it apart from sex
I wanted so much to show you them, but it didn't
happen

Believe me, the silver ring you left behind
Is too small a price to pay for your good luck.

32

SHE LOOKS ABOUT ELEVEN OR TWELVE. AUTUMN-wear jacket, knitted woolly hat. She walks out of the subway station and he tags along behind her. There's no one else around and she starts running, she doesn't even shout, just keeps looking back over her shoulder to make sure: the man isn't falling back, even though he didn't seem to be running. She look about eleven or twelve, not dressed properly for the weather, she's got the shakes, she runs along the street, she looks back over her thin shoulder, the snow crunches under her feet like the glass of broken bottles, she's in a hurry to get home, but she doesn't recognize these places. Façades with no walls behind them, the gaping windows of gutted buildings filled with the black night air, the festive lights pulsating jerkily in time to her breathing. She looks back over her thin shoulder, the snow swirls behind her, she's not dressed properly for this weather, she's got the shakes, she doesn't recognize these places, she scrambles over piles of broken bricks, dashes through dark courtyards, runs, stumbles, falls and runs again. The frozen door handle at the entrance, the four digits of the entry code, the gaping mouth of the elevator, melt water splashing under her feet. She looks back, she has the shakes.

Ksenia is waiting on the landing, she hugs the thin shoulders, says: "Don't worry, everything's all right, you know, you see, you got away, you got here, come on, let's go, here's the key, here's the lock, you're a big girl now, there's nothing to be afraid of, come in, take off your jacket, you're frozen through, come through into the room, you see, I got some presents ready for you, look – here's a cat-o'-nine-tails, here's a pair of handcuffs, here's a riding crop, a leather paddle, a set of sewing needles, a splinter from a mirror, a kitchen knife, and don't you struggle to break free, for God's sake, you're a big girl now, you ought to understand everything yourself."

Her heart is pounding, her T-shirt is soaked with sweat. Ksenia lies there, swaddled up tightly in the blanket, gazing into the winter morning twilight, wide awake before the alarm clock has even rung. After a dream like that, climb out of bed, run to the shower without looking round on the way, don't look in the mirror, turn on the water, wash off the cold morning sweat, try to forget your dream. Ksenia understands only too well what it means.

The subconscious speaks to other people in parables, thinks Ksenia as she stands under the shower, but it always speaks in plain language to me. Last night my subconscious told me: *you're guilty.* I know that's the way it is: I'm guilty. I've felt my own guilt for as long as I can remember. For Lyova having to sit with me and not play outside. For Mom working to feed a family of four. For her not divorcing Dad because of me, and for not being able to stop them getting divorced. For not going to college. For putting my name on my site. For everyone in Moscow telling Mom: *I heard your Ksenia on the radio, she was saying something about sex maniacs.*

My God, thinks Ksenia, standing under the shower. How tired I am of being guilty. All my life I've tried to make everything all right. So it would be interesting for Lyova to play with me, so Mom could work less, so she could be proud of me. How much longer can it go on, thinks Ksenia, sinking down on to the bottom of the bath, how much longer. I can't do anything, I can't even help Olya, today she'll go abort her child. Vika told me once what it's like, but I don't want to remember that, I don't want to remember today's dream, I want to stay lying here, on the bottom of the bath. I want to go to Olya, but I can't go to her, because it's her body, her child, her choice, She wants to do it all as if it's just a minor routine operation, nothing out of the ordinary, I understand her. Dear, dear Olya, I would like to be there with you today, to hold your hand, to stroke your hair, to say: *don't worry, everything's all right, you know I love you.* I'd like to be your mom today, to take you by the hands, lead you out of the hospital ward, take you home, put you to bed, feed you raspberry tea and pretend it's just a sore throat. Dear Olya, I probably couldn't even lift you up, let alone carry you home, but you can feel it, can't you, feel me summoning all the strength I have left to send you my love across the frozen city this morning? Maybe at least it will make the anesthetic gentle and the awakening less frightening, if there's nothing else I can do for you anyway.

Ksenia is standing up to her knees in water. The pipe has got blocked, that's what it is, the water isn't draining away. Sink down into the chlorinated Moscow water, curl up into a ball in a primal ocean of cold morning sweat and uncried tears. But no, she gets out of the shower, wipes the wet mirror with her hand (damp, steamy and warm), looks at her own reflection. Her wet hair has stuck to her cheeks, without makeup her big eyes have a helpless expression. She walks out into the room, comes back with her vanity case and draws on her face: hard mouth, severe eyes. She takes a critical look to see if it's all right. She steps back a meter, takes a sharp breath in and throws her clenched fist out in front of her, *kata-what's-its-name*, the way Lyova showed her. She freezes like that – hair stuck to her neck, hard mouth, clenched teeth, every muscle tense, sinews vibrating, little fist in the foreground.

A sob behind her as the drain swallows the remains of the water in the bath, the night sweat, the uncried tears.

She's practically twice my age, thinks Ksenia in the overcrowded subway car, she thinks as she puts her leather purse on her knees, looking at a white feather stubbornly creeping out through the black material of someone's Chinese down-filled jacket only twenty centimeters away from her face. *Twice my age, but if you divide her age between two, for her and the baby that is still inside her, in the airless darkness, you get seventeen,* thinks Ksenia, as a wet sheepskin coat covered in damp blotches takes the place of the Chinese down-filled jacket, *when I was seventeen, Lyova was the same age as I am now, so today Olya is my younger sister.*

Yesterday Mom phoned, Mom asked how I was getting on, I told her about Olya – listen, my friend's having an abortion, I'm terribly upset for her. Don't be such a little girl, said Mom, I had about eight of those abortions and there was no problem.

Two girls are standing directly in front of Ksenia. Lulled into a doze by the swaying of the train, she doesn't raise her head, but she listens to their conversation: "No, shit, this city's just the bloody end in winter, creeps on every bloody side, no matter where you look, the subway's packed, the streets are all jammed solid, the boss has got her menopause and there's a psycho lurking in the alley." – "So what's your beef, Lex asked you, didn't he, you should have gone to Thailand, everything's cheap there – they told me, you know, like wow, it's a hundred bucks a month, fantastic." – "Nah, think about it, me and Lex in Thailand? Are you nuts? This guy, last winter he was there, told me the local tarts give it away for nothing, well, maybe a coupla dollars at the most. Sure, that's a gas for Lex, but what good's that to me?" – "That's just great, that's neat, you don't even have to let him have it, like just go to the pool, or to the shops, like... shit, that must all be cheap there too." – "Nah, think what you're saying... why would I go to Thailand just for that? I don't even let him have it here." "Oh shit, now here's our change, we almost missed it." And they get out, grazing the metal corner of a briefcase across Ksenia's knees.

She raises her head. Through the gap left in the crowd she can clearly see a sticker on the window opposite her: a child's face chopped to pieces and the words "thou shalt not kill."

33

"LISTEN," WRITES KSENIA, "I HAD A TERRIBLE DREAM today. I dreamed I was a psychotic killer, can you imagine?"

"And what did you do in this dream?" asks alien. "Did you kill someone?"

"☺ ☺," replies Ksenia, "I don't think I got that far. But it looked like I was going to. A little girl, about twelve years old."

"And how were you going to kill her?"

"I took out handcuffs, a cat-o'-nine-tails, this leather paddle, and all sorts of other stuff."

"That's quite a collection you got together in your dream. A real sadomasochists' sex shop."

"☺ ☺," replies Ksenia, "I've got quite a real collection too. I like all that stuff."

"And are you *top* or *bottom*?" asks alien, using the English words.

"I'm more *sub* than *dom*," replies Ksenia, surprised at how much he knows about these things, but the phone rings and the security guard downstairs says someone's here to see her.

It's strange to sit and drink coffee with a woman whose articles she used to read when she was still a little girl. She's nothing like Ksenia imagined her: tall, thin, not at all like a sex symbol, a face with almost no makeup, hair trimmed short, practically a buzz cut.

"Maya," she says, thrusting out a skinny hand. Her grip is firm. Almost like a man's.

She takes a dictaphone out of her purse, a large one with an external microphone, no match for the small digital device that Ksenia sometimes uses.

She's wearing tight-fitting leather trousers and the boots on her feet have no heels. Ksenia sneaks a glance at her thighs, wondering what it was that quivered in sweet anticipation almost ten years earlier. She asks her questions calmly, looking into Ksenia's eyes, nodding benevolently. Nothing out of the ordinary: "How did you get this idea?", "What do you think about this man?", "Are the security services taking any interest in you?", "Aren't you afraid of being accused of this, that and the other?", "What will you do with the project when they catch the psycho?" She replies almost without thinking, it's all been said a hundred times before: "My colleague Alexei Rokotov took an interview, and we decided that… Of course, he's a sick man, he has to be caught as soon as possible. Yes, we cooperate with the police, they're happy to keep in touch. No, I'm not afraid of anything. I don't know, I haven't thought about it yet. Twenty minutes, is that it already?"

"Maybe we could have a coffee, Maya, if you're not in a hurry?"

"Yes, an excellent idea. I expect you're already tired of all these questions?"

"No, no, I've asked the same kind a hundred times myself. We're colleagues, after a fashion."

Maya takes a metal flask out of a scuffed leather rucksack.

"Cognac. Like to warm up a bit? But then, you still have to work."

Maya pours a shot for herself and just a little bit for Ksenia.

"You know, I used to read a lot of your articles once. In *AIDS-Info*, *Megalopolis-Express* and then somewhere else."

"Oh, back in the glorious nineties!" Maya takes out a cigarette and starts puffing on it. "It was a turn-on back then to write for the tabloids. I guess you can't understand, but for us in the Soviet Union, the tabloids, *Cosmo*, *Newsweek* – they were all the same impossible dream. It was really interesting to do all that. We thought our generation was lucky, we were going to create the new Russian journalism. Lay the foundation for democracy and freedom of expression. And now what's happened – some have gone into politics, some into TV, some are stars, and here I am – the old she-wolf of the yellow press. I won't even mention democracy and freedom of expression, you can see all that for yourself."

"But even so," says Ksenia, "you really did do something wonderful. My entire generation grew up on *AIDS-Info*. We used to steal it from our parents and read it. The fact that all my contemporaries are, I don't know, more sexually liberated, I suppose – that's your achievement."

"A rather dubious achievement, Ksenia, to be quite honest. Last week I saw one of my old school friends, her husband has left her for a twenty-year-old girl. Says he's found sexual happiness and harmony with her for the first time. So I was responsible for playing that dirty trick on my school friend."

"You know, Maya," says Ksenia, "I'd like to tell you my story, off the record. If you have five minutes. Just so you understand how much you mean to me."

"Go ahead," says Maya, "and I'll have a bit more cognac, if you don't mind."

As Ksenia tells her story she studies the other woman's face. Wrinkles round the eyes, dry skin, teeth stained yellow by nicotine. I wonder, she thinks, what this woman was like when she was young? Did she really have all those men she wrote about? Somehow I imagined her with big breasts – something about men liking to put their pricks between them – but now she looks as flat as an ironing board.

"Ye-es," Maya drawls, puffing out smoke sharply, "so do you still play 'You go to The Club,' and all the rest?"

"No, no," says Ksenia, "somehow I can't bring myself to go to the club. And it's not because I'm shy, or, you know, still in the closet... you can see, I've told you everything quite calmly and, believe me, you're not the first. It's just that it's very important to me that the man that, well, that I go to bed with, interests me in some way, that he makes me respect him, I suppose. It's stupid to go anywhere with the goal of finding a man just like that. And

I really don't want just anyone to beat me or, I don't know, pour candle wax on me, that's not a good idea. I can lash out if I don't like something" – and Ksenia smiles.

"Well, I don't really have much experience in this area," says Maya. "There was that one, my demon, then we split up, and for about six months I used to go to all sorts of dungeons and different games, I even tried it abroad once, in New York, and then I met a man who I guess was one of the best lovers in my life. You know, the kind of man who can guess absolutely every one of your desires. You know, like in that song by Cohen: 'If you want a lover / I'll do anything you ask me to / And if you want another kind of love / I'll wear a mask for you.' Well, I wanted him to be a cruel master, and he thought up things for me, that I don't think I really want to tell you about now. Anyway, I'm still thankful to him, but it all finished rather sadly."

"How?" asks Ksenia, and thinks that now she's the one taking the interview, as usual, the way things always are.

"You see, he was a wonderful lover, but I didn't love him at all. That is, I really liked him, and I still really like him, but I didn't love him. It's hard to explain, you know, you love a man as a friend, he's wonderful in bed, but you don't love him as a man. I wouldn't have understood it at your age, but maybe your generation really is different."

"Well, in general terms I can understand it," says Ksenia. "It sounds to me like an excellent basis for a marriage."

"Yes, we would have had a chance, but unfortunately he fell in love with me. Quite seriously. It's a rather strange story, really – the cruel master falls in love with his submissive slave and... and, basically, nothing. Because if he started giving me flowers and presents, then our relationship would immediately cease to exist. So all he could do was keep on thinking up various different new tortures for me. As presents, you might say. And as I said, he was a wonderful lover, with a good imagination, and so the moment came when he satisfied me completely. My masochistic side, that is. I didn't exactly wake up one morning and realize I didn't want to be flogged or hung from the ceiling any longer – I had a special hook, we took down the ceiling lamp and put in little spotlights to leave the hook free, it used to frighten my vanilla visitors a bit – well anyway, not all at once, but gradually I moved farther and farther away from BDSM, and now I'm a perfectly normal woman."

"You're frightening me," says Ksenia. "I'm terrified to think that one fine day I might lose the taste for playing. It helps with depression too."

"What helps with depression," Maya sighs, "is psychotherapy, or pills, if you need them. I've been through that too – so I can give you a phone number if you need one."

"Thanks," Ksenia replies, "but so far I'm managing. Maybe you could give me your friend's number instead? What happened to him, by the way?"

"He's still my friend, but I haven't slept with him for a long time. I tried once, after about three months – he was tender, considerate, technically adequate and wonderful in every way, but let me tell you, Ksenia, it's really horrible sleeping with a man's who's in love with you when you don't love him! And three months after that I got married, and my sexual adventures came to an end."

"Are you still married?"

"Yes, I am. I have two children now and I'm perfectly happy. I'll tell you something, although you won't believe me. This experiment, you know, playing, of course, it's tremendously exciting and all the rest of it, but you have to get past that. So you can live a normal life and be happy."

"I'm perfectly happy," says Ksenia. "I'm perfectly happy, insofar as it's possible to be happy in this world. And you know what, Maya, if you were interviewing me right now, I'd say: I made this site to prove that to myself. That the psycho is also part of the world, an integral part of the world. And the awareness that in this world there is suffering beyond all endurance, the kind these girls went through, and their parents go through, and all of us when we read about it, well, the awareness that that kind of suffering is inevitable can't stop me being happy. The pain I experience during sex brings me pleasure because that way my sex becomes a model of the world, do you understand, Maya? It's the only time I know I'm being honest with myself and I can allow myself to be happy. Because it's not hard being happy in a vanilla world – all you have to do is forget about what you read in the newspapers. Not just forget about the psycho – forget about the war in Chechnya, about the ecological disasters, about poverty, destitution and famine. But that's a dishonest happiness, Maya, and I won't accept it."

Maya says nothing, releasing cigarette smoke through her reddened nostrils, then she finishes the rest of her cognac straight from the flask and says:

"This is a strange sort of conversation we've had, Ksenia. It's a pity I turned off the dictaphone. But I can tell you that even your happiness is a dishonest happiness, because you pretend that a few lashes from a whip or jabs from a cigarette – I don't know what you prefer – can serve as a model for the pain and suffering that other people experience. But that's dishonest, Ksenia, because other people die from torture, and all you do is come. Because if you tell a mother who has lost her daughter: 'I understand your pain, I was flogged by my lover last night too' – she'll spit in your face and, I'm sorry, but she'll be right. If your idea is taken to its logical conclusion, in order to remain honest in your pleasure, in the end you have to die under torture. But I'd still recommend therapy."

"Thank you," Ksenia says rather coldly and pauses for a moment. "In any case, if not for you, I would probably have killed myself eight years ago."

"I'm sorry," says Maya, shaking the last cigarette out of the pack, "I have no right to pry into your life, you're right. But I'll tell you anyway, well, just so that you know. There are other ways to stay happy and honest. You understand, we live in a world where there is a war going on every day. It's the war between life and death. And suffering is on the side of death, and happiness is on the side of life. Pleasure is located at the point where they meet, but that doesn't mean we should play on both sides. Look at me. I'm forty-five years old, I had breast cancer, I lost thirty-five pounds on chemotherapy, and then they took off both my breasts anyway. My death lived inside me for a very long time, maybe it's still alive in there even now. But my two little babies, Max and Ilya, were there inside me once too, and they'll live in this world when I die. And so, by playing on the side of life, I've won. I won't have anymore children, but every time I make love with my husband, it's as if we're repeating those two times. And every act of love we perform contains the whole future life of our children until they die – including the pain and the suffering. You know, Ksenia, we make children – and absolutely nothing else is needed for us to regard every sexual act we perform as a miniature model of the universe and to come without any pangs of conscience and without any help from a whip or an electric shock baton."

Maya reaches into her rucksack, takes out a Kleenex tissue, wipes her eyes and gets up. Ksenia feels a little awkward, successful women shouldn't cry, although, of course, she understands everything. She catches up with Maya at the door of the cafeteria.

"I'm sorry," she says, "I don't know what to say to you, you know, I just wanted... anyway, thank you for talking to me today, thank you for everything that you said."

Maya puts her skinny hand on Ksenia's frail shoulder.

"Everything's all right," she says, "I'll send you the interview to read. And the therapist's number, just in case."

Ksenia watches her go and tries to imagine herself in many years' time as a famous journalist to whom a young woman says: "Oh, I grew up on your articles. Me and my friends in fifth grade watched your site about the psycho, really great!" – and then her imagination stalls, because even in this imaginary future, there's no way she can picture herself as a grown woman with a husband and two children.

34

"VERY GOOD," SAYS THE ANSWER FLASHING ON THE flat screen. What's good? wonders Ksenia, trying to remember, ah yes, "more sub than dom."

"Sorry, I went away for a while," she writes, and a minute later alien replies: "I was afraid I'd offended you somehow", she taps out her reply: "No, no, I'm not easily offended. It's just that I'm at work."

He already knows that she's a journalist, that she works with the news, that she has a friend Olya, who is having an abortion today, and a friend Marina, who stays at home with her little boy. He knows that this morning in the subway Ksenia saw a child's face chopped to pieces and thought about Olya. Now he knows that Ksenia is into playing, but even so he doesn't know that she has a lover and that she's the producer and senior editor of the scandalous site Moscow Psycho.

Ksenia knows that he has his own business, that he's not married, or rather, he's divorced, she knows that he lives in Moscow and in his free time he watches his favourite DVDs in his home movie theater, that he doesn't like *The Matrix* but he likes the films of Dario Argento, the Italian director who always filmed his own hands when he needed to show the hands of a killer. Now she knows he understands what BDSM is. And she still doesn't know his name or how old he is.

They chat every day, several times in the course of the day. This is probably the first time in Ksenia's life that a chance encounter in the internet has lasted for so long. Alien really is good company. He's interesting to talk to.

"How did you choose me?" Ksenia asks.

"I liked your name," alien replies. "It means the same as mine does."

"We can think of ourselves as brother and sister ☺."

"Then I'll be your big brother," he replies, "do you have a big brother?"

"Yes, but he's in America."

"Were you friends when you were children?"

"There was a difference of six years. I was too little for him ☺. He pushed me around."

"Did he hit you?"

"Sometimes."

"Well then," replies alien, "clearly, as your virtual big brother, I shall have to beat you virtually too."

"☺ ☺," Ksenia replies guardedly and waits to see what will come next.

"Don't worry, I'm not going to beat you today," writes alien, "but I shall demand that you obey me. Like a good little sister."

"And what do I have to do for you, big brother?" asks Ksenia, joining in the game and looking anxiously at the clock in the bottom corner of her monitor: it's almost midday, and the work isn't getting done.

"Dial 0804 on your cell phone and write to me what they tell you."

Ksenia obediently picks up her phone. A pleasant woman's voice offers to tell her about the weather. Ksenia types that.

"Well done, little sister," alien replies, "now go and work."

Ksenia smiles. She likes the way this man always knows when it's time to stop.

Two days later she's sitting on Marina's white rug again. Gleb is standing up, laughing, holding on to the bar stool on which the computer used to stand. Now there is a big plush rabbit sitting on the bar stool, a distant relative of the one that Ksenia sleeps with. Marina is still wearing the same robe with a dragon on it, they're eating Chinese fast food out of small bowls with chopsticks, it was bought from the Huáng-Hé River kiosk and heated up in the microwave.

"They say the Chinese food in China is completely different from anywhere else in the world," Marina says through her sweet and sour pork, with her cheeks bulging out and looking funny.

"They eat snakes and dogs," says Ksenia, "and grasshoppers, rats and absolutely anything that moves."

"Now I understand," Marina replies, "why that Chinese chose me. Back then I was interested in anything that moved too, although from a slightly different angle. And now there's only one member of the opposite sex I'm interested in. Gleb, want yum-yum?" – and she takes a piece of pork out of her mouth.

"Is that all right – straight out of your mouth?" asks Ksenia.

"I think so," Marina replies, "after all, it's my mouth, not yours. Go figure, kisses are all right, but a piece of meat, like, isn't? Especially from his own mother. That's the only way vixens bring food back: they eat something, then regurgitate it for the cubs, half-digested, so it's easier for them. It doesn't bother them any."

"Yuck," says Ksenia, "I hope my mom never did that."

"Your mom," says Marina, putting the pork that Gleb didn't eat back in her own mouth, "never did love you very much."

"How do you mean?" asks Ksenia, almost choking.

"You figure it out. You liked the dance studio – she stopped you going."

"Oh no, she wanted me to do better at school."

"Sure, sure." Marina gets up and puts her bowl and chopsticks on the windowsill, out of Gleb's reach. "It was your dad who liked the way you danced, and she divorced him. And you were the one who suffered for it."

"How do you make that out?" Ksenia asks testily.

"Why, everybody knew," Marina says with a shrug. "The dance studio's just a detail, of course. You can always see if a mother loves a child or not."

"I don't think that story has anything to do with love. On the contrary, the fact that Mom made me study is the best possible proof that she did love me."

"Poor Gleb," says Marina, "how is he going to know I love

him if I don't give him proofs like that? Well now, come to Momma, my darling little fox cub," and Marina crawls across the room on all fours toward Gleb. The infant is sitting in the middle of the rug and laughing.

"Marina," Ksenia begins in an icy voice, "you know, I've never taken the liberty..."

"All right, all right, I'm sorry," Marina says quickly. "I've been acting a bit dumb just recently." She picks Gleb up and goes back to her friend. "Don't get uptight, I really shouldn't have said that. Of course your mom loved you, who could ever doubt it?"

"All right, drop it," Ksenia says dourly. "Why don't you tell me if you've ever had any virtual affairs."

"How do you mean? Cybersex? In a special suit?"

"No, without any suit. You know, when you chat to a man you don't know on ICQ, and suddenly you realize you're thinking about him all the time, fantasizing... and so on."

"No, not with anyone I didn't know at all," says Marina, "but, you know, there was this one young guy from the East Coast. I saw him once at Vika's farewell party, if you remember, a tall guy in glasses, with beautifully shaped ears?"

"No," says Ksenia, "Vika and I happened to have a falling-out a week before she went away."

"Ah, sorry," says Marina, remembering. "Well, anyway, I danced with him and this and that, I was all set to go, but he was obviously feeling nervous, especially since I think there was some girlfriend or other of his there. And he was going away too, a week after Vika, he was in the same group. The farewell party was for both of them. Well anyway, Vika was going to Germany to marry a German, and Mishka was going to graduate school at MIT. Go figure, all we did was exchange emails, and I'd forgotten all about him, then suddenly a few a months later he pops up – hi, here I am, remember me?"

"And then what?"

"Well, one thing led to another, and he turned out to be a genuine sex addict. You know, absolutely great. He could go on about it for hours, like those novels in the pink covers. My powerful hands embrace your trembling body... well, and so on. I laughed at first, then I started getting turned on. Once I answered him something like 'my weak hands grab your trembling prick' – and then the floodgates opened. Go figure, it's their night, he's sitting there on his campus, everyone's asleep, and he's writing to me about how he undresses me tenderly, licks me passionately and screws me savagely. But go figure, there I am sitting in the studio like a fool, trying to work, with my hands literally shaking. I can't jack off at my desk, in front of everyone. I had to say, I tell you what darling, slow down. Why don't you get back in touch when it's our morning? And then, go figure, I set the alarm clock for eight, and go straight to the computer. And there he is already, all set for action. I use one hand on the keyboard and the other to work myself off – Gleb, don't you listen to this, by the way, you're still too young – well, after ten minutes, that was it! I don't know what he was doing all the time, probably the same thing. Well, I send him a tender kiss, hop in the shower, have breakfast, this and that – and by twelve I'm at work, fresh and relaxed after the morning."

"And where did it all lead?"

"Nowhere really, you know. He came to Moscow for the winter vacations. I met him in some café the very first evening, we talked, had a coffee, and I see – there's no way, he doesn't do a thing for me. Well, I'm not a little girl anymore, I have to finish what I've started: we caught a taxi, went to my place, got undressed, lay down and screwed. You know, all pretty average. A definite C plus. To be quite honest, I was expecting more. I could have been 'Like a Virgin' with him. He knew where to stroke, where to kiss, well you know. Well anyway, in the morning I wake up as usual when the alarm clock goes off – and go straight to the computer. And, of course, as you realize, there's nothing in the computer, because my virtual lover has devirtualized himself and he's sleeping just two yards away from me. What I really wanted to do was shake him awake and send him out to the nearest internet café. So, in short, that was how it all ended: while he was in Moscow I got out of the habit of getting up early. Now we meet occasionally on the internet and send each other greetings on public holidays.

9.38 alien	Are you there already?
9.38 Ksenia	Yes.
9.39 alien	Is there anyone else in the room?
9.39 Ksenia	No.
9.39 alien	Have you got any pencils on your desk?
9.40 Ksenia	Yes.
9.40 alien	Take the sharpest one, take out your breast and stick it into the nipple. But not very hard.
9.40 Ksenia	Hey, this isn't a very brotherly game!
9.41 alien	It's called a mammogram, little sister. So you won't get breast cancer. Do as I tell you, but don't make it bleed, or you'll stain your underwear.
9.42 Ksenia	All right. The left breast or the right?
9.42 alien	The left.

Pull up the sweater, pull down the cup of the bra, take out the breast, jab the pencil into the nipple that is already hard, then again, and again. How does he know, how can he feel what I need? A wave of warmth runs right through my body. Once again, just a little harder.

9.45 alien	Hey, I said once.
9.45 Ksenia	Sorry, I got carried away. You can punish me if you like.
9.46 alien	Don't get skittish. I don't need to punish you. You have to obey me anyway, I'm your big brother.
9.47 Ksenia	Yes, I'll obey you ☺
9.47 alien	Good. Put your breast away, put the pencil back where it belongs.
9.47 Ksenia	I never thought pencils had so much potential.
9.48 alien	There is no object that cannot serve as a source of pain
9.48 Ksenia	And pleasure.
9.48 alien	I'm not interested in your pleasure. Tell me what happened to you today in the subway.
9.48 Ksenia	Nothing interesting happened. Ah but yes, there was something. Two girls overtook me in the passage, one said to the other: "We'll be all right," and the

	other one said, just as seriously: "I hope we'll be all right." I remembered that for some reason.
9.49 alien	Maybe they were talking about a test or an exam.
9.49 Ksenia	Yes, or about some kind of reorganization. But I imagined they were talking about the psycho.
9.49 alien	It's not very likely. I've noticed that when girls talk about psychos they speak in a skittish, affected, jolly kind of way. I've never heard anyone talk about psychos seriously.
9.50 Ksenia	You haven't heard me.
9.50 alien	I hear you every day.
9.50 Ksenia	But there's no intonation here.
9.51 alien	I can guess it. But you're right. You're a serious girl. By the way, tell me something funny that has happened to you in the last few days.
9.52 Ksenia	Funny?
9.53 Ksenia	Well, yesterday I was at Marina's place, and she was playing vixen and cub with her son. Chewing up food and feeding him mouth-to-mouth. I don't know if that's funny, but at least it's strange.
9.54 alien	Is that the Marina who's turning herself into a Chinese woman?
9.54 Ksenia	Yes
9.55 alien	Tell her not to get carried away with the fox business. In China they think foxes are like werewolves. She doesn't want to turn into a Chinese werefox instead of a Chinese woman, does she?
9.55 Ksenia	☺ ☺ Wow! I'll tell her that.
9.56 alien	A great story. Now go and work.

35

You think it's easy – being a man like me?
You watched too many fashionable nineties movies,
I guess
Natural Born Killers and *Curdled*
And heaps of other B- and even Z-movies
For eight dollars they tell you
That being a serial killer is cool

Famous killers of the nineteen fifties
Charlie Starkweather and Caril Fugate
Were the models
For Mickey and Malory in *Natural Born Killers*
Charlie said when he was caught that he had no
regrets
That he still hated everybody
This is easy to believe:
He made love
To fourteen-year-old Caril on the sofa
Where he raped her mother an hour earlier
With the father's body lying in room
And when they were done
He went upstairs and put the barrel of his gun
To two-year-old Betty Jane's throat and –
No, he didn't fire – he waited
Until the little girl choked to death

He was real scum,
Theories of childhood trauma
Work perfectly in his case
But even after he said: "I still hate everybody,"
He still added: "and myself too"
Although, as you can guess
Introspection was never his strong point

Living is very hard when you hate yourself
And I had a happy childhood
I was a good little boy
From a decent Moscow family
I was afraid to watch the news, because
They talked about things too frightening for me
When I heard about the stadium in Santiago de Chile
Where they tortured and killed thousands of people in 1973
I was shattered for two weeks
I looked into people's faces passing by,
Trying to understand how they could carry on living
If they knew about this thing too

I still don't understand, to be quite honest.

Dostoyevsky said the harmony of the world
Is not worth a single tear shed by a tormented child
But a world in which there is no harmony
Is not worth anything at all
And this is the world I have lived in all my life

I have never believed in God,
Perhaps because I sensed
That Christ was not alone in dying for our sins
But every drop of blood, every groan of hunger
Every raped woman's scream
(once every fifteen minutes, remember that?),
Well, that all of this concerns each one of us

Chikatilo's wife also said
Her husband fainted at the sight of blood
How well I understand him.

I was a good little boy, you hear?
I was kind, and I still am kind
I love people, my pity for them brings a lump to my
throat
And when I squeeze a newly cut-out heart in my hand
My own heart contracts too, in tenderness and pain

A lump in my throat

How can a man like this live, when I know
The blood has eaten into my hands like coal into a
miner's hands
How can I live when my memory
Is like a torture chamber
In which every object –
Even the most innocent –
Can only inflict pain?

Once I woke up in the night
In my Moscow apartment
And suddenly realized none of them had existed
Not that teenager, the one with plump lips
That were torn to shreds when she screamed
Not that one whose eyes were burned out by the
magnifying glass,
Eyes so blue they looked like shards of broken sky
Not that one with the breasts so large
That I cut them off in thin slices for several days
Nor all the many others I recall so well

I realized none of them had existed
A wet and bloody dream
A masturbation fantasy, to make me come quicker
A murderous one-man play

I lay in bed, weeping tears of happiness
Repeating like an incantation:
"I haven't killed anyone"

Still weeping, I went to the kitchen
Objects lay on the table, no longer reminders of
torture and torment,
The fork on which I never wound the entrails from the
slashed abdomen
Of a living seventeen-year-old girl
Who screamed so loud, I was afraid
The insulation of the basement would not save us
The knife with which I never carved words of
tenderness and love
On the yellowish skin of a thin Kazakh girl
Whose breasts were so small, they both fitted in one hand
The cigarettes that I never stubbed out on the flat
stomach
Of a professional swimmer, tracing out the
constellation of the Great Bear
(I'm still embarrassed by that incident:
Stubbing out cigarettes on women is terribly vulgar,
Something only young street punks would do)

I stood and wept, repeating:
"I haven't killed anyone"
And my heart was filled with gratitude
If it is a dream, then I have been given one more chance,
Perhaps I will understand how to live differently in
this world

The sun came up and I carried on weeping
And promised myself that this would never happen again
I went to the dacha and collected all the souvenirs that
I had kept
The cut-off nipples, cut-out lips, eyes, even fingers
Took it all into the forest, buried it as deep as I could,
And then tried to forget that place

* * *

And then I carried on living, taking no notice of the black cocoon, of the objects that seemed to wink at me and ask "remember?", of the girls in the subway, in whose eyes I read a premonition of pain that would never be realized. I like to ride the subway, although I've had a car for a long time now. Under the ground electric light falls on people's skin quite differently, the subway is just another concrete basement. That's why the fates of all the passengers can be read so easily on their faces.

One day I was on my way to a birthday party, about six months after that night. At the change for the Circle Line a girl got in, wearing cheap trainers completely soaked through and wide trousers with numerous pockets and for some reason a raincoat, with water streaming off it. Her long, light-colored hair was sticking to her cheeks and neck, she unbuttoned the raincoat and took it off. She was probably a little older than twenty, and when she bent down to put the raincoat into a plastic bag, I saw the wet hair lying on her back like sleeping snakes. Light-colored hair, slightly wavy, damp from the rain.

She straightened up and saw that now her soaking-wet T-shirt was clinging tightly to her small but slightly drooping breasts. She raised her eyebrows and laughed – and at that laugh the train slowed down and people froze as if they had been caught in the gaze of the Medusa. It was the laughter, not the breasts, the laughter, the laughter, although even now I still remember that one nipple was right in the round eye of the letter R, a light-colored T-shirt, red letters. I bit my lips, squeezed my eyes tight shut – and before time was switched back on, I visualized every detail of the concrete basement, with a body crucified in the air. I knew her pubis was not shaved, she had a little gold ring in her navel, a rose tattooed on her buttock, and the light-colored downy fluff on her legs was so tender that I couldn't touch it without tears springing to my eyes. I knew in advance that she would die on the fifth day, her heart would give out.

I opened my eyes and the sound of her laughter was still in the air. I walked to the farthest door of the car and for the rest of the journey I felt as if I was limping and her severed head was attached to my leg with an invisible chain, like a convict's ball. Laughter on her lips, but her light-colored hair was like Medusa's snakes.

I got out at the next stop, walked up to the street and took a taxi. I felt as if all the objects were looking at me, the hairs on my body were standing up on end, I couldn't tell the noise of the cars from the noise of the blood in my ears. In the corridor a friend shook my hand: I twitched as if I'd got an electric shock. I took off my jacket and went into the room. The party was in full flow, lots of people I knew well, a couple of friends and a few girls I'd slept with some time or other. I drank with everyone else, joked and laughed. Then at a certain moment I got up, went to the kitchen, opened a drawer and took out a small knife from IKEA. Without even looking round to check if anyone could see me, I jabbed the knife straight through my jeans into my right thigh. The blood ran down my leg, but the flash of pain sobered me. The noise in my ears faded away, objects returned to their places, my skin recovered its usually sensitivity. I took a Band-Aid out of the first-aid kit, went to the restroom and covered the wound.

In the next month I killed three times.

36

DO EMPIRES REALLY COLLAPSE BECAUSE OF WOMEN? IS the shape of Cleopatra's nose really all that important? Was Anne of Austria the Duke of Buckingham's mistress and if so, how did that affect the siege of La Rochelle? How many men had Olga Krushevnitskaya had, and how many of them had been prepared to sacrifice anything at all for her? What was the most beautiful woman of the classical world called? What was the name of the greatest beauty of the graduating class of 1985 in the Faculty of Experimental and Theoretical Physics?

Olga gets out of her Toyota, nods to the security guard, takes the elevator up to the rented office. Five minutes till the start of the meeting. Sixty-five minutes to the moment when everything will be decided. If there is anyone who can pray for me, thinks Olga, let them do it now. Vlad, my brother, light a candle to Ganesha, burn some incense to your Buddha, or as a last resort simply smoke a few grains of hash to my success. Ksyusha, wish me luck.

They meet at the door of the elevator on the first floor. They ride upward without saying a word. They hesitate for a second before going in: the door is too narrow for two people. Grigorii gives way, Konstantin goes in and they sit down.

It's not possible to seat three people at a round table so that any two of them are not next to each other. They would have been glad to sit facing each other, but they end up sitting almost shoulder to shoulder – more like teammates than rivals – with their elbows touching, as if they are sitting at the front desk, at a seminar on quantum electronics or plasma physics.

She was called Helen, la Belle Hélène. Troy was destroyed because of her – and twenty-two years ago her namesake put an end to the friendship between Grigorii and Konstantin forever. Olga knows about this, and if she loses everything today, that means the shape of Cleopatra's nose is more important than conscious calculation, beauty is more powerful than will, old grudges are more important than reason.

Olga starts unhurriedly, approaching the subject gradually, as if they are having an ordinary business meeting. She shows them tables, moving the diagrams closer first to one of them, then to the other. She puts them in the middle of the table – and two heads are lowered over the quarterly balance.

"What's this, the statements for the tax office?" asks Kostya.

"Unfortunately not," replies Olga. "That's what we really have."

"Fucking awful," says Grisha and moves back from the table: he's seen everything and he doesn't want to sit beside Kostya anymore.

If this were a game of chess, thinks Olga, we'd have to play according to some weird set of rules. We have to reconcile the two kings, and all we have are the phantoms of pieces that were taken long ago and the shadows of pieces not yet introduced into the game. The board is practically empty: there are only three pieces on it.

How many tablets to take to begin with and how many later? How soon will the bleeding start? How painful will it be? La Belle Hélène didn't have to answer these questions – the method of drug-induced abortion was not widespread four thousand or even twenty years ago.

Olga carries on talking. She talks about why expenditure has increased, says that in a few months they can just close the business down. She realizes both the others know this just as well as she does – but she talks at a relaxed pace, as if she is trying to lull them to sleep. They're probably thinking: what a clueless bint. She's just wasting our time here. We should have told her to fuck off straight away. Now I have to sit next to this lousy creep.

They sat side by side the whole semester. Elbow to elbow, head beside head. For the whole semester they stuck to their guns and fought determinedly to win la Belle Hélène. They wrote her class notes for her and did her laboratory work. They brought her flowers and plied her with cheap sweet wine. La Belle Hélène smiled graciously and didn't grant her favors to either of them.

How many men were there in her life afterward? How many of them did she really love? Did she ever really love anyone? If she did, then that fortunate man wasn't Grisha or Kostya. By the end of the year they'd realized that themselves.

Here are the answers to the questions that Olga asked the doctor: first two, then three. It won't be any more painful than an ordinary period. Bleeding within twenty-four hours.

Her body works like a chronometer. Twenty-five hours have gone by and nothing's happening. Olga looks at Kostya and Grisha, at Konstantin and Grigorii, at the two kings, the two student boys.

"What are we going to do?" she asks. "I want to ask you as the major investors: do you have a comprehensive development plan? What can you suggest to cut costs?"

She knows the answer: they have to go back to the old system, make the old discounts available on banner ads in Grisha's holding company, make support available from Kostya's resources. She knows the answer and she knows they both know it.

Neither of them says anything, and then Olga launches her gambit with a cautious, almost meaningless move. It is no more than a vague threat, a feeler.

"For instance, we can sell the company. If we do it now, at least we'll get something."

She reads disappointment in their faces. Is that it? Is that what we were brought here for?

"Garbage," says Grisha, "nobody will buy it."

"No," Kostya says, nodding, "there aren't any players in our market who can support it properly. You can see for yourself what the costs are. Nobody will be interested."

Yes, it's not nice having to agree with each other, but Olga's suggestion is so absurd, there's nothing else they can do.

"Well, we can look for someone from the outside," says Olga.

Who was the newcomer from the outside twenty-two years ago? How did he enchant la Belle Hélène? Why did she get married in such a rush that her two suitors didn't even have the time to make peace with each other in the face of their common defeat?

Olga doesn't know his name. Everyone she has spoken to about this story has simply called him the "embassy boy" as if he had no individual features, only generic ones. Two weeks after the wedding the young couple flew off to join his parents in Paris – which, to Olga's philological turn of mind, gave the story yet another point of contact with the story of Beautiful Helen and Paris, the prince of Troy.

Unlike Menelaus, Grigorii and Konstantin were not able to pursue the fugitive. She and her abductor were securely shielded by the iron curtain – a far stronger protective screen than the one created by Aphrodite when she helped Paris and Helen flee from Sparta.

They were young and ambitious. Each of them saw the other as a witness of his own miserable failure. Their friendship ended, giving way to rivalry: the university faculty become too cramped for them, it was followed by trading in computers, and now the small industry of the Russian internet.

"I don't think anyone from the outside will be interested," Kostya says uncertainly.

"But if some wanker does turn up, we'll sell him the company, why not?" says Grisha.

And then Olga introduces a new piece into the game, a piece for which there is no term in traditional chess. An Outsider, a King from a different board.

"I have a buyer," she says.

"And what's his price?" asks Kostya.

"Does he want to buy our shares or the entire company?" asks Grisha.

"He only wants to buy one of your shares," says Olga, "and my share to go with it."

Is it possible to hold on to a company in which you don't hold a controlling block of shares? Is it possible to earn profit from it if you simply put in money but don't sit in the office every day as Olga Krushevnitskaya does? Do Olga's block of shares and the block of either of the other shareholders add up to a controlling interest?

Answers: no, no, yes.

"You mean he only wants to take a controlling interest?" says Kostya.

"And he wants to throw one of us out of the business," says Grisha.

"Yes," says Olga, nodding, "that seems logical to me. You don't want to work together any longer."

The two kings hesitate, the phantom of la Belle Hélène appears at the far side of the board.

"Please understand," Olga continues, "I am only doing this because I want to save the company one way or another. I don't want it to go under for no good reason."

Perhaps in chess that would have been called "stalemate". Neither side has a move that they can make. If one of them gets up and says "I'll sell my stake," the other will immediately name a lower price.

In this situation can you toss a coin? Or should you trust a random numbers generator? Perhaps it would be better to go away now and conduct a round of backstage negotiations? How obvious is their outcome?

Yes, it is obvious. The buyer, whoever he might be, has the opportunity to carry on knocking down the price ad infinitum. When there are two sellers, one buyer, and the item for sale is losing value every day, the price inevitably tends toward zero.

There is only one question left, and they ask it mostly as a formality, because it still seems to them that the answer to it is not all that important.

"By the way, who is he?" says Kostya.

And then Olga tells them the name.

"I only have a vague idea..." Grisha begins, but Olga says: "I'll explain everything."

She begins. Ksyusha remembered very well everything that Pasha Silverman dug up through his contacts. Olga repeats what she said, adding almost nothing from herself.

How many attempts have been made on the life of This Man? How many failed criminal proceedings have been instigated against him?

Two and three. Exactly like the tablets, although that, of course, is pure coincidence.

How much do the doctors play down the possible pain when they prescribe the tablets that induce a miscarriage in the early stages of pregnancy?

Answer: substantially.

Can it be regarded as coincidence that it was while recounting the criminal background of the new buyer that Olga experienced the first powerful spasm? Did Grisha notice that she clutched at the edge of the table? Did Kostya pay attention to how pale she turned? Had she said enough before excusing herself and leaving the room?

Yes, quite enough.

The two kings say nothing. Now the picture is clear: not only is it being suggested that they should give the company away for a song – it is being suggested that they themselves should introduce the wolf into their own fold. It is being suggested that they make a deal that will fundamentally change the balance of power on the internet market, bring in a player who will not stop until he takes away from them everything that they have.

Has even one contract killing been committed in the Russian internet in the 1990s and 2000s? How important is a negative answer to that question for the self-image of the players on the internet market? How often do internet businessmen resort to the services of gangsters and/or the law enforcement agencies in their competitive struggle? How do they feel, knowing that the answer to this question is "extremely rarely"?

The two kings sit there motionless at the round table. They raise their eyes to look at each other. Two phantoms hover in the room like pillars of mist: the specter of la Belle Hélène, which has almost melted away, and the specter of the Outsider, the King from a different board. He becomes more palpable with every moment that passes.

"In principle, we do have another way out," says Kostya.

"Yes," says Grisha, "we can not sell the company and go back to the old arrangement."

"I think that's the best solution," says Kostya, and holds his hand out across the table.

Grisha shakes it.

At that moment the IT manager, successful businesswoman

and executive director of the company that has just been saved, Olga Krushevnitskaya, is writhing in agony from an intense spasm as she waits for a pain killer to take effect.

Does she realize that she has won? Not yet.

Has she met This Man even once? No, not even once.

Has This Man ever even heard of the little internet shop? No, never.

Does he take any interest at all in the Russian internet? No, none at all.

Is it true what they say, that woman can save the world? Who will Jesus be, when and if he comes to Earth again? Are the radical feminists right when they claim that no man could endure monthly menstruation?

Did Olga Krushevnitskaya cry after her investors left the office of the company that had just been saved? And if so, what was the reason for her tears: physical pain? The bitterness of loss? The joy of victory? Is it really so very important for us to receive an unambiguous answer to that question?

37

11.23 alien	Are you there?
11.23 Ksenia	Yes, I'm writing a column. Are you busy?
11.23 alien	No.
11.24 Ksenia	Then ask me to do something.
11.25 alien	Ask?
11.25 Ksenia	I meant to say "order." I like it when you order me.
11.26 alien	Can you break off from work for five minutes?
11.26 Ksenia	Don't ask me. For you – always.
11.26 alien	The pencil you used last week, is it still on your desk?
11.27 Ksenia	I think so.
11.27 alien	You think so or definitely?
11.27 Ksenia	Definitely, definitely ☺ ☺ I'll mark it. I'll brand it with a special brand. Do you have a branding iron?
11.28 alien	You'll find out in good time ☺ Is it still sharp?
11.28 Ksenia	Yes, I don't use it.
11.29 alien	Very good. Then open your legs and stick the pointed end into your vagina.
11.29 Ksenia	E-e-er... Dearest brother, there are a lot of people here and I'm wearing trousers, so that's a bit difficult.
11.30 alien	Sorry, my dearest sister, you apparently need more detailed instructions ☺ Take the pencil, put it in your pocket, go to the restroom, go into a stall, lock

	yourself in, take off your trousers and panties and stick the pointed end of the pencil into your vagina.
11.31 Ksenia	That's too complicated, sorry. It will take more than five minutes.
11.31 alien	This is a very important game, my sister. We're playing gynecologist. Do as I told you – once; put it in and pull it out. That's two seconds. And don't even think of coming, you're too little for that. Don't forget, we're not tossing off, just playing.
11.32 Ksenia	☺ ☺ Okay, I'll try.
11.32 alien	I'll time you.

On the way back she meets Alexei and suddenly realizes her face is burning. Some important game that is! I just stuck it in once and pulled it back out. Shit, now how am I going to work?

"Are you busy this evening?" Alexei says.

"Yes, sorry" – and she edges her way through sideways to her desk, hurrying so she can answer before the five minutes are up.

"And in general – what plans do you have for this week?"

"Oh, I'm not really very clear on that right now," Ksenia says, and that, at least, is an honest answer. "Let's talk tomorrow, okay? But I think I'm all booked up, sorry."

"It's just that I'm missing you," he says, lowering his voice to a whisper.

Smile charitably, answer "me too", sit at the desk, type quickly "I'm here", oh, thank goodness she had the wits to close the dialogue box as she was leaving. Alexei is still there, looking straight at the monitor.

"Listen, you're stopping me working. If you've got nothing to do, go and check what Dasha's translated from Reuters, she messes up sometimes."

Phew, sigh in relief. Where are you, alien?

11.36 alien	Well done. You made it in four minutes. Next time I'll let you move the pencil about a bit more.
11.37 Ksenia	Bastard. Now I can't work.

11.37 alien	You're a slacker, little sister. You use any excuse to do nothing. Finish your column and then do whatever you like. Only that column had better be really good, understand?
11.38 Ksenia	We don't write any other kind ☺ ☺

I wonder why he never asks where he can read my stuff? Is he trying not to make me feel too important?

12.28 alien	Are you still there?
12.28 Ksenia	Yes, completely.
12.28 alien	How's the column?
12.29 Ksenia	I finished it.
12.30 alien	Then why don't you go and finish tossing off?
12.30 Ksenia	Dear brother, how can you use words like that?
12.31 alien	They're grown-up words, little sister. You'll have to learn them if you want to play with the big boys ☺
12.31 Ksenia	I'll be a diligent pupil ☺ I like it that you don't let me come. If you like, I won't come at all without your permission.
12.32 alien	I have lots of other things to do, sister, apart from arranging your sex life. Why don't you tell me what you did yesterday evening?
12.33 Ksenia	I went to the movies with Olya.
12.33 alien	How is she after the abortion?
12.33 Ksenia	She pretends nothing happened. And I don't bring it up either.
12.34 alien	Be gentle with her, it's hard for her.
12.34 Ksenia	I'll take special pleasure in carrying out that order.
12.35 alien	☺ And what are you doing today?
12.36 Ksenia	Do you want to invite me somewhere?
12.36 alien	In your dreams. I'm just asking.
12.37 Ksenia	You'll laugh, but I'm meeting a psychologist.
12.37 alien	For therapy?
12.38 Ksenia	No, to interview her.

Shit, why did I say that? Now I'll have to explain what the interview's for and what it's about. Maybe it's time I told him

I'm *that* Ksenia Ionova? A successful professional, an up-and-coming journalist, and also the producer and blogger of the "Moscow Psycho" site?

38

AT SEVEN IN THE EVENING LA BELLE CHOCOLATIÈRE café on October Square is crammed as usual and it's hard to find a table. Ksenia's feeling nervous, after all, it's the first time she's ever seen a real live psychotherapist. Medium height, well dressed, quite young. Could be some friend of Olya's. Entirely her style: the modern Moscow businesswoman. Only dressed less formally, and it obviously doesn't take half the evening for her face to thaw out after the working day. How shall I address you, formally by name and patronymic? Just Tatyana is fine.

It's the first time she's seen a real live therapist, should she ask some kind of personal question? Doctor, why do I like to be hurt? Oh no, some other time, today I'm working.

Switch on the dictaphone. Check the recording level, make there isn't too much noise. One, two, three. Now just a moment – no, everything seems to be all right. Let's get started, okay?

(Extracts from the article "Psycho: the psychologist's view" published on the Moscow Psycho site)

> Most serial killers belong to the class of sociopathic personalities or sociopaths. These are individuals in whom one of the most important aspects of personality is defective: they are incapable of understanding that there are certain things you must not do, not because

you will be punished, but because they cause suffering to others. In everyday language, they simply have no conscience, and this is not merely a metaphor, but a sad reality. Strangely enough, this state of affairs causes suffering to the sociopaths as well as the people around them: sociopaths are not capable of understanding other people emotionally, they are not capable of getting in touch with other people's feelings and sympathizing with them, and so they are terribly lonely and unhappy within themselves. When they kill, they do not perceive their victim as a person of flesh and blood, with his or her own feelings and desires, for them the victims are no more than figures out of their own fantasies. At the same time, a sociopath doesn't perceive himself as a living individual, but as a kind of abstract, powerful figure, the bearer of might and authority, an abstract aggressor who in fact is often endowed with the features of the aggressor whom he encountered in his childhood. As a rule, sociopaths are people whose childhood was devoid of emotional attachments and love. There was simply no one from whom they could learn to feel compassion, because they themselves never received an adequate measure of that compassion.

Sometimes killers have a tendency toward dissociation, that is, they have several personalities living inside them and, in principle, they might not even suspect each other's existence. This is a subject they love to exploit in the movies: one of the classic plots is Hitchcock's *Psycho*, the story of a man who thought he was his own dead mother and killed girls in a hotel, acting out that role.

The reasons for this kind of split personality have still not been studied adequately, but we can say with certainty that it often happens to people whose childhood involved some kind of severe suffering or serious psychological trauma. If the child is unable to cope with this himself, or he does not receive enough support from the people around him, then at some

> difficult moment his psyche attempts to deal with what is happening by splitting the personality, passing on the bad experience to someone else and starting over with a clean sheet. I must emphasize that dissociation is the result of intense suffering and serious pain. As a rule, these people cannot remember the trauma and they themselves cannot understand why they do certain things, for instance, why they become killers.
>
> But then that's a separate question – the distinction between sociopaths with dissociative features and dissociative individuals with a sociopathological component to their personality. It is of very definite importance when it comes to expert psychiatric testimony in court, but it doesn't change the way we regard what happens from a practical point of view.

Maybe I suppress part of my childhood experiences too? thinks Ksenia. Though I don't think so, I think I remember everything. But then – how can you check? Maybe I should ask her to explain one of my dreams? Yesterday I woke up and all I could remember was one phrase: "When I'm called, I'll come." Who's going to call me, and where to?

"As far as I know, in Russia most psychotic killers are declared sane, is that true?" Ksenia asks and finishes her coffee.

"To be quite honest, I'd rather not answer that question for the record, but if you're interested, I can tell you why it happens. The way I see it, of course. It's not even a matter of public opinion saying we ought to shoot these monsters. It's just that psychiatrists are only too well aware that it's possible to escape from hospital. That patients are usually only kept in high-security facilities for seven years – any longer is forbidden by law – and then transferred to the standard security regime, where the patients aren't actually guarded at all. They know you can leave the hospital when you're declared to be well. In short, there is absolutely no guarantee that these people will not kill again. If you have to take a sin on your soul, better take responsibility for a wrong diagnosis than for further victims. Mosgas, Chikatilo, and all the most famous serial killers – of course, they're all mentally ill, people with very serious disorders and a specific diagnosis. But they were declared sane and executed. And, to be quite honest, I can understand my colleagues for putting their names to that opinion."

"You mean these people can't be cured?" asks Ksenia, thinking that she would like to be like this woman: to understand killers with her mind, have all the answers pigeon-holed, explain all the reasons, know everything in the books, but not feel it with her own lacerated skin, her own heart.

(Extracts from the article "Psycho: the psychologist's view" published on the Moscow Psycho site)

> Many cases are known in which psychotherapy has helped such people to cope with their problems. But it has to be admitted that the case of serial killers lies in the realm of psychiatry and not psychotherapy: the transition from fantasies to real actions is usually the boundary beyond which the killer's personality changes irreversibly. But, of course, we must understand quite definitely that most sociopaths and individuals with multiple personalities are not psychotic killers. And neither are people who are obsessed by sadistic fantasies. In themselves, thoughts and fantasies do not make a person into a criminal – and in these cases the timely help of a therapist can be both appropriate and effective. The literature includes cases of individuals who went to therapy with an obsessive desire to kill. Many of them have managed to get rid of their own nightmares, others have at least managed not to commit any real crimes. I would like to use your site to appeal to people like that and tell them they will feel better if they can talk about their fantasies with a therapist.

"But surely a therapist should tell the police if someone who might become a murderer comes to him?" Ksenia asks.

"Well, you see, Ksenia, confidentiality is one of the fundamental conditions of a therapist's work. There are cases, very rare ones, when a therapist has the right to break this rule. For instance, if a child says that he or she is being systematically abused – then the therapist should inform the authorities, in order to protect this child and other children. But if someone comes of his own accord and talks about his problems, including his fantasies, his nightmares and obsessions, then he can be certain that no one but his therapist will hear about it."

I guess I'd be a good client, thinks Ksenia. I wouldn't hide anything, I don't have anything to hide. But then, I'm not likely to go into therapy, no matter what Maya Lvova says – after all, I'm perfectly happy. Especially just recently, when I have someone to talk with about what really matters to me.

She finishes her coffee and asks her final question:

"But what does the therapist feel, talking to a potential killer? How about you, Tatyana, wouldn't you feel disgusted or afraid?

"It's our job, Ksenia. If a man came to me with fantasies about killing little girls, as a woman and a mother I would feel loathing and anger. But as a professional, I would empathize, because I understand perfectly well that such fantasies derive from the experience of suffering. The therapist's attitude must always be based on a compassionate approach – that's another condition of our work."

(Extracts from the article "Psycho: the psychologist's view" published on the Moscow Psycho site)

> In conclusion, let me emphasize once again: an analysis of the causes of such crimes can in no way serve as an argument in favor of a "soft" approach to the killers. The understanding that so-called "psychos" are also human beings who suffer and perhaps need help should not be confused with a desire to justify them, yet alone to glorify them. Society has to be protected against such individuals, no matter how well we might understand the degree of their own personal suffering.

* * *

But what should I ask about my dream? thinks Ksenia. After all, I know the answer myself. *When I'm called, I'll come*. The answer's in the word "call." I guess I simply believe that my life has some kind of meaning, I have a "calling" and it will manifest itself when the time comes.

She switches off the dictaphone and says:

"Thank you for an excellent interview."

39

HE WALKS BACK HOME AFTER MIDNIGHT, FROSTY Moscow air, a full moon, snow crunching under his feet, powdered snow spiraling across the ground behind him. He ought to stop a car, walking through these alleys and yards you could freeze to death a dozen times over. Alexei switches on his cell, calls Oxana, lies that he fell asleep at work, an awkward kind of lie, but never mind that now. All his life he has wanted to fight against lies – and all his life he has lied to his wife. And now his own lies are heaping up into a snowdrift that all the pro-Putin media couldn't match in six months. But no, that was going too far. Every month there were more official lies, so many that it seemed like he was doing something very important by telling the truth about anything at all. Even if it was only the truth about the number of wounds on a dead body.

So he had phoned Oxana and lied again, but never mind that now. She could see anyway that something was wrong. Yesterday, when the children went to sleep, she came up, sat down facing him and asked what was going on. He'd put her off somehow, blamed his job, working on the project with Ksenia, did she think it was easy writing about the psycho day in and day out? But at least it meant recognition and a bit of extra money. I always wanted to do something big in the internet, you know, not just interview someone or write the occasional article. So this is my chance, and, well, we'll all have to put up with it for a while because, of course, you have to pay for a chance like this.

He raises his hand to stop a car. It's the first time he has ever gone home from his latest flame without feeling any joy or pride. Not even the slightest buzz. He shifts from foot to foot, waves his frozen hand, the cars drive by along the empty road, the powdered snow spiraling across the ground is like the strokes of an immense pencil. Outwardly everything had been as usual, with urgency and passion. He had easily got turned on, after all, this was the first time he had visited Irka for almost three months. He'd done everything the way he liked, this way and that way, they had even come together, which didn't always happen. But there was no joy in it, no buzz.

Why not just forget the car? Why not sit down here in a snowdrift, entirely sober, pull his jacket up over his head and wait for the spirals of snow to weave into a cocoon around him, fall asleep in it like a little larva and wake up as a butterfly – but already *somewhere else*, in a new life? Because it was pointless trying to deceive himself – no new life had happened *here*. The brand of a failure could not be obliterated by the two interviews he had given, or the money in the envelope, or the five evenings he had spent at Ksenia's. It could all be counted on the fingers of two hands.

He takes off his glove and looks at his open hand. If I were a palm-reader, he thinks, I could understand what's wrong here. Should I simply change my fate? Burn out all the lines of my life, obliterate them with red-hot metal, rip them off together with the skin? Write a letter, perhaps, to the hero of our site: dear psycho, I've done so much to make you popular and famous that I hope I can now count on a little favor in return. Remove the skin from my hands, it won't be the first time you've done it, allow me to deny my fate, to enter into tomorrow changed and renewed. I know you're not interested in men, but do this simply out of friendship, not for pleasure. If you like, you can make gloves out of my hands. We'll put a photo of them on the site, I can do an interesting interview with myself – the man whose hand was taken by the psycho – and bring the copy to Ksenia, I expect she would be pleased with it.

Frosty Moscow air, powdered snow spiraling across the ground, a car stops, the driver opens the door. "Get in, mate, you'll freeze out there. Where to?" He gives the address and flops back against the seat. "Going home then, are you? From work? Sure, you got delayed, right enough, it's half past twelve. Will the wife let you in?"

If Alexei liked talking to taxi drivers, he would have said that of course his wife will let him in, of course his wife understands that maybe he has a mid-life crisis, or maybe just an ordinary-type crisis. The driver would have told him that his brother had a crisis too, but then it turned into a long bender, so he had that stuff stitched into his stomach and the crises disappeared as if by magic, it was just a pity that a year later he got run down by a car at a bus stop. Some drunken idiot who obviously left it too late to get his stomach stitched. *It was clearly written in the stars that your brother would be killed by vodka*, Alexei would have said, and the taxi driver would have said, *well, there you go*, and they would have passed the time making this conversation. Maybe the driver would have come out with some piece of folk wisdom like *children are the most important thing* or *you should make do with the wife God gave you*, or maybe something else – Alexei always had problems with popular sayings and folk wisdom. But one way or another, if he'd got into conversation with the taxi driver, he might have stopped thinking about Ksenia, remembering the way she lay stretched out on her back, so touchingly thin, with the veins showing through her skin, lying there with her legs spread shamelessly, although, of course, what was there to be ashamed of if they had only just made love, or at least, he had made love, kissed the little scars on the folds of her elbows, rolled the little cylinders of her nipples between his teeth, gently, trying not to hurt her, run his finger across the fresh wound on the inner surface of her thigh (what's that? nothing, just a cut). Only just made love, you say? When was it, that "only just"? A month ago, at least. Tell me Ksenia, what happened? We see each other every day in the office, you're kind and friendly, but I can sense some kind of invisible wall growing up between us, and I can't understand what I've done wrong. And so all the way home he talks to Ksenia, instead of talking to the taxi driver, and that, as it happens, is a big mistake, because Ksenia doesn't answer him, and the taxi driver might have uttered some *bon mot* like *time heals what must be borne*, whatever that might mean, although basically it's clear enough, it means patience is all that is left to us and time heals. And it destroys too, as a matter of fact – which means either that it heals only what it doesn't destroy or destruction is in itself a part of healing. That's always the way with proverbs and popular sayings, even when their meaning is vague, check them out and you find they couldn't possibly be more banal. But even so, it would have been better to talk to the taxi driver, and then when he got his money, he wouldn't have roared off, leaving you standing in the frosty Moscow air, long after midnight, he would probably have asked: *Hey, lad, what's up, come to the wrong place have you, why are you gawping like that?* And you would have answered him: *Aw, shit, I gave you the wrong address, I'll pay if you get me away from this place*, that is, to be more precise, definitely take me home this time. And the taxi driver would have said: *Well, mate, that's incredible!* Or: *You really have been working too hard!* But one way or another, you would have got back in the car, and it would have taken you away from that place. But for that, it goes without saying, you would have had to talk to the taxi driver all the way and not conduct an interminable monologue directed at Ksenia, who couldn't answer it anyway, because just then she was at home with her laptop switched on, using one hand to answer alien's questions and the other... but then, you'd better not think about that or even know about it, after all, right now Ksenia isn't thinking about you and she doesn't know you're standing right outside the entrance to her apartment block and the powdered snow is spiraling over the ground round your feet, like someone's lifelines, lines that the wind changes with a single breath.

And there you are standing at her entrance and wondering what to do now, since you gave this address instead of your own, but you're not thinking about where to find a car, and what lie you'll tell to Oxana this time, when she doesn't really believe your last lie anyway, but about how, now that you've already come here, this is your chance to change your fate. And you mutter it to yourself – *change my fate, change my fate* – almost the same way you repeated that mantra several weeks ago – kseniakseniakseniaIloveyouIloveyouIloveyou – a mantra that no longer holds any promises of salvation, the shroud of anguish enveloping you simply becomes even denser, like the snow covering over anyone who decides to sit down in the middle of the night in a dirty Moscow snowdrift. And now you try to remember where the windows of her apartment are, what you could see when you stood at the window of her room and Ksenia remained lying there, stretched out on her back, so thin and touching with her legs shamelessly spread to reveal the mons pubis into which, it seems, you will never again introduce your jade wand or your sexual organ, or whatever you would have called it if you needed to use words to call it anything. And now, with your head thrown back, breathing in the frosty Moscow air, you see that both of Ksenia's windows are lit up, like a double lodestar, and then you realize that it is fate or, rather, a chance to change your fate – *change my fate, change my fate* – and, of course, you have to pay for a chance like this, but right now you are willing to pay any price, and I can tell you that's right, because, because no price will be too much for you. After all, if you, Alexei Rokotov, the husband of your wife Oxana and the father of two children, who have collected young lovers the same way your latest hero probably collects the lips and nipples that he cuts off, and more successful journalists collect photographs of the places where they've been or the autographs of the celebrities they have spoken to, well then, if you're standing here long after midnight facing the door of the woman who for the last month has been making it absolutely clear that she has absolutely no need of either your jade wand or your sexual organ, well then, since you're already here, go up, why don't you, and pay any price finally to put an end to this?

What could you have seen up there? Ksenia, bound hand and foot, covered with cooling wax – very convenient, despite the searing pain, melted wax leaves no marks on skin – or she could be lacerated by a lash or a whip, thrashed with a riding crop or swatted with a paddle. While you and she were putting the site together, you saw photographs of worse things than that: at least, whatever game Ksenia might indulge in, her eyes are still in place, and her nipples, although they're painful after the clamps (almost a hundred dollars in a specialized sex shop, this BDSM business is an expensive indulgence!) anyway, her nipples have not yet been added to anyone's collection, her lips, all three pairs, have not lost their ability to dilate with blood and function normally, her arms and legs are still whole, look, one hand is hammering at the keyboard and Ksenia is nibbling on the other one nervously, savoring her own astringent taste on the fingers. So don't be afraid, go up and ring the doorbell.

Ksenia gets up and looks through the spy hole. "What's happened?" she asks in a voice more alarmed than annoyed.

"Can I come in?" you ask in a very quiet voice, because on the threshold of Ksenia's apartment your courage has suddenly deserted you, together with your hopes of a miraculous change in your fate.

"Wait, I'll just put something on," says Ksenia, and at that point you could really have turned round and gone away, because even ex-lovers are not too embarrassed by being naked in front of each other, if they still remember that they were once lovers.

And now you stand there in the middle of the hallway, little Ksenia with no makeup, with a shirt over her naked body and old jeans, and Alexei Rokotov, the successful failure, that is, a man who has managed to turn even the major success of his life into failure. "What's happened?" Ksenia repeats, puzzled.

"I love you," you say and Ksenia sighs, completely at a loss, not knowing what to do with this man who is years older than her, the father of two children, the husband of his wife Oxana, whom she has never seen, except in photos in an online vacation album. She sighs again and wants to say something like: *Oh, come on, you just imagined it* or: *Listen, maybe you don't really?* – but then she looks him in the face and realizes that *no, he didn't imagine it* and *yes, he does*. So, she looks him in the face, reaches out her hand and strokes his cheek with her palm and then says:

"I'm sorry. I've fallen in love with another man" – and this answer is so unexpected even to her that she falls silent and carries on standing there as Alexei turns round and goes out without saying anything, out to the frosty Moscow air, the powdered snow spiraling across the ground, the car going his way that instantly appears. And there's Alexei sitting on the front seat, not saying a word to the driver, or Oxana, who is getting closer, or Ksenia, who is getting further away, sitting there genuinely silent, sitting there understanding that you can't scrape your fate off the palm of your hand, you can't burn it out with a red-hot iron, you can't take it off like a leather glove – and that's why being unfaithful to your fate is as impossible as being unfaithful to your wife. And as he thinks about this, Ksenia's image on his retina fades a little bit, although Ksenia is still standing there in the hallway of the apartment that he has just left, still holding her hand up in the air and repeating to herself: *I've fallen in love with another man*, as if she is trying out the taste of words that are new to her.

40

LARISA AND I ARE SITTING IN THE COFFEE INN. AS SHE hung her short coat on the hook behind her, I spotted the way she ran her palm over the smooth fur that is every shade of gray.

When we first met many years ago, she was wearing a fur jacket then too, artificial blue fur, jeans and an orange sweater with a diagonal zip. If you unfastened it, you could take out one breast and kiss it, but I didn't discover that until much later.

Larisa is three years older than me: that's a big difference when you're seventeen and you've just finished school. I was still a virgin, but that was normal: in those days everyone started later – although maybe that's just the way it seems to me. Larisa was my friend Yegor's big sister, and we were celebrating the New Year at his dacha. She was with a young guy from the faculty of law at the university, and after midnight they went off upstairs, saying they were tired. We exchanged glances, giggling, as if to say: we know what they've gone off to do.

We were wrong. I was convinced of that six months later.

The girl I had been dating since school told me she had decided to keep her virginity until she got married, and I was so furious I told her to get lost. We said goodbye in a cold park in spring, she hugged me and pressed her body against me and in farewell I stuck my tongue as far down her throat as I possibly could, as if compensating in this way for the penetration that had been denied to me. She sobbed and went limp in my arms and I was aroused because she seemed so submissive. It occurred to me that I liked this kind of behavior and if she always acted like that, I wouldn't mind carrying on seeing her. But when I asked for the last time if she would let me have it or not, she repeated "no" through her tears. I turned and walked away, feeling my prick tearing apart the material of my cheap jeans. I was seventeen and a half and still a virgin and so I decided: no more girls my own age. It was summer, and I went to Yegor's dacha again, after learning that Larisa would be there and she had just quarreled with her law student.

It was only later I found out that she quarreled with him because she had decided to keep her virginity until her wedding. Let me say straight away that she succeeded.

Larisa had dark hair and big eyes, a round mouth and heavy breasts. *Tits twenty-five pounds apiece*, as they used to say in the days of my youth. Since then I have weighed women's breasts a couple of times for the sake of amusement: seven and a half pounds was the absolute record. Larisa's would have been about six pounds. She was a good kisser and she probably gave me some of the finest blow jobs of my life. But then perhaps I was still too young and I didn't need very much. Before she took me in her mouth, she always removed her spectacles and handed them to me – I started putting them in my pocket after I almost crushed them in my fist as I came, my orgasms were so strong then. I can see it now, Larisa's blue-black hair fluttering like seaweed under the water as she swayed to and fro on her knees in front of me.

Since then her hair has turned platinum and it looks like a wig. She no longer wears spectacles and her gray eyes have acquired an unnatural greenish tinge, no doubt from contact lenses. Sitting in the Coffee Inn, I try to see this well-dressed, middle-aged woman as the girl I used to kiss on benches in summer and in hallways during the winter. I had to walk up the stairs to the very top floor, sit her on the windowsill, unbutton the artificial blue fur jacket and open the slanting zip fastener, then fumble to find the fastening of her bra as quickly as possible. Larisa always used to say: *Don't, what if somebody sees*, but as soon as I pressed my lips against her large brown nipple, she started breathing deeply and running her hands through my hair.

I used to have long hair back then. I used to dream of being a rock star, I used to listen to Yegor Letov, Nick Rock'n'Roll, the Sex Pistols and Iggy Pop. Larisa had graduated from a special English school, and a couple of times when I pestered her for translations she pulled a sour face and said the words were nothing but obscenities and she didn't like that kind of thing. She really didn't like obscenities, and her taste in rock and roll went no further than Queen, Aguzarova and Aquarium.

She probably likes Zemfira and Tori Amos now, although I think maybe it's okay for well-groomed ladies approaching forty to like Eminem, or even the band Leningrad. It's kind of awkward to ask, she might think I'm hinting that fifteen years ago my obscene musical tastes were more advanced than hers.

Fifteen years ago we sometimes used to go out to the dacha, where we would strip naked and spend hours at a time kissing on the divan that we had opened out, or simply on the floor. We were insatiable because we were young and we still had our virginity.

Three years of continuous petting – that's serious experience. I became a virtuoso in the art of bringing a girl to orgasm without penetrating deep into her vagina: I think I probably have Larisa to thank for being considered a good lover – with her large nipples and gentle hands and those especially sensitive spots between her shoulder blades and just above her buttocks, where her tail would have grown if she had been one of those animals that are used to make fur jackets for well-groomed ladies approaching forty.

We drink coffee. Larisa tells me about how she flew to London for Christmas and watched the last part of *Lord of the Rings* in English. We used to love that book, although now all I remember is the part where the dead faces gaze up out of the depths of the frozen swamp. And of course, I remember that sinister charm and the oppressive gaze that starts seeking you out just as soon as you put the ring on your finger. A feeling only too familiar to me now.

We put on our rings and lived together for three years. I guess we were just about the only couple in my circle who didn't get married because the girl was knocked up. My grandmother died and Larisa and I started living in our own apartment. I was already trying to *make money* and I used my first earnings to buy a VCR and a Japanese TV. We put them in the bedroom and every evening we used to lie in bed, watching video cassettes borrowed from friends or bought from the street traders. A three-hour cassette could usually hold two movies and if the first one was good the impetus of our interest usually carried us through the second one as well.

While we were hugging and squeezing each other in hallways and licking each other for hours at the dacha, I was certain that when the moment came and we made love *properly*, a miracle would happen. Unfortunately, I was disappointed. Larisa seemed to me like an excellent lover and now, ten years and dozens of women later, I can say that she really was, but there was still something wrong. We came together, sticky with sweat; I kissed her heavy breasts with the big nipples, she gripped my ear lobe between her lips and ran her always impeccable nails lightly along my thigh – and yet throughout the years of our life as a family I wanted to ask: is that all there is? Is this what they write books and make movies about? Is this what millions of teenagers all round the world dream about?

Larisa has been married for eight years now. I don't know if she loves her husband when she runs her nails across his thigh, if he knows the especially sensitive spot between her shoulder blades and how to kiss her palm to make her come. It's kind of awkward to ask about that, although I guess I really am curious.

Her husband earns a pretty good income, but even so I meet her every month to hand over an envelope with money in it: I love my son very much and I want to be a good father. It's eight years now since I last saw him.

Sometimes we used to make love in front of the TV. It didn't necessarily have to be porn, sometimes it was romances, action movies or even comedies. I remember we laughed like lunatics at *Airplane!*, at one point even forgetting that I was still inside her. I think we even tried making love to Ridley Scott and James Cameron's popular action movies of the time, with Arnold Schwarzenegger and Sigourney Weaver.

The best orgasm Larisa gave me was while we were watching some horror B-movie. A group of girl scouts, with the regulation huge tits – twenty-five pounds apiece – was trying to escape from a group of psychos armed with all sorts of weapons for butchering flesh, up to and including the chainsaw immortalized by Tobe Hooper.

(By the way, the original for Leatherface in *The Texas Chainsaw Massacre* was the same Ed Gein who inspired Hitchcock and Harris. I've read a lot about him: the man had a sense of beauty, a necklace of women's nipples really is one of the most beautiful things I've ever seen in my life.)

Larisa wasn't particularly fond of movies like that – she wasn't even afraid of them, just completely indifferent to what was going on. I guess she thought all these bloody stories about girls being butchered while they were still alive had nothing to do with her life, or maybe in her world, which was already artificial even then, these stories looked like an unacceptable intrusion of reality. Whatever, I don't know. Anyway, she was sitting on me with her back to the screen, moving up and down rhythmically. I was holding her heavy breasts in my hands and following the action on the screen over her shoulder. A second-string female character, obviously destined to be butchered, a blonde with hair the same color that Larisa is dyed now, was gazing around as she wandered through the woods where her two girlfriends had just been killed. In the regulation style for movies like this, she was wearing a highly revealing swimsuit, and I moved in time with Larisa as she rose and fell and waited for the blonde to get her throat cut. Suddenly a hand grabbed the girl's platinum hair and I saw a huge machete descend on her breasts.

It's actually very difficult to cut off a large breast with a single stroke. It takes practice – maybe the characters in the movie actually had it. But anyway, I didn't see what happened to the blonde's breasts – not because the camera skipped prudishly to her contorted face, but because at the moment when the machete entered the flesh I jerked spasmodically, grabbed Larisa's breasts tight and came abundantly.

Usually I could hold out for quite a long time; Larisa didn't like condoms and we used to practice *coitus interruptus*, so she swore, jumped off me and ran into the bathroom. I lay there on my back for a while. My heart was pounding and my body was trembling convulsively.

I guess Larisa's probably put in a coil now or she takes the pill. Whatever, but she doesn't have any other children, and she's not likely to: America's the place where businesswomen have children when they're approaching forty. I'd like to ask her about that, but it's kind of awkward.

When we separated I was twenty-four and she was twenty-seven, but now it seems to me that we were complete children who knew nothing of our own desires and were afraid of our own feelings. I wanted to be a rock star, she wanted to be a zoologist, like her mother. She's ended up as a manager in a large Western firm that produces animal feed. I guess that's zoology too.

A little less than a month later we learned that my sperm had not gone to waste: the regulation period was followed by the birth of Denis, my son conceived from a stroke of a machete that severed those breasts so similar to the breasts of his mother.

I think that now Larisa's heavy breasts have sagged even more and the fat has probably built up on her thighs. She was always afraid of getting fat, so maybe she has liposuction, follows Dr. Volkov's method for slimming or goes to Fitness Planet twice a week. I'd like to ask about that, but it's kind of awkward. She's getting old, all women get old and they try to hide it. Time deals mercilessly with their flesh that is so beautiful in its youth – they get old and covered in wrinkles, put on fat and then die. But the girls I have killed will stay young forever.

Larisa drinks her coffee and says they make good coffee in the Coffee Inn, but not as good as I once used to make. Really? I've already forgotten how I used to brew coffee back then. Since then I've become highly skilled in this art, especially with all the new kinds that have appeared. Does her new husband know how to make coffee? I'd like to ask about that, but it's kind of awkward.

It's hard for me meeting Larisa. Usually I just call into her office, but today she suggested getting together for lunch and I couldn't refuse, especially since I've been in an excellent mood since early morning. After all, she is the woman I loved for six years – longer than any other woman in my life. I used to dream of waking up together every morning and going to sleep together every night, every month breathing in the smell of unborn children leaving her womb when their time came and then, when we started to get old, watching every day as the gray hairs sprouted through her black tresses.

I was very young and I knew nothing about myself, but that's not so very important. I licked her body for three years, I knew every square inch of her skin and could tell if she had started menstruating the moment I caught sight of the figure in the artificial blue fur at the far end of the subway platform. Today I look at the artificial platinum hair, the too-regular teeth, the green-tinted eyes and I can't reach the Larisa I once used to love.

Now she's telling me that her old friend Mashka – I remember her: a skinny woman with chestnut hair and incredibly beautiful arms – almost got divorced, but she and her husband went to a marriage counselor and now they're perfectly happy again.

We got divorced when Denis was a year old. Larisa went back to work and she was sent to Europe for a week for training. I stayed home with the child. In the evening, when he was already asleep, I used to lie in bed, masturbating. During the first year of our life together I hadn't done this very often: the door to the shower didn't lock, and I was frightened by the thought of my wife finding out that I wanked like a teenager. We never talked about it and I was sure she never masturbated herself. If we'd met as adults, I could easily have asked a direct question, but now it's kind of awkward.

During Larisa's pregnancy I rediscovered the taste for masturbation that had almost been lost since my schooldays. Early toxicosis was followed by the danger of a miscarriage and then by late toxicosis, it was a difficult birth and there was no question of sex for three months. It's curious that it didn't occur to either of us to recall our rich experience of petting. That night when Larisa was on her training in Europe I came quite quickly – and when I returned to reality, I heard Denis, who was standing up in his little cot, shouting: "Daddy, Daddy!"

He could hardly have seen anything. Most likely he had got hungry, woken up and started crying. I got up. My right hand and the lower part of my stomach were covered in semen. I darted into the bathroom, swearing and holding down my prick that still hadn't wilted. For a second I remembered how Larisa had sworn and darted into the bathroom on that night when we made our son. Denis is eleven years old now. He calls Larisa's new husband Daddy, and I think that's a good thing. Larisa tells me our son recently won some kind of prize in the academic competitions at school, and I don't know if I can feel proud of this: after all, I'm not raising the child and my entire contribution to him amounted to a few cubic millimeters of semen released into his mother when I saw a blow from a machete sever a woman's heavy breasts.

That night I realized that we had to separate. As I held the bottle that my son was sucking on, I was acutely aware that right now I was doing something monstrous, perhaps more monstrous than everything else that I was going to do. A man who has just ejaculated, picturing to himself a woman with her eyes gouged out and her breasts covered with stab wounds from a corkscrew, has no right to feed a child. He has no right to hold a bottle of breast milk in his hand, even if it is artificial breast milk, as artificial as Larisa's blue fur and her greenish eyes.

I was a very good father. I loved my son very much. I didn't want to hand on to him the hell in which I had lived all my life. That hell was hidden so deep that I forgot about it myself, and only occasionally an image in a movie, a phrase spoken by someone, a dream out of nowhere plunged me back into it. Perhaps I got it from my father – I'd have liked to ask him about that, but it was kind of awkward. What answer would he have given me? Yes, son, I have also lived in hell all my life? I'm sorry you ended up with a piece of it? I didn't want my son to have even a part of the hell that I lived in. I thought it would be better if he never saw a man who knew that his appearance on Earth had resulted, not from the melding of two loving bodies, but from a machete blow that severed his mother's breasts.

"I wonder," Larisa suddenly says, "if we'd gone to a counselor, would that have saved our marriage?"

I shrug. It would have been awkward for me to ask about this, especially since Larisa still doesn't know why I divorced her. Luckily for me, a month later she had a casual office affair, and she repentantly confessed her first infidelity to me. I pretended to be shattered and that evening I left home and went to Mike's place, and two days later I rented an apartment. I'm ashamed to admit it today, but for an entire year, while our divorce was going on, I took pleasure in the fact that Larisa felt she was guilty. I remember that one day she came to my place slightly drunk and tried to persuade me to come back. I played the offended husband, kept repeating "no, no," and then she went down on her knees and crawled toward me, whining. While she was unbuttoning my fly, it occurred to me that I liked this kind of behavior, and if she acted like that all the time, I wouldn't mind carrying on seeing her. Since then, many girls have stood on their knees in front of me, crying, but the first time is always special. The blow job didn't turn out all that well, though. Maybe because she was still crying, or maybe because she didn't take her spectacles off.

That Larisa, tearful and drunk, is even harder to see today than the twenty-year-old girl whose heavy breasts I used to fondle on the top floor of all the apartment blocks in the neighborhood. I feel ashamed of that last blow job – but what else could I do? Larisa always acted up when I bought the latest volume of de Sade, who had just started to be translated extensively, and she walked out of the room almost as if she was making a point when Mike and I watched *Ilsa, She Wolf of the SS* or some other movie of the same kind. As if I'd said to her: dear Larisa, the only things that arouse me are blood and violence, blood and violence. The marriage counselor would have been very surprised too.

"I don't know," I say, "it was so long ago. We were mere children, we didn't know what we wanted. I dreamed of being a rock star and you dreamed of being a scientist. So it's hard to imagine now..."

"But do you regret now that you got divorced?" she asks, and I realize that the old resentment is still alive. I don't think she has ever stood on her knees, crying, in front of anybody else.

"Of course I regret it," I reply, "the way things turned out with you was stupid, and I loved Denis very much. And you?"

This time she shrugs.

"No. Everything's just fine with me. Denis calls Oleg Daddy. I guess it's actually good that things turned out the way they did..."

At that moment, just for a second, I imagine that she already knew all about me back then – about masturbating in the shower, about de Sade, about my fantasies, about the machete slicing off the breasts on the TV screen, she knew, but regarded it as endearing eccentricity, nothing serious. Maybe all my friends know and they simply don't take any notice? People have all kinds of fantasies.

"Everything's absolutely fine with me," Larisa repeats, "but how about you – are you happy with your life? We meet every month, but we don't ask about the most important things."

It would be awkward for me to ask about the most important things, and for a second I freeze. Not because I'm trying to weigh up if everything's okay with me, but because at that moment I see you. You're standing on tip-toe so that the sharp point of the stake is jammed into your crotch and your arms, raised above your head, are chained to rings set into the ceiling.

That's how I left you this morning and I think your legs must be tired by now. You're starting to sink lower, little by little, the stake is entering deeper, the blood is flowing onto the floor. You have beautiful, slim thighs, with no cuts on them – yet. I'll come back late, untie you and wash your wounds, I'll caress your left breast and remember Larisa in her artificial blue fur jacket. I'll feed you the best dinner I can cook, pour the wine, and then tell you a story about a little boy and a little girl who grew up in a country far away. They were afraid of sex, they felt ashamed in front of each other, it took them three years to lose their virginity. Since then they've grown up, I'll say, matured a great deal, come to understand many things, but they will never be able to talk to each other about this. *This* is the most important thing. I'll ask you to give me a blow job, in memory of the days when Larisa still used to wear spectacles. And afterward I'll brew coffee, which I know how to do, and pour it – straight from the pot – onto your face.

"But how about you – are you happy with life?" Larisa asked. I remembered you and replied:

"I'm happy."

* * *

I used to dream of being a rock and roll star. Of screaming out the injustice of the world and my own suffering. Of standing on a stage, covered in blood, like Iggy Pop or Nick Rock'n'Roll. I guess my dream came true.

I became a serial killer.

41

TRY A PENCIL WITH A SHARP POINT. TRY MASTURBATING for exactly twenty seconds once every fifteen minutes. Time yourself and report on your performance. Try putting the clamps on your nipples before the daily briefing and sitting like that for an hour. Don't faint. If you do, tell him about it when you come round. Try typing with just your left hand for a whole day. Try buying the very heaviest earrings you can find. Go to a workshop and ask them to make some even heavier. Try to feel the pain in your ear lobes every moment.

Try simply talking to him.

14.26 Ksenia	Do you want me to tell you something funny?
14.26 alien	Yes. I like your funny stories.
14.26 Ksenia	I read it yesterday in a forum, I don't know if you'll find it funny, but Marina and I laughed a lot. A girl wrote that she was walking home and she thought a psycho was following her. But luckily she met some of her friends who were really drunk, coming back from a party. She ran up to them, told them what was going on, and the whole bunch set off to escort her. But the man, the one who was supposed to be a psycho, carried on following them. And then one of these guys said: "shit, he's really pissed me off, I'll go and sort him out." He walks over to the man, says something to him

	quickly – and the man immediately turns round and runs away. Well, everyone asks him what it was he said. Of course, the young guy acts stubborn, but then he confesses: "I leaned down to him and I said: you're a sex maniac, and I'm a sex maniac too." That's all.
14.28 alien	☺☺☺☺
14.29 Ksenia	Just imagine if he was some ordinary passer-by! How frightened he must have been: a group of drunks, some young guy who comes over and says he's a sex maniac.
14.29 alien	☺☺
14.29 Ksenia	I realize it's a rather specific kind of humor...
14.30 alien	No, it's fine, I liked it. I understand, it's a professional thing with you.

Try loving a man without any flesh. Try living every day dashing from one computer to another. Try seeing it, even as you go to sleep, that yellow ICQ rectangle blinking in the corner of the screen. Try picturing a man when you don't even know his name. Try explaining all this to your friends. Try not being offended by their jokes.

22.12 Marina	Maybe he's a freak? An invalid with only one finger?
22.12 Ksenia	No, he types too quickly.
22.13 Marina	A Chechen war veteran with no legs. A ninety-year-old impotent. Actually a woman. The mannish lesbian sadist type.
22.13 Ksenia	Just a little bit longer and I'll agree to meet, even if that's all true.
22.14 Marina	Even all of it at once?

Try to explain. Try to find the words. *So what if I've never seen him. Women love with their ears.* Yes, yes, their ears. With the lobes of their ears. With the tips of their fingers. With a lip bitten so hard that it hurts. With aching nipples. With the inner surfaces of thighs, jabbed all over with a sharp pencil. With a damp throbbing between their legs. With their entire body.

Try to tell him about yourself. Try not to hide anything. Try to find the words. Try to remember everything: Mom, Dad, Lyova, Nikita. Try not to hide anything. Try to tell him about your work. Try to tell him your name. Try not to be disappointed that it doesn't mean anything to him. Try to accept that all fame has its limits. Try to come to terms with the fact that journalists exaggerate the importance of their work.

Try to describe everything that you have at home. The cat-o'-nine-tails, the whip, the riding crop, the nipple clamps, the gag. Try to tell him how all these objects can be used. Offer several different alternatives to choose from. Promise to go to the special sex shop and buy what's missing. Try to make sure that afterward you have enough money to last to the end of the month. Try to list the ordinary objects you used to use before. Clothes pegs, hair pins, sewing needles, shards of glass. Try to think up a few more. Suggest that he could bring something with him.

Try not to talk about sex. Try not to talk about playing. Try simply to talk. Try not to get aroused while you do it.

14.46 alien	Good. You told me a funny story, and now I want a frightening one.
14.46 Ksenia	A frightening story about the tortures you're going to subject me to?
14.46 alien	No need for that. Just some frightening story.
14.48 Ksenia	All right then. During the war in Yugoslavia a female journalist ended up beside a sniper. He was lying in an attic somewhere, the windows looked out onto a large square, with a clear view of everything. They were talking about something, and suddenly a woman carrying a box of food appeared in the square. The town was under siege, there wasn't much food, so she carried the box with great care. The sniper took aim, and the journalist said to him: "Hey, what's this, are you going to kill that woman?" – "No," the sniper replied, "I'll just frighten her." He fired into the box and the food scattered across the ground.

But the woman wasn't frightened and she started gathering it up. And then the sniper killed her with his second shot.

14.48 alien — A good story. Why do you think it's so frightening?

14.49 Ksenia — Because you can feel it has a hidden meaning that you can't quite grasp. At first I thought it was a parable about the way we cling to material comforts when our very life is at stake: if the woman had run, the sniper might not have shot her.

14.50 alien — And maybe he would have shot her anyway.

14.52 Ksenia — Yes. And then, I told you the town was under siege, and maybe she was taking that food to her children – in that case she wasn't just picking up what had fallen, she was trying to fight to the very last moment. And then I realized that this story doesn't have any moral, it's just a situation with a choice – and that choice is a parable about our life. There are three characters here: the victim, the killer and the observer. And when we hear this story, every one of us subconsciously associates himself or herself with one of them. So, I started talking straight away about what happened to the victim. I guess if I were a genuine journalist, I'd have asked if my colleague carried on talking to the sniper afterward, what she asked him about later, what his answers were and where the interview was published. At the very least, I would have tried to understand what makes journalists go off to war.

14.52 alien — I think they don't understand what war is.

14.53 Ksenia — You mean, they're trying to find out?

14.54 alien — No. They don't understand that what they find in war can be found without going outside the Moscow ring road.

14.54 Ksenia — Risk? Adrenalin?

14.54 alien — No. The most important thing about war is the insanity. Any war is a moment when lots of people

	are suddenly informed: listen, you've always been told you mustn't do this, and this and this. Well, now you can.
	And people start killing, raping and torturing.
14.55 Ksenia	You mean to say that war is simply the moment when all of us are allowed to understand serial killers?
14.55 alien	Yes. It's that kind of insanity on a mass scale. And so you've only been in a war if you've been inside that insanity. When you've realized for yourself that it's possible to torture and kill people. But I'm not sure there's any need to go to Yugoslavia or Chechnya to understand that.
14.55 Ksenia	But what if you're outside it? If you take the position of the observer?
14.56 alien	In that case, I think there's no point. It's no different from watching the news on TV.

Try to work – at least sometimes. Try to turn off ICQ for an hour at least. Try not to rush back to the computer during lunch. Try to avoid the word *addiction* when you think about this.

Try to understand what you're *really* talking about. Admit to yourself that you're not really talking about playing, or about handing over control, or about sadomasochism, or about submission and domination, or about sex games. Try to find the words. Cruelty? Fear? Violence? Horror? Insanity?

14.52 alien	In actual fact there's an important difference between us and the characters in this story.
14.53 Ksenia	What's that?
14.54 alien	We can choose who we would like to be and attempt to analyze our choice, but the characters don't have that opportunity. We have freedom, but they don't. The journalist, the woman and the sniper can't change places, even if they all want to. They can't see any possibility of choice for themselves. The woman can't help starting to gather up the food, and the sniper himself doesn't

know why he fires. They each have a set position.

14.54 Ksenia But they ended up in that position somehow!

14.55 alien Yes. That's why I agree with you. It really is a frightening story. A story about the fact that while we remain outside a situation we have freedom, but we can't use it because every choice seems equally terrible to us. And when we're inside a situation, we still can't choose, because we've lost our freedom.

14.55 Ksenia But is there anything we can do to avoid being there?

14. 56 alien Of course. For instance, the woman could have taken a different route. But the key element of this parable is that as a rule we learn that a situation exists when we're already inside it. Or, even worse, we don't even realize we're inside it and simply stop noticing other possibilities. And then we bend down to pick up the food or press the trigger.

14.57 Ksenia But tell me, dear brother, can you and I find ourselves in the situation "two live people in the same room"? Or, if you don't want it to be in a room, perhaps in a basement or some other place?

14.58 alien We can find ourselves in that situation. At least, I don't see any particular physical obstacles to it. But I think the time's not right yet.

Try to love a man without any flesh. Try to ask less and less often to meet him. Admit that his refusal is a demonstration of authority. Try to imagine what he looks like: thin or fat, with broad shoulders or a stoop, with brown eyes, like Nikita? Transparent eyes, like Marina? Dark eyes, like Olya? Pampered hands, like Vlad, or rough hands like Sasha? Try not to ask him about this. Try asking. Accept his refusal to talk about it.

Try to tell yourself that external appearances don't matter. Try to imagine you will meet sometime. Imagine how you will live when the malleable, pliable image with no specific features, hardens into a man over thirty years old. Imagine how you will try to find the alien who has said "hi" to you every day when you turned on the computer under the veil of his flesh. Imagine that your meeting is inevitable.

Get him to give you more orders. Try putting the laptop on a stool at home and typing, standing on your knees. Ask if you should scatter broken glass on the floor. Answer "ok" when he says "not yet." Try standing on your left leg in the subway on the way to work, and on your right leg on the way home. Try to understand why he orders you to do precisely this.

Feel the pain in your tense muscles. Feel like a puppet in his hands. Regret that you can't make all your body hurt at the same time. Accept this pain as love. Try to feel this love in every muscle, every square inch of skin, every bruise, every wound. Try to love even more strongly.

11.26 alien   have your lovers ever made you cry from the pain?
11.26 Ksenia   No. I never cry.
11.27 alien   But I cry easily ☺
11.27 Ksenia   You're my big brother, you can do whatever you like.

Try to hide your trembling from the other people in the room. Try not to go to the restroom too often. Try not to freeze over your cup, gazing into the empty cafeteria with unseeing eyes. Try to see yourself from the outside: blank stare, hair over your eyes, black circles from insomnia, nails bitten right down to the quick. Try not to tremble when Alexei touches your shoulder. Answer him: "Yes, I'm just fine."

Feel how the hairs on your body standing up on end, notice the world scrolling up around you, pay attention to the way your hearing has become more acute. Imagine that you have no skin at all – your body is so sensitive.

Remember if it was ever like this before. Remember all your lovers. Remember your most intense orgasms. Remember your deepest depressions. Remember the moments of insatiable arousal. Remember the tortures that were inflicted on you. Remember all the instruments you have encountered. Admit that words replacing each other in a white rectangle have proved more effective than anything else. Remember the word *subspace*. Learn once and for all that it means simply what it says, and not "submission space" as you always used to think. Say thank you to him for telling you that.

Say thank you to him for visiting you on ICQ a month ago. Say thank you for all the orgasms he has given you. Say thank you for the pain. Say thank you for the pleasure. Say thank you for everything he has told you, for everything he has made you tell him. Say thank you to Someone Unknown for the fact that you met.

Do not be surprised that the word "meet" no longer means a meeting in the real world.

Try to lure him out into the real world. Try promising not to touch your clitoris until he touches it himself. Offer to have your nipples and vulvar lips pierced, offer to put on a chain, so that he can control you like a puppet. Offer to give him a severed nipple when you meet him. Offer him the choice of which breast he'd like it from. Try to admit you are really prepared to do this.

Try not to think that he might get bored with this game. Keep him here. Find the words. Talk to him. Don't let him go away. Ask questions. Answer the questions he asks you. Make conversation with him. Be a smart girl.

15.16 alien	Have you even gone to a club for players?
15.16 Ksenia	No, never. I think it's vulgar. Black leather, masks, rituals ☹
15.17 alien	Right. It's like an amateur choir meeting or a gathering of new school graduates.
15.17 Ksenia	☺ ☺ Perverts!
15.18 alien	In fact the worst thing is that these people try to pretend everything's all right, hunky-dory, safe, secure and consensual. Some boys like girls, others like boys, some like to wear high heels and some like to flog their fellow-creatures with a whip. It's all voluntary, no animals have suffered in the course of the filming, nobody's been hurt or offended.
15.18 Ksenia	☺ But that's really the way it is, isn't it? Some like one thing. Others like something different. It should all be safe and by mutual consent.
15.19 alien	No. That is, yes. It's not important. You know,

	when I talk to you, not only about sex, but anything at all – about politics, your friend Olya, the Moscow Psycho – I get a transcendent kind of feeling.
15.19 Ksenia	A feeling of the tragedy of what's happening?
15.20 alien	Yes. The tragedy. And when I tell you "go down on your knees, raise your arms, and don't dare toss off," I can tell you that, and you can do it, because this feeling of tragedy unites us.
15.21 Ksenia	Yes.

Try to understand him. Try to imagine his life. Listen carefully. Grasp the meaning of every word. Try to prepare yourself to meet him. Understand what really interests him.

15.21 Ksenia	And pain? Why is pain so important?
15.22 alien	Because pain is the language in which this tragedy speaks. The language in which life speaks. And for me the most important thing is to know that I am participating in the cycle of pain. That we are participating.
15.22 Ksenia	On the other hand, we can't avoid pain.
15.23 alien	True, but when we do what we do – we do it voluntarily. We accept responsibility for the pain – and ultimately it doesn't matter which one of us inflicts it. You can inflict pain on yourself. The important thing is that the moment comes when you can no longer say to yourself: "suffering exists in the world, but it has nothing to do with me." No. It is your responsibility. Suffering exists because you accept the responsibility for it.

Try a pencil with a sharp point. Try the nipple clamps. Try to stand on one leg. Try to stretch your breasts so far it leaves bruises. Try to take the pain to the limit. Make it even stronger. Try to feel that this is your choice. Try the word *responsibility* to see what it tastes like. The word *suffering*. The word *voluntary* and the word *pain*. Find other words.

15.25 alien	These people say: "look at the great time we're having," but I say "every day I burn in hell." We can never understand each other. You can't have a great time in hell.
15.25 Ksenia	I think you can.
15.26 alien	It's my own personal hell, what can you know about it? ☺ But there's certainly no room in it for a crowd of fifty people dressed in leather and wearing masks.
15.26 Ksenia	☺

Imagine his life. Imagine that he's never spoken to anyone about it before you. Imagine that the doors into his personal hell are firmly closed. Imagine his hell as a cupboard or a closet that he's afraid to leave. Remember the expression *in the closet.*

Tell yourself: *every one of us lives in hell, but as long we hold out, we're doing fine.* Remember that if you don't hold out, then immediately the cuts start, the suicide attempts, the fits of feeling sorry for yourself and despising others. Repeat: *we're doing fine, we're holding out.* Imagine that there is a personal hell tightly constrained by the straitjacket of your body, feel it beating inside your ribcage. Listen to it pounding in your temples. Repeat: *I must hold out.* Tell yourself: *I must not allow all this to burst apart the cage of my ribs and break out.* Tell yourself: *so far I am managing.*

Think about him. Imagine his life. Say thank you to him.

Feel happy.

15.35 Ksenia	are you there?
15.35 alien	yes
15.36 Ksenia	I wanted to say something about your hell.
15.36 alien	well?
15.37 Ksenia	I want to come to you, into your hell. Could you open the door for me?
15.37 alien	all right, I'll open it.
15.38 Ksenia	and then we'll have one hell for two, won't we?

Try to love a man without flesh. Try to explain this. Try to find the words. *The most important man in my life.* Ignore

Marina's smiley. Repeat again. *My most important man – like Gleb is for you.* Admit this man is so very important, it doesn't matter if he turns out to be a lesbian woman. And even if she's not a lesbian – it doesn't matter.

Remember this very well. Remember the pain. Remember the arousal. Remember the trembling. Remember. Know: someday all this will end. Look at the screen. Read the little black letters in the white rectangle. Masturbate if you like. It doesn't matter. The most important thing is – remember.

Try to find the words. Don't tell anyone, just find the words. The words will stay when it all ends. Say them to yourself – and try to remember them. What did you say? *The love of my life.* Like in a romantic novel, right?

Yes, exactly, like in a romantic novel.

42

RECENTLY IT SEEMS TO OLYA THAT EVERYTHING around her is shedding leaves, as if it's not winter outside, but fall, and she herself is a tree that is no longer very young, losing leaf after leaf. Two weeks ago, on the evening of that day when Grisha and Kostya shook hands with each other, she stood in her own bath, reflected in the mirror walls, and looked at the bloody clot in her hand. For some reason she thought it had two little tails because she had taken exactly two tablets, although what connection is there between tablets and an embryo's tails? That is, of course, if that lump really was the embryo.

Olya turned her hand over and the unborn infant fell into the pink water, a reddish-brown blob. At that moment she felt very, very strong. For the first time in recent years she didn't feel like a traitor. All my life I have behaved correctly, she whispered, I have always been right. I have nothing to reproach myself with.

She knew she wouldn't call Oleg anymore, she would put his number on the blacklist in her cell phone. The old love had gushed out of her in streams of blood, leaving a resonant, joyful emptiness in its place.

This emptiness was the cold emptiness between the branches of the trees in fall when they have lost all their leaves, one after another. Grisha and Kostya had flown off to Thailand together, to cement their renewed friendship with a joint vacation. Vlad was still in Goa. Mom hadn't called since the information about Ksenia's site reached Peter. And Ksenia herself had become so deeply immersed in her virtual romance that Olya hadn't seen her for ten days. And that was why today after work she was going to collect Ksenia from the office and then they would go off together somewhere for dinner. Afterward maybe they'd go to a movie, or maybe they'd stay on in the restaurant until late in the night.

All day long, in the gaps between business talks, Olya tries to reach Ksenia on her cell phone, but there's no answer. Eventually she asks her secretary to find the number of Evening.ru and connect here with Ksenia Ionova.

"Hello," Ksyusha says in a voice that immediately makes Olya's branches drop a few more leaves, as lifeless and withered as Ksyusha's voice.

"What's wrong with your cell phone?" asks Olya, and Ksyusha answers like an echo.

"What's wrong with my cell phone? I guess I forgot to pay."

Of course, she could tell herself that it's just February. That of all the months in the interminable Russian winter, February is the cruelest. Sometime, a long time ago, when all the leaves were still green, when you could drink coffee outside in the street, Ksyusha and Olya had agreed on that: yes, as Eliot says, "all the instruments agree," there's no month in the Russian calendar worse than February. Ever since we were kids we have the idea in our heads that we have three months of winter, February's the last, then supposedly spring begins. But every year in the middle of February, you suddenly realize there's still a very long way to go to the end of winter, and you feel like a tree that has been stripped of all its leaves, and the new buds have no intention of opening yet. This is a month when you don't even want to live, and maybe Ksyusha is right to have invented a virtual love for herself and fled from the cold Moscow streets, where the snow has long ago turned into dirty frozen slush and the leaves that fell from the trees in the fall have rotted, and not even the trees can recognize them any longer when they bow their heads down to the chilly, hoary earth.

But no, Olya drives away her melancholy thoughts. You have to move, to keep holding out, like the enterprising frog in the old parable, you have to whisk up the unsavory milk of the Moscow slush and the February cold into sour cream. You have to move, take yourself in hand, remind your body that it exists. That's why in the heart of February there are so many melancholy girls in the Moscow clubs, propped up against the bar with an air of anguish. In reality these are not girls, they are trees in an autumnal copse. They have lost their leaves and are waiting for spring to come back, or at least for the fine country folk to deck their broken branches with pennants and garlands. And that's why the flags of the sheets in the men's bachelor apartments flutter so alluringly, why the one-off wedding wreaths of the fluffed-up pillows beckon, blessing the heads of the bridal couple for a single night. At this time of year men don't make love with these girls – murmuring sweet nothings in their ears and rocking the frail boats of the beds – they merely remind the trees broken by winter that they will live until the spring – if, of course, they are not killed before then by the woodman's axe, the bitter frost, or some forest disease. But then, it's best not to think about diseases, especially in February, when it's already hard enough to remind your body that it exists.

And that's why, thank God, apart from the dubious sexual acrobatics to which Ksyusha and Olya are both indifferent, there are other forms of physical activity, and let's go to Fitness Planet, you can get a one-off ticket there, and I have a club membership card, and we can work out a bit on the exercise machines – of course, only if we feel like it! – and then have a swim and afterward we'll definitely sit in the sauna and come out relaxed and refreshed, almost happy, reminding ourselves that February really is the last month of winter so spring isn't far away. Well then, are we going?

Ksyusha's objections rustle feebly in the phone – swimsuit, tracksuit, and what else? – no, no, today Olya's in a determined mood, no, no, no, we'll call round to your place for the swimsuit and the tracksuit, and if you say you haven't got a good swimsuit, you've only yourself to blame, we'll go and buy you a new one in next summer's fashion. And if you try to say you haven't got any money, I'll have to give it to you as a present. All right, we'll call round to your place for the old one.

They take little keys for adjacent lockers and get undressed, listening to the conversations of the other girls. Which is better – Pilates or yoga? Should women go to aikido, or is it just a sheer waste of time? Is it true that working on exercise machines without a personal trainer for ten dollars an hour is just throwing away your time and money? This is great, thinks Ksyusha, what nice girls they are here. No one's talking about psychotic killers. No one's aroused by the thought of being hung by their feet from a hook hammered into the ceiling. You feel like a normal human being. Almost wholesome and healthy.

Ksyusha and Olya run on adjacent running machines. Ksyusha runs easily, controlling her breath, only sometimes tossing the hair back off her face, although there isn't really anything much to look at here. After three minutes Olya already starts sweating, she finds the smell of her own armpits unpleasant, and the thought hammers away in her head that she needs to lose an entire five kilos, not just two, and in general, maybe it's still too soon for her to exercise so hard after recent events.

Ksyusha jumps down off the running machine flushed and happy. "Shit," she says. "A pity it's so expensive, or I'd come here every day!"

"Let's go to the pool," says Olya, but Ksyusha can't stop now and she wants to press weights over there, and then check her muscle stretch and then there's this, and that, and that too, and then:

"All right, let's go to the pool." So Olya stands and watches Ksyusha as she presses iron – up-and-down, up-and-down – like Sarah Connor in the old film, and her tousled hair sticks to her forehead, but now look at that, the old familiar gleam is appearing in her eyes and so Olya watches and thinks that Ksyusha isn't really all that thin, she's actually more trim, that's what it is, Olya thinks and she feels a little bit proud of Ksyusha, and a little bit like a not very youthful mother keeping an eye on her child from the edge of the playground, not daring either to leave him alone or to climb up herself and slide down, without giving a damn for her fur coat, the way we did, remember, Ksyusha, at New Year, right? That was great, wasn't it?

"Yes," replies Ksyusha, catching her breath, "now let's go to that pool of yours, only look how crowded it is, I think the aquatic aerobics has started, aw shit."

So they come out an hour later, two young, interesting girls, successful professionals, local celebrities of the Russian internet, who have almost forgotten about fallen leaves and the black branches of February, get into a car and discuss where to go for dinner, because their bodies, roused by the health club, are demanding food, and although Olya was intending to lose weight, her body is demanding it even more loudly than Ksyusha's, which instead is looking forward to the way all its muscles will be aching tomorrow, and they choose the Yakitoria near Ksyusha's apartment building, and over dinner Olya tells her how she's looking for new staff, and all the boys are such dorks, and all the girls are excellent, organized and businesslike, although not like Ksyusha, of course, but even so there's no comparison with the boys. "So tell me," she asks, "in your generation, are all the guys useless? Just look, in our IT business there are lots of girls, more than twenty, and not a single boy."

"I guess so," replies Ksyusha, "nowadays all the guys with smarts get an MBA or study to be lawyers."

So they have dinner in the Yakitoria, and after dinner they decide to go to Ksyusha's place, especially since it's so close, and Olya doesn't want to drive all the way across the city on this black ice, you know, she's so relaxed after the pool and after dinner, she's even afraid she might not be able to handle the car, and it would be stupid to die in February, when there's no time at all left until the end of winter.

At Ksyusha's place, Olya goes to put the kettle on as if she's at home, and Ksyusha immediately switches on her laptop and reads her mail, and when Olya comes back, Ksyusha's standing there, gazing at the screen, standing there frozen, scarily motionless. And Olya immediately goes up to her, presses her cheek against Ksyusha's cheek and looks at the screen too, and glimmering in Ksyusha's eyes is the reflection of an *auto-da-fé* in which all the frozen trees of February have been burned alive.

43

KSENIA, KSENIA, KSENIA.

I don't know how to begin this letter.

Perhaps in the most banal manner possible? Ksenia, I love you.

I first heard about you from a chance acquaintance. A friend who had come back from America as a masochist with an MBA dragged me to a BDSM party in Moscow, just to keep him company. There were quite a lot of people there, I lost sight of him and sat down at a table with a young guy who seemed even more perplexed than me. It looked like it was his first time there too. We started talking and he told me about you. His name was Sasha, and he spoke for a long time about how you met, how you split up, how you made love, he said you didn't answer his calls, that he always read your online newspaper, because he recognized the intonation of your voice in every article, and now you had done a site about the Moscow Psycho, and yesterday he'd heard your voice on the radio in his car, and he had to stop driving, because he almost started crying. And so he told me all this, and it was clear that he was still in love with you, and I suddenly realized you were the one I have seen in my dreams all my life.

When I was ill, you sat beside me, invisible, wiping the sweat off my forehead; and when the black cocoon enveloped me like a cloud, like suffocating spirals, like the hair of the Medusa, you held my hand and cried with me. When my heart was bleeding, you cut your body so that our blood mingled.

Finding your ICQ address wasn't difficult. That's how we got to know each other.

Ksenia, Ksenia, Ksenia

It's me, alien. I'm talking to you, Ksenia, from my home, from out of a shattered ribcage, *de profundis*, from out of the depths, from my own pocket hell, too cramped for one person. I'm calling you, I'm talking to you. Do you want me to tell you the whole truth?

You have been following my trail for six weeks – well then, hello. I realize you won't believe me, there are plenty of idiots willing to pretend to be killers in order to show off to a girl. But I know that some of the girls' bodies have still not been found – do you want me to tell you where to look? Let it be exclusive information for your site. If the birds and the beasts haven't pulled them to pieces, of course.

Today you asked if I could let you into my personal hell. Welcome.

You promised it would be one hell for two, remember?

You must realize I could easily have met you without saying a word about my secret life. Made you my lover or, on the contrary, taken you to the dacha, to the concrete basement where the things you tried to seduce me with would seem like games for children.

I start to get aroused, thinking of the tortures that would have been in store for you. But I love you too much to take you there – because no woman has yet left my basement alive.

It was pointless to kill them. I was trying to explain what they simply couldn't understand – but you always knew. I was trying to take the materials at hand, women's flesh, metal instruments, chains and ropes, and make an astral sister for myself, a twin sister who would understand my pain. Now I can stop the torture – because I have found you.

I didn't have to tell you anything, but I know you're the one I've been looking for all these years. My astral sister. More than a sister. And it would not be brotherly to deceive you. I don't think I need to put a smiley here.

I don't know what you will do now, but I implore you, don't leave me alone. We were made for each other, all the things I have done and all the things you have done are like two sides of a single coin, yin and yang. We are both writers, only you write in bytes on a screen, and I write in blood on a human body. These are both rather non-traditional techniques.

You are so close to me that sometimes I think I've gone insane and you never existed. That I made the site myself and I'm writing to myself, to you, my *anima*, my astral sister, my secret self.

I tried for so long to create you out of all those women. And sometimes I think you don't exist, that ultimately, I made you – out of tears distilled by the pupil of an eye, out of despair, out of the same stuff as my wet dreams are made of.

Sometimes I think you will forsake me forever.

On the site you appealed to me to see a psychiatrist. Then on ICQ you said it would be a genuine American happy ending: the Moscow Psycho site helps the Moscow Psycho find the path to healing. But I can't go to a psychiatrist – not just because I don't want to be locked away in a loony bin, but because I simply can't imagine what I would say to him. How could he work with me, while feeling horror and loathing? And if he doesn't feel those things, then I haven't done enough yet.

But we share our horror and loathing with each other. I believe you will not spurn me. I believe we can be happy together. Like Hannibal Lecter and Clarice Starling, like Mickey and Mallory, like Cameron and Janice Hooper.

That is the only way a happy ending can look.

Would you like me to promise to try not to kill you? And you try not to die with me, all right?

Do you remember, once I asked how you would like to die? And you answered: "Rip open my ribcage and take my heart." And after writing this letter, I can feel it is my ribcage that has been torn open and my heart that is trembling on your lips.

I love you

alien

44

JUMP UP, SLAM THE LAPTOP SHUT, DASH ACROSS TO your purse, rummage through the pieces of paper, mutter: *there should be a card in here somewhere*, don't look at Olya, don't hear a single word, say: *there it is, at last!* Dart over to the phone in three quick bounds, pick up the receiver, dial the number, listen to the ringing tone.

Don't look at me like that, Olya, don't look. Can't you see I'm a grown-up, responsible woman performing her civic duty, I'm helping the police, I'm saving the lives of girls who haven't been killed yet. Don't look at me, don't say a word, I can't hear words anyway.

Nobody answers, of course, nobody answers. It's an office number and it's night time, there's nobody in the offices, the investigators have gone home, they're putting their children to bed, singing lullabies to them, reading fairytales to them before they go to sleep. The children are snuffling in their sleep, the toys are sleeping in the nursery and the files are sleeping on the shelves in the offices, the photographs of dead bodies are sleeping, the experts' reports are sleeping, the witnesses' testimonies are sleeping. The investigators are embracing their wives and mistresses, going to bed, preparing to make love. They leave their work outside the home: looking at their naked lady friends, they don't think about dismembered corpses scattered through the forests outside Moscow. The photographs are sleeping in the files, the email from the killer is sleeping in my laptop, the hundreds of kilobytes of our correspondence are sleeping in the computer at work. In the morning I'll burn them to a CD and call again, this time during working hours. We have come into possession of invaluable material, I'll say, conversations with the killer. Your experts are sure to be able to find some lead.

Eventually hang up the phone, turn toward Olya, shrug casually, say: *No one there*. Look at her in amazement, explain: *The police, who else?*, go into the kitchen, on the way checking the latch on the door, as if it means nothing, just like that, sort of automatically, maybe it's a neurotic habit of mine, checking to see if the door's locked when I walk past it? Yes, it's locked. Brew tea in a cup, ask: *Shall I make you some?*

Don't look at me like that, Olya, don't look. Don't you remember – we were going to drink tea. Aren't we going to drink any now, then? What's happened that's so special? Don't look at me like that, please.

Tell her how to track down the killer. Don't call him alien, call him the killer. Find Sasha's number in your address book, say: *He must have remembered him*, eventually hear at least a few of the words Olya says, answer: *Well yes, he was always an infantile, irresponsible blabbermouth. That's why we split up.* Remember the word "responsibility" and immediately forget who was the last person to say it to you.

Drink tea, try to listen to Olya, answer offhandedly, matter-of-factly. Refuse to close down the site, refer to the advertising contracts, the high traffic, your own *business reputation*, pretend nothing has happened. Explain: *And anyway, we've hooked him now, we've got him. The police will have to thank us.*

Don't think about the conversation with the investigator. Don't think about the fact that he'll read our correspondence. But no – think about it, prepare yourself, be imperturbable, not even slightly embarrassed, we all have our own different tastes, don't we? Pretend you suspected something from the very beginning, imagine it all as a big journalistic investigation. Pretend you were going to publish extracts on the site. Do something else, do it right now, ring Pasha, say: *We've found him*, no, that's probably going too far. Don't call anyone, pour more tea, eventually sit down, keep calm.

Don't look at me like that, Olya, don't look. Better don't say a word, don't mention that name. if you say *love letter*, if you say *he's in love with you*, if I so much as hear that word *love* – I'll hit you, believe me. Don't look at me, don't console me. There's nothing to console me for, nothing's happened.

Say: *Probably time you were going, isn't it?* Be surprised she wants to stay, Ah, yes, the black ice, I forgot, sorry. Say: *Thank you for a wonderful evening*, take clean sheets out of the cupboard, open out the divan bed, let her into the bathroom first, wash the two cups. Left alone in the kitchen, realize that you're shaking. Of course – it's cold, winter, February.

Say: *Goodnight*. Once again: *Thank you for a wonderful evening*. Go into the bathroom, lock the door. Soon Olya will fall asleep, soon the investigators and their lady friends will fall asleep, their children are sleeping soundly, the toys are sleeping in the nursery. The clues are sleeping, the testimony is sleeping, the photographs are sleeping, the letters in my laptop are sleeping. Somewhere in cold February Moscow there is one man not sleeping. He's looking at a monitor, waiting for my reply.

Go back into the room, switch on the computer, apologize to Olya, move him to "ignore," apologize again and go back to the bathroom, get undressed, sit on the edge, close your eyes.

Olya isn't sleeping, she's listening to the silence in the apartment and thinking: *Ksyusha's really holding out very well, I wouldn't be able to do that*. Trying not to think what she would do in Ksyusha's place. Thinking: *It's a good thing I came with her.* Imagining Ksyusha sitting in the bathroom now. As still as a dried-out tree, like a huddled bird, like a stone Mexican god.

Ksyusha lowers her hands, starts moving her fingers, tries to summon up in her imagination one of her usual fantasies. Instead of arousal, nausea rises higher and higher, like a lump in her throat, nausea, nausea, shame and guilt. *Other people die of torture, but all you do is come*. Every orgasm for the last month floods her face with the color of shame. As if she has come to the morgue where the bodies of the murdered girls are lying stretched out on the tables, come to the morgue and masturbated for a long time beside each one of them, carefully examining the marks from the burns, the deep cuts, the bloody abrasions.

Hideous, hideous. Ksyusha stops moving her hand, raises the dry fingers to her face, shrugs, glances round for something that can cause pain. A solitary hairpin is lying on the mirror-bright floor. Ksyusha sets it against her nipple, winces and puts it back down. It hurts. It just hurts. The same as for normal people. Pain and pleasure are no longer transformed into each other. The lump in her throat is like a nail hammered into her neck. The nausea is like a knife in her solar plexus. She sits motionless on the edge of the bath, small, with tousled hair, hugging herself in her arms, a huddled bird, a sleepless, broken toy.

45

ALEXEI GOES DOWN ON HIS KNEES AND KISSES THE fingers that seem to have almost no nails left. My God, he thinks, feeling for the fastening of the skirt, what's happening to her? Might as well not bother to ask, she answers my questions, but it's as if she doesn't hear them, as if she only knows answers that she's learned off by heart. *Okay, everything's fine, good, absolutely*. And then again: *Thanks, I'm grateful to you, sorry, please, oh no*. Maybe now at least, thinks Alexei, maybe in bed I'll be able to get through to her. Let her shout and swear and cry, just as long as she says something! I was so glad, he thinks, when she asked on ICQ what I was doing this evening, I answered: nothing, although Oxana had asked me to come home a bit earlier, well never mind, I'll tell her some lie or other. And she wrote: "will you call round to my place?" and I answered "yes!", and now here I am down on my knees in front of her, her skirt's lying on the floor, I'm carefully pulling the panties down off her thin thighs and pressing my lips against her mound of Venus.

So how long are we going to keep on doing this? thinks Ksenia, but he's making an effort, so let him. Maybe I should tell him I don't enjoy it that way, I don't like it with the tongue? But then, it seems like I don't enjoy it any way anymore. It's hard to make love when you feel like a nail's been hammered into your neck. *You need to unwind somehow*, says Marina, *have a screw, maybe*. Have a screw! Easily said. Ksenia stands there with her legs parted, her hands resting on the head of the man bending the knee before her, and she listens closely to herself. Yes, it seems like sex is no more help than masturbation, something inside has broken, the usual fantasies don't work, as if someone has switched off the mechanism that makes the body respond to the touch of hands, the touch of a tongue, the images flickering inside your head. Better not start thinking about what's inside your head. A nail in the throat, a knife in the belly. And there she stands, like a fool, in the middle of the room, with her legs spread wide, so that Alexei can move his tongue about comfortably down there, stroking his bowed head – and feeling absolutely nothing at all.

My God, Alexei thinks in amazement, she always used to get aroused so easily, what's happening to her? He tries with his fingers, then his tongue again, running it all over her body, but Ksenia lies on her back, almost completely motionless, small and frail, as if she's broken. When was the last time I felt so helpless? thinks Alexei. Probably it's what they call love, he tells himself, the kind when it's impossible to have sex with the woman you love. Especially if she doesn't love you. Don't think about the fact that this is Ksenia, it's just a woman, just a skinny body, with protruding ribs, with fur below the belly and two breasts that jut out. The usual business: kiss, touch, caress. Try to arouse pleasure in her, don't think about love. It's just sex – and Alexei runs his fingers over the cold skin again and again, runs his lips from Ksenia's toes to her soft, defenseless lips that respond mechanically to the kiss.

So how long are we going to keep on doing this? thinks Ksenia, but he's making an effort, so let him. But then, if he waits for me to come, we have an interesting night ahead of us. Why did I invite him, can you tell me that? You can't treat other people like that, after all, he's a living human being, not a vibrator, why do I treat him like this... It will be hard for me to find lovers now, thinks Ksenia, well all right, I'll live alone. The fun and games are over. Who needs sex anyway? Maybe I should tell him to start screwing me properly, thinks Ksenia. I've got to work tomorrow, and I'm tired already. She tries to sigh more naturally, breathing out as she exclaims: "Take me!"

My God, thinks Alexei, moving inside Ksenia, how long have

I waited for this evening? I wonder what I'll say to Oxana, but never mind, I'll tell her some lie or other. He moves smoothly, varying the rhythm, covers her face with kisses and runs his fingers over her body. What's happening to her? He tries to remember the way she made love a month earlier – and it's as if a completely different woman is lying beside him.

So how long are we going to keep on doing this? thinks Ksenia, but he's making an effort, so let him. Poor thing, now he's stuck in this mess too. But at least I know this kind of amusement isn't for me right now. Maybe some time later... She lies on her back with her eyes closed, remembers her visit to the police. They didn't believe me, they decided I was tying to hoax them. They took the disk, of course, but I could tell from their eyes that they thought I was a muddle-headed idiot, a hysterical oversexed girl. What a great erotic fantasy – a visit to the cop-shop. But then her other fantasies were no more help – in the last few days she'd realized it was better not even to try: nausea, a lump in her throat, a nail in her neck, a knife in her belly. She opens her eyes: Alexei is swaying intently to and fro. Poor thing, thinks Ksenia, maybe I should play along a bit, I have to go to work tomorrow, and I'm already tired – and she starts moving her hips to meet him, gradually lengthening the swing, curving her body up and moaning with her head thrown back, clutching at his shoulders with fingers with the nails bitten down to the quick – and feeling absolutely nothing at all.

My God, thinks Alexei, I was almost ready to give up. I guess I really am a good lover. Moments like this make it worth living, he thinks, living to give pleasure, thrusting your tongue deep into her mouth, swaying toward each other, finding the best rhythm, listening to the vibrations of the other body. Now that's my Ksenia, he thinks, ah, my God, yes that's her. Lifting himself up on his hands, he leans down and kisses her on the lips again. "I love you," he whispers, "I love you." But all the same – what was wrong with her?

So how long, thinks Ksenia, how long, how long are we going to keep on doing this? She's already flailing hard, her body moving of its own accord, as if in response to an electric shock, the shock of a sudden blow. For a second Ksenia seems to be floating above the bed, she sees the broad male back hanging over her, her own closed eyes, the convulsive movements of her own body, her white lips and tipped-back head. She feels neither joy nor pleasure nor pain, there's just something inside her hammering away at her ribcage, seeking a way out, making her arch up, twitch, shudder. What's happening to me? Ksenia thinks. Why do I feel so bored? No, it's not possible to make love with a man who loves you if you don't love him at all. I guess it's time to moan and put an end to all this, I have to go to work tomorrow, I'm tired, oh shit, she gives a long, drawn-out moan, twitches one last time and stops moving. Feeling absolutely nothing at all.

My God, thinks Alexei, that's all. He rolls the condom off his drooping penis, ties it in a knot, goes to the rubbish bin, then into the bathroom and washes himself wearily under the shower. That was a great screw we had, he tells himself and tries to figure out what he's going to say to Oxana when he gets home. We took a long time today, he thinks, but it was a great screw. I'm a good lover, after all. He stands there, and the shower slowly washes away his former love and his former delusion. A great screw, Alexei repeats to himself, and he almost believes it already.

He's taking a long time in there, thinks Ksenia, but then let him. What is happening to me, after all? A nail in the throat and a knife in the belly. Maybe Olya really is right and I should take a vacation, say somewhere by the sea, take Alexei with me, stay in some cheap hotel. Screw like this in the evenings and in the afternoons lie on the beach... no, it's not possible to make love with a man who loves you if you don't love him. Especially if you love someone else and you've lost his address from your address book and marked him "ignore" in ICQ because you never want to hear about him again.

46

THE PEOPLE WHO INVENTED THE ADVERT SHOWING flowers made of thin slices of meat have absolutely no imagination, and I feel embarrassed for them every time my eye falls on the poster in the subway. Don't forget that posters of half-naked girls leave me absolutely cold, no matter how provocative they might be. Over there on the wall there's a girl in red, covering her breasts with hands in leather gloves, advertising the magazine *Moulin Rouge*. I could imagine that her nipples have already been cut off and her hands are red with blood – but looking at her smug face, that's hard to believe. Advertising in general leaves me cold, maybe because what it offers is what's on the market.

Sitting in the bathroom at the apartment of one of my young girlfriends, I read a thing or two in a left-wing journal. I dislike left-wing types in general: the thesis that the world should be drowned in blood for the sake of some idea or other seems like arrant hypocrisy to me. To drown the world in blood, no ideas are needed: blood is attractive enough in its own right.

Anyway, in this journal I read a phrase from some French lefty. Comfort, he wrote, will never be comfortable enough for those who seek what is not on the market.

I guess that's why the only adverts I like are the famous series by Benetton, with soldiers' shirts soaked in blood, handicapped and wounded people, cripples. It's a shame it was never displayed in Moscow. If I was really rich, like Abramovich,

Berezovsky or at least Patrick Bateman, I'd cover the entire city with images of death and suffering. Then I would never have started communicating with the world in the way I do now. I guess that's why I'll never be really rich. The real money is only made by those who help people to forget about death – and give them the joy of lapping up what's on the market.

Basically, in my view, there's only one good thing about Russia: the Orthodox Church still continues to regard abortion as murder – but it's still common all over the place. With my CV, I like living in a country where one woman in ten knows that she's a murderer.

If they asked me how I see the perfect society, I'd reply: it's a society in which pain and suffering have equal rights with happiness. And more than that, they're acknowledged as valuable in themselves: not pain and suffering for the sake of something else, but pain and suffering in their own right. In that society I probably wouldn't feel so lonely.

I think Ksenia understood me. She had a taste for pain, a sensitivity for suffering. It's not a matter of masochism: I had a masochist lover once, and I split with her after the very first night. I was sickened by her desire to make pain comfortable and enjoyable. With Ksenia, everything's different; I loved her for the way she looked at the world. For the stickers she noticed in the subway. For the stories she told me. And for the site she made, too.

I wrote and told her I really do think of her as a sister: that's the way it is. She's my second half, the female hypostasis of the alien who lives in my chest.

Every morning I look at the little ICQ flower in the corner of the screen and wait for her, repeating: *Good morning, dear Ksenia, wake up!*

She didn't reply to my letter, and she blocked me in ICQ. I guess she was scared – I don't believe that she rejected me, that she didn't understand: she and I are one and the same, mirror reflections, different-sex twins, platonic soulmates.

She wanted my hell to become a hell for the two of us. Words like that are not easy to take back.

But now that she's gone silent, my hell has changed. It's no longer a matter of sudden seizures, black spirals and intense despair – no, it's a continuous, steady feeling, a nagging pain 24/7, a gray veil in front of my eyes. Last week I didn't leave home for three days, and today I woke up because I was crying.

I haven't killed for two and a half months. That's a long time for me: as a rule, I've never held out for more than five weeks. But I wanted Ksenia so badly that there was no place for other women in my fantasies. I imagined the tortures she wrote about and then in my dreams invented more and more new ones together with her. I saw us in our old age, after living together for many years, somewhere in India or Thailand, a decent climate, nobody interested in murders committed fifty years ago on the other side of the world.

Sometimes I imagined us killing together. It certainly happens: girls with a submissive nature willingly assist men with these things. I remember that Karla Homolka gave her fourteen-year-old sister to her lover, Paul Bernardo. The Canadian press dubbed them Ken and Barbie, they were young, beautiful and in love. Caril Fugate herself chose the victims for Charlie Starkweather – I don't remember if they showed that in *Natural Born Killers*.

And even if Ksenia didn't want to kill, she and I could have got a slave girl, kept her in the basement and had fun thinking up various amusing little tricks. Women can live quite a long time in conditions like that: seventeen-year-old Carol Smith lived with the Hooper family for seven years, and she spent three of those in a special trunk under the bed. Cameron and Janice screwed literally right above her head. Janice gave birth in the same bed – and Carol was lying in her trunk at the time.

There were so many ways for us to be happy together!

Now my life has been transformed into hell again. Today I thought: maybe it would have been better if I'd never known about Ksenia? Never let my fantasies deceive me?

The black cocoon wraps itself round me tighter and tighter, I can hardly breathe, the pulsing of the blood in my ears is like the blows of a hammer. I don't have the strength to take it anymore.

This morning I parked my car by one of the exits from the subway. I walked hastily down the steps, like a sick man hurrying to get to the pharmacy when it opens. I knew that under the ground I would find my medicine, the woman who would help me forget my pain.

And now for hours I've been changing from train to train, merging into the crowd on the escalators and in the passages, listening closely to myself, trying not to miss a single woman. I know the most insignificant detail can suddenly serve as a sign. It's not the age that's important, or the length of the legs, or the size of the breasts, or the prettiness of the face. It's not the body you choose – it's the person.

But today all the girls look to me like goods on the market, goods that I don't need.

A few years ago Mike fell in love with a young girl of seventeen. He hid the whole thing from Lyuba, but the girl left him anyway, and he started moping. I advised him to pick up a girl at a club and go to the sea to chill out, but Mike said with tears in his eyes: "When you love someone, you just can't get it up for other women." Mike in despair – a ludicrous sight, but that's exactly the way I feel today.

There are two girls sitting opposite me, one who looks like a southerner, dressed in black, plump, with big breasts. Every now and then a red bra strap creeps out from under her dress. Her friend is a thin peroxide blonde with coils of hair on her head, as if she's just got out of the shower, wearing a blouse with red flowers and a black bra that shows through it. There they sit, like positive and negative images, twittering about something – I can't hear what.

The brunette reminds me of a girl
Who once stopped my car
Near Semyonovskaya subway
A few hours later I found out
She had fine black hairs
Covering all her body
Legs, stomach, back, even the breasts
It often happens with southern women
But Moscow's a northern city:
She must have felt really shy

I left her in the basement,
Tied up, down on her knees,
And next day brought a present –
The very finest shaving cream there is
I covered her in foam, white as a bridal veil,
And shaved her smooth, from ankles to armpits
Legs, stomach, back, even the breasts

I shaved her with the razor
I used to skin her later

Today the brunette sitting opposite me completely fails to arouse me. The combination of red and black is terribly vulgar. And apart from that her sweat would smell sour and sharp. Not even the smell of fresh blood would mask it.

Positive and negative, positive and negative. The blonde laughs, pulling her white down jacket tight round her. She looks weak and frail, but I know what girls like that are capable of.

Once a girl who looked like her
Hung in my basement three weeks
I had problems at work,
Suppliers delaying deliveries,
I spent almost every day in Moscow
So I couldn't give her enough time

At last she started menstruating,
A strange sight, the dark uterine blood
Flowing down her legs,
Mingling with the fresh blood
From the cuts I'd just made

When I cut out her womb
It was smooth and firm

Positive and negative, red and black. They carry on twittering, I turn my eyes to the girl beside them. She adjusts her spectacles as she reads a cheap magazine, leafing through the pages with hands in old knitted gloves. A tired-looking face, beautiful plump lips, big brown eyes. Worn boots on her feet and a plastic bag lying beside her. A woolen skirt with neatly darned holes and a long Chinese down jacket, patched in several places. If I look more closely, I can see she could hardly be older than twenty-five. It's just that she's very tired.

She reminds me of my first woman,
A young girl walking through the forest
To her dacha,
Carrying bags of food

That time too I sat opposite her
In the commuter train
And examined her face

I came at the moment
When I shattered her head
With a piece of metal pipe
I'd found on the road.

That was a hasty death,
Like having hasty sex

The first time, yes

A few tomatoes rolled out of a bag
Running off, I stepped on one
The juice mingled with the fresh blood

They sat there facing me, as if they were in a shop window. Goods offered on the market. Even now I enjoy remembering the others, the ones who were like them. The ones I have killed. But today they fail to arouse me. I imagine them in my basement, I try the tortures Ksenia invented on them, listening to their breathing as they die – and I feel nothing.

Once the subway used to welcome me with open arms, once I used to read the signs. Once time used to stand still at the sound of a woman's laughter, at a passing glance, the turn of a head. Once I used to know in advance how each one of them would die. Once I used to think every one of them was worth taking trouble over. Once I used to think they were all beautiful. Unbearably beautiful.

But now I'm telling you goodbye. I won't be coming down into the subway anymore, suppressing my trembling, standing transfixed on the escalators, standing motionless in the overcrowded cars, following girls to entranceways, trailing them on dark evenings, pushing in the needle of the syringe, barely managing to catch the falling body, carefully putting it in the trunk of the car. This evening you will go home to your loved ones, parents, little children, and you'll never know what I wanted to tell you.

There's only one woman I want. And I'll wait until she summons me. Summons me herself. She can only come to me voluntarily.

The tired girl opposite me gets up, picks up her bag and walks to the door. There's a sticker on the seat, where I couldn't see it before. An image slightly worn by people's backs, a child's face chopped to pieces. The words say: "Thou shalt not kill."

47

THE SAME THING EVERY TIME FOR THIRTY-FIVE YEARS, but every year it still comes as a surprise. In the morning it's winter, cold, snowy, loathsome. But in the afternoon you glance out the window, go outside, and – whoa! – the sun's shining, the birds are singing, the snow's melting, winter's on the way out. Every winter you think: *Oh, if I can just survive until spring!* – not, of course, because you're actually planning to die. It's just that in February it's not possible to believe winter will ever end. But every year it's the same thing: something in the air changes elusively, a half-forgotten smell breaks through the stench of gasoline – and suddenly an invisible wave of happiness floods over you.

God only knows when the snow will melt (more will fall in May anyway!) There's still a long time to wait for the first greenery, it will be a while before you hand your fur coat in to the special cold store to protect it from the heat and buy summer dresses, but even so, you suddenly realize that it's over, finished, you've lived through another winter. That evening you go to bed with a man – and you don't care that he'll leave you and go straight back to his wife; you go to bed to sleep alone – and you don't feel lonely; you open a book and you don't even try to read, you smile over the open pages, you say: *I think it turned out fine*, but what it is that turned out fine, you don't even know yourself.

A believer, thinks Olya, would probably call it "God's blessing," but I don't have any special words for it. As a girl with a philological education, I declare authoritatively that if there are no words, none are needed. It's enough to know that every year, no matter what, you have a day like this coming to you, a day that justifies the other three hundred and sixty-something days in the calendar year. A day of entirely spontaneous happiness.

You get up in the morning, go into the shower, look at your reflection in the mirrors – after all, you're a beautiful woman, aren't you? Not a sterile model from a glossy magazine cover, not some twenty-year-old chick who has no idea of her own worth; no, a lovely, beautiful thirty-five-year-old woman, open to the world and to new love in the future. Hey, hear this – Olya turns on the shower and even makes the water a little colder – hear this, I, Olga Krushevnitskaya, am standing here in the bathroom, wet and happy, ready for new love. I'm all clear, I'm free, I'm lovely, I love myself, I'm happy, I deserve to be happy.

It was a tough winter, Olga tells herself, opening a fat-free yoghurt and rolling the word "was" across her tongue, tough, but it brought results! She came out a winner, no matter which way you looked at it. The presentation unfolds in her head, in PowerPoint: Olga Krushevnitskaya, Winter Results.

In proper sequence, point by point.

1. The Business – preservation and development.

Photo: Grisha and Kostya in Thailand. Graph: expansion plans proposed on their return to Moscow. Tables: schedule for receipt of initial tranches of new investment. La Belle Hélène is nowhere in sight: the expert Thai masseuses had probably banished her ghost forever. Ah but no, I beg your pardon, what had young Thai tarts got to do with it? It was her, Olga Krushevnitskaya, thirty-five years old (photo in business suit), successful business-lady, subtle psychologist, maestro of the chessboard bluff – yes, she was the one who had driven out the phantom of the ill-fated Helen. So, the business: expert appraisal – five out of five.

2. Family – stability and harmony.

Small but loving. Photo: Olga with Vlad beside her, half-smiling. At the bottom of the screen – the outline of the

Admiralty building in Petersburg, a little snapshot by Mom. Lines indicating contact by telephone connect it with Vlad and Olga. Next slide, please. Vlad and Andrei beside the ocean. Goa State, India. The house I hope to get to next winter. Another slide: Sheremetyevo-2 , to which Vlad will fly back in a month. So, family: expert appraisal – four and a half out of five.

3. Love – freedom and independence.
A blank white screen. No: Olga Krushevnitskaya in her best dress, looking like all four lead characters in *Sex and the City* at the same time. Seductive. Romantic. Sexy. Confident. Next slide: a man's silhouette with a blinking question mark. A pity she can't show that he has no wedding ring – to symbolize the fact that the affairs with married men are finished forever. So, love: expert appraisal – five out of five, yes! Refer all questions to the experts.

She pours the coffee out of the little Turkish pot, smiles contentedly. What do we have left? Ah yes, friendship. Kind of hard to think up a slogan. Make it "closeness and constancy."

4. Friendship – closeness and constancy.
Slide show: Olya and Ksyusha at the Yakitoria, Olya and Ksyusha at Fitness Planet, Olya and Ksyusha on a snow slide, in the Coffee House, at a chessboard table in the Atrium, with two other people at the Coffee Inn. Skip the next slide, please – oh, no, it didn't work, there it is, nothing to be done about it now: Ksyusha with her eyes empty and her face frozen, a small, disheveled, huddled bird, a broken toy. And the next one, quickly: Ksyusha with a suitcase at Sheremetyevo-2, Olya seeing her off to Prague: she managed to persuade Ksyusha to take a break after all, to travel toward the European spring.

A sharp flash of memory: Ksyusha's face nestled between her breasts, black tousled hair, Olya runs her hand over it, whispers in a low voice: "Don't worry, Ksyusha, everything will be all right, you know." How's she getting on? thinks Olya, how's the nail in her throat, the knife in her solar plexus? Have the spirits of the Prague alchemists managed to draw the cold iron out of the warm flesh? Have they managed to transform despair into hope, grief into fearlessness, ice crystals into pure tears? She spoke cheerfully on the phone, well, never mind, another two days and I'll go to Sheremetyevo to meet her. Ksyusha flying back and winter already over. That's happiness, real happiness.

Olya drops her dressing gown on the divan and walks toward the wardrobe. I forgot to include the increase in salary, she thinks with a smile, the increase in salary and the promised loan for a new car. She dresses in front of the mirror, thinks: *That's good, it's high time to change the Toyota. It's almost seven years old, it makes me look bad, I ought to get something new.*

She takes a long time choosing her makeup. After all, what day is it today? You could call it the first day of a new life. Maybe she'll meet the man of her dreams, why not? Who will he be like? He could even be like Pasha Silverman. We'll be a lovely couple, two successful business people, almost exactly the same age. Especially since he really helped me in that business with That Man, the Big Investor. And Ksyusha... yes, I think he really loves her. Like a father, I mean. And the two of us will be like Ksyusha's mom and dad.

Olya looks herself over in the mirror once again, tells herself: okay, all's well that ends well. Ksyusha will come back and she'll be just fine, everything will be like it was before. Even better. On a day like this it's impossible not to believe it.

She picks up her purse and checks – cell phone, apartment key, car keys, license, safe key, what else? – and she walks down the stairs without waiting for the elevator. She parked the Toyota on the other side yesterday, there weren't any spaces – in winter that's annoying, but today she actually feels glad of a chance to stretch her legs. The reflection of the sun, shifting from window to window, follows her all the way to the corner. She moves into the shadow – the snow will take a long time to melt there! – walks over to the car, gets into the driving seat, locks the door and turns the ignition in a single movement, and tries to drive out of the parking lot.

What the hell! She gets out, swearing to herself: well now,

would you believe it, on a day like this! Someone's punctured two of the tires. If it was just one, she could have put on the spare and driven to the tire shop, all fine and dandy. But now what? Call a tow-truck? Olya looks at her watch. No, that would take till evening, she'd miss the whole day. She glances into the car again – has she forgotten anything? – turns on the alarm (a lot of good that was last night, when the tires were flattened!), hangs her purse over her shoulder and walks out into the side street.

The first car stops. Olya gives the address and makes herself comfortable on the front seat. Well all right, she thinks, I've hardly lost any time at all, and this evening I can have a drink and come home in a taxi. But I can't have any drink! I have to get the car sorted out! Ooooh, she sighs, and then immediately smiles: on a day like this it's not possible to sigh for long. The sun is shining straight into the windscreen, Olya shades her eyes and turns her face to the spring sunlight. They say you can't get a tan in a car, she thinks, well so what, there'll be time for a tan later. After all, there's the whole summer ahead.

48

THE PLANE GAINS HEIGHT AND THE AIRPORT terminal building, the meandering ribbon of the Vltava, the gothic spires, the narrow little streets, the statues on the Charles Bridge, the crowds on the Old Town Square, the spring flowers on the slopes of the Castle Hill are left behind down below. March, and everything is green already, no snow, would you believe it. Ksenia smiles.

Olya was right, a week in Prague was the best medicine. If you thought this thing through, it was no more than a failed virtual love affair, almost like Marina's. A wonderful lover on ICQ, but a monster in real life. That was almost poetry.

The ghosts of Prague had scattered the phantoms of Moscow. Dead girls, flayed skin, severed hands... Ksenia jiggles her shoulders. It's not hard at all to teach yourself not to think about it, shove it into a dusty corner and forget about it forever. I guess that's what everybody does. There's too much suffering and pain in the world already, what's the point of thinking about it all. You have to live without letting the phantoms into your cozy little world. That's the way everybody lives. There's Marina, raising her son without thinking about how the boy will live his life, turn into an old man with white hair and then be a handful of dust in a rectangular box with a name on a plaque.

Thank you, Olya: she bought Ksenia's ticket, booked the hotel, arranged for friends who lived in Prague to meet her, make her welcome and show her the city. Olya's friends – a man with the funny surname Karmodi and a girl with the amusing first name Allena – *not pronounced "Allyona," in the Russian fashion, don't get them mixed up* – led Ksenia round the narrow streets, bought her beer, gave her hash, did the rounds of the tourist spots and concerts, and gradually Ksenia thawed out, the nagging pain passed off, as if someone had pulled out the nail stuck in her throat and taken away the knife sticking out of her belly. On the second day she got drunk and told them the latest Moscow jokes, disregarding the fact that her kindly hosts had also read them on the internet at Anecdote.ru. They drank beer in Žižkov – at Plato's Cave, Amsterdam, and The Seven Wolves, they played table soccer in a beer garden, tried to spit into the Vltava from the giant metronome in Letná Park, bought grass at the Château, smoked it in the basements of the Barrel Wine Bar and went to watch a movie at a multiplex in the Andêl district.

On Friday they attached themselves to an international group in the Central Lounge – three Americans, one Frenchman, a couple from Germany, two girls from Austria. When it was getting near morning, lanky Jean-Pierre with the flaxen hair tried to hug her and puckered up his lips, and she recoiled so sharply that she even frightened herself: a few moments longer and she would have hit him. "You can just say no," he said in English, pale-faced.

"I'm sorry," said Ksenia, "I have problems with my sex life, Jean-Pierre, I'm really sorry." How easy it is to say in English, how ludicrous it sounds in Russian – "I have certain problems with my sexual life." Problems? Why problems? Maybe everything's perfectly normal, in fact. Look for yourself: you had an affair, you split up, you're suffering. You're not ready for a new relationship, and so, hmmm, well... And then, you can't even masturbate either, and nothing arouses you, and in general, doctor, I think I'm frigid now.

Ksenia reaches out for a glass of apple juice: "Can I have some water as well? Thank you." I guess I should be glad it's all over now. I guess it's better to have no fantasies than that kind. Maya told me masochism was something you had to get over in order to start living a normal life. Get married, have children, one boy and one girl, no, better two girls, call them Marina and

Olya, live a happy life. Make a good career, then get married and have two girls. Right, now it's clear how we're going to live from here on. Very good.

Or I could become a lesbian, thinks Ksenia. I have no memories connected with women, women have never tied my hands together with a clothesline or dripped wax onto my bare stomach. How repulsive it is, really. She puts her empty glass on the tray and smiles at the air hostess: snub nose, broad cheekbones, bright-painted lips, she gives a well-practiced smile, but Ksenia thinks it seems warm and sincere. Right then, marry a woman, be the wife, she thinks. Or, on the contrary, be the husband. Marry Marina, say. But no, better not Marina, Marina would be unfaithful, screw with their mutual female friends and bring men home. Better marry Olya. Olya's grown-up, independent, experienced. She would be a mother to her, sometimes a daughter, or a sister – for an instant the word "brother" flares up in her brain, triggering a sharp pain in her neck, stop, Ksenia tells herself, no more brothers, enough... right then, instead of a sister, instead of a husband, instead of a wife. She tries to imagine Olya and herself making love. There probably wouldn't be any point in pretending, you can't fool a girl. If I don't feel like it, I'll simply say: "Sorry, I'm not getting it on," Olya will understand. Olya's beautiful, Ksyusha likes the way Olya leans her head sideways in conversation, draws on her cigarette through a long holder, smiles with the corners of her mouth and swings her well-groomed hand smoothly through the air. She drove Ksyusha to Sheremetyevo and kissed her before she checked in. When they said goodbye, Ksyusha stuck her face between her breasts, Olya stroked her hair and whispered in a low voice: *Don't worry, Ksyusha, everything will be all right, you know it will*, and it's come true, everything is all right, thank you for Prague, thank you for Einstürzende Neubauten at the Archa Theater, thank you for this week, for pulling the knife out of my wound, getting rid of the nagging pain in my neck, for the goodbye kiss, for not sleeping that night when I came out of the bathroom, sitting beside me until morning, stroking my hair without saying a word.

"Yes, MK, please." The newspaper rustles, she looks through

the window at the clouds, as yellowish-gray as the Moscow snow. Thinks: it will be spring at home soon. Just why were we born in such a cold country? We fly into Moscow and tomorrow I go to work, I wonder how they're getting on there? The site, oh, I don't even want to think about the site. Olya's right, we ought to close it down. Or give it to Alexei, not take any money, just take our names off it? But what if they've already caught him? thinks Ksenia. Then I could just forget the whole business completely. She leafs through the newspaper, looking for the crime section: that would be a real welcome home present. "Moscow Psycho captured." And not think about the fact that I loved that man, not think about it. That isn't what I went to Prague for.

She turns a page – and instantly, as if all the pain that had gone has suddenly come back, as if someone has hit her in the face with a hatchet, chopped off her hands, ripped open her breasts, smashed her ribcage, taken out her heart, she screams, screams, the apple juice gushes out of her throat in pink foam, the startled man next to her recoils, the air hostess comes running, Ksyusha squeezes the sheet of newsprint between her bitten fingers, clutching it as if she's still hoping to wake up, scream, scream, howl like an animal, anything not to see the small print right down at the bottom: *Another victim for the Moscow Psycho? The body of a young woman with indications of sexual violence and torture has been found in the Bitsevo forest park. From the nature of the wounds and the location of the body, experts believe this could be the latest victim of the psychotic killer who has been terrorizing the capital for the last six months. The dead woman has been identified from her documents as thirty-five-year-old Olga K.* Scream, scream, choking on your sobs, writhe in the arms of the air hostess, cry, cry.

But no – Ksenia sits there without moving, reading it over and over again, no longer hoping for anything, not believing it's just coincidence – there must be plenty of girls in Moscow called Olya, with a surname starting with K, thirty-five, the director of a well-known internet shop! – she sits there without moving, not a single tear, the sky above Europe, clouds as dirty as the Moscow snow.

49

I'M TRYING TO THINK UP A HAPPY ENDING FOR THIS story – but I'm not getting anywhere.

Even when I was killing Olga, I didn't get aroused at all. The first time in my life.

She was an interesting woman, I used to like working with women like that. Beautiful breasts, eyes filled with sadness, delicate skin on her hands.

I kissed her on the palm before I chopped off her hands.

I hacked, burned and sliced, but I didn't feel a thing. When I killed before, it felt like I was using a woman's body and my own skill to create genuine works of art. This time I felt like a crude artisan.

Usually the time passes quickly when I work, but I tired quickly – maybe because Olga failed to arouse any feelings in me – no sympathy, no admiration, no pity.

She simply did not interest me.

I took a drink of water, splashed some on my face and went back into the basement. Olga was lying on the table with her hands severed, skin hanging in tatters from her lacerated thighs, her right breast transformed into bloody pulp, blood oozing from her left nipple. Leather straps held her body on the table, her widely parted legs were tied to rings set into the wall: between them I could see a pool of blood. The instruments were scattered in disorder on the table beside her – scalpel, pruning knife, several whips. There was a blowtorch lying on the floor, rope nooses caked with blood hanging from the ceiling. The walls and the floor were covered in blood too – I used to make my prisoners tidy up the basement, but the last couple of times I haven't bothered with that. There are probably severed body parts still lying around here, forgotten: there's an oppressive smell of rotting offal. Strange, I've only just noticed that.

Olga was lying on the table, her mouth lacerated by the gag, her eyes closed. She looked like a broken toy dumped on a garbage heap, not a work of art. I thought of how she was Ksenia's closest friend, a woman whom Ksenia loved. I walked over to the table, took the gag out of her mouth and lay down beside her. It was only then I noticed I was still clutching the hatchet in my hand. I put my arms round Olga and tried to kiss her. Suddenly she jerked her head up and sank her teeth into my lip. I pulled back sharply and hit her in the face with the hatchet.

My blood gushed out onto my chest. I dashed to the hand-basin, and washed the wound, crying.

I've been afraid of pain ever since I was little.

I didn't know what to do with Olga after that. My penis was impotently limp, my imagination was exhausted.

What I really felt like doing was leaving her to die from hunger and her wounds, and collect the dead body after a couple of weeks. But I didn't want to wait: I had to send a signal to Ksenia.

I suddenly realized what I should do. I gathered up the instruments, gagged Olga again and set to work. I don't usually feel tired when the work is approaching its conclusion, but this time I sat down to rest twice. Afterward I realized I'd broken my usual habit and not even checked whether she was still alive or not. So, to be quite honest, I don't know at what moment Olga died.

Finally the job was done: I tossed the remnants of the shattered ribs out of the wound, hacked off the scraps of flesh and skin round the edges – and tore out Olga's heart.

It was the very death that Ksenia had wished for herself.

50

A CLOSED COFFIN, YES, OF COURSE... THEY SAY HER face was disfigured, almost unrecognizable... and is it true what they wrote, her ribcage was broken open and her heart had been removed...? yes of course, it's him all right, who else...? she made the site about him, didn't she...? yes, as if she had a premonition, an incredible coincidence... it must have been fated... thirty-five years old, still young, really... I think she's the first person in our business to be killed... yes, this business we're in isn't really serious: the first killing, at this stage...! and even then it's some psycho, not some adult problem, like restructuring the market...

The sound of voices, they move from table to table, the official funeral banquet "Olya always loved this restaurant." Really? I didn't know that, I never came here with her, well, that doesn't matter anymore. They walk up, express their condolences, as if she's the closest relative – a daughter, a sister – as if they really had got married and lived in loving harmony for many years, lived happily for years and years, had children, two girls, with each other. She didn't need to have the abortion, thinks Ksenia, she wouldn't have had to raise the child alone anyway, she didn't need to be afraid. But maybe it's a good thing there was nothing but clots of blood left in the darkness of her womb. Just imagine what that's like: dying together with your child, even if it hasn't been born yet! She can't imagine it, she can't even imagine that Olya's gone, a closed coffin, she didn't even see her one last time, she can't imagine, she can't think about how she died. She always used to say she was afraid of pain, she said: "I'm a terrible coward, I'm so afraid of pain, not like you," not like me, yes, it would probably have been fairer if it was me, not her.

Pasha walks up, squeezes her arm just above the elbow: "Ksenia, please accept my condolences, I know that you were very close." It's the first time he's spoken so formally to her, as if Olya's death has made Ksenia older, as if some of Olya's years have been transferred to her. She answers: "Thank you, yes, very close." Not a single tear in two days in Moscow, not a single tear in her whole life.

She's a strong girl, thinks Pasha, she won't break down, I know. Pasha only needs to see a person who has lost dear ones, and he knows all about them. After all, didn't almost all his childhood friends lose someone? the statistical base is more than adequate. He's still holding Ksenia's elbow, he says: "Can I talk to you for a moment?"

"Yes, of course, but what is it?" They move off into a corner, sit down at an empty table, Pasha glances back over his shoulder, takes a small pistol out of his inside pocket, puts it on the table.

"There, take it."

Ksenia looks at it wearily. "Pasha, what are you thinking of? Why would I want a pistol?"

He takes no notice, shows her carefully. "Do this, do that, put your finger here and press here. And put it in your purse." She looks at him blankly. A beautiful girl, thinks Pasha, but she looks a lot weaker this last month, as if she's grown old, but how can you grow old at twenty-three? You can only grow up. "Take it, take it, it's a legit shooter, don't worry. Consider that an order from me, your boss." She shrugs her skinny shoulders, puts the gun in her purse. "Right, that's good." She goes back into the hall, Pasha watches her go, thinks: if anything happens to her, I'll never forgive myself. I just knew they shouldn't do that site. I tried to explain, but obviously I didn't explain clearly enough. It turns out words are just as unreal as advertising, as the rectangular banners on rectangular screens. Inanimate machines are more reliable. A cartridge, a detonator, a trigger mechanism.

They move from table to table, the sound of voices, the quiet whispering, her mother came from Peter for the funeral, but she didn't come to the banquet, you can understand that, she's lost her daughter, it's terrible when parents bury their own children. Yes, yes, but Krushevnitskaya didn't have any children herself, if I remember correctly? No, no one. Her only relative in Moscow is her brother, he didn't get back from India in time, it's hard to contact him, they wrote, but obviously he doesn't read his post every day. What a life he has, if I don't check the inbox at least a couple of times every day, I start going to pieces. Yes, drop everything, go off to India. The sound of voices, from table to table.

A young man comes up to her. "Can we step outside just for a moment?"

"Yes, of course, but what is it?" Where has she seen him before, damn it? Her dry eyes don't want to recognize people anymore. "Ah, sorry, yes, indeed, today I'm, well, you understand.

"Yes of course, Ksenia Rudolfovna, I understand. We read your correspondence, I regret that we didn't do it sooner. We contacted Alexander... er, Sasha, as you suggested. He gave us a description, well, the height, the build... Unfortunately the man was wearing a mask, but nonetheless I'd like to ask you to put a photofit on the site, it's very important."

"I'm sorry," says Ksenia, "I've closed the site. I'm sorry, I really feel very awkward... Why don't you put it out on Tickertape.ru? They have more traffic."

The words freeze on her lips. Traffic, rating, views, clicks, hits, hosts, banners, pop-ups, title sponsorship. Olya, Olya, Olya. She took Ksyusha to Sheremetyevo, kissed her before she checked in, ran her hand through her hair, *everything will be all right;* it will never be all right now, never again. No riding down slides, no drinking saké in the middle of the night, no chatting on ICQ, no burying your face in the fluffy sweater. *Don't cry. I'm not crying, it's the snow. Oh, sure, your face is all wet. I never cry.* There, you see, you didn't believe me, but there really isn't a single tear, even now. You see, I wasn't lying to you, all my life I've believed there's no point in crying, you have to fight, tears won't help your grief, crying means admitting you've been defeated. Well, and so on. But what could help with this, what could you fight against? If I could at least cry. But even if I wanted to – I can't. Maybe if I'd seen you dead, I'd finally have believed it, if not for the closed coffin, if I'd touched your hands, kissed you, run my hand through your hair. It will never be all right now, never again. Dry eyes, not a single tear.

He comes up, takes her by the elbow. "Olya told me so much about you, you're Ksyusha, aren't you." Who's this now, dark suit, tear-stained face, expensive watch on a broad wrist, holds her elbow like he owns it.

"I'm sorry?"

"Oh, I haven't introduced myself, we haven't met, I'm Oleg, here's my card, I thought Olya told you about me, you were her closest friend, she must have spoken about me, yes, what a nightmare, we'd been seeing each other for four years, true love, a terrible blow." He wipes his eyes, sobs. So he's crying. What right does he have to cry here? Ksenia thinks angrily. Where was he when Olya aborted his baby? She suddenly remembers: *domestic violence and psychotic killers are the two poles of male coercion.* She thinks: and somewhere between the two are married men who start convenient affairs that last four years and act like widowers at the funerals of women they used to screw once a week.

She pulls her hand away and tries to leave, Oleg overtakes her, grabs her elbow, looks into her eyes, sobs. "Ah, Ksyusha, if you only knew how much she meant to me!"

At the last moment she holds back her raised fist, but she can't hold back her shout. "How dare you call me Ksyusha, are you fucking stupid, or what? I was only Ksyusha for her, do you hear me? She aborted your child, and you didn't even notice, didn't even realize what had happened, you weren't even surprised when she stopped calling you! Go back to your wife, what are you doing here?" People are looking round, someone's already bringing water. "No, there's no need, no, I'm not hysterical, I'll calm down in a moment." Dry eyes, not a single tear.

Marina makes her way through the crowd, black T-shirt, black jeans, puts her arms round Ksenia's shoulders. "Thanks, thanks, I just flipped, got really furious, I have to get a grip, thanks, Marina, thanks, yes, let's go."

51

ALEXEI WATCHES THEM GO, POOR LITTLE GIRL, suddenly it's clear: she really is a little girl, still a child, a *lost little girl*, like in that Doors song. The most important thing to happen to him in ten years, yes, a real war, a fight in which he thinks he held his ground. Or maybe he didn't, in that kind of action you never know if you won or lost. But the former delusion has disappeared: she doesn't exist anymore, the Ksenia whose windows he stood under when the taxi simply took him there, the woman whose name he wants to repeat like a mantra, adding IloveyouIloveyouIloveyouIloveyou. There's just a twenty-three-year-old little girl who has lost her friend.

He phoned her the day before, said "I'll come round," brought a bottle of Stoli, they drank without clinking glasses. Then they sat in the kitchen without speaking, she only started talking after the third glass, remembered how she first saw her, friendship at first sight, she wanted to be like that herself, in about ten years. Closer to her than anyone else, apart from Mom.

They sat in the kitchen, drank vodka, not a single tear, dry eyes. Sitting there hugging herself. Poor little girl, tenderness, tenderness and pity, he tries not to touch her unnecessarily, so she won't think he came for sex. He's had better sex, to be quite honest, but this – yes, this was love, it was frightening to remember: January, snow swirling across the ground, a huge pencil tracing out spirals on the empty roadway. In the hall, as he was leaving, he took hold of her hand. "Ksenia, I have to tell you, even if it's not important, but everything I said that time, here, when I came that night, it all really was true... I guess it's still true even now. And if I can do anything to help..." She forces herself to smile, answers: "You've helped me a lot, thanks." Dry eyes, not a single tear the whole evening, she stands there, leaning against the wall, with her arms round herself, a little girl, a broken little bird, beloved.

Oxana didn't even ask where he'd been, instead she just started crying and wailing. "I told you right from the start I didn't like the idea, you don't really care a damn for me, do you, always up to your neck in some kind of shit, you didn't go to Chechnya, so you jumped into it in Moscow instead, what if it's your turn next?" He lowered himself wearily onto a chair, took hold of her hands, said: "We've closed the project, and anyway, Oxana, he doesn't kill men, he's strictly heterosexual. I'm perfectly safe."

Calming down, she answered: "Well, then he'll kill me."

That night they made love with amazing tenderness, then lay there with their arms round each other, pressing themselves together tightly, in the light of the streetlamp outside the window Oxana's hair glinted gold and silver, and as he ran his hand over his wife's head, Alexei thought he knew what project he would do next, he would do it, even if they didn't give him any money. It would be called *Ruined Moscow*. Photos of facades with no walls behind them, the gaping windows of gutted buildings filled with the black night air, amateur snapshots transformed into historical records, places where he used to wander in search of fleeting love, in ludicrous attempts to assert the substance of his own reality, places that had been transformed into ruins, as if there really was a war going on here. Using the things he knew how to work with – news, interviews, photos – he would put together a requiem for the Moscow of his youth, a Moscow of hasty infidelities and chance liaisons, basements where water slops, steps where the glass of broken bottles crunches, a requiem for a ruined city that feared neither God nor the devil, not a single tear. Yes, maybe Ksenia will agree to help, but Pasha probably won't want to tangle with the Moscow authorities, well, never mind, we'll think of something, and I'll ask Marina to do the design, she's good at it, she's good to work with in general. She has a nice smile, thinks Alexei, innocent and at the same time somehow... And he falls asleep without finding the right word, falls asleep picturing Marina smiling, falls asleep hugging his wife, with his face buried in her hair, gold and silver, gold and silver, ghostly light pouring in through the window.

52

"I CAN'T BELIEVE SHE'S GONE," MARINA REPEATS IN Ksenia's kitchen, pouring herself the final shot of vodka left in the bottle from yesterday. "I hardly even knew her," says Marina, but she was so sweet and she loved you very much, you could feel it.

Ksenia sits there, hugging herself, a huddled bird, repeating over and over: *It's my fault, it's my fault,* stares into empty space, sways from side to side, tousled hair, skinny and small. Yesterday Mom phoned, shouted down the line: "There, I told you it was a crazy thing to do, what if it's your turn next? Think about me for a change, I didn't like the idea from the very start, I'm still ashamed to look people in the eyes, I thought my daughter would be the best in the world, but you have some rubbishy kind of job, what kind of profession is a manager – surely you don't enjoy being up to your neck in all kinds of shit all the time, now look where it's got you, and anyway, who was this Olga?"

"Mom, I've told you a hundred times: she was my closest friend."

"Ah, a friend." She hung up, now Ksenia's sitting there, repeating, *my fault*, *my fault*.

"Don't talk nonsense," replies Marina, "you didn't know anything, why torment yourself? Why don't you think about Olya?" says Marina, "you know a martyr's death is really good for the karma, so think about Olya flying toward a clear light, sitting in a lotus at the feet of the Buddha, remembering nothing about us, or sadness, or suffering, or anguish."

"You know," says Ksenia, shrugging her skinny shoulders, "you know I don't believe in all that. We just die and afterward nothing happens, don't try to console me, don't talk nonsense, there is no clear light."

Marina doesn't say anything, she's not sure about the martyr's death herself, maybe she just made it up on the spot. And in general, it's fine to prattle about karma with the men, pull the wool over their eyes, make herself out to be *a girl with a rich inner world*. But what's the point now, when Ksenia just sits on the chair, saying nothing, staring blankly with her dry eyes. I can't go up to her, take her hand, sit beside her, run my hand over her head, saying over and over, *don't worry, everything will be all right*. Marina doesn't even believe everything will be all right, she doesn't know how to sit beside Ksenia, saying nothing, holding her hand: she thinks she ought to do something, help in some way, cheer her up, no, shit, not cheer her up, of course, but at least shake her out of it. If Ksenia was a little girl, really little, just a year old or, even better, a little boy, then Marina would know what to do. She'd toss her up in the air and catch her, toss her up and catch her, and Ksenia would start laughing, and there wouldn't be any sadness or suffering or anguish left. But you couldn't toss Ksenia up in the air, you couldn't kiss her little tummy, you couldn't tickle her, whispering tender words and stupid nicknames.

"Maybe you should go to bed?" Marina suggests, simply in order to say something. They walk into the room and Marina struggles hard, trying to think what she used to do before when Ksenia was shattered like this, and she remembers, she says: "Listen, maybe what you need is another sadist, like Nikita that other time?" – and in reply Ksenia suddenly retches and throws up right there in the hallway, on the very same spot where Vyacheslav, aka Stanislav, puked.

Then Ksenia sits in the kitchen, Marina wipes the floor, feeling glad that now at least it's clear what she should do, and Ksenia apologizes, says she finds it hard even to think about sex recently and it's absolutely impossible to think about playing, seems like it's over for her, after all, all things pass, look, Marina must remember how wild she used to be before she got pregnant, but now she's a sedate lady, a kind of family mother. The sedate lady stands on all fours with her bottom jutting up in the air and her straw-colored hair falling into her eyes, squeezes out the cloth into the bucket, laughs. "What kind of sedate lady am I, I'm the same as ever. I just have a child instead of sex."

"And I'm the same as ever too," says Ksenia. "I guess instead of sex I've got my job, or Olya's funeral, or everything all together."

Or maybe not everything, but nothing, she thinks. A good word, "nothing." A truthful, good word. With no falsehood, no deception in it. Nothing. A word for the silence in an apartment at night, for the darkness in a lonely room, for the blankness in open eyes. A good word for answering any question. What's left of Olya? What will be left of Ksenia? What's left of a computer file after it's deleted? What do people have inside their heads?

Why was it Olya he chose, thinks Ksenia, why not me? I know he smashed her ribs, took out her heart, as if he was remembering once again what I said – *break open my ribcage and take my heart*, like leaving his signature. And that means he did it for me. It means it's my fault, it means I killed Olya. It means I was killing her when I made the site, when I answered that very first hi, I was killing her every time I wrote to him, every time I masturbated, every time I came, every time I hurt myself, I was killing her when I read his letter. I killed Olya. It's my fault.

She lies there in the darkness, Marina's gone, Ksenia lies there without closing her dry eyes, not a single tear, lies there in the darkness, repeats to herself: *it's my fault, I killed Olya*, picturing over and over again the smashed ribcage, the dead heart encrusted with blood, like a signature at the bottom of a letter – a letter she had been forced to read, a letter you couldn't just dump in the waste paper basket, kill on the server, block out with a filter. If I hadn't shifted him to "ignore," Olya would still be alive, thinks Ksenia, that means it's my fault, I killed Olya. That night I came out of the bathroom, walked over to the laptop, said: "sorry, Olya" – and killed her.

Blank eyes, a silent apartment, a dark room, nothing, there's nothing I can do. Nothing I can change. It's my fault, I killed

Olya. What's left apart from that thought? Nothing.

Round and round the same circle, without stopping: *Olya, ribcage, heart, letter, signature, my fault, I killed Olya.*

Ksenia sits up in bed, hugging herself. In the ghostly light of the streetlamp pouring in through the window the room looks gray, the space is curling up at the corners, like torn wallpaper on a damp wall, it's hard to concentrate.

He sent me a letter, thinks Ksenia, what answer should I give him? Nothing.

If I could delete him from life, she thinks, delete him like a file in a computer memory, go back into the past, kill him at birth, kill him before he starts killing... but what can I do now? *Olya, ribcage, heart, letter signature, my fault, I killed Olya.*

Letter, signature. Olya sat right here on the divan, and she, Ksenia, ran around with the phone, calling the police, pretending to be a responsible grown-up woman, but Olya just sat there, she already knew the answer to *what can I do?* There's nothing I can do. Nothing I could have done. I can't lie down and go to sleep, I can't stop thinking. *Olya, ribcage, heart, letter, signature, my fault, I killed Olya.*

Think about something else, Ksenia tells herself, think about Mom, think about Marina, think about Pasha, about work, if nothing else helps. Think about how tomorrow you'll arrive in the office and start editing the latest news. Think about the news. About Mikhail Khodorkovsky, about the Chechen war, which doesn't exist, about YUKOS, which soon won't exist, about the doubling of GDP, about international politics, leisure and sport. Don't think that sooner or later the crime news will remind you once again: *it's your fault, you killed her.* Now every woman he kills will be a letter to you. And he'll keep writing until you answer.

What can I answer him with? A silent apartment, a dark room, blank eyes.

He'll kill again, Ksenia tells herself, and somehow this thought seems to offer hope, it seems like a way out of the circle. She doesn't understand why it's so important, just repeats to herself: *he'll kill again.* Think, Ksenia, think, ask yourself the question you're so afraid of, the question to which you already know the answer.

Who will he kill?

You know the answer, she tells herself. He writes to me, he's going to kill for me. He killed Olya. Now he'll kill Marina.

Ksenia goes across to the computer, prods a key with one finger, looks at the clock in the corner. Two o'clock. Even so, she knows what she has to do.

The long beeps of the ring tone, five, six, seven. No one answers. Surely she can't be too late? Surely Marina can't be...? Surely the cybernetic gods of the old altar would have warned her, the Great Bear-Mother would have shielded her in her white fur, the cryptic Chinese symbols would have protected her?

"Hello," Marina replies in a sleepy voice, speaking over a child's crying, "who is it?"

"It's me," says Ksenia, "are you all right?"

"Apart from the fact that you woke Gleb up, yes, I am," Marina answers. "What's wrong?"

"Lock your door properly," says Ksenia. "And in general – take care. You're the only friend I have now."

"So?" – Marina still doesn't understand.

Of course she doesn't. She hasn't been lying in the darkness, repeating hour after hour: *Olya, ribcage, heart, letter, my fault, I killed Olya.*

"He's killing my friends," Ksenia explains. "That's how he talks to me."

Marina says nothing, then she answers, already wide awake:

"All right, I'll put the door on the chain."

Ksenia hangs up, walks round the room. She feels cold, there's a buzzing in her head, it's hard to concentrate. *Attagirl*, she says to herself, *attagirl*. Mom was right, there's no point in crying, you have to fight, you have to do something. See, I phoned Marina, made sure everything's all right, warned her, attagirl, go to bed, you've done everything you could, go to bed. Tomorrow morning call the police, ask them to give Marina protection, let them watch over her, let them catch him...

He'll kill again, Ksenia tells herself. Maybe he's already broken into Marina's apartment? Maybe he knows everything I'm going to do? Maybe he can see me right now? Ksenia closes the laptop, checks the door to the apartment, turns all the lights on. All the things she does won't stop the killer. He wants to talk to her – and he'll kill again. The police won't be able to protect Marina forever, he'll bide his time, lie low, pretend he's given up killing, but he'll be waiting. *He'll kill again.*

Ksenia walks round the apartment, the lights are on everywhere, she thinks there's something moving in the corners, something rustling in the silence, something flickering on the very edge of consciousness. There's a buzzing in her head, it's hard to concentrate. Calm down, she tells herself, go to bed, what can you do now? Nothing.

Nothing? Ask that question again. *What can you do?* Ksenia Ionova, successful IT manager, senior editor in the news department, twenty-three years old – *what can you do?*

I have to kill him, thinks Ksenia. Kill him. Out loud she says.

"I'll kill him."

No, she doesn't believe it herself. How can she kill him? He's a strong adult man, and she's a little girl. The entire police force of the city can't catch him, how can she kill him? It's like the story about the sniper, thinks Ksenia: there's a killer, his victim and an observer. And already there's nothing you can do. This is the same. He's a killer. She's an observer. What can she do?

I have to do something, Ksenia tells herself, I have to fight, I have to do something. Think about the sniper, the woman and the journalist, she tells herself. The woman's the victim, she's walking along the street, she doesn't know anything, she has no choice. The sniper's under cover, he has a rifle, he can kill. The journalist is sitting with him, they're talking. Why does the sniper decide to shoot? Out of boredom? No, he's not bored. He's sits there under cover and talks to the journalist, and then – then he says: "I'll fire." He fires for her, he writes her a letter.

Ksenia feels like the solution's somewhere close. She stops noticing the shadows in the corners, doesn't hear the rustling or the murmur of the blood in her ears. She walks round and round the room, faster and faster, as if she's trying to catch up with herself. Think, Ksenia, think!

He writes a letter. A letter is written to someone. The sniper kills because there's an observer. The journalist can't kill the sniper, she can't stop observing. If she'd got up and walked out a minute before the woman appeared, nothing would have happened.

That's right, thinks Olya, that's what I tried to do. I got up and walked out. And then he killed Olya.

That means she can't walk out. She's the observer, he's the killer, he'll carry on talking to her and killing again and again. What can she do?

Nothing?

Ksenia walks round the room, round and round. Think, she repeats to herself, think. How can you stop being an observer, if you can't walk away? If you can't kill? What can you do? Once again: observer, killer, victim. The observer and the killer are unique. The victim can be anyone. Anyone who walks down the street. The killer will shoot. The observer will watch. The victim is the point at which bullet and gaze meet. What can the observer do?

She feels like the solution's somewhere close. On the very edge of consciousness, in a blind spot, in the corners of the room. Round and round, what can you do?

Once again: observer, killer, victim. The observer and the killer are unique. The victim can be anyone. Anyone who walks down the street. Anyone who goes out in the street. Anyone.

Stop.

Ksenia stops walking. Her hair is stuck to her forehead, her hands are shaking, her sunken eyes are glittering.

The observer can't walk out. The observer can't kill.

The observer can only become the victim.

Ksenia smiles. That's the solution. That's the answer. Now ask again: what can you do?

You can die.

"That's good," Ksenia thinks, and again: "That's good. There'll be no one to write to. Marina will be safe, everything will be all right."

"Did you want me to answer your letter?" Ksenia says out loud. "All right, I'll answer. Did you want me to come to you voluntarily? All right, I'll come. Did you promise not to kill me? Fine, but I'm going to try to die. We'll do things my way this time. You will kill me after all. And everything will stop, everything will be all right."

Did you say *responsibility?* Yes, all right, let there be responsibility. You kill, I die. To each his own. I can't kill you, not even for Marina's sake – I can't. But I can die for her sake. A man can kill, a woman can die.

Ksenia smiles. No more need to hold back, no more need to hold out. She knows what to do.

So, we'll meet tomorrow, she mutters. I used to dream about that meeting, remember? Now I don't want to remember, I don't want to talk about tortures. I invented them myself, what a fool. To be quite honest, I'm a little bit afraid. Although, what do I have to be afraid of? I used to hurt myself so I could come. I hurt myself so I could forget myself, at least just a tiny bit. Tomorrow you'll hurt me so I can die. So Marina will live. So everything will stop. I'll see it through, won't I? It won't take very long, will it? I'll try to die quickly. And Marina said a martyr's death is good for the karma. Now I'll find out.

Ksenia smiles. Sits down at the table, types the address from memory, writes: *Dear brother, I'm very sorry I didn't understand before how much we need to see each other. Unfortunately, I don't know where I can find you, so please, find me and take me. If we really are two sides of the same coin, we have to try. I don't know if we'll manage to be as happy as Hannibal and Clarice, but if the invitation to your personal hell still stands, I'm waiting for you. Your sister Ksenia.*

She reads it through, yes it's fine. No matter how clever he is, he won't guess she's going to trick him, trick him and do things her way. She hits "Send," the letter is converted into ones and zeros, goes flying off through the intricate network of wires and optical fibers and a few seconds later it reaches the addressee. That's all there is to it.

What can you do now? Ksenia asks herself. Nothing. Just wait.

And this time "nothing" doesn't sound so frightening.

Maybe, thinks Ksenia, I should write a farewell letter? Wake up Mom and say goodbye? Poor Mom. No, I don't want to, let her think it was an unfortunate accident, a whim of malevolent fate. Malevolent fate? I don't think so. Ksenia smiles.

Maybe she should write to Lyova in New York? *Dear brother, I'm really sorry I didn't realize sooner just how much I miss you.*

Dear brother, I'm very sorry we'll never see each other again. A fine letter. But no, let Lyova think his little sister died a pointless death in a distant northern country where the local police can't even protect their own citizens.

If Lyova was here, thinks Ksenia, everything would be different. He promised to come back, but he's still there. They'll be coming for Sarah Connor soon. I just hope it's very soon. Or else, God forbid, the police will realize what's going on and put me under protection, condemn me to the role of the eternal observer, stop me dying, stop me winning.

"I just hope you're quick," Ksenia says to the brightening window. Then she goes into the kitchen and puts the kettle on. It's stupid to sleep on your last night. Don't think about death, she tells herself, just think: I did what I had to do.

53

KSENIA, KSENIA, KSENIA.

I received your letter. I'm waiting for you, waiting so eagerly, that all the forgotten fears are coming back to me.

I've never seen your face, the only photo I found on the web was five years old, a young girl, almost a teenager, black hair hanging loose down to her shoulders, a boyish figure. I can't match this photograph up with the woman who answered me on ICQ.

Somehow when I think of you, I remember Karina, the first lover I had after my divorce. I was a faithful husband, so Karina was my second woman. I remember we arrived at my place, and I walked over to the bar to pour the wine, and she immediately started taking her clothes off, and when I turned round I saw her slipping her unfastened dress off her shoulders. Her skin looked radiantly white to me, and Karina herself was like the Snow Queen when she came for Kay. It was so beautiful and so frightening that I squeezed my eyes shut and squeezed my nails into the palms of my hands so hard that it hurt.

Ksenia, Ksenia, Ksenia, when I think of you, that fear comes back to me again. I think you're so beautiful that I won't be able to stand it. You sat with me when I was sick, you cut your skin when I cried in pain – and I'd like to repay you. When you come, I'll cut the skin off my own hands, cut out my own eyes, tear the skin off my own flesh in strips, eviscerate my stomach, break open my ribcage. I can do it, dear Ksenia, believe me. I'd like to pile a heap of nails torn from fingers, severed nipples and lips turned inside out at your feet, and I'd crown this pyramid with the slippery spheres taken from my own eye sockets. This is me, dear Ksenia, this is me, laid open to my deepest depths, the only gift I can bring to you. Tell me you will not reject my gift.

I'm afraid she won't accept my gift. I'm afraid our meeting will kill me. I have a rich imagination, and I've pictured our meeting many times before, but recently I haven't been able to.

I'm trying to invent a happy ending, but I can't.

I have a rich imagination, but recently it's been letting me down. I find it harder and harder to believe that Ksenia loves me, harder and harder to picture her. Ksenia Ionova, IT manager, senior editor in the news department of a fictional newspaper, a local star of the Russian internet, a woman who liked to be hurt. Skinny shoulders, fingers with the nails bitten down, black hair. The woman I love. A woman who never existed.

My astral sister, you wiped the sweat from my brow when I was sick, you cried with me when the suffocating spirals of the black cocoon enveloped me, like a cloud, like the hair of the Medusa, you cut your skin when my heart was bleeding. My beloved, I invented you. I invented you from beginning to end, from the artificial trill of the microchip to the lonely night after the funeral.

I invented your newspaper, I invented your site. I liked to imagine the way people shuddered when they saw a banner saying "psycho kills here" – like the word MOSGAS hanging over the calm city. I really do want people not to forget about me. To try to understand.

So that all these killings will not have been in vain.

Yes, I confess: I invented you, dear Ksenia. And so you won't come to me tomorrow, and I shan't kill you. Will that be enough to give the story a happy ending?

Or maybe I should admit to everything? Say there weren't any killings. I was always a kind boy. I was kind, and I'm still kind. I love people and my pity for them brings a lump to my throat. I faint at the sight of blood. I cry at the thought of someone else's pain.

So, nothing I've told you about ever happened. There never was any basement torture chamber, there were no dismembered corpses, none of the girls that I invented one after another existed. No successful failure Alexei, no business-lady Olga with her well-groomed hands, or her gay brother Vlad, or frivolous Marina with her little Gleb – none of them ever existed. What about Mike? Mike was real, and so was the fox-terrier girl: and I really did pick her up in a club and screw her, but nothing like the way I told it here – we were too drunk, and I don't even remember if she came.

Oh, all right then. I've never managed to pick up a girl I don't know in a club. I confess: there was never any Mike, or any Alice. And no such club exists, although that's not important.

There never was all that blood, those severed hands and feet, gouged-out eyes, necklaces of nipples, torn-open ribcages. Nothing. Just the silence in an apartment at night, the darkness in a lonely room, the blankness in open eyes.

Now that really is a happy ending, isn't it? The delusion has been dispersed, you can walk the streets again without being afraid. The Moscow psycho doesn't exist anymore, and he never did.

I invented it all.

But that's not right. There was one incident, just one.

I walked into a kitchen, opened a drawer, took out a knife and stuck it in my thigh.

Only that, nothing else.

Only the black cocoon of anguish, only despair and hopelessness, only fantasies and dreams.

If a man kills, he's a psycho, a monster and a murderer, he doesn't deserve pity and compassion.

But if a man dreams about killing, who is he? Say he has a wife and kids, he goes to work, watches movies, reads books. And only sometimes, in the middle of the day, in the subway, at home, in a café – he suddenly sees the flesh peeling off a living human body, slice by slice, petal by petal. A machete descending on a woman's breasts. An eye that has been cut out, rolling around in a stomach that has been ripped open.

Imagine these visions pursuing you night and day. While you chat with your colleagues. While you make love. While you play with your children.

You don't know where these visions came from, all you know is that somehow they're connected with what's most important to you, with what makes you human.

You have a job, a wife you love, children and friends, and one fine day you go into the kitchen, take a knife and stick it in your own thigh.

A man standing there with blood flowing down his leg.

And that's all.

Maybe we ought to regard him as a murderer?

Then we can rush the police in, arrest the criminal and end our story happily.

This morning I stood at the window and watched two girls swinging to and fro on the swings in the yard. They were about seventeen years old, they took their jackets off and the two bright spots of their summer dresses soared up into the air and back down again. Their long hair fluttered in the wind. When the swings started slowing down, I noticed one of them had red underwear that showed through the white fabric. I could distinguish her eyes, as blue as shards of sky, her slightly swollen lips, her left ear, with either three or four earrings in it. Her friend was standing with her back to me, and all I could see was wave after wave of ginger hair moving up and down with the swing.

I watched them for a long time. They were beautiful.

I didn't want to kill anyone.

54

A STUPEFYING, SICKLY-SWEET SMELL. SHE FORCES HER eyes to open, the pain feels like something exploded inside her head. A low ceiling, dirty concrete walls covered with brownish-red streaks, light as bright as in an operating theater, a large zinc table in the middle of the space, and lying on it Ksenia's purse and her raincoat, covered in mud, absolutely ruined. She turns her head, battling against the throbbing pain in the back of it: metal rings in the walls, nooses of rope on the ceiling. Strangely enough, she's not tied up: she's sitting on a metal chair, her thin hands with the bitten-down nails are lying on her knees. She hears a voice: "I'm sorry it had to be like that." She doesn't remember anything, a sharp pain, the dirty snow of a Moscow sidewalk. So that was the way it was done. She looks straight at him, says: "Well, never mind now." He stands there, leaning against the dirty wall. She pictured him to herself so many times: as a psychotic killer, as alien, as a man who wrote "I love you," but he's not like what she imagined. He stands there, leaning against the dirty wall, smiling faintly. "I'm a bit anxious, I don't know what to offer you. Maybe you're hungry? Would you like me to cook dinner?"

The nausea surges up her throat. Ksenia shakes her head. Still smiling the same way, he asks: "Maybe you'd like to make love straight away?" I want it all to be over as quickly as possible, thinks Ksenia, and she doesn't say a word. "Look what I've got here for you, look." He walks over to the table, moves the raincoat aside, puts a metal box down on the zinc surface, opens it and starts taking out instruments.

"This is a scalpel for cutting, this is another one, look how sharp it is, these are tweezers, for pulling out hair, do you know how much time it takes to pull out all the hair on a mons pubis? This is a hacksaw – for sawing through bone, these are pincers – for tearing skin, this is a hammer and nails, a hatchet and a pair of pliers, a chisel and a cutthroat razor. This is a set of gags, all sizes, look, even with spikes on the inside, they go into the tongue, the important thing is not to choke on the blood, these are hooks, these are needles, these are chains, this is an awl, knitting needles, clamps, look, you've never seen anything like this, you can't buy this in a shop, come over here, let me help you up."

He holds out a firm, strong hand. Ksenia always imagined the psycho as small, skinny, pitiful. Ksenia doesn't take the hand, she gets up on her own, wincing at the pain in the back of her head, leans on the table and watches as he takes out more and more instruments, lays them out under the bright surgical light, repeating: "Now isn't that just beautiful?

"And this is a set of lashes, feel them, no – just feel them, these aren't your leather toys, one blow with these can split the skin to the bone, and this here is an iron rod, if you aim right, you can reach the heart with it, and these are pegs for hammering in between the fingers, this is salt to sprinkle in wounds, this is acid, this is a little bit of gasoline, this is caustic soda, these are syringes for injections, these are forceps for the fingernails, a pity they're not appropriate for you, these are pincers for pulling out teeth if the mouth is small, well, you know, it helps with fellatio, these are darts, specially sharpened, these are more knives, look, touch them, the genuine article, razor-sharp."

Ksenia reaches out her hand, touches the nearest knife, a long one with a curved blade, and alien apprehensively takes her by the elbow. He's afraid of me, Ksenia suddenly realizes, he's afraid too. And indeed, he takes the knife with a gentle but insistent movement and cautiously pushes it away to the far end of the table.

Suddenly her head feels all right, as if someone switched off the pain. *He's afraid of me.* Ksenia still doesn't know what that means, but she feels the answer is close. What should you do? She asks herself. Think, Ksenia, think. *He's afraid of me.* The delusion has been dissipated.

"Well, let's begin," he says, still smiling the same way. "To start with, I would hang you on the rack and show you how the whips work. What do you think of that?" Ksenia doesn't say anything, and he shrugs his broad shoulders and says: "Just imagine, I'm nervous too. After all, it's the first time a girl has come here voluntarily. Maybe I should ask you what you want to start with, is that right? I don't know the ritual, give me a hint, why don't you say something?" *Think, Ksenia, think.* "I understand, there's so much to choose from. I guess you're already aroused, right? I always dreamed of a woman who would get aroused with me. You can't imagine how glad I am that we met. And this is all for you, all for you."

Ksenia is absolutely calm now. She asks:

"So you think I came here voluntarily?"

"Of course, well, practically, yes, voluntarily. You wrote to me yesterday. You're the first woman who's come here voluntarily – and you're the first woman who's ended up here that I don't intend to kill."

"And you intend to live a long and happy life with me?"

"Yes, yes, till death us do part," he says, smiling very calmly, "yes, they lived happily together and they died on the same day. Just like in the stories, a long and happy life. Like brother and sister, you know."

"Let's write a marriage contract," says Ksenia, "so I never forget I came here voluntarily, and you never forget you took me in voluntarily."

Still smiling as calmly as ever, he nods:

"Yes, all right, let's. The adult approach, a stop-word, all the works?"

"Yes and a stop-word too."

"I once suggested using a stop-word with a girl," he reminisces. "The stop-word we had was 'kill me!' And I warned her that when she said it, I really would kill her."

"Did she say it?"

"Yes, but I still didn't kill her straight away. After all, the most interesting part comes after the stop-word, doesn't it?"

"I guess," says Ksenia, "then my stop-word can be 'I love you,' all right?"

He smiles and nods.

"Yes, very good. Shall I go and get some paper?"

"I have some," says Ksenia, and she reaches for her purse, "I have some," she repeats, "I am a journalist, after all."

He twirls a short, narrow knife with a light-blue handle in his hands, the table is between them, his eyes are calm and thoughtful, he carries on smiling, he's still smiling when Ksenia shoots him twice in the chest without taking the gun out of her purse. As he falls, the knife in his hand catches his right thigh, but he doesn't feel pain anymore, he falls, falls, falls through the time that is standing still, tearing through the black cocoon, through the dark cloud of anguish and despair, falls as space curls up like tattered wallpaper, windowpanes melt and flow, doors scream in horror, falls, falls, falls, and in the final bright flash he sees a female figure of unbearable beauty and royal bearing, a white radiance, a grinning mouth, dripping saliva, the flesh shreds apart, the jaws gape wide, jewelry made of skulls, clear light, a corpse under each foot, a wrathful deity, the Snow Queen, he falls, falls, falls, feeling something crunching and breaking inside his chest, something leaving his body, forcing its way out toward the radiant light, he falls, falls.

Ksenia comes to when she hears the dry click of the empty pistol. She doesn't remember coming round the table to be beside the dying man, doesn't remember emptying the clip at almost point-blank range. He fell, the knife in his hand caught his right hip, the blood is still oozing from the wound. His ribcage is ripped apart as if someone had smashed it with a single blow. Ksenia looks into the dead face: forty years old, plump lips, wide-open eyes, receding hairline, touches of gray.

"You didn't understand anything," Ksenia tells him, "you didn't understand anything. You didn't read what I wrote to you carefully enough. Even for my most powerful orgasm, I wouldn't pay with somebody else's life. I'd give up any pleasure not to have you living in the same world as me."

Ksenia is still holding the pistol in her hand, she tosses the knife further away from the hooked fingers with the toe of her boot and goes back to the table. She looks at the tattered remains of her purse, the items of makeup scattered among the knives, forceps and clamps. She touches the cold metal with a cautious finger. Something's wrong, not the way it ought to be. Something almost forgotten rises up from within her, moving through her body in a warm wave, clumping together into a heaviness below her belly. Ksenia automatically picks up a scalpel, yes, alien was right. She is aroused. For the first time in weeks she feels the itch, so strong that she can hardly move. As if the arousal locked away inside has finally broken out and filled Ksenia's body, trying to burst it open, demanding release.

Ksenia goes back to the metal chair, sits down, lifts up her skirt, slips her hand under the elastic of her panties – and encounters the dead gaze of open eyes staring at her in reproachful surprise. She gets up and walks over to the corpse, still holding the scalpel in her hand. There's a hole in the chest, on the left side, into which Ksenia emptied the entire clip, and it occurs to Ksenia that the alien who used to live in this body must finally have escaped. I don't even know his name, she thinks, and brushes the palm of her hand over the dead eyelids.

As she gets up, Ksenia notices something glittering in the shadow beside a leg of the table. Gathering up her skirt, she steps across the dead body – and picks up Olya's bracelet with the dark-red stones.

Playing at snowballs, like little children, riding down slides and laughing in taxis, side by side jogging on running machines, four of you at the Coffee Inn; the baby on the rug, saying "ma-ma," behind you "I'll be back" getting closer, what should you do? The boy hears the trembling sound getting louder, out of the bathroom comes Mom in her robe, puts her hand on your forehead and asks: "Are you hot?"; "No more dancing for you, you've got to study"; "I love you so much, and I sacrifice everything"; "What will people say, it's pure filth, you're my daughter!"; "No point in crying, you just have to fight"; what should you do? A wet face against a warm fluffy sweater. "Your mascara's run." – "That's the snow, Olya, it's only snow."

Ksenia, Ksenia, lost little girl, beauty who killed the beast, you're twenty-three years old, squat down in the dirty, blood-soaked basement and cry, don't stop, please, please cry, cry.

ABOUT THE AUTHOR

SERGEY KUZNETSOV was born in Moscow in 1966. In the 1990s he achieved a high profile as one of the pioneers of the internet in Russia, and has written for *The New York Times*, *Harper's Bazaar*, *Playboy*, *Vogue* and *L'Officiel*. His groundbreaking thriller *Butterfly Skin* has been translated into six languages, and in 2001 he became the first Russian journalist to receive a Knight Fellow scholarship from Stanford University. Besides being an entrepreneur and writer, he is editor-in-chief of *Booknik*, an internet publication on Jewish literature and culture. He lives in Paris.

ABOUT THE TRANSLATOR

ANDREW BROMFIELD has been a full-time translator from Russian for more than twenty years. He was a co-founder and original editor of *Glas*, a journal of modern Russian literature in English translation. His numerous translations include Mikhail Shishkin's *Letter-Book (The Light and the Dark)*, works by the Strugatsky brothers, Vladimir Voinovich, Pavel Pepperstein, Olga Slavnikova and Andrey Kurkov, as well as most books by Victor Pelevin and Boris Akunin, Mikhail Bulgakov's *A Dead Man's Memoirs (A Theatrical Novel)* and *A Dog's Heart (An Appalling Story)*, Leo Tolstoy's *War and Peace – the Original Version* and the two-volume *Russian Criminal Tattoo Encyclopaedia*.

ALSO AVAILABLE FROM TITAN BOOKS

KOKO TAKES A HOLIDAY

KEIRAN SHEA

Five hundred years from now, ex-corporate mercenary Koko Martstellar is swaggering through an easy early retirement as a brothel owner on The Sixty Islands, a manufactured tropical resort archipelago known for its sex and simulated violence. Surrounded by slang-drooling boywhores and synthetic komodo dragons, Koko finds the most challenging part of her day might be deciding on her next drink. That is, until her old comrade Portia Delacompte sends a squad of security personnel to murder her.

Now Koko is on the run in the sky-barges of the Second Free Zone, and falling in with Flynn, a depressed local cop readying his nerves for a sanctioned mass suicide known as Embrace. Can Koko and Flynn outfox her hunters until she can confront Delacompte?

"wild ride... breakneck pace... great fun"
Booklist **(starred review)**

"I felt so completely immersed in such a perfectly realized world of the future. Kieran Shea is the breath of fresh air the science fiction genre has been looking for."
Victor Gischler, author of *Ink Mage* and *Go-Go Girls of the Apocalypse*